M000288401

TETHERED

Echo Green

ISBN: 978-1-7356351-0-1 (eBook)
ISBN: 978-1-7356351-1-8 (Paperback)

Library of Congress Control Number: 2020916470

Any references to historical events, real people, or real places are used fictitiously. Names,
characters, and places are products of the author's imagination.
Artwork and design by Marko Curk.
Interior formatting by BookBaby, Inc.
Printed by BookBaby, Inc., in the United States of America.
First printing edition 2020.

https://evermoredeadening.wixsite.com/echogreen

To those of us forgotten

The lost

The hopeless

To all of us that were told we couldn't

The broken

The afterthoughts

Never stop

CHAPTER ONE

Her anger was intoxicating; it washed over me as self-hatred devoured her. I could taste her hopelessness heavy on my tongue, fortifying me. She was exactly what I needed after two days off. There were nights that I came to work and didn't feed, but this was not one of those times. My patient was seconds from coding, her voice shrill and fists poised to hurt herself or someone else – which would mean calling security, restraints, and enough sedatives to put a person into a coma. The key, I'd learned, to feeding from the ill was to do so gently. Breathing in her chaos, I ingested her emotions slowly. It was the only way to keep her from complete unconsciousness, and myself hidden.

Her name was Maize, and she'd tried to kill herself three days ago. Oozing wounds covered her body from head to toe; her body stank of old blood. Every inch of her was covered with scars, her form misshapen from years of mutilation. It was evident the doctors had given up suturing long ago; jagged lines of staples were the only things holding her together anymore. Thankfully I'd found a way to exist without the blood – for now – which was good because her anemic and withered frame couldn't afford any more blood loss.

What I needed was her suffering. What I wanted were her emotions, the one thing she had in abundance. It was a small price to pay for peace. The mentally ill were easy prey, I just had to find a way to draw them in and force a connection. Physical contact was the easiest way to grab hold; it solidified their focus on me and allowed me to ensnare them. Fortunately I'd taken care of Maize several times before now, which made hijacking and her mind and entwining myself within her that much easier. I had quickly become her favorite nurse; there was just something about the way only I could calm her soul. All she needed were a few kind words, maybe some guided imagery, a gentle but supportive touch… and she was mine.

It felt like I was tapping into a live wire as I fed on her turmoil and took from her the anxiety that drove her to cut, the crushing depression that sapped her will to live, and the fear that kept her imprisoned. I fed freely on her excess trauma, ingesting every emotion just as quickly as it was created. I was better than any antidepressant, better than therapy, and the only relief Maize had ever known. Unfortunately this relief was only ever temporary.

I took until her mind spun; exhausted and sapped of the awful energy she thrived on, I provided her with true salvation: the medications she never remembered to take and a good night's rest. I hoped, as I tucked her in, that tomorrow would be better. Her pain, once so fresh, was now masked by a mixture of fatigue and sedation as her blue eyes closed. I felt renewed by the forty beautiful minutes I'd been afforded to meticulously strip away Maize's excess emotions. It wasn't always so easy. Some people were completely closed off, especially here. The level of trauma that some of my patients experienced had completely destroyed them; there was nothing left. Not for me or for them.

No one tells you how to be a vampire, or at least no one stuck around to tell me. What I did know was that there weren't a lot of us, because not a lot of us survive the exchange. For those of us who do exist, we are as different from one another as fingerprints. The only constant is that we all need to feed. Dark thoughts played at the back of my mind like dirty fingers digging into my skin, thoughts that I had to work hard to ignore. I'd found a way to sustain myself, but it wouldn't be enough... not forever. Knowledge not my own spoke of a need I would not be able to gratify with the passive ingestion of people alone.

For now it was enough; it had to be. Luckily, feeding this way was easy, especially because all I had to do was come to work. I'd been a nurse at Oceanside Behavioral Health since before everything happened to me, and I hoped I could keep up the charade until I figured out what to do.

"Hey, good job with her. Did you give her something?" Quin asked from over my left shoulder, startling me.

I was just able to stifle a curse. Per his norm, Quin was leaning over me. He draped his arm across the back of my chair, forcing me to lean back as his weight counterbalanced my own. Quin was one of the rare few I'd never been able to read, but unlike my patients, his mind wasn't foggy, it was just blank.

"Yeah, it's amazing what a healthy dose of antipsychotics can do to calm the soul," I responded passively. "A little Ativan doesn't hurt, either."

I tried to hide my apprehension as he read over my shoulder. The heat from his body was distracting, and despite having just eaten, I was hungry. That was the problem: I was always hungry and no amount was ever enough. It was a constant battle as I struggled not to pry apart the minds of everyone who crossed my path. If I wasn't careful I would force feed: taking freely without consent or concern. That kind of feeding didn't go unnoticed.

A few months ago Quin, a couple of security guards, and I had all been stuck in an eight-by-eight seclusion room together. An obtuse man was kicking the locked door with enough force to bend the metal frame. Anger spewed from him, free and abundant, and nothing we tried helped. I wasn't able to subdue him as his rage suffocated me. It wasn't until he broke loose from security and his fist connected with the center of my chest that I lost my temper. My own irritation and anger ignited and before I could catch my breath I tore into him and everyone else nearby.

I inadvertently placed my patient into a stupor, forced the guards to stumble, and brought Quin to his knees at the entrance of the seclusion room. My patient recovered quickly but with evidently less conviction. The security guards, too proud to admit they'd almost fainted, returned to their task of restraining the madman. The problem was Quin. He'd put two and two together, and the look of amazement and curiosity that crossed his gaunt features made me instantly uneasy.

Since then, he'd been trying to get me alone, questioning my *exceptional* management of even the most psychotic patients, insistently trying to figure out how I did it, and finding any excuse he could to encroach. All of it was made worse by Quin's immunity to me, which made him a one-in-a-million pain in my ass. For months now he'd been sneaking up on me. I almost wished he'd just get it over with and ask. At least then I'd have an idea of what he knew. This ultimately was the problem of feeding without consent: they could feel me consuming and ripping into their mind. Unintentionally, I'd forced my consciousness onto Quin and took a part of him into myself, and now he wanted more.

Every night, Quin eventually relented and returned to his own work. I'd hoped that with enough time he'd lose interest, but so far it seemed that it had only amplified his curiosity. This, I knew, was going to be a problem – and while I didn't know why, every instinct told me the only way I could be safe was in hiding. I spent every shift avoiding him.

Finally my twelve hours of servitude had reached its end. Finishing the last of my notes, clicking the last of my boxes, and fumbling through hand-off; I'd made it through another shift without discovery.

Overcast skies and cool mist greeted me as I left the hospital; the smell of rain always cleared my head. I turned my face to the sky, enjoying the feel of it on my skin. It was ritualistic in nature, my need to detach myself from my shift and other people's need of me. This moment was for me, a second of reflection as I left work. In spite of my best efforts, I was getting out of work late. Regardless, the empty parking lot brought with it a welcomed silence as exhaustion and light exposure weakened my senses. It was time to rest and reset.

Keys in hand, I tossed my lunchbox into the passenger seat – had to keep up appearances. That's when I felt him, Quin's mind a brief and bright flash across mine just before he pinned me to the side of my car. The impact forced the air from my lungs; the sudden squeak of an exhale and jangling keys broke the previous silence.

"Easy way or the hard way?" Quin asked, the tenor of his voice loud in my ear.

I reacted, instinct making me fight for the room required to take a breath and escape. That's when I felt the knife slip between my ribs. Slow and sharp, the pain engulfed me as the knife nestled into my intercostal space.

"I guess silver does hurt," Quin said as my overcast sky went black.

———

The smell of blood and dirt woke me; my uniform was caked reddish-black from the mixture. Sitting up, my vision blurred. At least it was dark here, wherever here was. Best guess: I was in an unfinished basement. From the looks of it, this place wasn't part of the original floor plan. Crates made up the stairs that led to a rough-looking cellar door. Scooting back, I propped myself against the cool cement wall of the make-shift basement and began the tedious work of removing my scrub top.

"I guess silver does hurt… felt like lava." My snide remark and mockery of Quin did nothing to decrease the pain.

The tank top underneath was saturated, the blood here fresher. I quickly went to work, ripping the fabric of the scrub top into bindings. What I wouldn't give for clean water, gauze, and an ace wrap. Hissing, I cinched the fabric around my waist. I closed my eyes and let my head fall back, exhausted. I could just make out the low rumble of male voices from inside the house. Starvation was heightening my senses, and for a second I thought I could smell them through the floorboards. Regrettably, I hadn't been imagining it, as the scent of them grew stronger, pouring over me just as light flooded in from the cellar door.

I hadn't been afraid until now, and I did my best to press myself against the far wall, wishing that I had been blessed with the power of invisibility. The man who entered the basement looked to be around 5 feet 10 inches and 180 pounds of pure rage and muscle. He gave me nothing, his mind completely immune to my probing. He held wicked-looking gun loosely in his right hand. The black steel was every bit as menacing as the obsidian of his eyes. I'm sure I looked absolutely pitiful pressed tight against that wall, my left arm tight under my chest as I desperately fought to control my bleeding.

Slowly, the gun in his right hand leveled with my face. Heart racing, I felt my breath catch in my throat like a bowling ball. If this man was afraid of me, it never showed. He moved cautiously but with purpose before crouching beside me, the muzzle of the gun pressed hard against my sternum. With his free hand he pulled my arm away, inspecting the wound and my binding. I stared unblinking and terrified of the man in front of me. Eyes watering, I felt tears streak down my dirt-covered face.

"Show me," he demanded, his voice deep and just as stoic as his demeanor.

I fumbled with the knot, eyes never leaving his face, but he was impatient. Shoving my hands away, he ripped hard against the fabric. I bit back a cry, the muzzle of his gun providing me with a welcome distraction. The force required to rip the binding away sent searing pain spidering through me like breaking glass. Again my vision swam; I could feel new blood burning its way down my side. The smell made every fiber of my being come to life. It took me a second to realize that it wasn't my blood I smelled, but his. It took everything I had to restrain myself and fight the hunger that urged me to feed, to devour, to survive…

"Don't scream." It was the only warning I received before he dug his fingers into my side.

White-hot pain erupted through my body; weakly, my right hand grabbed his arm, desperate for him to stop. He flinched at my grasp, dark eyes meeting mine as he pressed the gun harder against my skin.

"By all means…" I loosened my grip, letting my arm fall away.

After he was done performing what felt like a lobectomy, he stood up, looming over me for a second before finally leaving. Good. Maybe now I could focus on healing and sleep; it was clear I wasn't going anywhere for a while. Feebly I rubbed my sternum and the deep circular imprint left behind – a stark reminder that the worst was yet to come. That day I dreamt of the coven, of the night my life was ripped away and this one had begun.

———

Quin waited in the kitchen for Marc to return. Fingers tapping against the tabletop, he played a lazy drumbeat on its surface. Patience was not his strong suit – that and he was exhausted. Quin's normal diet of caffeine pills, cigarettes, and energy drinks just wasn't cutting it today. The adrenaline high from earlier certainly hadn't helped either. He was running on fumes, especially after twenty hours without sleep. Nothing quite got him excited like the chance of injury. Quin had been at Oceanside since its beginning; he guessed wrangling the mentally ill and meth heads just wasn't doing it for him anymore. It'd been a long time since he'd felt so exhilarated.

Apparently he was the only one, because when Marc finally returned, he was pissed. Fists clenched, jaw tight, Marc affixed him with a vicious stare. Quin spent a lot of time around agitated people and he knew in that moment that Marc wanted nothing more than to hurt him.

"Why did you bring her here?!" Marc all but yelled.

"Where else would I take her?" Quin asked, pushing himself away from the table, creating a bit more distance between himself and Marc.

"You work together, and you abducted her from the parking lot? What the fuck were you thinking?" Marc spat the words.

"Okay, I get it, you're mad." Quin sighed, rubbing his left hand through his black hair. "I thought we could use her, that she'd be able to help us."

Marc stared at Quin for a long time, trying to understand. "So you stabbed her? Why would you think that was a good idea, Quin? She's bleeding out down there; do you know what happens when a vampire becomes feral?"

All Quin could manage was a nod. "I didn't know if I could get her here otherwise. I've seen her feed every night; I guess I thought she'd be stronger."

"That wound isn't healing; if she ate every night, it would have closed by now," Marc said, matter-of-fact.

Quin shrugged, straddling the kitchen chair, he tapped his feet nervously. At a loss for words, he rubbed his temples; fatigue had started to make his head pound.

"How has she fed, Quin?" Marc pressed, annoyed by the uncharacteristic silence.

"It was a few months back; we had this guy that needed restraints. He managed to pull away, hit her square in the chest." Quin struck out with his own fist for emphasis. "About knocked her on her ass. Thing was, before security or I could regain control, she had us all on *our* asses."

"How do you mean?" Marc asked.

"That's the thing, I don't know! It felt like the air was being ripped from my lungs, and she never even moved. But she leveled six grown men." Quin was standing now, trying to give more emphasis to his stature. "I see her do it every night. Patients in full-blown psychosis are suddenly out cold where IM medications couldn't even touch them."

"You know I don't know what that means—"

"Intramuscular. A shot with sedatives, the kind serial killers use to abduct people," Quin spouted quickly.

"Did you ever see her bite people, or was it always from afar?" Marc asked, lost in thought.

Quin shrugged again and saw Marc's temper flare. "From afar, I guess. I never noticed if she did and there was never any blood."

"What's your plan here, Quin? From what I can tell, she's not healing. If your goal was to kill her, then congratulations. If a vampire doesn't feed, they can't heal."

Bile rose in the back of Quin's throat, forcing him to clear it away with a choked cough. Panic and exhaustion made it hard for him to concentrate. He'd been so sure; he just had to get her here and then…

"I didn't know. I thought maybe if I weakened her it would be easier," he admitted, "She was supposed to heal, Marc; it wasn't supposed to matter."

Relaxing, Marc unclenched his fists. "Listen, I know you're new to this, but we aren't hit men. You can't just go around stabbing people and non-people."

Quin nodded tiredly. "They're usually harder to kill. I thought she'd heal; you told me wounds don't count if they aren't lethal."

"Don't blame me for your stupidity; you only hear the parts you want to hear. You're like a damn ten-year-old. If I didn't know better, I'd say the only reason you joined was because you thought it'd be cool to kill vampires like Van Helsing." Marc berated.

"Alright!" Quin shouted, launching the chair out from under himself. He was in Marc's face before he knew what he was going to do. "I fucked up, okay? But I can't kill someone, especially not her. I – I work with her."

He wasn't so much angry as he was scared; his thoughts raced. Adrenaline was definitely playing its part in shutting off the thinking parts of his brain. Crossing his arms, Marc stared down at Quin; his dark brown eyes appeared black in the dimly lit kitchen. This time though, he wasn't glaring.

"Why her, Quin. Why'd you pick her? Why bring her here?" Marc's voice had taken on a softer tone.

"I knew her from before. She hasn't changed," Quin relented, letting the remains of his anger fall away as he spoke. "I mean, she has…" Quin took a step back, "I can't just let her die."

"Okay." Marc said, acknowledging Quin's words. He'd finally gotten some truth. Even if Quin's *how* in getting Eryn here was wrong, his *why* wasn't.

———

The terror of the coven plagued my sleep – the smell of them, the blood, his dead eyes… the sound of teeth scraping bone. I was trapped in that dark room again. Reliving my death as they took more and more from me, as they took him… Those eyes didn't see me any more than his skin could feel my touch. I had stopped fighting, waited for my turn; there was nothing left that could be taken from me – or so I thought.

When I awoke I was still in a dark room, but this wasn't the one in my dreams. Here I wasn't alone. Quin sat on the makeshift stairs; he was half in and half out of the basement, leaning forward with his arms resting on his knees. His sapphire eyes fixed on me. Meeting his gaze, I sat up slowly, watching as he revealed the shotgun cradled in his lap. Unlike the other man, Quin just wanted me to know it was there.

"I can feel your pulse. Tell me, are you scared for me or because of me?" I asked, absently tapping my leg to the beat of his racing heart.

The smell of his guilt was sour in my nose as his feelings of remorse seeped through the cracks in the brick wall that was his mind. It wouldn't be long before I couldn't stop myself.

"Please, leave or use that gun," I urged. My veins were on fire as I struggled against the need to eat and my instinct to survive.

"I'm sorry. Try not to fight, okay? I'm going to fix this. Trust me." Trust… His guilt crashed into me, overwhelming my senses as four men descended into the basement. "Don't fight," were his words, but his emotions told me something different: *'I don't want to kill you.'*

12

I could see him clearer than I ever had before, his barriers falling away to reveal his turmoil, his pain, and the life he'd led – disappointment after disappointment as he self-sabotaged, all alone. His memories flooded my mind. I was paralyzed as he leveled the shotgun and four men stepped around him, each one restraining a limb. It was my heart that raced now as Quin's psyche overtook mine.

'*Trust me*', his thoughts urged. It was all I could hear as he confined me within his mind, forcing emotion after emotion into my head.

'*You're distracting me?*' I thought, watching as Quin visibly flinched.

It'd been working up until the moment I felt the prick of the needle puncturing my skin. The sharpness of it focused my mind just enough to pull away from his. Why was he starting an IV? Saline wasn't going to help me. Realization lifted the fog of his mind from mine. Line primed red, I began to fight.

———

"You'll be killing her. Are you sure?" Marc watched as Quin paced. "If I'm right and she hasn't fed before, you'll be completing the transformation. Are you sure that's what she even wants?"

Quin stopped a moment, covering his face with his hands while he collected his thoughts. "No one wants to bleed out in a basement."

"If you do this, your life will be tied to hers: tethered. Whoever she becomes after this, it becomes a part of you, too." Marc knew what Quin was going to do; he just hoped he understood the consequences.

Tethering a vampire intertwined their life force with the hunter's. That is if the hunter was even able to survive the exchange and not be completely consumed. If it worked, Eryn would be forever bound.

With any luck she and Quin could learn to control the impulses and hunger that she would become.

"You're sure?" Marc asked again, fearful of the possibility of failure, and of success.

A sly smile played across Quin's lips. "I know what could happen if I can't control her, but there's a chance."

Dark curiosity burned in his eyes, it was this curiosity that would be Quin's downfall, of this Marc was certain. "Get ready, then. We have seven hours until nightfall."

———

Sticky, red liquid filled the once clear IV line. I watched in horror as Quin flicked the clamp open in one precise movement. Gravity would force the cold fluid into my veins drop by drop, sealing my fate.

"No, Quin, you can't!" I screamed, fighting desperately to dislodge the IV, pleading for him to stop as I lashed out, tearing at the corners of his mind.

If he was going to be in my head, then he was going to understand. I would make them all understand as I forced every memory of that night into their skulls. It was the way their teeth ripped into me, the smell of their putrid breath, and the pressure of their bodies as they overtook mine. It was the pain I felt as I watched the life fade from Alexander's eyes. But if Quin understood, if any of them understood, they never showed it. All I heard was Quin's voice low and hypnotic – I couldn't make sense of what he was saying. The sound of his voice was on repeat as he overwhelmed me.

There was a reason I'd never truly fed, a reason I sustained myself on the emotions, a reason I fought. I knew that if I fed, that the death that lay dormant in my veins would be awakened. I'd be just like the monsters that had killed my husband. Anything left of my humanity, of me, would be lost.

"Please," I hated the fear-seeped tone of my voice, but it was too late; as the blood entered my veins I never wanted it to stop.

In that moment, being held down and forced to consume, the coven won. Drop by drop I was erased, any control I had left was consumed by my need. I hadn't realized my existence before now was like being trapped underwater. I'd been holding my breath, the full agony of it realized as soon as I took my first breath. Suddenly the hands that held me didn't feel as heavy as they did before. Lashing out, I watched as the man who'd been restraining my left leg crumpled against the far wall.

"Quin!" a familiar voice yelled, dark brown eyes meeting mine; it was the man from before.

"Marc," I said curiously, liking the feel of his name. I'd claimed this knowledge of him before he could slam his mind closed to me once more. That was fine; Marc couldn't keep me out forever.

It was hard to focus though with all of Quin's chanting. The persistence of his tone quickly reclaimed control of my attention, demanding my focus. He was distracting and despite my best attempts to rip apart his mind, I couldn't disrupt his hymn. The only crack in his armor was the pain that sparked in his blue eyes. Maybe I could break him.

Before I could try pain sharp and abrupt tore down my arm. He'd opened an uneven line – first in my flesh, then his own. Blood spilled from him and onto me. The deep red of it burned across my skin with every drop. Blood connected us, jagged cut to jagged cut, as he clasped my arm in his own. I was lost again, this time by the merging of my memories with his.

I was four again; my mother lay comatose in her bed as I built castles out of her pill bottles. I was five, and my grandparents cried and prayed over me at the foster home. I was six, and my father showed me to my bedroom – tea sets and Barbie dolls. I was ten; the babysitter was lifting up my pajamas, asking if I wanted to play a game. I was twelve, tucking my brothers in before my dad came home drunk to yell at me. I was fifteen, swallowing pills before I went off to bed – hoping there wouldn't be a tomorrow. I was sixteen, and suddenly there was him… *Get out! Get out, get out, get out of my head!*

CHAPTER TWO

Quin startled awake, he was drenched in sweat and couldn't remember how he'd gotten out of the basement or why he was sleeping in the bathtub. His body was on fire. The last time he felt this bad he was a freshman in college, or maybe it was that time he caught the flu from a hobo. Looking back, it was definitely the time he'd caught hobo flu.

Quin quickly realized why he'd been placed in the bathtub. Vomit lined the toilet and dotted the bathroom rug, yellowed from bile. He felt pathetic as he struggled to stand and peel his sweat drenched clothes loose before showering. Thankfully the hot water dissolved the ache in his bones and eased the tension of his muscles. It was still hard to dress himself. His limbs were weak and traversing the stairs was near comical. He white-knuckle gripped the banister the whole way down, afraid his legs might give out.

The smell of coffee filled the air, and while normally he hated the smell, this time it made him feel oddly at home. Marc sat at the kitchen table, and from the look of things this was also where he'd slept last night. A blanket lay crumpled on the floor beside him, his clothes disheveled. Corner to corner the table was covered with binders of hunter lore.

"Mind if I have some of that?" It wasn't a real question, as Quin was already pouring them both a cup.

"If you puke, you clean it." Exhaustion thickened the timbre of Marc's voice.

Nodding, Quin settled in beside him. "That's the nicest thing you've said to me all week," he joked, pretending not to notice Marc's smile. "How is she?"

"What do you want me to say?" Marc sighed into his coffee. "You saw what happened to her, what the coven did. She didn't want this, you did. But you already knew that though, didn't you?" The accusation hung in the air, Marc's dark eyes daring Quin to tell him otherwise. "I'll be bleaching this place for weeks. Don't pretend you weren't planning this since you joined. You just had to wait for the right opportunity."

"It worked, didn't it?" Quin pointed out, ignoring Marc's question.

"Yeah." Marc's voice no longer held its earlier softness. "And at no cost to you. Eryn will have to feed now, and not like before. It will be your fault if those bodies stack up. That is, if she doesn't eat you first."

"Why are you always busting my balls? I saved her," Quin scoffed. Marc's "smarter than thou" speeches typically didn't get under his skin.

"NO…" Marc was standing now, his full height towering over Quin. "You used her. You're tethered. That makes her hunger yours now. I hope you can control it better than she did."

———

I felt Quin's intentions before he even made it to the basement. My head felt like it was splitting in two as I struggled to shut him out.

"Stay out of my head," I hissed, covering my ears with my hands in hopes of drowning him out.

'*Sorry.*' The thought bounced around in my head like a bullet; he was sitting on the crates again, half in, half out. "You don't have to stay down here."

"Does it matter? I'm trapped no matter where I go." The theatrics in my tone made even me cringe.

"I guess not," he conceded, "but you're starting to stink."

Quin's statement caught me off guard. "Are you always so dismissive?" There was no answer as he sipped his coffee, and for a second I thought I could taste it.

"Stay down here if you want; it stinks." The disinterest in Quin's voice caught me by surprise.

"Wait." I felt lost and more than a little indignant. Every fucked up thing I'd ever done, every regret, every piece of me that someone had taken away – he knew. "What do you get out of this? What's the point? Why keep me alive?" I waited, watching as Quin finished his coffee. I knew I'd tasted it on my tongue that time.

"Short answer?" he said before leveling his eyes with mine. "Power."

"You saw it didn't you, the things they did to me? The way they took without regard? That's what I am now. That's what you did." Each word was a battle as I struggled to speak, panic blurring the edges of my vision.

The absurdity of his answer horrified me as my breath caught. The space around me suddenly felt too small, like the walls were closing in. Shattering glass softly muted in the dirt below, Quin had dropped his cup, his hands desperately loosening his collar and the hold of my anxiety from around his neck. His panic mingled with mine before a sense of calmness overtook me. Quin had regained his composure one breath at a time as he vanquished the feel of me in him.

"Warn me the next time you feel like going emo, okay? I almost fell off the crates." Annoyed, Quin gathered the pieces of the broken cup. "Come on. Let's go."

He was right. It was beginning to stink down here, and the smell, unfortunately, had nothing to do with the basement. Hesitantly I followed, finding Marc waiting just outside the crawl space. Hyper focused, I braved the makeshift staircase and entered the kitchen. I was pretty sure he had a gun pointed at me from underneath the table where he sat. His dark eyes were just as cold as the expression he wore on his face.

"I don't want any trouble," I said pitifully as Marc sized me up.

That's when Quin stepped between us. Quin's gaunt, 5-foot 8-inch frame easily blocked my curvy, 5-foot 5-inch build. "I've got this," he assured.

His words surprised me. Maybe it was the familiarity of his tone or maybe it was the way he defended me. Cautiously and without protest from Marc, Quin ushered me to the nearest bathroom.

"Go. You stink," Quin teased lightheartedly, like nothing had changed between us. It was insulting. He'd made a choice that wasn't his to make.

"If whatever you're trying to do doesn't work, you need to know I can't – won't – be just like them." I didn't know yet the extent to which my words held conviction or the strength of the threats within, but it didn't matter because in that moment, as I shut the bathroom door in his face, so, too, did I close the connection of our minds.

I wasn't sure how I'd done it; maybe my resolve and need for silence had created a barrier even he couldn't weasel his way through. All I knew was that I was alone again. Disrobing, I sat in the shower until the water ran cold. I was mesmerized by all the new sensations. Every cell in my body hummed with a strength I'd never known. My body, once marred by the hideous and hungry scars of the coven, was healed. I was new and it scared me.

Could I still be myself after becoming the thing I was now? Water heater sufficiently tapped, I turned the shower off and stepped out to find a bag of clothes waiting just inside the bathroom door. Dollar store specials from what I could tell, but anything was better than blood-soaked and torn scrubs. Settling on a pair of high-waist yoga pants and a fitted gray blouse with an open back, I was surprised by the fit of the clothes. My curves had been accentuated by the recent gain in muscle that worked to both slim and define my shape. If only it made me taller; that seemed to be the only feature unchanged.

Even the color of my eyes had changed; my once deep green shade was now vibrant and luminescent in the artificial light of the bathroom, almost as if they were backlit. It was odd, this new sense of self. I enjoyed the ease with which I could move, as every muscle in my body ached for action.

Emerging from the bathroom, still in awe of myself, I found Marc. He stood watching me from down the hall, his presence but a flicker in my mind. I wondered how long he'd been there, waiting. Fixated, I wondered if I could catch him and if I was quick enough. I tried to pull from him any inkling of emotion or passing thought. Not surprisingly, his mind still gave me nothing, but I was beginning to see the cracks in the armor. Maybe if I forced – pain, instant and hot, seared my palm. The smell of burnt flesh sharp in my nose; but when I looked, there was no damage to be found.

Looking up, confused, I realized Marc had escaped. The acrid scent of melted skin pulled me down the hallway and into the living room, where I found Quin. He sat stretched out on an old sofa with a lighter in hand. Marc stood skewed, just from view, on the stairs that led to the second story. Seeing me, Quin held his hand out, a smiley face shaped burn branded in the same place I'd felt my own skin burn.

"I guess that got your attention," he said, the grin on Quin's face sinister.

"Why?" I asked before plugging my nose.

"You were trying to play cat and mouse with Marc. Trust me, you'd lose," Quin remarked before blowing on his scorched palm.

"I'm not so sure," I responded as the pain etched in my skin faded.

Excitement as clear as day sparked from Quin as he turned his palm toward me once more, marveling at the new skin where burnt flesh had just been. His face said it all: he'd never been so happy in his life.

"Congratulations, you've got exactly what you wanted. Make sure you keep her fed, or you're both dead," Marc announced before taking his leave of us.

"Well that wasn't ominous," Quin mocked. "What do you want to do?"

His words weren't so much a question as they were a dare, his dark curiosity evident to me. I couldn't help but smile, and a part of me wanted to see what I could do. I felt restless in my need to run, to move – anything, really, but stand still.

"Cat and mouse?" I suggested, remembering Quin's earlier comment.

"Give me a head start?" Quin asked, before darting out the front door.

A mix of delight and anticipation made my heart race as I counted the seconds. I had to force myself to breathe and to wait, feeding my own excitement until I couldn't stand it any longer and I tore after him. My bare feet hit the pavement as the space between the front door and the street blurred. I surged forward with a burst of energy. Instinctually, I knew Quin felt the same way and wondered if this energy was just mine.

It didn't take me long to reach the rundown industrial area of this neighborhood, the stink of it overpowering. I hadn't realized until now that I'd been tracking Quin by his scent. He smelled faintly of honey, vanilla, and tobacco. It was an overall pleasant smell, and though it told me that he had been here, it didn't tell me where he was now. Without thinking, I reached out, probing for his thoughts, his excitement, or anything that would tell me where he'd gone.

'Cheater.' The word dashed across my mind, quickly vanishing before I could pinpoint any clue as to where he was hiding.

I laughed. '*There is no such thing as fair, Quin.*' I let this truth, my truth, ring out in my mind as I leapt for a low hanging fire escape.

My fingertips just managed to encircle the bottom rung. I climbed it with ease, making my way up before it could fully descend to the ground below. I'd never felt more capable or sure of myself than I did now. Once at the top, the smell of tar and birds completely erased any remaining hint of Quin's scent. That was alright, because if I focused I found I was just able to make out the sound of his ragged breathing.

My senses sharpened and homed in on every breath he took, the burning in his lungs my own as he fought to slow his breathing. His amusement washed over me, the sound of his heart pounded in my ears. It was better than any concert I'd ever experienced. I crept closer, consumed by the sound of it. Crouched low, I rounded a large roof-mounted air conditioning unit.

"Well, come on, then. You haven't caught me yet," he urged, the lights of the city silhouetting his frame, his sapphire eyes gleaming even in the dark.

That was all the permission I needed to charge forward, his reflexes against mine. Too slow, his arms braced across his chest as we collided. I heard his head bounce with a wet crack as the smell of blood filled my nose. I was on top of him in seconds, taking advantage of his downed form. My knees pressed into his chest, left hand around his throat as I held him still, leaning forward to take in the scent of him. Both of his hands pried at my fingers, desperate to maintain his airway.

"Go ahead, it's what you want isn't it?" He wheezed blue eyes like steel, daring me.

Curious, I lowered my face to his, squeezing my left hand until I felt him squirm. I wanted to see the steel of those blue eyes shatter.

I wanted to see his fear. Always so cocky, it was funny, considering how weak he was. That's when he laughed, his left hand darting from his throat to meet the back of his skull. A blur of red as his open palm met my face.

I panicked, tasting him on my lips, and suddenly I couldn't get away from him fast enough. My fingertips smeared red as I wiped my face frantically. Quin turned instantly to his side, coughing and gasping for air. His teeth bared as he smiled up at me. I was back in that dark room again, but this time the monster was me, and all I wanted was to see him bleed. My chest felt tight as I struggled to breathe against the smell of him all around me.

What had I been trying to do? The fog of predatory instincts faded from me slowly as I realized, a little too late, that I didn't want to play this game. This time I was the one caught off guard as Quin swept my legs. The force of the impact stole the air from my lungs. The silent pain was excruciating, no air moving in or out as my body absorbed the shock of it.

"If you're going to act like one of them, then I'll treat you like one. Get up." His words were as hollow as my lungs.

There was no second warning as his size-ten met my stomach. The force of the impact lifted me from the ground. I'd never been hit so hard in my life. The pain held me captive, muscles screaming from the impact as I fought for air. Quin struck out again but this time my hand met his ankle, stopping his steel-toed boot before it could meet my ribs. I shoved his leg wide and away from me, staggering his gait.

It wasn't much, but it afforded me with enough time to flee. I hadn't realized until now that I wasn't the only one who had changed. His clothes fit tighter against his now full frame. He was less gaunt and wiry. By the look of him I was pretty sure I'd rather be kicked by a horse than him again. It didn't take Quin long to regain his balance and continue his onslaught. Helpless, all I could do was back up, dodge when I was able, and absorb the pain when I couldn't.

Everything in me screamed to feed, to take, to consume. It terrified me, my need of it and the horror I felt as hunger ripped through me. All I saw was red as my hands shook and I struggled to break away from him, distracted. Quin pushed me back until there was nowhere left to run.

"Stop," I breathed, I knew I couldn't escape him even if I'd wanted to.

"It's only going to get harder if you fight it. It feels good, though, doesn't it, delaying the gratification. How 'bout we just get this over with?" he spat, clearing his throat.

This time it was me that was pinned as Quin slammed me against the oversized AC unit I'd originally hidden behind. His arm was like metal across my throat as my feet dangled, the weight of him suspending me. His size advantage had me trapped. Eyes watering, my vision blurred against the force of him against my windpipe, the tables completely turned.

"Easy way or the hard way?" he asked before pulling a pocket knife. "Stupid question?"

Quin drug the knife across the forearm directly under my throat. If I'd thought my senses were overloaded before, blood was all I saw now. The sweet smell and taste of it in the air was tantalizing as it dripped down the front of my shirt.

"Smells good, right?" The teasing tone was in his voice again as the pressure of his mind invaded mine.

I couldn't shut him out while I was battling for control over myself. Instantly his urges and desires combined with my own.

"Here, let me help." His fingers traced the cut, forcing their way past my lips and along my clenched teeth.

Fireworks exploded behind my eyes as I struck out, physically and mentally pushing him away. Quin's body recoiled from mine, shoved back with enough force to drop us both. I was gasping for air, the taste of him thick across my tongue. I couldn't get far enough away from it or him. I knew there was no escape as Quin smiled at me, blood dripping off his fingertips. He slashed his arm through the air, effectively splattering me with blood like shrapnel.

This time he wasn't going to let me go. Scrambling on his hands and knees, Quin took full advantage of my stupor and in seconds he had hold of me again. My back pressed forcefully against his chest as he wrapped his legs forward and around mine. His right arm tight around my waist as he pinned my arms at my side and his left hard against my mouth, the pain of it forced my jaw. I was trapped, unable to resist the hunger any more than I could fight Quin.

The ache of my thirst ripped through my veins like razor blades; there was no way to hide from it and no other choice but to drink. I sighed against his skin and the delicious release he provided. For the first time, I fed. It was more than just the taste of him – dark and complex across my tongue. It was the feel as his pulse synched with mine – a rhythmic tempo the likes of which I'd never before enjoyed. It was the smell – mineral and alluring in its promise as I consumed and in turn was consumed by it. I felt his hold loosen, allowing me to replace his grip with my own. Surprised when he relaxed, leaning back as I drank him in.

"You know, you made this a lot harder than it had to be," his words played around my periphery, lost in the focus of my feeding.

It wasn't long until Quin repositioned, returning us fully upright before placing his right arm through the triangle that my arms had created in order to hold his left to my mouth. He forced my jaw once more, pressing hard to feed the bite. I had no choice but to release, his right arm quick to pin my arms back to my sides. The loss of him was agony.

"Breathe," he urged, his left hand clamped like a vise under my chin to prevent me from biting him again.

I wished I'd never known what it was to feed, because in the relief of it was the need for more. The searing heat of Quin's blood had melted away the torment of my constant thirst. It was the cost of what I was as the need for more ripped and tore at the remnants of my self-control.

"Why?" I finally managed to ask through clenched teeth. "Why be like this, knowing what could happen?" I was breathless as I focused on the smells of the rooftop, the humid air of the city, anything but the smell of him too close.

"Honestly?" Quin considered my question, his hold never wavering. "I've always wanted to know what it felt like to feed."

It was then that I became acutely aware of a need not my own. It wasn't as intense as my own, but it felt just as dark and infinite. One ragged breath followed another until I could no longer feel Quin's pulse hidden within my veins. It took me longer to relax against the pressure of his fingertips digging into my skin, but when I finally did, I reveled in the freedom of him. Scurrying away on hands and knees, I was elated by the chance to distance myself from him.

Something told me personal space wasn't something he understood well. Settling, I looked back to where Quin sat, completely unperturbed by our interactions as embarrassment burned my cheeks.

A knowing smile played across his face. "You're as easy to read as a book. We'll work on that next."

"You never answered my question, not really," I pointed out, doing my best to hide my discomfort.

"We can't fight them: vampires," Quin began. "Not well, at least. If I wanted things to change, I needed to change. Now, the stronger you get the stronger I'll be. The way Marc explained it, hunters used to tether vampires all the time as a way to extend their own lives and provide their benefactors with a sustainable food supply. That and being tethered keeps you from losing your connection to humanity."

I listened intently, noticing just how breathless Quin was by the end. I hadn't thought too much of it until he moved to stand. His first attempt was foreshadowed by a low grunt before he quickly fell back down. His second attempt was more fruitful, though, as I watched him stumble, sweat beading his brow. Instinctually, I reached out. Panicked, I scrambled to my feet, his elbow grasped in my hand.

"Sit back down before you fall," I urged.

"I'm fine," Quin laughed as the color slowly returned to his face. "It doesn't always work you know – the exchange. Sometimes the hunter is consumed by it, their life forfeited. Sometimes we even become ghouls. Really wasn't looking forward to rotting skin and viscera eating." He shuddered before gawking at the nearly healed wound on his arm. "It's too bad we can't heal patients like this. But then we'd be out of business. Your blood is only good for poisoning people now. The human body rejects the stuff, almost like anaphylaxis. Guess we both got lucky."

Blood loss was making him ramble; the lack of red blood cells was clearly affecting his faculties. It'd been a long time since I'd seen this side of Quin. For the first time in months I felt normal, not realizing how nice it was to be able to speak openly instead of hiding.

"How long did you know what I was and what had happened?" I asked before relinquishing my hold on him.

"A while, I guess. I don't know. I wasn't sure until the day you floored me outside the seclusion room." His tone was characteristically teasing again, "Come on. We should get back; Marc's probably tired of looking at you through a scope."

"What!" I yelled after him, but Quin was already halfway down the fire escape, cackling the whole way. Thing was, I wasn't so sure he was joking.

The walk back to the house was sobering; everything up to this point had felt surreal and almost like one bad dream after another as I stumbled through months of uncertainty. I really wasn't sure how I'd made it this long alone; that's the part that still didn't feel real. A familiar pain settled in my chest, threatening to restrict my airway as I blinked away the tears. I wondered if it would ever get easier. Tendrils of daylight had begun to chase away the last of the stars in the sky by the time we reached Marc's. I'd need to find a place to sleep, and soon.

"Hurry up," Quin called from the porch where Marc leered, an affront to the doorway. I could just see the strap of the soft gun case slung over his right shoulder, the length of it taller than me.

"Motherfucker…" I whispered under my breath, stopping short at the steps that led inside.

I might as well have been staring at a brick wall. If it wasn't for the expression on Marc's face and his body language, I'd have no way of knowing his intentions. How was it he could mask himself so completely? Soft hues of white and baby blue spilled into the streets, heavy against my skin as morning fully bloomed. That's when I felt the full weight of my exhaustion set in. My head began to throb as my vision blurred and my body ached. I'd never felt so weak. Cautiously, I reached out, using the porch railing for support as a wave of nausea threatened to double me over.

"Are you pissed because you didn't get to shoot her or because it worked?" Quin jested, pushing his way past.

"The others will know soon enough, Quin. You leave after tonight. Don't make me hunt you down next." What Marc's non-threatening tone lacked, his eyes made up for in his unyielding gaze.

"Okay." Blue eyes met brown, both men unyielding.

Something told me this conversation wasn't over between them, but eventually Marc moved aside to allow me entry. I'd just made it inside before collapsing, everything hurt, as I tried to shield my eyes. My stomach churned, this pain gave me a whole new understanding of morning sickness.

"Puke on me and I'll drop you down the stairs." I tensed as Marc picked me up.

'He feels like marble,' I thought as the faint smell of cedar and vermouth emanated from him.

"Marble, really? What are you, twelve?" he mocked as Quin laughed from somewhere in the living room.

"Are all of you mind readers?" I spoke indignantly, my face pressed against him as I tried to escape the pain exploding behind my eyes. "I can't help it when you're this close."

"You need to focus," Marc scolded as he prompted me to stand again. He kept one arm around my waist as he set my feet back on the ground to pull open an attic access door. The metal ladder clanged to the floor like machine-gun fire inside my head. "You're pushing your thoughts to the surface; makes it hard not to hear what you're thinking. Can you get up there?"

"Yes." I nodded feebly. I'd be damned if I was going to let him sling me over his shoulder. It was slow-going but I managed. The relief I experienced within the darkness of the attic was instantaneous as my eyes adjusted. "Thank you…"

Marc looked up at me, eyes cold and distant, and I couldn't tell if it was pity or sorrow I read within them before he turned, leaving me to my solitude and darkness of the attic. I pulled the latch closed quickly before I withdrew to the hollow pit growing in the center of my chest. Maybe, just maybe, I'd get to see the only person that ever made me whole: Alexander. God knows I'd had enough of the nightmares.

Looking around I couldn't help but smile when I found clean bedding. Marc had intended to let me hide away up here all along, his tough exterior all a charade. Ritualistically, I curled up under the blankets, sealing myself within as I covered my ears with my hands. The demons couldn't reach me here as long as I remained under the covers. Secured within, I imagined his arms around me. Alex had always been able to hold my broken pieces together; maybe I could pretend just until I succumbed to sleep.

It was the low sound of voices, the scraping of chair legs on hardwood, and the smell of coffee that woke me, pulling me from my dreams. I wished that I didn't know when I was dreaming. I'd give anything to forget, even for a second, that Alex wasn't really dead. Tears stung my eyes; I hadn't escaped the nightmares either. Flashes from the night I was born and the coven had tainted my dreams of him. My head ached from the memories; they felt sharp behind my eyes. Still half asleep, I could hear their voices pulling me back to them. I didn't understand why they'd made me just to kill themselves; what was the point? My mind felt foggy as I tried to pull the dreams to my waking mind, desperate to make sense of the words they'd etched in my veins with their blood.

Transference…

The word was there and gone, spoken as if from just beside me. I sprang from my cocoon of comforters. I could have sworn I felt the vibration of the word in my ear, but no one was here. The voice was familiar yet distant in my mind. Absently, I twisted my wedding ring around my finger; I needed to get out of this attic and my own head before I heard anything else whispered to me in the darkness. I was starting to creep myself out and couldn't shake the heavy feeling of the presence that had called out to me. That voice. I'd heard it somewhere before. My hurried descent and clattering of the ladder was enough to announce my presence to the dead. Luckily neither Quin nor Marc were dead or asleep, their eyes on me as I entered the kitchen.

"What's wrong?" Quin's voice mirrored the confusion I felt.

"Have you ever heard of transference?" I asked, rubbing my temples as if it would help clear my mind.

Marc looked up from what he'd been reading. "What did you see?"

"It doesn't make sense. That night plays out in my head, over and over. Sometimes it's through my eyes, sometimes I feel like it's through theirs; their memories and emotions. It's how I knew not to feed, that I could sustain for a while like I was. But that's all it's ever been, jumbled memories and pieces." I shook my head, trying to force myself awake. "This morning I felt it. That word, as clear as we're talking now."

Marc tensed, eyes wide, before he darted past me. He cleared the stairs in three long strides. Quin and I shared a look of confusion; from what I'd seen of Marc, he wasn't one to startle. It wasn't long before he was bounding back down the stairs.

"Put these on," he demanded, presented me with bulky head-phones. "I can't explain, but I need you to block everything out. Do you understand?"

I nodded, his panic like electricity against my senses. I did as I was told and took the headphones, placing them tightly over my ears. Marc connected the jack to his phone, making me wince instantly as pop music assaulted my ear drums. Thankfully, he turned down the volume, motioning for me to listen and do so carefully.

You need to concentrate, he mouthed, before returning to Quin.

I lowered myself to the floor, trying to anticipate the verses of the songs as I listened carefully to the chorus. It wasn't my favorite genre of music, but it worked in a pinch. A dull yet insistent pain had begun to build just behind my right eye. It quickly became sharp and throbbing, the beat of it matching the tempo of the music in my head. I must have made a noise because Marc turned toward me. Quin moved as well, rubbing his temple on the same side I had felt the pain growing. This connection we shared – it was odd the way it manifested at certain times but not others.

Tethered.

The voice overrode the music in my ears and again I felt the breath of the word, and this time it sent goosebumps down my arms. Quin tensed, wide-eyed. He'd heard it, too. In that instant Marc was crouched, his face inches from mine. He held my jaw tight in his right hand. The pain broke my fixation with the word.

Concentrate, he mouthed again.

I felt the force behind the word as his breath hit me in the face. Marc's brown eyes were unblinking, warning me to do as I was told, afraid that I might not listen. The pain was in my temple again, burrowing through my right eye to settle in my skull. The lyrics felt distant in my ears, muddled and distorted by the pressure in my head. Quin almost doubled over, hand to his right temple. Marc's grip tightened, that's when I closed my eyes.

There was nothing but his grip as it bruised my skin, my breathing – slow and purposeful, and the sound of the music flooding my every thought. Eventually his grip fell away and I pulled my knees into my chest. I focused on the sensation of the music as the vibration and sound dulled my other senses. With every breath my sense of self was returning, the previous fog lifting. I waited for the pain behind my eyes to completely subside before opening them again. Marc was still crouched in front of me; the attentiveness of his gaze was alarming. He tapped the side of his head, motioning for me to remove the headphones.

"You both need to leave." His normally irritated tone now worried.

"What do you mean?" I asked as he ripped away the headphones.

"Transference occurs when a vampire is created. It's the shared knowledge of the coven passed through the blood. It protects the new bloodlines if the coven is destroyed or separated." Marc was standing, glancing between Quin and me nervously. "To read the emotions and thoughts of others is one thing; to speak is another. I've only heard of it occurring between vampires tied by blood, much like tethering between hunter and vampire, but stronger. Before you, Quin couldn't even listen in. That's why you have to leave; your maker is looking for you."

"That doesn't make sense, they're all dead. I saw them." I spoke truthfully, Marc's panic sparking my own. "Marc, I don't have a maker."

"I hope you're both ready." Marc looked down at me from where he stood, the same look of pity from before.

CHAPTER THREE

er name was Mira, and she was screaming in my face. Her hot saliva against my skin and the smell of her grimy hands twisted in my uniform dissolved the last tendrils of my patience. I had tried it her way and now I was done.

"Hands on." I spoke the words out of habit; the two security guards beside me had restrained Mira the second she laid hands on me.

Piss and vinegar, she fought the whole way, a mix of paranoia and fear trapped her in a cycle of violence, hospitalizations, and incarceration. Two more security guards met us in the padded seclusion room; I was accompanied by one other nurse and an aid. Like a well-oiled machine: orders were placed, doctor present and Mira pumped full of enough Haldol, Benadryl, and Ativan to completely derail the negative feedback loop she was trapped in. The door was shut and locked before my code even reached the ten minute mark. It was a new personal best. It couldn't have happened at a more opportune time; I had just under an hour left in my shift. Charting would take about that long and then I'd be free. I couldn't stand the smell of unwashed bodies and stagnant air much longer.

"Hey." Quin's voice was low, stern almost. "Can I talk to you about that code?"

And just like that, everyone gave us the desk; there wasn't a nurse alive that didn't fear those words coming from a charge nurse's mouth. I didn't bother to stop typing my note, I barely acknowledged him with a shrug.

He stood over me, one arm on the desk as he leaned in. "What the hell was that?"

"I medicated her; she wasn't going to be able to manage without some sort of intervention."

"So why didn't you calm her down instead? You let that code happen." The seriousness in his tone was hard to ignore, especially when he rarely used it.

"Yeah, I did," I answered pleasantly.

That made him angry; it burned like acid in my throat. "Are you even a nurse anymore?"

"She needed medication; ignoring that just to make your job easier doesn't help her. She would have just re-escalated." I stood, leveling my eyes with his before he could stand up and use his height advantage to look down at me. Luckily, he backed off. "I have to clock out, Quin."

It'd been a week since I'd heard the voice in my head, and I'd only grown more irritable waiting. I knew they were out there. Unfortunately it didn't take Quin long to catch up. His footsteps close behind as I swiped the time clock with my badge. In this last week I'd gotten better at sensing him and keeping him out of my head.

"If you try to stab me again I won't still be your friend this time." I sighed, exhausted.

Quin laughed, the sound of it easing my tension. "Anything new?"

"No," I replied quickly, slowing in my pursuit of escape only long enough to hold the doors for him. "I haven't even been dreaming. I feel this shroud around me, though. I can't tell if I'm making it up or if it's them."

Quin's mind reached for mine, almost like a caress, it was hard not to completely recoil from him. Reluctantly I gave a little; it was a lot like removing a piece of armor as I expose a part of myself. It scared me just how easy it was becoming to hide and bury my emotions.

"I can't tell," he admitted sheepishly. "I'm sorry about earlier. You were right. I just expect you to, you know, not let them get so bad."

I closed myself to him. "Their emotions are hard not to internalize, I can't pull away like I did before. I take a piece of them with me when I delve now. I feel like I could lose myself if I'm not careful."

I spoke truthfully, stepping from the hospital entrance. The fresh air was a gift to my senses as it purged the smell of the homeless. It didn't take long for Quin's guilt to make my stomach churn. This time I reached out. He felt responsible, knew this would happen, and that he was supposed to... tether. Quin forced me back, wincing with the effort.

"You should probably get back. They're already wondering where you are, and the guards are watching from the third floor."

Quin peered up, waving as they scattered. "I'll see you later," he resigned, his concern apparent.

I gave a noncommittal nod as he turned to leave; I contemplated the weight of my keys for a moment before ultimately tucking them back into my pocket. It was a good night to wander. Since changing my schedule, I was able to go to work at night and return home at night. Oceanside Behavioral Health owned me from eight at night until four in the morning three nights a week. It was my only option. The exhaustion I felt from sun exposure was crippling since Quin intervened. Plus not needing food, health insurance, or to save for retirement really cut down on my cost of living, so it didn't matter that I only worked a measly twenty-four hours a week. That being said, there were three hours of night to be had before I needed to worry about getting home; that and the night air felt amazing.

Gradually I made my way toward the waterfront. The city lights danced off the river, creating a dark and distorted image of the city in the black water below. I'd been here before, walked the pathways that framed the waterway. Tents littered the underpasses here; in a lot of ways it smelled like the hospital – unwashed feet and excrement. Thankfully the breeze carried the scent away, leaving me with the earthy smell of the river and plants; and except for the occasional police siren or car horn in the distance, the city was quiet.

I had a strong desire to sit at the docks. I needed to look out across the water and feel the mist created by the wind against my skin. The city was waking up on the other side of the river. Shop lights were slowly replacing the glow of the street lamps. A curious thought crossed my mind, and I wondered if the reflection in the water could replace the reality that was in front of me. If I jumped in, would it all be different there?

"I don't suggest that; you might not come back up."

I looked back, lost in the moment. A tall woman stood, cool eyes taking me in. Her face was blank yet not unkind. Her voice was the same one I'd heard before, soft and velvety in my ears. But this time it wasn't just in my head, this time I had really heard her. Moving, I turned to face her on the metal dock. My mind was racing. I was angry, hurt, betrayed, and confused all at once. Angry that she was here, that she was the one who took Alexander away from me; hurt by her presence, by the loneliness and emptiness I felt in my heart; betrayed in this moment by my need of her and her negligence; lastly, confused, unsure of myself and my need of her.

"He'd still be here if it weren't for you." My voice was just a whisper, barely louder than the river beside me.

"Come now, you know that's not true." She was in front of me now, her hands framing my face like a parent, trying to get a good look at me. "I killed the coven for what they did to you and your husband."

Her breath was thick with the sweet smell of iron, her very presence blanketing me. I couldn't pull away from her, didn't understand why I was so captivated, or how her touch brought me relief. She pulled me forward, leading me to the rocky beach; the stairs that led to the dock formed an alcove just out of reach from the water. The smell of blood was stronger here as it soaked the rocky sand under my feet. The waves frothed pink with it. How had I not noticed the smell before?

"They haven't been feeding you. Eat." Her words compelled me forward.

A man lay just propped against the cement base of the stairs. Even if I hadn't seen him, the smell of alcohol would have given him away. He was drunk, too drunk to understand why he was here, why he was bleeding, or why the sand was soaked red from his friends.

Grinning up at me, he was too drunk to fight as I traced the crimson trail in the sand to his throat. His skin was cold against my lips, his blood blistering by comparison. It scorched its way down my throat as he reached out and groped me with dirty fingers, oblivious to the danger he was in. It didn't take long for his grip to fall away as unconsciousness took him, his heart slowing just as I was ripped away.

The world spun around me as the alcohol in his system became mine. It was unlike anything I'd ever experienced, warming my stomach like a shot as it burned its way through my body. I laughed, the sound of it sad in my ears; being drunk shouldn't feel so good. Regrettably, the sensation was already fading, the sway of the world slowing as I metabolized the alcohol.

"He's calling to you." I could taste her distain, bitter on my tongue. "Don't lose yourself in him. That's not why I saved you."

Her smile faded as she left me on the riverbank, gone just as quickly as she had arrived. There was nothing but the sound of the dock rocking against the black waves and the labored breathing of her victims around me. I could just sense Quin's panicked confusion as my head cleared. He must have felt me feeding, probably even felt drunk himself as he sat at work. The pale bodies around me shivered in the cold; drained and drunk, they'd wake tomorrow a little worse for wear. My nursing judgment told me they were in no immediate danger as I stumbled back to the docks.

This is where Marc found me, using my phone to track down my location. I don't know what I expected, but the look of disgust and disdain was exceptionally venomous as he approached; luckily, I was still too drunk to care. So I just pointed him in the right direction, giving him all the evidence he would need to condemn me and justify his hatred. Oddly enough, I thought I could see relief on his face when he returned, his phone already to his ear.

"I found her," Marc said into the phone. I laughed, feeling Quin's relief wash over me. "She's drunk. I can smell it on the guy… Well I guess her tolerance isn't as high as yours. Listen, there are five people down here with her… Find me after work."

He said nothing to me as he hung up; turning from me, he was already halfway up the dock by the time I called after him.

"It wasn't all me, Marc. I didn't mean to." The words felt thick across my tongue as I struggled not to slur.

I had to all but run to keep pace with Marc's long stride as he pulled away from me. His anger swelled. I felt it heavy in my chest as it shrouded him in a dark aura. For a second I was taken aback, not completely sure that I wasn't hallucinating. When had it become easier to see past his calm façade and read his emotions? That's when I felt the weight of the woman's presence against mine, heavy like a blanket as she held me back.

"You see him now, don't you?" Her voice preceded the warmth of her touch as she spoke softly in my ear.

Marc stopped cold in his tracks, turning to look back at me. She grinned up at him from over my shoulder, her eyes like embers against her porcelain skin. Marc moved, just too slowly, as she spun away from me. She'd shoved me to the ground as she charged. The sidewalk cracked and smoldered where we'd been standing, the bullet molten hot in the depression it had created. She had Marc pinned against the cement column of the underpass, his arm twisted at an impossible angle beside him. She held it twisted there, immobilizing him as the gun clanged to the ground beside his dangling feet.

The energy that poured from both of them felt like static before lightning strikes. Marc's was that of pure rage, black and all consuming. Hers was white light, playful and mercilessly blinding against his anger. It was a game to her, no fear or regret clouded the emotions I read from her.

"Calm down, hunter, it's unbecoming." Sharp teeth lined her smile, unapologetically true to her nature. "I do hope you'll start taking better care of her. I can't have you hurting her."

Marc fell to the ground, no longer suspended by her grasp around his collar. He coughed hard, struggling to catch his breath as she crouched beside him. I watched as she inhaled the scent of him curiously.

"You still smell of him." She paused, her sharp smile fading. "I'm sorry."

Marc spat on the ground between them, pain piercing his psyche. "Fuck you."

Her energy faded from me then, her features stoic as she withdrew. Sighing, she took his twisted right arm in her hands. Marc fought weakly before she sharply twisted his right arm, forcing the dislocated joint back into place with a sickening *POP*. Marc cried out, collapsing onto his side to cradle the now straightened limb.

"I forgot how fragile your bodies are. Tell Quin I'll see him soon, hunter; at least he won't suffer as you have."

I felt a chill go down my spine. Her words were like ice as she left him there, only stopping for a second to peer down at me. Her eyes were cold, the embers from before gone. They told me to prepare, though for what I was unsure, as she left me there again. I felt the weight of her leave me once more. Defensively, Marc scrambled for his gun, only finding me in its sight by the time he forced his left arm to level his aim. Instinctually, I threw my arms up, cursing.

"Sorry," he hissed, lowering his gun as he pulled his right arm into his lap.

"Let me take a look," I urged, reaching for him.

"Do me a favor," Marc snapped, pushing past me as he stood. "When she comes after Quin, at least try to defend him."

His dark eyes leveled with mine; there was the hatred I'd been sensing from him all night, no longer veiled by his perfect mask.

"I couldn't move," I finally managed, hurt by his accusation. I didn't know how to explain it, the effect her presence had on me.

"You'll *feel* his death if that woman gets to him," he said, the pain in his eyes palpable. "Like a piece of your soul is being shredded."

His attitude was infectious; instantly I was just as pissed as he was. "What would you know?" I spoke the words like a curse. "I didn't ask you to come here."

"Maybe," Marc all but spat in my face. "This isn't about you. Has it occurred to you that maybe, just maybe, I'm trying to protect my friend?"

"None of this would be happening if it wasn't for him!" I met every ounce of his anger with my own as I pushed him back, the weight of him nothing against my fingertips. "So back off."

Marc stumbled back, eyes wide. I could tell he was looking for a fight; something must have made him think twice because he didn't advance again. The fight in him replaced with a somber ache.

"If you don't decide who you are, it will be decided for you." His voice had lost its edge. "You might think you know what it feels like – being alone – but nothing will prepare you for this loss. You didn't have a choice before, but you do now. You need to talk to Quin. Don't make me come after you again. I don't miss twice."

Marc's voice hung in the air. He'd simultaneously warned and threatened me before turning to leave; the cold shoulder he gave me was the only true farewell. At least my apartment wasn't far and my buzz wasn't completely gone as I made my way back home. One drunk step after another, I let the alcohol erase the feel of Marc from my mind. My pace inevitably slowed, rigor mortis was setting in by the time I finished climbing the stairs to my apartment. I dropped my keys twice before I could manage to unlock the door and enter the sanctuary that was black out curtains. I barely managed to get out of my scrubs before I collapsed onto the blissful cold that was my silk sheets. With a full belly and a bit of alcohol left in my system, I didn't dream of anything.

It was the sound of slamming cupboards that finally drug me from the abyss... 'Quin?'

"Yeah, yeah, 'bout time you woke up." His voice rang out loud and clear under my bedroom door.

I rolled out of bed, immediately feeling sick, it was still daylight. Asshole was getting back at me. I took a moment, tossing an oversized t-shirt over my bra and underwear. Fuck him. It was my apartment; I didn't have to get completely dressed.

"I'm ordering pizza; you should really buy some groceries. Or... I could just get some whiskey? Then we can both drink dinner."

I could barely open my eyes wide enough to glare as I plopped down on the couch. "Get the whiskey."

He smiled his best cheesy grin as he pulled a bottle from a brown bag. "Pizza's already on its way; you're buying."

He sat down next to me, not even bothering to grab a glass. A fifth of discount whiskey in his lap, he unscrewed the top and downed a third of it instantly.

"I'm not cleaning up after you if you puke." The smell of it made my eyes water. I didn't understand how he was just chugging it.

He chuckled. "I'm not cleaning up after you if you puke, lightweight. Marc told me you were sloshed; bet that guy last night didn't even blow a point-O-six. Let's see if I can get to point three before my buzz disappears." He tilted the bottle back, his eyes challenging me to call his bluff.

"Why would I buy groceries? Just to watch them go bad?" I yawned, rubbing the sleep from my eyes.

He put his hand up, motioning for me to wait until he finished, letting out a burp that could have blown up the apartment had there been an open flame. I blew at him, waving my hand through the air, desperate to dissipate the smell of it.

"So you look normal, and when people come over you can offer them – me – food," he answered, incredulous. "Alright, you have ten minutes until that whiskey hits me, it won't last long. My metabolism is insane now." His cheesy grin was back. "Don't get any crazy ideas and try to take advantage of me."

I was honestly caught off guard by him, and this had him giggling now. The look on my face must have been good, either that or the alcohol was hitting him faster than he anticipated. I couldn't help but laugh at him, shaking my head at his utter childishness.

"Wouldn't dream of it," I finally managed to say.

Sure enough, ten minutes passed and Quin was already slurring his words, pizza at the ready as he recapped his phone call with Marc. Thrilled to retell his momentary drunkenness at work and the short-lived excitement it had created in his otherwise boring night. Done talking, Quin pulled out a pocket knife, probably just as hungry as I was. He dropped it twice before I took it from him.

"Say something mean." I held the knife poised at his forearm.

"I don't know why you don't just bite me, you wimp."

And just like that, I didn't feel bad about putting a one-inch incision through all three layers of his skin and into the fascia below. He winced slightly, but otherwise didn't care what I did. There we sat, side by side. He ate pizza and rambled while I drank. The thirst was always present, and if left unchecked it could become all-consuming. It was hard to stop once I started. I had to concentrate, forcing my awareness of Quin's pulse and the way his breathing changed instead of just my need of it.

This was better than the night before; feeding from Quin allowed me to tap into his sensations and him into mine. I felt the alcohol's effect on him and within me as I drank. His interest was always the same; he fixated on my urge to feed and its intoxicating effects within me. In a lot of ways, my feeding from him was like a drug. The only time the pain stopped was when I ate. Emotional and physical, I could let myself be swallowed by it. Nothing else mattered and there never seemed to be enough.

Quin always allowed me this solace, only pressing his consciousness against mine when it was time to stop. This allowed me to focus, to become aware of him once more and not just the relief he provided. His heartbeat, once even and slow, pounded in my ears as his body fought to oxygenate, each breath deep and purposeful. His mind pulled at mine, forcing me to listen, to slow, to release. The loss of sustenance was always painful, my body and mind aching for more. I had to physically distance myself from him, from the temptation. I stretched out across the couch, shoving Quin to the far end with my legs as I let the alcohol numb my mind.

"I didn't know I could still get drunk," I said, closing my eyes, enjoying the warmth of the whiskey as it coursed through my veins.

"Well, I'm not a cheap date. I can barely afford to get drunk anymore thanks to you," Quin scoffed through a mouthful of pizza.

"It's a shame it doesn't last," I sighed, feeling my buzz lessen with every passing minute. "Whiskey was his favorite," I remarked, glancing at the empty bottle. "He had better taste than you."

"Obviously not," Quin countered, eyeing me sarcastically.

I smiled, kicking out at him jokingly. It was odd watching him eat, since changing the idea of eating food had never once crossed my mind. The shared memories from the coven had warned me that the outcome would be less than ideal should I try. Occasionally, though, I picked up on the memories of food through Quin. Maybe it was how he could enjoy my act of feeding despite the vast difference in diet.

"If I made food, would you eat it?" I asked casually.

"Probably," Quin answered slowly. "Why?"

"I don't miss eating, but sometimes I just want to remember." I paused, unsure of where my memories were going to take me. "I want to remember the taste of coffee. Alexander... He wasn't an addict like me, but it was something we enjoyed together. There are other things, but that's just what comes to mind right now."

"Sure," Quin responded lightheartedly.

I was thankful he didn't probe further. As he finished eating I looked around my one bedroom apartment. This wasn't the home I had made with Alexander; it was just the remnants of what was left now that he was gone. Sparse knickknacks and artwork outlined the life we'd had together, but no pictures. The sight of him just brought me back to that night as I watched the life leave his eyes. I had to settle for seeing him in my dreams, but even there the outcome could be rigged.

"Yesterday, the one who made me, she said you were calling to me. How could she know that and why didn't I hear you?" Quin shook his head; he didn't know any more than I did. "It all feels like a dream now, I was by the waterside, almost like I was sleepwalking. I remember going to the dock, but I didn't really know why." I propped myself on my elbows, desperate to explain. "Then I saw her. I was angry, but more than anything I felt hurt and confused by it." I could feel the tears welling in my eyes, my anger and frustration getting the better of me. "I know what she took from me, but a part of me needed her, and I didn't even realize it. When I was at the dock with her, I wanted to hate her, but I couldn't. I couldn't get away."

"You were compelled. All I could feel was her. I had a general idea of what was happening, but it didn't feel like you," Quin said plainly. "It's the hold she has on you; the connection only goes one way, though. That's the difference."

"What will happen if I can't fight her, fight *this*?" My tears made sense to me now.

Since being tethered my emotions became less and less meaning-ful. I felt blunted, almost like the parts of me that could feel emotions and cared about who I was before were being erased. Only the stron-gest emotions seemed to spark a true response from me. I found less meaning in normal, everyday activities, and I didn't care. Existing the way I did before felt, at times, trivial. It was this thought that terrified me. How long until I could no longer recall Alex or the way he made me smile, or the reasons I loved him more than I ever did myself?

"You get it now?" Quin's voice every bit as somber as I felt.

CHAPTER FOUR

Quin tossed his hoodie on before leaving Eryn's apartment; he planned to stumble around downtown for a bit and see what kind of trouble he could get himself into. He wasn't drunk anymore; his stumbling was just for show. People seemed to tolerate a lot more bullshit or leave you alone altogether if they thought you were drunk. It was just after midnight and the light from the moon cast a mysterious glow over the moss-covered streets. It was still just cool enough for Quin to see his breath; he loved this time of year. The rainy season washed the old streets clean, taking with it the smell of pollution. The city sparkled, the roads mirrored with rain like glass. Quin loved the city on nights like this, but it was nights like this that made it hard not to use. He could smell it in the streets even with the rain, just catching the scent of it on the air before disappearing. Before old habits could trump his better judgment, he ducked into a nearby bar.

"Double of your cheapest whiskey and whatever's on tap." Quin downed the whiskey immediately, tapping the bar with his empty glass. He'd probably need another on standby in case the first didn't do the trick.

The bartender cast him a sideways glance but did eventually refill the glass. The whiskey burned the whole way down. Usually he'd sip it, taking the time to enjoy the taste as it warmed his bones. That was not a luxury he could afford right now. The beer was just easy to drink as he waited for the liquor to hit his system. Out of habit Quin started tapping his feet, forcing his attention on the sound of it and the taste of his drink. Anything would do so long as it distracted him from worse habits.

It was getting harder, because in a way he had found a new drug. It was just too bad it made him crave all the others. There was nothing quite like the oblivion of being fed on.

"You alright man? Can I get you something else?" The bartender sounded genuinely concerned.

Quin smiled; this guy was cute, probably years younger than him. "No, just need a few more drinks and I'll be fine." Quin made a point to reach out for his shot glass with a shaking hand.

Standing, Quin downed his sufficiently shaken shot before leaving. It was hard not to laugh at the concern on the bartender's face. At least his little prank had bought him enough time to kick-start his second buzz of the night. This time when Quin stumbled back into the street, it wasn't pretend. He'd successfully smothered one addiction with another.

It wasn't the same high he got when Eryn fed, but it was going to have to do. Marc had told him what it was like, their blood lust and the desire that blinded them, but he'd never told him how good it felt. If feeding her was the cost, she could take every drop.

"Damn it," Quin cursed.

He was getting himself worked up all over again. The cold night air helped to clear his mind but the user in him only wanted one thing – to use. Quin pulled out his phone; scrolling his contacts until he found the number he'd been looking for.

"Can you meet me somewhere before I do something stupid?" Quin's tone was earnest, spoken from a place of desperation.

Quin's buzz was completely gone by the time Marc made it downtown; he'd been sitting outside, letting the rain drench him. The ice bath kept him from thinking about anything other than how fucking cold he was. Marc eased in next him on the curb; he'd dressed for the downpour, unlike Quin.

"I didn't expect you to call me for this shit," Marc said callously.

Quin tried to laugh but it got caught in his throat. "What can I say; I like my vices."

Marc took a deep breath. "If I'm being honest, I thought you might have trouble with this. I just hoped it would replace your need for anything else."

"Was it like this for you?" Quin tried not to notice when Marc tensed.

"Yeah," Marc admitted quietly.

Quin stared, astonished he'd actually elicited an answer from him. Marc usually just avoided the subject.

"Their hunger can consume you, better than any drug…" Marc continued.

"Better than sex?" Quin teased.

Marc looked at him. "Huh. I would have thought you two would have passed that point by now."

"What?" Quin scoffed in disbelief.

"It's not better than sex, not even close," Marc said absently as he stood.

"Don't tell me that shit; you know her husband died, right? Now I'm going to wonder."

Marc just laughed. "It was different for me. Who knows, maybe you two will find a different connection. No two hunters bond in the same way. It's hard to say what you'll become."

Marc looked around before picking a seemingly random direction in which to head, gesturing for Quin to join him as he went. It was too cold to sit in one place, especially without cover from the rain.

"Is that what brought all of this on? Were you there tonight?" Marc prodded, trying to keep his friend distracted.

Quin was stiff from forcing himself to stay in one place. He'd been too afraid to wander; he knew where his feet would lead him if he let them. It felt good to be moving again though; sitting still wasn't one of Quin's strengths, and Marc's long strides forced him to keep a brisk pace.

"Yeah. You know you never told me it would be like this. No wonder they can't control it." Quin let out a shuddering breath. "When she's eating, that's the only time she doesn't think of him. There isn't room for anything else."

Quin rubbed his forearm absently, remembering the feel of her. Sharp at first, then nothing but her need of it; it was better than that first drink in the morning, just so you could brave the day. Marc looked back, regarding him suspiciously before continuing their conversation.

"Eryn won't stand a chance if you become an addict. Hunters don't talk about the need for blood after they become tethered; it's something that is shared in the bond. There aren't a lot of us left, Quin; even fewer are successful at creating a bond. For those of us that do make it, the makers often destroy the connection." Marc grimaced as he spoke the last part, his eyes distant.

"I'm sorry; I didn't mean to bring it up. I didn't know. I mean I thought maybe," Quin admitted carefully.

Marc waved away his apologies. "I don't know when that woman is going to come for you. I think she was just trying to send a message and meet Eryn. Did she know her maker was still around?"

Quin thought for a second, reflecting on the mirage of memories that had passed between Eryn and himself. "No. Whoever she is, she made a point to stay hidden."

"Figures. Whoever she is, she's old. She knew Eryn was tethered and could sense you." Marc rubbed his right arm at the memory of her. "She knew I'd been bonded."

"How could they know that?" Quin asked, skeptical.

Marc thought about it for a while, considering his answer. "The exchange changes us more than we realize. We're human, but something in us is never the same."

"How long has it been?" Quin asked, not wanting to outright ask how long Marc had been alone.

"Thirty years." Again, Marc hesitated, unsure whether giving Quin more information would be more harmful than good.

"How old are you? How long have you been like this?" Quin all but shouted his inquiry, his interest sufficiently piqued.

Marc was instantly remorseful. "A long time. I'm still aging, just slower. Like I said, something in us never goes back. Some of us even turn. You never know how much of yourself will be left." His gaze became cold and unyielding. "If you'd tried this with the others, they would have killed you and her. The maker isn't your only enemy, Quin."

"We're dying enough as it is without attacking each other," Quin said, completely disregarding Marc's warning. "Hell, you barely made it out yesterday. How are we supposed to fight them if we can't even stand on level ground with them?"

"You're missing the point. Too many of us were dying, being consumed, or turning. Half of the new vampires being created were coming from us and the hunters that were tethered."

"You never told me that." Quin felt disgusted. "Hopefully they've all killed themselves."

That was exactly the wrong thing to say; Marc had Quin by the collar of his sweatshirt. "Don't. I've been a hunter longer than you've been alive, while you prance around here like some fucking superhero. The hunters didn't decide to change." Marc released his hold on Quin. "The makers found great pleasure in using our tricks against us. It's easy when you're already halfway there."

Quin took a second, mentally counting to ten. Marc was always finding some way to put him in his place or one-up him. He was getting really tired of being pushed, but now was not the time to press the issue and he knew it. Quin knew he'd been insensitive. That being said, you'd think someone almost a hundred years old could take a joke, even if it was in poor taste.

Being a psych nurse meant that discussing death, suicide, and even homicide were common topics of conversation. He had to admit that sometimes he forgot to censor himself. Joking helped it all seem less real, pushing aside the constant threat, and in a lot of ways it took the power away from the thoughts.

"My bad, okay? No more joking about dead friends." Quin put his hands up as a sign of surrender; he was good at half-assed apologies.

The truth was, he'd lost friends too; sometimes it was easier to pretend otherwise, never acknowledging the loss or pretending it was their fault. If they'd been smarter, trained harder, or asked for help, maybe they'd all still be here. Quin hid those thoughts away before they could overwhelm him. *Fuck them.* He wasn't going to be another dead friend; not now. He'd found a way to stay alive and beat the bastards at their own game.

"How do I keep us alive?" Quin asked, all joking aside.

Marc turned to him once more, the same distant look in his eyes. "I wasn't able to. Sometimes it isn't up to us."

"Then what do I do differently? I don't have time to make everyone else's mistakes, especially with all of mine waiting to happen," Quin pushed, exasperated.

Marc chuckled. "That might be the smartest thing I've heard you say."

Shrugging off the insult, Quin lowered his voice: "What happened to you?"

"Creating doesn't always happen on purpose; usually victims just die in the exchange. Sometimes, though, they survive. This leaves a lot of orphaned monsters to roam the streets."

He waited patiently for Marc to say something he didn't already know. Marc was like a walking history book. At least he knew why now – he'd actually lived through most of it.

"The orphans are easy to recruit, abandoned by their makers; hunters are quick to get a hold of them before they kill someone." Marc found a relatively dry bench to sit on, the overhanging trees providing an adequate cover from the rain before he continued. "When I met Michael, his maker had disowned him. For weeks his sire had tortured him, tried feeding his family to him until there was no bloodline left to kill. He must have gotten bored because when I found Michael he was alone in an old warehouse feeding on himself." Marc paused, reflecting on his memories. "He'd been trapped for so long, just starving… I couldn't bring myself to kill him. I found his family buried around him, corpses rotting in shallow graves. The smell…"

Quin watched as Marc cringed, lost in thought. He wondered if the smell of decaying bodies ever really left your nose; he didn't intend to ask and hoped he'd never know.

"He was so far gone by the time I'd found him, I didn't know if I could save him. Usually they can't survive that long without feeding; even Eryn fed on the subconscious." Marc was leaning forward now, elbows resting on his knees. "It about killed me, saving him. He'd been starving for so long. I didn't have the luxury of bagged blood, either." Marc pulled up the sleeve on his jacket to expose several silver and white crescent moon scars across the dark skin of his left forearm. "Turns out we can't heal from everything."

"He was really cannibalizing himself to survive? How did you bring him back if he was that close to being feral?" Quin asked, incredulous; he'd had no idea a vampire could feed from itself.

"You told me that when your mind linked with Eryn's, her memories overtook you; but what about your memories to her?" Marc paused, taking a reprieve from his memories.

"I don't know; not really, I guess. I got pulled in and before I knew it I was a part of her past. It felt like I was living her life. I've never felt anything like it," Quin answered plainly.

"That doesn't make any sense. Did you let her in?" Marc's tone was that of genuine confusion.

Quin wasn't sure why Marc's inquiry made him uncomfortable. "I didn't really think about it, I saw her life and the shit she'd been through and I guess I just wanted to know more. When I woke up, I remember her yelling at me to get out of her head."

Marc's face quickly informed Quin just how wrong his answer had been. "Figures you'd find a way to turn something as intrusive as that into a one-sided gain."

"She didn't pry. What was I supposed to do?" Quin responded defensively.

"Maybe back off and stop ripping apart her mind long enough to allow her to think? How do you expect someone to trust you when you're the only one holding all the cards?" Marc sat back, peering up at the green canopy overhead. "You have to be vulnerable. It's uncomfortable. It was probably one of the worst feelings, to share myself completely with another person. Having every secret I've ever kept ripped away from me. The only thing that makes it better is not being the only one standing there naked in the end."

"Thanks for the lecture; they never get old. Tell me again how I've messed up, but maybe this time you can tell me how to fix it, too." Quin sneered.

"Your sarcasm never gets old," Marc sighed. "The next time she feeds, drop your guard. The blood connection increases the bond. Just try not to pull away."

"Alright, fair enough. Is that how you got Michael to let go of you?" Quin asked, desperate to change subjects.

"Not quite. A funny thing happens when you let the lines that divide you from another person blur. I was able to use his memories against him. Nothing I could do or say was going to bring him back once he'd latched onto me. I had to find the piece that the blood and hunger couldn't take away." Marc was smiling, the faintest curve played across his lips. "If you keep yourself separate, you won't be able to pull her back when she loses sight of herself."

"So after that, the two of you lived happily ever after? You already told me the sex was great. What happened to him?" Quin was eager to get to the point of their heart-to-heart.

Marc shot Quin a look that said *'If you're going to be an ass, I'm done here'*. Again, Quin put his hands up, gesturing for Marc to continue. He was starting to think that he liked Marc more as the cold silent type.

"His maker came back for him, furious, finding his protégé tied to a human. Jealous that Michael had used the life he'd given him to deny him." Marc was rubbing his temples, a scowl playing across his face.

Quin felt Marc's emotions wash over him: anger, regret, and remorse; never had he seen Marc lose control, let alone been able to sense it so clearly. It was just a flash, but Quin could swear he saw Michael's face flash in his mind's eye. Little pieces of the pain Marc had endured burrowed into his chest; it felt like his heart was being ripped open.

"I couldn't stop it. They tore each other apart. I was so angry for what he'd done to Michael that I lost control. I broke myself trying to destroy that man." Marc had his elbows back on his knees, leaning forward with his hands clenched together in front of his face. "I play it over and over in my head, and for the life of me, I don't know how it could have ended any differently, Quin. All I know is we were both consumed, feeding off each other's anger. In the end neither of us was in control."

Quin felt a dull ache settle in his chest; this pain was Marc's, but he felt it all the same. Slowly the sensation was replaced with a sobering sorrow.

Quin rubbed his chest, trying to rid himself of the sensation. "You feel like this all the time?"

Marc looked up from his clenched fists, confused before he realized what Quin was referring to: "How long have you been able to read emotions like that and not just overhear?"

"I don't know. It started off just as sensations. Lately, though, it's been flashes of images and the emotions attached. Why?" he asked, relieved that the change of subject had rid him of Marc's grief.

"That's how she survived so long. Eryn's abilities manifested psychically at first. That's why you're starting to see the memories and feel the emotions." Marc's tone was that of excitement and dread.

"What's your point?" Again Quin found himself growing tired of Marc's prolonged narratives.

"The last hunter who had that ability controlled others," Marc concluded.

Quin smiled, his earlier disinterest replaced with dark curiosity. "Controlled them how?"

CHAPTER FIVE

"If there was a night to call in sick, it was tonight," was a saying spoken every night. Regardless of the workload, it always seemed to ring true.

Everyone at the nurse's desk, including me, mumbled our agreement. It was turning out to be an especially painful night; a part of me almost felt bad that I was leaving in a few hours. Mid-shift had its perks. It felt like we'd been putting out fires all night. It started off with my intoxicated patient who reeked of alcohol trying to code on me. He'd been seconds away from needing chest compressions by the time the ambulance arrived and pushed two rounds of epinephrine. After that it was borderline personalities feeding off one another for staff attention, self-harm, and a few patients even managed to tip their recliners when they climbed out of them backwards.

The unit was buzzing with energy, energy that I freely took in, easing patient anxiety and putting out fires slowly. It felt like a full moon of a night and all of us wanted to know who had used the Q word. Healthcare was steeped with superstition. If you said it was quiet, the night would be anything but; if one person died, there were going to be two more to follow; and if you didn't knock on wood, it would be too late for you.

The only reprieve came in the form of medication optimization. Everyone was just now starting to metabolize their medications. Five hours into the shift and all of the medication-tolerant patients were beginning to feel the full effects of our pharmaceuticals working together to provide them, and us, with much needed rest. The wonders of adjuncts and polypharmacy were creating bliss for all involved.

It was a bit strange to feel the energy of the unit change. The earlier chaos felt like I'd downed four cups of espresso. Usually I only felt this lively after actually feeding. It had become effortless, preying upon the hurt of others. I didn't have to think about it anymore as I freely took in the excess. Now that everyone was settling in for the night, the earlier high was subsiding. It was bittersweet.

I could feel the pull of sleep settle over the unit like a warm blanket. Interestingly, I found that if I paid close enough attention I was able to catch glimpses of their dreams. Sometimes it was just a jumble of thoughts mixed with old memories, but more often than not it was nightmares.

Tonight, there was an especially bad dream that caught my attention as I did my rounds. Her terror was like a car horn on a silent night, and before I knew it I was looming over her. She was grimacing in her sleep as she tossed back and forth, trapped within the nightmare. I could just see it, foggy and distorted at first, but eventually her fear brought forth bursts of clarity.

I could see her; she was probably eight, an older woman screamed in her face. Then she was being held down, the weight of her assailant crushing on my chest. I could feel the woman's breath hot on my face as she spat her words. I felt the guilt as it consumed the patient, the words as sharp as any knife: *It's your fault he left!* My body felt every bruise left behind as if they were mine. Her pain resonated with my own nightmares. Those words were like poison when spat from a mother's mouth.

Captivated, I found a place to sit amongst the patients in the oversized living room that was my psych ward while I shared in her nightmare. Over and over again the words replayed in her head: *it's your fault.* I watched as those words destroyed her life. It may have started when she was eight, but time did nothing to ease the trauma and the ache within her soul. I coaxed her regrets from her. Everything in her life that she destroyed… *it's your fault…* until the women I felt heavy on our chest and screaming wasn't her mother anymore, but herself.

Her shame was tangible. Flashes of her life played before me: pills, alcohol, anything to ease the pain until all that was left was the needle in her arm and those words as she screamed them. This time, though, the girl on the floor was her daughter. *It's your fault he left!* She believed the lie absolutely, making it her truth as everyone left. She projected the blame so completely that she couldn't see how she'd destroyed herself and continued the cycle of violence. Any connection or understanding I had originally found in her was erased and replaced with repulsion.

'*Pathetic*,' I thought, disgusted by this woman who had justified hurting her own child in the same way she'd been hurt, '*You became just like her.*'

In that moment I wanted her to understand, to truly see herself and the terribleness she'd brought down on her own family. So I showed her the nightmares, but this time through my eyes. No matter the reason for her actions, I couldn't condone what she had done. By the time she woke, tears streaked her face from bloodshot eyes.

I watched as panic consumed her, her mind desperate for solace and understanding, but all she found was me. Her eyes pleaded with me, she was up and across the room, her fingers digging into me desperately.

"Let me go." My words were cold, precise, and knowing; a power resided within them that I'd never felt before.

"It wasn't my fault," she wailed.

Within seconds the staff was on their feet. Their hands pulled her away from me; she was horrified as she fought for purchase in my skin, frantic for understanding… for forgiveness that wasn't mine to give. I didn't move, just watched her, feeling her chaos as she fought the truth of her lies, unable to blame and hide away.

"Are you okay?" A security guard and fellow nurse stayed by my side as the other staff handled the now hysterical woman.

"She startled me. I just froze and before I knew it she had a hold of me," I lied, pushing past their concern. I needed to distance myself from the turmoil of her mind.

It was the child in me that hoped she was swallowed whole by the realization of what she'd done. I knew I wasn't able to be objective in this moment. The images of her child, just as broken as the mother now, made me want to punch a hole in the wall. How could a parent purposefully hurt their child? How had mine?

"I need to get out of here." Suddenly all of the thoughts, the dreams, and the nightmares were suffocating me. "My charting is done. I gave Dawn report already."

I was clocked out and running through the hospital. I couldn't breathe inside of the walls anymore. I pulled desperately at my collar, the cold October air hitting me full force as I left the warmth of the hospital. My chest and throat were tight, panic overtaking me. I'd let all of their voices in, the pressure of them eradicating my ability to think, to hear. I felt his intentions before he even reached me. His name was Myer.

"Eryn, right?"

I must have looked pathetic, leaning against the building as I tried to catch my breath; I nodded, acknowledging his question.

"Bad night?"

"I just let them get inside my head," I breathed, standing upright. "I'm usually better at not internalizing it, but it got the better of me tonight. A patient just reminded me of someone."

I could feel his concern, desperate to find the right thing to say.

"Thanks for listening, I'm fine now, just needed to catch my breath." I smiled faintly, hoping it was reassuring. "I'll see you next week."

With that I was off; the last thing I needed was another person's thoughts in my head. I'd had enough of that tonight. Regrettably, I wasn't quick enough to escape him completely: *all alone*. I never liked knowing what people thought of me, it wasn't any of my business and it honestly made me feel crazy. Trying to understand everyone's perception of me made it hard not to try and constantly justify myself. To Myer I was sad and alone.

And? I thought, pissed by his assumptions and angry that he'd been able to read me.

This was the second time this week I'd left my car at work. I couldn't bring myself to drive home. The feel of the car around me after being stuck inside just wasn't appealing. Most nights I wandered the city, exploring the old buildings and watching the inhabitants of the city. It was strange how distant I felt from all of it and everyone. I was beginning to understand that it wasn't just the loss of my husband that made me want to disconnect. It was hard to be around people when you could hear every thought and feel their every emotion. It was unsettling. I was beginning to find just how little I cared for any of them, even my patients...

There was a time when being a nurse was who I was; now it just felt like a dance I knew the steps to but no longer appreciated. My job wasn't hard, especially not now. Maybe that was the problem? Work had quickly become a place to snack more than it was a place of healing and for a moment I wondered how hard it would be to just disappear. All I needed was a place to sleep... and blood?

The sweet smell of it just reached me as I neared the railroad tracks; it was faint and nearly overpowered by the creosote-soaked railroad ties, but it was there. The coppery tinge of it was unmistakable. Sliding through broken chain-link I entered the maze of old rail cars, reaching out cautiously as I went, prodding Quin awake. I felt him stir, his mind slowly responding to mine. His initial confusion quickly melted away, succumbing to my curiosity, uncertainty, and the enticing smell of blood as it pulled me farther into the shadows and rail yard beyond.

Moving slowly, I became aware of another smell. Acrid, Rancid. Rotten. This was the smell of death, the kind of smell you never forget as an emergency room nurse trying to save the remains of a person after a car accident. It was created when the organs and bowels ruptured, mixing innards with piss, shit and blood. More troubling than the smell was the sound of something eating, chewing, and crunching.

'*Ghouls*,' Quin thought, his dread acidic across my palate. I curled my lip, spitting.

Every fiber of my being homed in on the sound as I crept closer. I'd pieced people back together, held crumbled limbs with gravel for bones, and seen the inside of chest cavities. What I found as I rounded the last rail car wasn't human. The smell of rot and infection belonged solely to the creature before me. It gulped and chewed with primal urgency as it clawed at the remains in front of it. I wasn't sure how I had smelled the blood before I'd smelled the rotting thing before me.

It was skeletal, leather skin taught around the bones, its stomach bloated from gorging. Other parts were bulbous, almost like it was decaying from the inside out. This was a failed attempt at creating a vampire. Why, then, had its creator not just killed it? Surely this option was not better than death. Its spiked spine was hunched forward over its buffet, too preoccupied to notice my approach.

"Don't." The word whispered sounded like a shout, I froze. The ghoul thankfully took no interest in the noise. Before me sat a lithe man poised atop a distant rail car. He sat motionless, just watching. Circling carefully, I climbed, joining the man atop his perch.

"Are you feeding them?" I asked softly.

"Yes." He never took his eyes from the ghoul. "Why do you smell different, almost human?"

I sniffed absently at my uniform, but doubted that was what he was referring to. "They aren't alive anymore. Can't you smell the rot?"

"Yes, I can." His eyebrows furrowed, accentuating the lines in his face and under his midnight eyes.

"You need to leave." I urged. Quin's consciousness weighed heavily in my mind; he was close.

A part of me knew that I shouldn't let him go; it was the part that knew feeding a person to a ghoul was inhumane, even inhuman. The other part of me saw the loss and understood his need to keep his malformed companion alive despite the futility.

"She used to be beautiful." His voice broke as he struggled to recall the way her face had been before death had claimed her, hollowing her cheeks and rotting her eyes. "I couldn't do it."

His emotions played out before me. He'd failed her, failed himself. He hadn't been able to save her and now he couldn't bring himself to end it. Images of her flashed in his mind, transposing her previous beauty over the disgust and rot that she was now. That's when I realized a part of him was broken far beyond anything I could hope to understand or reason with.

Without hesitation, he dropped to the ground below, having heard Quin's approach. A mix of excitement and nervous energy sparked in my chest as he grew near. The vampire below wasted no time as he grabbed the skeletal frame of the ghoul. One arm encircled her waist as he turned her toward him. His mind's eye no longer wavered between images of her. She was beautiful. Long black curls framed her once full, oval face; eyes the color of warm honey stared back at him. He'd placed his other arm under her chin, keeping her dripping and broken jaw from clamping onto him. His laughter was musical as tears streamed down his face. His mind completely fractured. Chaos washed over me as all the bliss and madness of his loss destroyed him. He couldn't accept that he had been her undoing.

Crunching gravel and hasty footsteps, Quin came upon them; the shock and confusion at what he was witnessing froze him. Two corpses danced upon a dance floor of carnage, slick and jagged beneath their feet as they turned. The ghoul snapped madly at her captor, frothy pink sputum spattered the vampire's face and clothes. Still, all he saw was her oval eyes and her full lips smiling back at him. Two shots rang out. No more laughter, no more madness. I let the gun fall from my hand, watching as they both turned to ash.

I didn't remember jumping down from the rail car or the feeling of landing. I couldn't recall how I'd taken Quin's gun or the weight of it in my right hand. What I did remember was putting my finger on the cold metal trigger and squeezing it twice. I needed the insanity to stop; I couldn't listen to his maddening laughter for one more second as she broke in his arms, fighting to destroy him as he had her.

The next thing I remembered was Quin picking his gun up from where I'd dropped it; he was mumbling some sort of disapproval, but I couldn't hear him. I let the deafening ring from the gunshots drown out my hearing, praying the laughter wouldn't return once it stopped.

"Did you hear me?" He was standing right in front of me, gun held out to me.

"No." I looked up at him. From the tone in his voice, he was trying to scold me.

"If you're going to use my gun, try not to drop it in whatever the hell that was." He announced angrily as he presented it, gore and bits smeared the black metal.

I pushed past him like he wasn't even there, annoyed by his tone.

"Hey!" He yelled. I had inadvertently shoved the gun against his chest as I passed, painting his jacket red.

I had to get away from this place. I knew if I stayed much longer, I'd see them again, hear that laughter. Picture her face both beautiful and broken.

"Why are you upset? You put that poor bastard out of his misery." His tone grated at me.

I was running now, one foot in front of the other until I was through the broken fence and being bathed in the city lights. No more rot and no more laughter, just the smell of car exhaust and the sound of horns blaring.

"What's your problem?" Quin's annoyance had grown exponentially.

"You didn't see them, Quin; if you had, you wouldn't be asking me that," I snapped.

"You're upset about them?" He ridiculed. "Did you see the body on the ground or what was left of it?"

"Shut up." I forced the words through gritted teeth.

"Maybe you should have kept them both as pets, then, huh? Fed them people off the streets just so you could save them, is that what you wanted?" Quin continued, each word testing my last nerve.

Our anger grew, fed by the other's annoyance. He held his arms wide as he confronted me, his gun held loosely in his left hand. It was a dare and I took it, shoving him back. He stumbled, hitting the chain link. His blue eyes blazed once he regained his footing, but I didn't give him a chance to move. Fed up and tormented, I let him see exactly what I had.

Slamming the memory against him just as hard as any physical strike, I wanted it to hurt. It wasn't just the images, no. I gave him all the chaos and turmoil I had felt watching them. Pain contorted his features, his hands clenched against his temples as he fell to his knees. I tore into his mind. The pain of the exchange mirrored back to me through our connection.

"You didn't see them, Quin," I repeated, releasing him.

"You think you're the only one who can do that?"

Just as quickly as he spoke the words, my world was black; all I felt was the gravel biting into my skin and the weight of him behind me. His knee dug into the center of my back as he twisted my left arm to meet my right shoulder blade. The old familiar feel of a gun barrel pressed against my skin. It took everything I had to push his mind away from mine, my vision returning slowly. It didn't matter, he had me pinned, and there wasn't much to look at from the ground.

"If you keep letting them get under your skin you'll be just as mad as they are. You can't take every sob story personally. Not everyone can be saved, and every dead body isn't Alexander." Quin spoke his words like knives, sharp and to the point.

"Don't say his name!" I tested his grip, causing searing pain to erupt in my left shoulder, "You don't know."

"Don't I?" He pressed the gun hard against the back of my neck.

Again his mind took hold of mine, but this time my vision didn't go black; this time I saw his memories as he recalled my grief. I saw myself through his eyes from before I'd lost Alexander to now. What upset me most was the way Quin experienced my pain, it hurt him in all the same ways it had me. All he lacked was context.

"Don't." My voice broke.

The pain I felt wasn't just Alex's absence, it wasn't that simple. It was the loss of myself and of my identity when he died. It was every morning waking to him, every night falling asleep with him. I lost the language we'd cultivated from fifteen years of marriage and our dumb humor only we understood. It was the way he held me together when I fell apart. All the times he kissed me good night. It was his knowledge of me and the fact that I never had to explain myself or who I was, he just loved me. It wasn't just the loss of him I felt; it was the loss of my history and of my best friend. From our first kiss at his house before we went to Jazz Band when I was sixteen to our last...

Quin relinquished his grasp on me, sliding beside me to sit in the gravel. Internalizing what I had given to him.

"I get it. I still don't agree, but I get why you reacted the way you did." Quin sighed, rubbing his temples. "There have been six bodies found just like that one, nothing left but pieces of ground meat and splintered bone. I don't care why he was feeding that thing."

His resolve was absolute: no doubt, no pity, and no confusion. I breathed it in, letting his resolve calm the hurt I'd let creep in and overtake me.

"I shot them; I needed it to end, just to get them out of my head. I know what I did was right." Sitting up, I wiped the dirt from my face, hands shaking. "I can't turn it off and I'm afraid that if I do, if I shut off that part of myself. The part that still cares, that can care, I'll never get it back."

"Come on, let's get out of here." Quin's tone was hesitant. I could feel the same nervous energy from before. He didn't look at me as he stood. "I never asked you what you wanted before all of this, and I'm sorry I didn't give you a choice."

I paused, taking him in as I digested his apology. The weight of it hung between us uncomfortably. I realized Quin probably didn't have any more of a plan day-to-day than I had before all of this. Also, we were never really friends before and even now, after all he knew about me, I still wasn't sure.

"What you did, even though I didn't understand it at the time, gave me a chance. My choice wasn't taken away by you. Besides, a part of me knew that I wasn't going to be able to fight forever; the need never stopped eating at me. I honestly just hoped I'd find the courage to kill myself before then."

Quin looked at me now, taking in my words. His apology had been sincere, spoken from a place of regret. That was an emotion I knew well, and if left unchecked it could destroy even the strongest mind.

"Maybe this isn't what I wanted, but you bought me time to figure it out." I couldn't tell if my words helped. "It hasn't been all bad." A sad laugh escaped my lips before I could help myself. "That's hard to admit. Call it survivor's guilt, but it just doesn't feel right to be happy without him."

The sound of sirens erased the tension between us; someone had called in the body. It wouldn't be long now before this place was crawling with cops.

"Time to go." Quin announced, extending his hand to me.

I took him up on his offer. My body felt heavy, exhausted by the events of the night and hunger. He knew this, though. He always knew. I think a part of him needed it just as much as I did. Slowly, we made our way back to my apartment, taking side streets as we went. Luckily the cops were too excited to get to the body to take notice of us.

As expected, Quin flipped on every light in the living room and kitchen, I'd turn them all off again when he left. I was better suited for the dark and didn't need the spike in my electric bill.

"Maybe this stuff is easier for you because you were with some-one for so long." Quin was looking around the apartment, distracted, almost like he'd never been here before. "Our lives aren't that different, but those times you found your mother with the pills or watched as your father drank, I joined in with mine. I've been in control for a long time, but you and I both know that addicts never really change."

He wasn't saying these things to me so much as he was telling it to the walls. This wasn't something he knew how to say to someone else; maybe it wasn't something he'd even said out loud before. I just stood, watching him from the doorway as I kicked off my shoes. Quin walked the perimeter of the living room, each step precise. When he finally made his way back toward the doorway, I felt something in him shift and I understood why he had been nervous. The hunger I'd been feeling all night was different somehow, like a craving. This was why he was talking out loud, so I would understood why he was already opening a vein in his arm with a pocket knife.

The smell of him filled the apartment. I didn't want to want it as badly as I did, but I was fixated on it as it ran down his arm. It was his need that pulled and twisted my hunger into something urgent and dark. If this was what it felt like to be addicted, to crave drugs and the escape they provided, I didn't know how anyone stopped. Every fiber of my being ached for it and I knew that if I just gave in, it would all be better. I wasn't strong enough to resist – not him and not the blood.

CHAPTER SIX

He was six, and the sound of his parents' laughter drove him from the comfort of his bed; it was a party. Everyone was dancing; his parents lifted him in their arms. He didn't know why, but they were always happy when these other people were here with them. He loved waking up to find the fun parents. He was ten, and he waited until they all left, pretending to be asleep when they checked on him. Mirrors covered the coffee table, white powder dusting the surface like snow on Christmas. That was the first time he'd done a line, recalling how his parents closed one nostril before inhaling, rubbing the remaining residue on their gums. They wouldn't be home for days; that was more than enough time for him to clean up after them.

He was thirteen, selling to the kids at his school, and it never crossed his mind that he was doing anything wrong. Hell, it was how his parents paid the bills, so what did it matter if he sold what he could steal from them? Occasionally, he'd keep some for himself. He was fifteen, and he could hear them partying again, but something was different. When he came out of his room, he didn't see the dancing, though the music blared just the same. A man he'd never seen sat among the limp bodies of his parents and regular house guests. Tan powder sat carefully guarded on a scale. This wasn't the last line he ever did; it was his favorite, though – especially when he didn't want to feel anything.

He was eighteen and his mom was helping him push off for the first time. He could hear her coaching him and laughing as his head lolled back against the couch. Everything was bliss and his body felt weightless. This was the best he'd ever felt. This was a different kind of high; he knew it would never be this good again.

'I'll be chasing that high my whole life.' Quin's voice floated through my mind as his memories played out before me.

He was twenty, life was fuzzy – one hit after another just trying to get through his day. It didn't matter what it was, so long as he wasn't sober. Life was boring when he was sober; chaos was the only way he felt alive, and chaos was all he found.

Quin's memories became a blur with every drug. I felt them inside me, tasted them in my mouth, felt them in my veins. With every high there was a low; it took more and more until there was no more of himself to find in the bottom of the baggies, at the end of the syringe, or after every pill he followed with a drink. It no longer got him well; it was just the thrill of the chase and the ache that was left in his hollowed bones.

I could feel his need overtaking me, both of us intoxicated by the exchange. It would never be enough. His arms trapped me, my back to his chest; I could feel his eyes on me. As he fed me, I, too, fed him; the intensity was blinding as I took more of him into me. I bit down, needing more. I wasn't in control anymore; Quin was, and he was pulling me further down the rabbit hole with him.

His blood seared through me, and with every drop I could feel myself getting well, nourishing his high. I was drunk on him, lost within the pleasure of feeding. Nothing else mattered but the taste of the blood on my tongue and the distraction it provided me. The lines that separated him and me faded, giving in to our mutual need of each other. I felt his breathing slow, the strain becoming my own as his heart fluttered within my chest.

My energy became his as I steadied his heartbeat, the exchange shifting until I was finally able to release him. In control of myself once more, I severed my connection with him. Fleeing before he could pull me back under. The effort it took was extraordinary; his control clung to me like wet cement. Every nerve in my body was raw with the loss of the drug he provided. It was unbearable. My muscles shook as sweat beaded my skin. Too hot, too cold, and in complete agony; this was the withdrawal he felt at the loss of me. This was the drug that I in turn created for him.

"You son of a bitch." The realization of what had just transpired between us made me sicker then I'd ever been, his need still burning in my veins.

He'd used me. Angry and disgusted, I struggled to control my trembling limbs. No matter how I tried I couldn't get him completely out of my head; this pain – his need – never wavered.

"I haven't used in ten years, not until you," he said, matter-of-fact, his tone controlled and flat.

Guilt and self-hatred overwhelmed me; he'd completely over-ridden my self-control. I couldn't get him out of my veins, felt him coursing through me even now; our connection changed. What had tethered us before was but a tendril; what I found now were roots. I had to fight to keep myself and my feelings separate from his. I was desperate to rid myself of the drug he created within me and how much I still wanted it. The urge to use tore me apart; it was worse than the withdrawal and pain that crawled under my skin. I would have given anything to escape it, to never know.

He reached for me, but I pushed away, striking out at him. What I saw when his eyes met mine made me falter. He held my wrist tight in his hand but this strength wasn't his, it was mine, and what I saw when I looked back at him startled me. The deep blue of Quin's eyes reflected back the green of mine. He leaned in then, his face stoic and calm as he locked his haunting mixed eyes on mine.

His emotions flooded my psyche, my disgust and self-loathing completely erased by his unapologetic self-enjoyment of whatever poison would sustain his escape. He showed me time and time again the hatred that others had showed him. Family, friends, and any self-righteous asshole who thought they needed to shame him in their attempt to save him. He didn't stop because of their pity or support of him; he had stopped because he wanted to and not for anyone but himself. A part of him always wanted the escape that drugs provided. The break from reality helped keep him sane, and now he had that release again in me.

Relinquishing his hold of me, Quin leaned back, enjoying what was left of our exchange. A part of me understood; this was his life, his truth. It was who he was. He looked at me without really seeing me, the green fading from his eyes to reveal blue once more. I realized this was the first time I'd truly seen Quin for who he was. We'd changed. His consciousness was soft against mine where it had only ever been abrasive and restricted. I felt more a part of him, more aware. We were no longer quite as separate as we had been and it scared me.

Both of us looked without seeing as we took in the shared awareness of one another. It felt like I could see myself through him, feel the soft carpet against his palms as if I was touching it myself. We'd become an extension of one another but the connection felt foreign despite the ease of it. The sensation wasn't entirely unpleasant though and for a moment I didn't feel so alone.

This connection hadn't been cultivated over years of friendship and understanding but by the forced bonding created in the blood. Quin, who was not usually perturbed by closeness and lacked any understanding of personal space, shared in my feelings of awkwardness. This was new territory and both of us seemed equally uneasy with the level of closeness we now shared within each other's minds.

Standing, I purposely distanced myself from him as I mentally assessed him. I absorbed the sensations of his body as my own, making sure I hadn't hurt him. I had taken more from him tonight than I ever had before. I did all of this instinctually, realizing just how intrusive it must have felt, surprised that he hadn't recoiled. Blue eyes placid, he just sat there looking up at me. His psyche fit against mine like a puzzle piece, and suddenly I wasn't sure if the sensations were mine or his. I winced. The mixing of our perspectives was disorienting, and the discomfort drove my mind from his.

"It's a two-way street. Don't poke around if you don't want me doing the same." Quin laughed.

"I wasn't trying," I answered indignantly.

He smiled up at me, finding continued enjoyment in my embarrassment. It was with slow focus that he moved to stand, visibly straining to do so without falling. He swayed briefly before ultimately finding his balance. Sweat beaded his forehead as he focused on breathing, his vision speckled black.

I grabbed him, tucking myself under his arm. "Come on, you can stay on the couch."

He leaned against me, each breath calculated as he forced oxygen into his lungs, trying not to pass out. I could feel the true extent of his exhaustion as his consciousness pressed against mine. His eyes took on the same blue-green hue from before, and with each breath he grew stronger, drawing on my energy. It was an odd feeling; I psychically fed on those around me, taking bits of their stamina as a way to sustain myself. Quin was unknowingly doing the same, taking from me in order to heal. I felt his exhaustion ease, his strength and color returning slightly before he withdrew both mentally and physically from me.

"Did you know you could do that?" I inquired.

Quin shrugged, making his way to the couch. "Half the things I do happen on accident."

I reflected on this, thinking about how my own abilities had been evolving. "Have you been able to see people's memories?"

"Yeah, once or twice, but usually just yours. Marc, he's always been able to read people. I just get feelings." Quin was a bit more animated now, excited by the topic of conversation. "I can tell when a patient is getting ready to swing at me."

"How were you able to keep me out of your head before?" I knew in his current mood, he may just tell me.

A smirk affixed his features. "I didn't keep you out of my head; there just wasn't anything there for you to find."

As he said this I felt something change within him. He was systematically turning off his emotions, denying his exhaustion and thoughts purchase within his mind. Nothing mattered to him in this moment; he was void of need or want, merely existing within himself. There was peace within the nothingness. Leave it to Quin to oversimplify something so complicated. It was meditative in nature, the way he let go piece by piece. Taking a deep breath, I allowed myself the space to just be and exist for a moment without the weight of worry. For just a moment it was okay to just be.

"Exactly." Quin yawned as he stretched out across the couch. "Most people try to imagine a wall or create a loop in their head. You'd probably pick up on that easily enough, but you can't read what isn't there."

"I'll try to remember that." I yawned back. "Stay as long as you need. And Quin?" I stopped at the entrance to my bedroom. "I don't want to feel what you shared with me tonight ever again."

The veil over his mind rippled as he stared at me from across the living room. I could tell he didn't understand.

"I'm not an addict. My parents were and you are. I'm not. Don't force that connection again and don't ever manipulate my need to feed like that." My tone was venomous.

Quin's earlier smile twisted, it was every bit as hostile as my tone. "Don't pretend you didn't enjoy yourself. You might have liked it even more than I did."

I felt his anger twisting inside of him, dark and spiteful as his mind lashed out at mine. My head spun at the pull of his blood within me, the force of his addiction kindling my hunger again. It was always present, but somehow he magnified it within me. His anger was familiar, he'd be damned if he would be shamed for who he was. I shared in this sentiment, but now was not the time to be sympathetic, his anger forcing mine.

"Don't." The warning hung in the air between us.

I felt my control waver once more to his as hunger clouded my mind, demanding payment. Quin's mind was unrelenting; he'd rather be right than alive. My senses were on fire. I heard his heartbeat – a kick drum in my ears – and I smelled the blood just under his skin, watched the pulse in his neck, and tasted the remnants of him on my lips.

The look in his eyes told me he knew exactly what he was doing; his smug smile infuriated me. I yet held control as I forced my body to relax, every muscle within tensed from the terrible pleasure and pain that was my bloodlust.

Don't – her voice was soft in my mind.

If Quin had heard her, he gave no indication. I could feel my hunger fading slowly, like waves washing away footprints in the sand.

The hunger is not his to control, it is yours – her voice guided me, easing my mind and allowing me the reprieve required to regain my composure.

Quin felt the loss of our connection then, all green fading from his eyes as I exhaled the last of him from me. It was then that I became aware of a new sensation, and suddenly I could feel the connection of the blood between him and me – and me and her. Leveling my eyes with his, I read the uncertainty within as I took hold of the blood that tethered us: my blood, not his.

I pulled it tight, seizing the blood within him. Fear ignited in his eyes, stripping away any notion in his mind or mine that I was still human. Any slack he'd held was completely torn away before exhaustion forced my release of him. Quin rolled from the couch, landing on his hands and knees. He coughed, gripping his chest before erupting in sputtered and choked laughter. It was unnerving how quickly his fear could shift and contort into excitement.

He met my gaze, curiosity burning within the pools of his blue eyes. "How did you do that?"

"Leave me alone, Quin," I managed, exertion robbing me of my conviction as I sank to the floor.

My legs were trembling under me. I was truly surprised my body had failed me and it was terrifying and new. Quin's laughter grew; though less maniacal, he was giggling at me on the floor where we had both found ourselves. He moved as if to sit next to me, but something about the way he had forced himself into my mind triggered something primal in me. Panicking, I pushed away as I struggled to stand. The way he had elicited my hunger, forcing it, Quin had been so determined to be right that he was willing to risk himself and me.

His willingness to self-destruct had almost destroyed my ability to stop myself. It brought up memories I'd long forgotten, of a girl who believed death was her only release, refreshing the hopelessness I felt at being alone. It was a darkness that played around the edges of my own vision, waiting for me to give in. Quin, though, he lived with it – letting the darkness shape his recklessness. He was willing to destroy himself and me; perhaps what scared me more was the ease at which he pretended it hadn't happened as he moved to help me.

Hand extended, I warded him off as I forced myself upright. Quin stopped short, bewilderment marred his features before settling into concern and hurt. We stayed like this for a moment too long: him in confusion and me in defense until he finally withdrew. His form resigned to the couch and I withdrew to my room. This was the first time since Quin had abducted me that I'd been afraid, unsure of the person I saw before me and what I might have to do to keep myself safe. It was in the cool darkness of my room that I found solace and comfort.

CHAPTER SEVEN

I awoke to an empty apartment; the only inkling of Quin's presence was the mess of throw pillows and blankets scattered across the couch and floor. I could just feel the last rays of daylight fading into dusk as my body slowly returned to normal. The weight of my forced hibernation was losing its grip on my muscles and reflexes. I wished I had a reprieve from work and Quin. The uneasiness from our last encounter settled in and filled me with dread.

Thankfully I still had an hour to kill before I had to think about work or the discomfort of facing Quin again, so I let the mindlessness of routine take over as I prepared for work. This used to mean breakfast in front of the TV with Alexander, cuddling until I was forced to dart out of the house, praying I made it to work on time. Now, routine meant a scalding shower, letting the water wash away my worry, thoughts of the day to come, and days that had already passed.

It was something I'd always enjoyed; water had always been a means for me to cleanse my soul – even if just temporarily. The warmth and sound of it hitting the ceramic tub was rhythmic and soothing. Very little time was actually spent washing. All I really wanted was to sit in the tub and let the fifty-gallon water heater run out. I liked to pretend it was rainfall as I closed my eyes, allowing it to dance down my chest and pool between my bent legs and stomach.

By the time I was done, the edges of the mirrors were hazy, blurred by the moisture and heat. I took a moment to look at myself, taking in the changes that had occurred since my awakening. I'd never been particularly fit – always a little soft around the edges – but now that had all changed. I was leaner. Smooth, strong muscles defined my physique now, revealing my hourglass waist and athletic build that was both strong and feminine.

Though subtler than the changes of my body, perhaps the most significant change was that of my face. My features were somehow more full, yet strong, and my eyes were more predatory. They'd taken on a deeper green than before and they held a luminescent glow within. Even in the dimmed lights of my bathroom they were bright against the warm hue of my skin and dark hair.

The other changes, while I had taken notice, were imperceptible. I don't know what I had expected, two long fangs? All my teeth had taken on a sharpness, the edges of them angled like a blade – not a visible change, mind you, just one I felt as I ran my tongue over their razored edges. I remembered Quin questioning why I didn't just bite him. He must have known how easy it would've been for me to break his skin, which made me wonder how many times he'd been bitten before me.

Satisfied with my secondary inspection of myself, it was with bored and practiced familiarity that I finished preparing for work. Clean scrubs – check, hair up so no one could pull it – check. All that was left to do was prepare a lunch so people thought I ate. It was high time I threw away the peanut butter and jelly that had since grown moldy inhabiting my lunch box. Someone was bound to get suspicious or at the very least search out the smell. Hastily, I made a turkey sandwich; processed meat lasted forever and limited the amount of money I'd have to waste on food no one ate.

Routine completed, I grabbed my keys and my raincoat. My roughly twenty-minute walk to work would likely be the last bit of solitude I'd get in the next eight hours. I had learned to hate the quiet nights spent with my coworkers; their polite questioning and invitations always put me on edge. All I wanted to do was work. Put in my time and leave. Even then, I wasn't entirely sure why I showed up. Sure, I was helping patients, that part was undeniable; it was the effort I had to put forth not to hurt those around me that made me question the viability of working.

I often felt like an open and exposed nerve around so many people. I wasn't able to completely close myself off from all of their thoughts and emotions when surrounded. It was a double-edged sword, providing me an easy way to feed psychically, but at the cost of my stability. Anxiety, soft yet present, crept over me and reminded me of my first day of nursing.

I'd been terrified walking through the ambulance bay doors. I was so certain I couldn't handle whatever waited for me inside the hospital walls, positive I'd freeze during my first medical code, desperate to remember all the information I'd been force-fed over the last five years, and scared at the prospect of having to watch my first patient die because I somehow wasn't prepared.

These memories made me smile; all that worrying only ever amounted to undue stress. I never froze, and while people did die in my emergency room, it was never from a lack on my part. I had learned a long time ago that just people die, no matter how hard they or I fought. This was an undeniable truth that used to fortify me, but now, the idea hollowed me.

He was going to die no matter what I did… The thought came and left, dark and true as it resonated through my soul.

I felt a dissonance within my psyche. One part was dark and ominous; it fought to be heard as memories and whispers of hurt played at the back of my mind, just out of reach, while the other part tried desperately to scrub the ink of the first one away. Anxiety, cold and sure, picked and pulled at the edges of my mind, fighting for purchase. This was something hidden but not yet forgotten.

I tried to focus on the encounter with my maker, thinking back on her words and the way she'd been able to read my anguish and pain. I was so sure she was the one who had taken everything away from me – knew he'd still be here if it wasn't for her… *Come now, you know that's not true.*

The memory of her words stopped my forward momentum. Halting, I covered my ears the same way she had at the docks. There was a memory, foggy at the back of my mind, something I needed to remember now. I'd stopped halfway across the steel bridge, leaning against the railing to peer at the water below. I focused on the sound of my breath, raspy in my ears as it mingled with the endless noise of the city and rain against steel. I closed my eyes tight against the migraine that was erupting in my skull.

"Stop." I heard her voice, serene and calm against my chaos. "Stop, child, before you hurt yourself."

She leaned beside me, placing her gloved hand over mine as she crossed her other arm in front of my face so she could pull me toward her. A faint smile played across her red lips, the pale blue of her eyes like that of the sky after a storm. Long blond hair spilled from the hood of her coat to frame the right side of her face.

"You're still so human." She said fondly a she closed the gap between us. "Now is not the time to remember."

The scent of her surrounded me: ocean, woods, and blood. She stood two heads taller than me, the warmth of her enveloping me as she lifted my face to look at hers. She forced my focus. The intensity of her gaze and mind on mine erased everything from me but her. I was nothing and no one. A look of sadness and relief played across her face as she leaned down, bringing my face to hers. The taste of her blood sweet and thick on my tongue, it reminded me of a dessert wine. The flavor was complex, robust, and yet still delicate as it coated my throat.

The taste of blood on my lips alarmed me. I wiped my face, but found no trace on the back of my hand, I must have bitten the inside of my mouth, but it didn't taste like mine.

"Are you alright?"

I turned to find a few coworkers approaching me; I was in the parking lot of the hospital, the SWISH of the automatic doors startling me, causing me to jump as they walked past and inside. I needed to stop daydreaming when I walked. This wasn't the first time I'd found myself across town without realizing how I'd gotten there. Brushing off the feeling of déjà vu, I entered the hospital to start my eight-hour shift. It would be over before I knew it, and I could get back to my wandering.

There were twenty minutes left before my shift started, so I took my time hanging up my coat and putting my lunch away before making my way to the gardens. Impulsively, I licked my lips; any trace of the earlier taste was gone. The faint glow of city lights were just peeking over the tall garden walls. Everything here was built to keep people in. Without my keycard I too would be stuck behind these walls. All of it was built to keep the public safe or those within from hurting themselves. For a hospital it was hard not to think of it like a prison sometimes, just with better scenery and food. It had been raining all day, continuing its downpour even now. I loved the way it cleared the air, washing away the usual smell of exhaust and the homeless that often plagued bigger cities.

Typically flowers, shrubs, and trees filled the garden with color, but this time of year they were all hibernating, and bare branches littered the usually perfect landscape. Fall weather had stripped them of their vibrant leaves. It was perfect like this, I thought, as I settled under the awning of a bench.

"What are you doing out here?" Quin's voice cut across the silence of the garden, disrupting my peace. "It's freezing out here."

He closed the distance between us quickly before settling beside me.

"Is that my sandwich?" I asked knowingly as Quin smirked, amusement playing across his face and eyes before he took a bite.

Purposefully and with a mouth full of turkey, he said, "You weren't going to eat it."

I should have left the moldy PB&J for him. "I came out here so I could have a moment before I had to deal with people." *Like you*, I thought.

I could tell he was thinking of something to say as he ate the sandwich. Almost in a panic, I excused myself before Quin could formulate any semblance of conversation. I'd rather be surrounded by other coworkers and the mentally ill before I was alone with Quin again for any long period of time.

"Enjoy the sandwich," I managed awkwardly as I waved a goodbye over my shoulder.

I was quick to gather the necessities of work: favorite pen, stethoscope, lucky pen light, and a note pad. I missed the days of saline syringes, sheers, and alcohol pads. Behavioral health was a different beast from medical. Tonight I was filling in for triage; I tried not to be relieved, but this meant no patient load other than initial intake, and I got to work alone.

Blissfully mindless work and no small talk with coworkers pretending like we cared about each other's lives sounded like a good night. I liked to pretend my isolative behaviors were new, but they weren't. I'd always been bad at finding meaning in the lives and needs of others – unless you were dying and needed medical attention that was. Guess I just enjoyed feeling like a hero, like I was a good person by doing good.

I laughed at myself. I didn't actually believe in good and bad, at least not in a black-and-white way. I'd cared for enough people to know we were all a little bit of both and could just as easily be one or the other. Thankfully, when I reached Triage, it was empty, just the way I wanted it.

"Eryn right?" Most day shifters never learned night shifters names. I was surprised.

"Yeah, guess I'm up here tonight?" I poised my words as a question, politely allowing for between-shift conversations.

"Quin said you could cover so I don't have to stay over. Addison usually works, but she's sick. Someone will be here to cover before you go home – or at least I hope so," he joked, waiting out the clock.

"Me too," I agreed pleasantly. "Jason, right? Anything I need to know before you head out?"

He smiled wide and eager to show me a thing or two about the art of Triage. I got a "master of the castle" vibe from him, but he happily set me in the right direction and shared how he managed Triage to optimize down time.

"You'll be fine; you've worked medical before, so triaging will be second nature to you. Plus Quin can pop up and help you if you need it." His statement caught me off guard. My confusion must've been evident on my face because he clarified by stating, "All of the charge nurses are trained up here. I'm sure Quin won't mind helping you if it gets busy."

My earlier excitement faded; this shift had now become a hostage situation, and I was trapped up here where Quin could come and go. Being charge nurse meant he could have my tech step onto the unit to help while he stayed behind in Triage. It was going to be just him and me.

"That's good… Have a good night, Jason."

He patted my shoulder assuredly before he left, mistaking my apprehension as work jitters.

"Fuck." The word slipped out before I could contain it, causing the tech to look at me questioningly before returning to his phone. I busied myself with chores: checking equipment, stocking, safety checks, and cleaning. Glancing at the security cameras I was thankful to see the main unit in a state of controlled chaos; it meant Quin would be too busy to check in. If the night continued like this I wouldn't have to interact at all – or so I thought, until the phone rang. The extension that lit up belonged to the main unit. A quick camera check confirmed the culprit: Quin.

"Triage. This is Eryn." I feigned ignorance.

"Can you come help us deescalate a patient?" Silence filled the line between us; I knew what his words implied. "Please?" His tone was sincere. "I don't want someone getting hurt."

It was an honest request, selfless. He was worried. I could feel his anxiety like butterflies churning in my guts. I checked the cameras for the source: a man had barricaded himself in the bathroom. From the look of the milieu and the noise transferred from the phone line, he was causing quite a commotion.

"Have the medications ready." I hung up. "Page me if we get a patient," I managed before leaving the minimally engaged tech to man our post.

I couldn't help but smile as I navigated the sally ports and keyed doors to my unit; in spite of myself I was excited. Give me your aggressive, the combative, the dying, and bloodied, for I am a nurse. Quin met me in the office, quickly filling me in on the situation.

"His name is Rey. Cops brought him; he's on a public safety hold. From what I can find in his chart, this is probably his first psychotic break. He slammed the door on his nurse when she tried to get him to leave the bathroom. Paranoid delusions. Security is getting ready to pull him, and he's not going to go down without a fight. Listen, I don't want us or him getting hurt." Quin finished in a hurry, eager to get me up to speed.

I nodded, assessing the situation before I gloved up and met security just outside earshot of the barricaded restroom. "He's scared, paranoid, and in a new place. I'm going to open the door and see if I can get him to walk out here. If he can't, try to wait until I say 'hands on' before you move in."

I paused only long enough to assign the remaining roles and talk through plan B should things go to hell. I made a point to ensure the restraint chair and restraints were close at hand, even if I didn't need them. I still had to model safe care practices. Everyone in agreement, we moved as one.

"Rey, my name is Eryn. I'm a nurse, and I'm here to help." I spoke as calmly as I could with everyone's nervous excitement swirling around me; we were all adrenaline junkies here.

Carefully, I opened the door. The man named Rey was tracing the seams of the walls within, trying to find an alternative way out. He was trapped, eyes wild as he continued his search. *Easy* – I thought, allowing the calm of my psyche to press against those around me. Quin was the only one I felt guard against me. The tension eased slightly. I felt it in the way the security guards relaxed, bodies less tense, and the way Rey paused, not as frantic in his search for a trapdoor. His calm was short-lived, though, as his eyes drifted toward me, seeing his safe space breached once more.

"Stop," I demanded, catching Rey before he could move to slam the door. I made a point to present my empty hands, both outstretched to protect myself and to show him I had nothing to hide. "You're safe, Rey. I'm here to talk; let me help."

He stood tall – perhaps 6 feet 8 inches – at the back of the room, and he looked like a construction worker; his calloused hands clenched and unclenched as he intermittently eyed me and searched for another way out.

"I need to get out of here before they find me. I don't want the medicine; it makes me tired. That's how they find you, when you stop moving." He spat each word, pressured and childlike in his tone.

"You don't like the medicine; neither do I, Rey." He turned to me, hearing my words. "Let's see if I can help you without it. But first I need you to come out of this bathroom. Can you come with me to a different area where you can be safe and others can feel safe until I can help you?"

He considered this; I had stepped into the bathroom with him, the door behind me obscuring the hoard of security, staff, and emergency medications from his view. His mind felt like barbed wire against mine. I could just make out flashes of his thoughts as they cut through his forced calm. I'd seen this before.

"Are you a veteran, Rey?"

His eyes cleared a moment. "I served five years in Iraq." War flashed in his mind, the smell and taste of gunpowder, metallic and sulfuric.

I was instantly humbled in my earlier assumptions of this man. He wasn't in a hospital right now; he was seven thousand miles away in a warzone. I took a deep breath as I pressed against his psyche, focusing as I drew on the strongest of his emotions. I could feel him underneath it all, confused, scared, and fighting to make sense of the flashes in his mind. Little by little I pulled at his broken pieces, fighting to take hold.

"I don't know where I am." Rey spoke low. "I can hear them, smell them all around me. I can still *see* them." He was rambling, the earlier feral look in his eyes now pleading and confused as he struggled for understanding.

Every time he said "them" I saw the flashes of other soldiers. Their bodies and the bodies of the people he'd killed. I heard the gunfire in the back of his mind as it mingled with the never-ending screams and acrid smell of burning plastic.

"You're at Oceanside; it's a hospital. You're home now." I had to wait for him to look at me again. I needed a stronger connection with him before I could convince him. "Rey, you are safe. You aren't in Iraq."

His eyes wandered, seeing things that only I knew before finally meeting mine again. I had him, the tendrils of my mind holding fast to his clarity as I dissolved and digested the war within.

"Follow me, Rey. We're going to a seclusion room." My voice was low and controlled.

His eyes clouded as I stole away his fear and replaced his need to escape with the desire to follow. I could still feel him just under the surface, stronger than I gave him credit for. I led him out slowly, holding tight to his consciousness as we went. I was thankful in that moment for Quin as he directed the others, allowing me to concentrate. I compelled Rey forward like it was second nature. I hadn't expected this outcome. I'd imagined just wearing him down until it was safe for us to redirect him. This was new, and a part of me was desperate to fix the man before me. I saw the trauma in his mind: canyons carved in a landscape; this pain ran deep and tore at the foundation of his mind.

The walk was slow, his will to escape almost stronger than my ability to keep him and the others safe. Reluctantly, I tore that strength from him, depleting his resolve to force his compliance. His energy came in waves, intense at first but short-lived as his pain and fear hit him in flashes. We rounded the corner to the padded seclusion room, the mood of the staff completely renewed.

Most takedowns occurred here when the patient realized there was no escape and that he was, in fact, going to be locked away. Thankfully I met none of that resistance in Rey. I'd been carefully feeding upon his delusions, paranoia, and confusion, acting as a substitute antipsychotic to numb the visions of the battlefield.

"I need you to sit down in there, Rey." I withdrew from him slowly, allowing his clarity to return.

He nodded, tears threatening to spill from his dark brown eyes. "Did I hurt anyone?"

I turned to Quin, unsure how to answer. He looked like he was trying to piece something together: the truth, but in a digestible and thoughtful way.

"You were brought here by the police; do you remember why?" Quin asked sincerely.

Rey covered his face with his hands, on the verge of hysteria. "Did I hurt them?"

Quin's expression changed, softening as he knelt beside me in the seclusion room. "No. They're fine, Rey, but you're not. We're here to help you."

I could see Rey struggling to compose himself, the tears flowing freely now. "I didn't mean to pull the gun on them. I just... I'm not myself sometimes."

I saw it all play across his mind. He'd been outside with his family when someone set off a barrage of fireworks. It was in that volley of pops and explosions that Rey found himself back in the desert. The arid air and dust biting at his skin once more as he shouldered his rifle, ready for a fight. He had disassociated. Carefully, I fed Rey different flashes of our tenuous journey to the seclusion room. These fragmented memories where mine, but to him he'd see it as an out-of-body experience. I was trying to help him understand what had happened, lending him some insight to his current situation.

Quin took over from here. "I have to give you medications, Rey. You weren't able to be safe; that's why we're here."

Rey nodded again. "I know. I'll take anything if it'll help."

I felt the chaos just under the surface; he was fighting to keep his paranoia at bay. It was clear on his face as he eyed us. Unsure if he could trust us or even himself anymore. Quin sensed my urgency, explaining the medications quickly before giving them and locking the door behind him. Within ten minutes Rey was pounding the door, lost in his war again. It took a full hour for the medication to take hold. Rey was sedated but still lost. Even his dreams wouldn't let him rest. He had a long road ahead of him. The truth was: medications would probably only mask his symptoms. He and his family would need a lot of support on the road to stabilization.

"You need to keep on top of him," I warned Quin when he returned to reassess. "He isn't able to keep himself rooted in the present right now."

"Thanks for your help." It was all the leeway he needed to follow me into Triage.

"Anytime," I answered absently, not meaning to make it sound like an invitation to continue the conversation.

Phase one of the hostage situation was about to be under way, and it wasn't even midnight. As expected, Quin ushered my tech away to help do safety checks. I'd never seen a grown man roll his eyes the way the tech did at Quin; god forbid he actually work or put his phone away.

Shit-eating grin in place, Quin leaned over the desk at me. "That was insane. How did you persuade him to walk to the seclusion room?"

Quin's eyes gleamed with excitement; apparently I wasn't the only one high on the mixture of adrenaline and chaotic energy. I had thought that Quin was privy to the exchange between Rey and me, although maybe he was just being observant and read my needs instead of the patient's.

"I didn't really have to persuade him. I just had to give him a push and provide the clarity needed for him to act," I answered quickly.

"That's not what it felt like to me," he said, his tone dark and suggestive.

"Oh?" I looked up at Quin, curious now; was he beginning to see and feel the psychic exchanges as they happened?

He didn't answer right away, choosing his words wisely. "I felt your mind take control of his; there were two of you, then poof. Just you. I think I see now what Marc meant about being able to control people."

His excitement made sense to me now; his motives were always so clear to me once I remembered why Quin had bonded with me in the first place. Power. That uneasy feeling from yesterday settled back in; tethering me gave him everything he wanted. It was beginning to make me feel used and more than a little misled. Was every interaction between us solely a gain for him? I couldn't be sure after the way he'd acted last night, and I was afraid. Afraid he was just as out of control as I was.

"I never lost touch with Rey's mind; you couldn't feel him resisting the whole way to the seclusion room. I didn't erase him." I paused, trying to understand exactly how I had controlled him. "I replaced his will with mine, just for a second. I gave him a task."

"Ah, but that's different than what you said before," he pointed out. "It's like I said, there were two, then just one."

I didn't like the excitement in his voice or his skewed perspective. "I'm not a monster, Quin. I did what I thought was right to keep him safe. That's why you called me. I didn't just take over his mind and force myself on him."

His eyes met mine, staring at me with a sinister knowing. "But you did."

His words felt absolute in my ears, like anything else I said would simply be negated because despite why I had done it, I had taken over Rey's mind. I knew that where Rey's mind was trapped was hell, cycling through his trauma over and over again. Quin was right; I hadn't given him a choice. Instead, I acted, hoping that my call was the right one. Wasn't that what we did every day as healthcare providers? I couldn't be the only one just trying to do my best.

"We both know why you called me and what it was you wanted me to do." I tried and failed at hiding my frustration.

"Just don't pretend you aren't doing what you're doing. It doesn't make any sense, and you aren't fooling me," Quin said, eyes locking with mine.

Now I was pissed; it wasn't my intention to lie to him or myself. "It kills you to know that if we traded places you'd be the better monster, doesn't it? You can't stand that I don't give into my nature; that's why you tried to push me into it yesterday, isn't it? So you could somehow prove that you can control it and me?"

If Quin was surprised by my outburst, he didn't show it; in fact, it may have been exactly what he was hoping for. I could see him thinking long and hard on what I'd said, perhaps unsure of how far he should or could push me at work.

"Maybe you're right," he said finally, voice low and humorless. "Maybe I am pushing you. Maybe I want you to accept your *nature* so you can stop pretending to still be human." His words were becoming more and more pressured as he went. "Maybe I do want to prove I can control whatever you throw at me, no matter how lost you become. And maybe, just maybe, I already am a better monster than you. What makes you think I can't handle your demons, too?" Quin stepped back from the desk, anger flickering in his eyes. "Try me. I've done things you can't even imagine, hurt people in ways you'll never know."

I watched as Quin collected himself, thinking over his next words. "You aren't better than me because you fight your urges, Eryn, and I'm not a bad person for enjoying mine."

Having said his peace, Quin left almost as quickly as he had shown up. I was confused, unsure if I'd misread Quin by overcomplicating his intentions with my own uncertainty. Maybe there hadn't been any intended malice except that which I assumed. I thought back on his memories, trying to remember anything other than the feel of his addiction. Had I only taken from him what I wanted to see, oblivious to his intent and the nature by which he had survived?

His earlier words played through my head again, reminding me of the night I'd turned and how he had pushed me, forcing me to feed. I was so afraid of what I had become, but he never doubted it or what he had to do for a second. Was he still doing that now? Pushing both our limits in order to become stronger, because otherwise what was the point?

This last thought resonated with me and the memories I had of Quin. His whole life had been spent just trying to live his life the way he wanted and having the strength to do so without consequence or worry. He didn't care if he became a monster, which was evident when he bonded with me and risked his life. He was unapologetic in his goals, because life was short and he was going to live it the way he wanted.

"Shit." I covered my face, cursing into the palms of my hands as I tried to collect my thoughts.

It wasn't Quin I hated; it was myself. Every time he pushed me I fought so hard to deny him. Maybe he was the better monster, but not because of who he was or the things he'd done; it was because he didn't hide from it. He was learning control while I practiced denial, afraid to let go of the fact that I was never going to be the person I was before. I was letting my fear shape the person I was now. Truth was, I didn't know what was right or wrong anymore; I was just instincts and hunger. The world wasn't the same as before and I needed to relearn what it meant to live within it if I was going to survive.

CHAPTER EIGHT

Selene watched from afar, ever curious and protective of her new-born. She didn't completely understand why Eryn clung to her ritualistic human duties, but she knew it was important. Selene had watched her like this before, perched upon the neighboring build-ings, waiting to see how her night had gone. Some nights Eryn would emerge with her face turned upwards to the rain, rinsing the night away before returning home. Selene admired that about her. For a human, she was able to find peace and serenity within the simplicity of life.

Selene had learned to admire this about her human turned kin, but it wasn't why she'd fallen in love with the creature before her now. It had been the smell of death that first lured her to Eryn. It had hung around her like a shawl, wrapping her in mystery. It was a curious mixture of ozone, chemicals, and the sickly odor of decay. These smells Selene would forevermore associate with radiation, chemotherapy, and cancer. Death was an insatiable driving factor for Selene's kind and she had found it, not just in the smell of her new obsession, but in Eryn's mind as well.

Serving as an unofficial bouncer, Selene was occasionally required to redirect the would-be patrons of Oceanside. She would suffer none of them tonight and her fledgling need not be disturbed – so she warded them off, sending them away to seek help elsewhere. Selene cared not what happened to them so long as they left well enough alone at Oceanside. Tonight, after all she had seen unraveling within Eryn's mind, she couldn't have someone ruining her hard work and triggering the memories she'd suppressed.

This place was odd; most hospitals Selene encountered reeked of healing wounds and the dying. The only thing this one was filled with was noise, even to someone such as her who was not an adept channeler. There was a constant, insistent hum of agony and turmoil the likes of which Selene only knew in warzones. Once upon a time the noise emitted from within Oceanside would have ignited her hunger, but now all it gave her was a headache. By all accounts Eryn was a channeler, which meant being in that place was not just loud but painful.

"Why not just take her back? You want her. Why not call her back to you?" Derek called, interrupting her train of thought.

Selene turned to meet the black eyes of her firstborn. He stood apart from her on the balcony. His clothes gave tell; specks of blood glistened against the dryness of his attire. He hadn't come alone. It was not that long ago that their roles were reversed and she had been the one feeding him. Selene peered past Derek and into the darkness of the apartment. She could smell them.

Stepping away from her post, she found two young women held within. The terror she found in their eyes was exuberating. They knelt bound by blood. This was Derek's gift; the small kisses from his blade decorated their bodies, allowing him control over their essence. It delighted her, these treats he brought her.

"The hunters will come for you through her," Derek continued, insistent.

"She is not you, Derek; you welcomed me. To her I am a reminder of her loss. She is not ready." Selene answered absently, "And the hunters stand disjointed, alone, and shunned for their practices."

"It is their practices that scare me," he remarked, his tone disdainful.

Selene waved away his concern before pulling the first girl forward; delicious terror was the only thing still paralyzing her. She admired the woman; Derek had a type, hunting the same beautiful girls every night. Caramel eyes, mocha skin, and full pouty lips. Selene entwined her fingers in the tight curls of her hair, forcing her tear-streaked face away from her before ripping her throat open. Her teeth were sharper than any knife, the tissue below giving way without resistance.

Blood-choked moans gurgled to the surface as Selene fed, sweet and gone too fast. Terror always made the heart beat faster, speeding its inevitable collapse. It was the adrenaline in the blood that Selene was truly after; just as each vampire had their own gifts, so too did they have their own vices. The second girl cried out as Selene dropped the first in a twitching heap on the floor. Smiling, Selene reveled in the second woman's fear as she struggled against Derek's hold. Alas, the more she fought, the more she bled, strengthening Derek's hold and feeding their excitement.

His obsidian eyes watched his prey emotionlessly; Selene knew this was part of his vice. Derek would trap them for days, taking them little my little until they begged for the end. He'd drink in their death slowly.

"Share her with me. I'll save the end for you. I'll make her want it," Selene promised with a blood-stained smile.

Derek stepped forward in agreement and together they fed, Selene at the woman's throat and he at her wrist. Compelled, the girl stopped her screaming and leaned back into Selene's arms and razored mouth. Adrenaline still poured through the woman's system, just slower now that they both asserted their control over her. Selene would give this one a sweet end, playing with her mind as she swallowed away her life.

As promised, Selene pulled away, giving the end to Derek. She watched as he held the woman to himself, her smile faint, believing the lies placed in her mind by him. She welcomed him as he took her very last breath, feeding himself on whatever emotions he had created within her. Selene had never seen a vampire work as hard as Derek did for his blood.

Returning to the balcony, Selene left Derek his corpse to play with. It had started to rain again, the big droplets lazy in their assault. She considered Derek's earlier statement. His words of caution weren't completely unfounded.

"One of them is shattered; whatever is left of his bond barely makes him a threat," she called back to him. "The one now, Quin, makes a mockery of the powers he has stolen. He'd sooner break himself against the limits of his body than hurt one of us." Selene peered out across the balcony once more, taking in the glow of the lights and the life that flourished despite the chill in the air. "Have you another perspective?"

Selene waited patiently for an answer, allowing Derek to take in the pleasure of his kill. Once finished, Derek stepped out into the rain alongside her. He always looked at peace after eating; perhaps it was because he waited so long between feedings? She'd watched as he starved himself for weeks just to prepare his meal. His picky eating habits astonished her. She had made the mistake of watching him truly feed once, curious of his vice's compulsive need, and had not enjoyed the taste of it on her tongue.

"They have *her*, Selene; they are strong because of her," Derek said carefully, understanding what he was implying.

Selene's anger sparked like a match, the rain hissing against her; she knew now why he had hesitated. He was afraid of upsetting her, but it was too late. Derek was suggesting that Eryn was already lost to her, that her youngest would come to destroy her. The glow of Selene's eyes reflected purple within the abyss of his. She reached out to him, caressing his face with her hand, watching as he winced against the warmth of her. He dared not pull away.

Carefully, Selene smothered her anger, preventing the ember within from fully igniting. She felt Derek's fear within her: colicky and acidic. His fear was not of her, but for her. How naïve he still was to need her so much after all these years. Selene knew not why he clung to her for she was as warm as she was cold and as cruel as she was kind.

"Perhaps you misunderstand altogether," Selene suggested, stepping back from him. "She is no more theirs than she is mine. She has always and *will* always belong to him… the one who came before."

It hurt Selene to reveal this to Derek for she too mourned the loss of her unborn child and the pain it caused Eryn. Selene's sorrow settled heavy in the pit of her stomach, fully extinguishing her earlier anger.

"They were supposed to be together forever." Selene's words were hollow, spoken to no one but herself.

The people below scurried about like rats in a downpour; soon she could leave. Until then, she watched the mortals, peering through the wall of glass that made up the front of the hospital. It almost reminded her of an ant farm or a beehive. Selene pulled herself from her thoughts; sensing the hunter before she saw him. Derek stepped forward as well, focusing his vision on the one below.

Quin had ducked outside, hiding just under the overhang of the ambulance bay, cigarette in hand. Derek made a noise low in his throat reminiscent of a grunt as a snarl played across his features. Selene imagined what it would feel like to gut Quin where he stood; his very existence felt like a slap to the face. He'd robbed her of the chance to teach and provide for Eryn. It was Selene's right and duty to teach her children how to feed, when to kill, when not to, and how to hide it. For this trespass, she would never forgive him.

"He smells of her." Derek's words were forced; the realization of the hunter's transgression truly repulsed him.

Curiously, Selene watched as Quin looked around; he knew someone was watching. It was hard to tell if this was hunter instinct or the product of his bond. She could sense the changes within him; much like the other hunter, he wasn't completely human anymore.

In all the times Selene had come to watch over Eryn, she had never seen Quin linger like this before. He was waiting for her, of this she was sure. Concentrating, Selene raised her body temperature one degree at a time. Her blue eyes brightened to lavender until they were saturated red. Derek retreated; the closeness of her was both painful and hazardous.

Selene waited for the right moment to put doubt in this hunter's mind. The rain that had earlier cleansed and soaked her clothes was all but gone; it would not be enough to extinguish the rage she felt within. This hunter liked games, so did she. Embers sparked bright against the night. Quin's cigarette: it would be her catalyst.

"I think it's time I introduce myself," Selene declared.

She was over the railing of the balcony and crossing the street toward the parking lot of Oceanside Behavioral Health within seconds, her eyes meeting Quin's just in time to engulf his cigarette in flames. His startled response brought a sharp smile to her lips.

"Hello, Quin." Selene curtsied, never letting her eyes leave his.

Surprise quickly turned into daunting realization as Quin faced her, his features hardening. He knew exactly who and what she was. What he didn't realize was that he didn't stand a chance. Yet he still approached, reeking of overconfidence.

"You aren't going to attack me in the street; that wouldn't be good for either of us." He matched her wicked smile, daring her to prove him wrong.

Selene withdrew, allowing the heat of herself to die down, but she never let it leave her eyes. She never gave away an advantage, besides it served to unnerve Hunters. Quin stepped a bit closer, feeling the heat of her fade.

"You're the maker, the one who attacked Marc." Quin spoke without question.

His accusation made Selene laugh. "He attacked, I just won. And you are the thief."

"Yeah." Quin shrugged. "You left her for months. She didn't even know you were alive."

Selene met Quin and in one swift movement he was face to face with her. The heat of her returned as the fingers of her left hand encircled his throat, burning his flesh as his airway closed. Her right hand just caught the upward motion of Quin's left; he was faster than she'd anticipated, but not fast enough. Blisters erupted everywhere she touched. Selene had his undivided attention now, her red eyes holding his unblinking gaze.

"You are only alive because of her." Selene leaned in, whispering her words into his ear. "This is going to hurt."

His pupils were pools of black lined in blue as she bit hard into his exposed forearm. Quin's blood tasted of fear, anger, and Eryn... Selene smiled as she relinquished him, spitting out the chunk of flesh she had rended from him. He swiped at her desperately with his free arm, but she was already gone. His choked gasps and burnt flesh brought her great joy as she returned to the shadows.

Selene had gotten more than she'd hoped for; now she had him. Selene left behind the slur of curses that Quin threw, his anger only serving to amuse her. He'd heal soon enough.

"Why?" Derek called from overhead, leaning over the fire escape above to look down at her.

Selene was too excited to explain so instead she beckoned to him. "Come, and taste him."

Derek did as told, joining Selene on the ground. She was smiling wildly, the remnants of Quin's blood still thick across her tongue. She pulled him to her, bestowing it to Derek excitedly.

"He is the blood of my blood. Can you taste it? Can you?" Selene held tightly to him, her fingers tangled in the lapels of his jacket.

Derek pushed away, forcibly removing Selene and her excitement from his immediate vicinity. "He tastes like a vampire, one of us but not; it's a trick of the blood. Why does this excite you?"

"I can *feel* him, Derek." Selene reveled in this; she felt Quin within her, sensing his confusion, irritation, and humiliation. Their connection, albeit fleeting, was undeniable.

CHAPTER NINE

I felt Quin's fear before the pain, before the searing and scorching; white-hot pain set into my throat and left wrist. It brought me to my knees. My lunchbox clattered to the floor. I couldn't breathe, the pressure around my throat a noose as the smell of melting flesh accosted my senses. Instinctually I tucked my arm into my chest, desperate to protect it.

Quin was hurt and I could feel him drawing on me, trying to protect himself. I scrambled from the break room, cursing the key card doors as I made my way back through triage and out the ambulance bay doors. The smell of burnt skin and hair led me to the parking lot. What scared me, though, was the smell of Quin's blood, sharp and fresh against the stink of charred tissue.

Bounding from the ambulance bay, I could just see him pacing the far edge of the parking lot. Blood dripped from his forearm, a crescent shaped chunk of skin ripped away. He was cursing himself, oblivious to me as I reached out. The silvered blade in his hand met no resistance as it bit deep into my palm. Teal eyes flashed at me, and for a second I thought he was going to strike again. Reflexively, I pulled away, not realizing at first that I had been cut until the blood welled, spilling forth into my palm and down my wrist. That's when I felt the pain, sharp and intense.

"What the fuck, Quin!" I cursed, our blood combining on the sidewalk.

His eyes focused, realizing quickly what he had done. I turned away from him defensively when he tried to examine the damage he'd done.

"I thought you were – I met your maker." Quin interrupted himself, distracted.

His voice was low, cautious. He was so focused on his surroundings; the adrenaline coursing through his veins preparing him for the next attack. His mind felt just as sharp as the knife as he fed on my strength, drawing on me forcefully. I watched as the blisters on his wrist and neck faded. His consciousness collided with mine. I was instantly aware of him. It was a truly unique sensation to be two people at once, unsure of where he began and I ended. I was breathless, watching as the last of his wounds closed while mine bled and throbbed with each beat of my heart. I was dizzy from the exchange, my palm searing as blood trailed like fire from my fingertips.

Quin's blue eyes met mine and I stumbled, his connection with me severed. The loss of our combined senses was startling and abrupt. He must've been better at differentiating between what was his and what was mine because his stance never swayed. Almost as an afterthought, he held his hand out to me, a pool of red cupped within. I stepped to him, wishing I didn't need it as his fingers curled around my face and I drank it in. I didn't understand how all of this was just second nature to him; nothing ever fazed him; not my need, not the changes, and not the fact that he was feeding me now. It was unsettling.

"How did she do that to you? It felt like you were on fire." I thought back on how she had dispatched Marc, ragdoll-ing him at the docks.

"I've never seen anything like it." Quin remarked in a daze as he rubbed his wrist. "Her eyes."

I caught a glimpse of her through him and felt the heat of her on my skin again. They were the same red eyes she'd shown Marc. I was the only one who had seen the ice blue of them at the docks.

"I have to get back. I don't know what this means." Quin was uncharacteristically serious. "She could have killed me."

He had started to walk back across the parking lot and away from me. "What do I do, Quin? What am I supposed to do?" I called after him.

"Go home and wait, I have to talk to Marc." Just like that he was gone, leaving me in the rain, worse for wear.

'You'll feel his death… nothing will prepare you for this loss.'

Marc's words came back to me. At the time they hadn't meant much – a warning that fell on deaf ears. Now, though, feeling the fear that had ripped through Quin, and feeling his pain, I couldn't shake the weight of the dread that was settling in my chest. Anxiety threatened to take hold of me. Every sense was heightened as I bled, fear and hunger skewing my perceptions. I needed to get home before my impulses got the better of me.

The memories from the blood, the only good thing that came from the coven, told me what would happen if I allowed myself to lose control. I shouldn't have let Quin draw from me the way he had, but I'd been too worried about his injuries to safeguard myself. That was a mistake.In my panic I had left my coat and lunch box inside. They weren't worth the trouble, so I resigned myself to a wet walk home. Crossing the parking lot, I made my way toward the bridge that would take me across the river and home. I wasn't concerned about the rain or cold; they felt distant, unlike the hunger. My vision blurred at the smell of my own blood, sickly sweet as it hit the ground.

I couldn't escape the smell; it was everywhere – in the people that passed by and in the air around me. In desperation to escape it I covered my nose and mouth, quickening my pace as I went. Rounding the nearest corner, I quickly stepped from the main street. There were too many people between myself and home. I had to catch my breath. Focus. Calm down. Stumbling into the closest alleyway, I leaned on the wet brick building for support as I went. I was drunk on the aroma of the people around me.

"The hunger will blind you if you let it," a voice warned. A man stood before me, eyes like obsidian. The smell of blood poured from him to me. It was the same smell I'd been trying to escape. Underneath it all was the scent of the ocean and the woods; there was something strangely familiar about it. Though his words carried no threat, they scared me nonetheless. This man wasn't human, at least no more human than me. "If you don't eat, you won't heal," he said, his tone even and indifferent.

He made no move toward me, but still I was unsure if I was in danger. I was caught between two worlds and I didn't know to which I belonged, or to which I owed loyalties. A part of me was deeply curious of the man before me though. He and I were the same, yet different, and I couldn't help but wonder who he was.

"What do you want?" I spoke carefully, trying to match his earlier indifference.

"I wanted to meet you," he said plainly, circling the alleyway slowly; he was closing the distance between us without trapping me.

Old me – human me – might have felt threatened, but the new me, the one who felt so unsure of who and what I was, was thrilled. I stood rain-soaked, right hand cradled just under my chest, and I took him in. There were tells to spotting one of my own, and the easiest tell was the eyes. There was a light, a hunger that back-lit even his black eyes. It was also in the way we moved. I'd never noticed it before, but the more I encountered others like me, the more I saw it.

"Who are you?" I moved slowly from the brick wall, turning to face him. "And why do you smell so familiar?"

"Derek." He smiled faintly. "We share the maker Selene."

I couldn't help my feelings of neglect; I didn't understand why his words should hurt me, or why my earlier excitement for another of my kind evolved into a sense of loneliness. Did he know her? If so, then why was I alone?

'Why' I thought, 'does the absence of her hurt me?'

His smile broadened. "Because a part of us will always need our parents."

I physically and mentally recoiled from him. "Don't."

I had been so eager to find connection that I had forgotten to protect myself. It had become easier and easier to create a radius in which my mind could wander, feeling those around me without taking in every emotion. Being alone here with him I didn't have the all-consuming weight of other peoples' minds pressing in on me, which made me forget myself. I'd allowed my presence to seep forth, both uninhibited and unprotected from others. It was like flexing a muscle; the more I exercised these abilities, the easier it became to block people out, consume energy, or just listen in.

He looked at me curiously; it was an expression much different than that of Quin's. Derek held an honest interest that lacked the malice I'd come to expect.

When he finally spoke again he said: "I am not a telepath. I can't read your thoughts."

"How then?" I asked skeptically.

"It is not my gift. Perhaps you are projecting?" He suggested.

I considered his words, wincing when my head began to swim. My muscles ached, cramping from hunger. Reluctantly, I returned to the brick wall, reaching out for support before sliding down it to rest on the ground.

"You need to eat." I was caught off guard by his concern.

The smell of him never left me and again I cupped my hand over my nose and mouth, desperate to escape it. I could see the traces of red on his clothes. It was mesmerizing: the flecks seemed to dance across the dark fibers of his jacket like bursts of rust. They threatened to consume my mind, tempting me the longer I stared. I knew whomever the blood belonged to hadn't survived. The thing that scared me most about this new hunger was that I didn't care about the life lost; all I wanted was to do as Derek had and stain the world red.

Everything in me screamed to fight it. It was this voice that held me, calling out louder than the pain of my hand and the razor-sharp hunger. It was all that was left of my humanity; it was the part of me that knew if I gave in I would never come back.

"I can't." I pleaded, desperate his understanding.

"If you don't soon, you won't have a choice." Derek's tone had evolved; it was soft and knowing, and I could hear the inflection of his own pain within.

I gritted my teeth against the smell of him, nodding my understanding when he moved closer to crouch beside me. The darkness of his eyes matched his short, well-kept hair. Everything about him was precise and calculated. I got the feeling he knew how to hide in plain sight. It was startling, having him so close; he acted like we were old friends.

"Show me." Derek reached out, motioning for my hand.

I hadn't noticed how much I had been guarding it, mourning the loss of its warmth as I turned it over to expose the cut on my palm. Blood saturated my uniform underneath. His skin was warm against mine as he inspected the wound.

Derek made a noise low in the back of his throat. "Why did he cut you?"

I tensed, his grip suddenly like iron around my wrist when I tried to pull away. I was innately aware of my mistake, instantly afraid of his closeness and the danger I had put myself in. If he knew about Quin, then he also knew I was tethered. Instinct told me that being tied to a hunter would make me an enemy to others like him.

"Let. Me. Go." My eyes met his, each word spoken in defense.

The air between us changed, both of us waiting for the other to make a move. I was acutely aware of his every breath, the rhythm of his heartbeat, and the pressure of his grip on my skin. I didn't know if I could get away – and if I could, at what cost?

"Your eyes are like emeralds, so different from hers and mine." Slowly, he let me go. "You can't trust them; they mean only to use you."

He lingered, hesitating for a moment longer before leaving me just the way he had found me: alone. I sat, taking in the alleyway, fixating on the dirt and grime of it. For a just a moment, I contemplated how nice it would be close my eyes and never open them again. Would I see him again? If I focused hard enough, could I trick myself into believing Alexander was still here with me? What would he think of me now?

I sat with these thoughts, finding only emptiness before I could let it pass. One shuddering breath in followed by a long exhale. I let the rain wash it away. Alexander didn't have any thoughts, hopes, or dreams – not for me and not for himself. I liked to think, though, that he'd be mad if I gave up here. I focused on the ridiculousness of it, and my pain, as a way to distract myself before continuing home.

I was more than a widow, more than this curse, more than my weaknesses, and I was beginning to wish I'd driven to work. The mile-and-a-half walk home had felt more like ten as I ascended the stairs that led to the solitude of my apartment, and away from the smell of people.

While I could shut out the temptation, I knew I could not escape the need of my hunger as easily. I closed the front door behind me; blood and rain dripped from me to settle in the carpet as I undressed. I was exhausted from the effort and redressing wasn't any easier. The cotton top and silk bottoms of my pajamas clung to me in much the same way as I wasn't able to muster the energy it would take to dry off. I stumbled through the living room, unable to catch my breath. I collapsed. At least it was warmer here than the alleyway had been. Settling where I landed, I watched the world spin through the sliding glass door that lead to the balcony.

The blood that seeped from me was thicker now and almost black in color. I wondered if it would taste as nauseatingly sweet as it smelled. My lips were cool against the searing heat of the laceration. It was thicker and richer than Quin's blood. The ache within me ignited at the taste of it. I didn't know how long it would sustain me, but at least the only person I was hurting was myself.

CHAPTER TEN

Quin counted the minutes until he could leave; the sooner he got out of this hellhole the sooner he could figure out what the fuck had just happened. His wrist still burned; the nerves hadn't completely healed yet, but he'd have to worry about that later. For now he was just trying to get through shift change without anyone figuring out how angry he was. Feigning interest was not skill he possessed.

He was perseverating on the feeling of the woman's burning grip and the look in her eyes when she had bitten him. He was pissed she'd been able to get that close to him, and he hadn't even put a scratch on her. Those red eyes burned him every bit as much as her touch. She'd loved every second she'd held him. It was unsettling how quickly she'd been able to come and go. Marc had said she was strong, but this was like nothing he'd ever seen before.

He knew that, alone, should scare him, but she hadn't come to kill him; she'd come to introduce herself. Quin had to admit it was one hell of an introduction and he still didn't know her fucking name. His eagerness to leave work hadn't gone unnoticed; neither did his gathering of Eryn's forgotten belongings. It was getting harder and harder to avoid their looks. Some congratulated him while others shamed him for taking advantage. It made him laugh; if they only knew the things they did when they were together.

Ducking out early, Quin shrugged his coat on as he went, not bothering to hide Eryn's things from prying eyes. Maybe this was the real issue of working with so many women. Ninety percent of nurses were women after all. It created an interesting work dynamic a few times a month; nothing was worse than being in charge of a group of women who were all synced, hungry, and mean. Keeping the peace was not easy.

The cold night air slammed into Quin like a sledgehammer. He coughed against the sting, sharp like ice in his lungs. He spotted Marc's brooding frame at the far end of the parking lot. Car exhaust created a white, plume-like fog around him.

"Where is she?" Marc asked after they were both inside the car.

Quin took a second to warm his fingers on the dash. "I don't know, she didn't stick around after attacking me. I couldn't really go after her."

"What?" Marc gave Quin an all-too-familiar look of confusion. "Where is Eryn?"

Quin shrugged. "Her shift ended, she went home."

"Her maker came here, attacked you, and you thought it would be a good idea to what, just send Eryn off alone?" Marc spoke slowly, each word louder than the last.

Quin didn't have a response for Marc as he threw the car into gear. Marc's anger translated into road rage and barely concealed curse words. Quin underestimated his friend's ability to turn a short drive into an uncomfortable and hostile situation, and he considered tucking and rolling as they neared Eryn's apartment building.

"If that's her blood on the sidewalk, she isn't going to be able to heal what I do to you." Marc slammed the car door.

"Calm down." Quin knew these words said to anyone rarely did as suggested, but he was beyond tired of Marc's shit.

As expected, Marc did not calm down. "You left her alone after– "

"Save your lecture," Quin interrupted. "It's my fault she's bleeding. It was an accident, hero, she's fine."

Before Marc could formulate a response, Quin tucked his hands into his pockets and shouldered past him on their way inside and up the stairs. He wasn't in the mood for one of Marc's never-ending lectures, so he took the steps two at a time in an attempt to create a bit of distance between the two of them – even if it was only temporary. Quin tried to ignore the reddish-black spots and Marc as he made his way to Eryn's apartment.

As Quin suspected, the trail hadn't gone unnoticed. Regarding the blood suspiciously, Marc joined him on the landing outside Eryn's. He was clearly fighting the urge to scold Quin as they pushed their way in, neither bothering to knock. Distracted by the tangling of wet clothes at his feet, Quin hadn't immediately noticed the smell of blood that permeated the apartment. Once it reached them, the scent froze him and Marc alike in the entranceway. Eyes adjusting, Quin could just make out a wet sucking noise he associated with feeding. That's when he found her green eyes in the dark; blood covered her face, dripping down her arm and into the carpet. He'd never seen a vampire self-cannibalize. Eryn had bitten and torn into herself in a desperate attempt to keep from hurting another. The sound of it was horrific when he considered the cost of feeding this way.

The horror of it was second only to the look of terror and hurt on Marc's face; his expression was something Quin would never forget. The pain that resided there was palpable and Quin knew he didn't see Eryn in the corner anymore. He saw Michael, weak and desperate to survive. Quin glanced between them, unsure how to proceed. The look in Eryn's eyes was predatory; the haunting green of them lacked any recognition as she stared them down.

"Stop," Marc spoke softly. It was a whisper of a word and though weakly spoken, held powerful sentiment.

Quin reached out, grabbing the cuff of Marc's jacket before he could move closer. Maybe he couldn't understand the full gravity of the situation, but he knew in his bones that they were the ones in danger. Call it an ancestral instinct; he couldn't explain the certainty of his fear in this moment. All he knew was he didn't want Marc to get any closer. Marc ignored Quin, pulling himself free as he moved forward, pleading with Eryn to stop.

"Don't." The word was wet and muffled against the wrist of her right arm.

But Marc wasn't going to stop – couldn't. He didn't see the blood on her face, ignored the sound of her feeding, and was oblivious to the hunger in her eyes. Impulsively Quin stepped forward – his movement too fast – and instantly regretted his actions. He'd drawn Eryn's full attention from Marc and to himself. Training and fear guided him then as he drew his blade. The weight of her mind descended on them just as quickly as he'd drawn his steel. He and Marc collapsed, driven to their hands and knees as the floor creaked underneath them. His joints screamed for reprieve.

This was her strength, her anger, her fear. Quin had no idea how to reach her. From the second he'd stepped through the door he hadn't felt a shred of their connection. He realized this power, her power, wasn't something he controlled. It was something she shared with him and not something he owned or that even resided within himself. Quin had been so sure of himself and his abilities, but this made it twice in one night his ego had taken a hit.

Her control over them weakened as her strength wavered, and for a second Quin felt Eryn's mind against his, their connection tangible once more.

'I can't, I can't, I can't; can't control it, can't lose control. I can't.' The force of her words hurt him every bit as much as the earlier shift in gravity.

In that moment he saw it, saw her. Quin was sure Marc could as well, because even though the pressure that forced them to the ground was gone, neither one could stand as Eryn's fear ripped through them. These memories weren't unlike the ones he'd seen the night they'd been tethered, but unlike those memories he could *feel* these ones. He felt their hands on him, ripping at his skin as their mouths tore into him. He smelled the dirt and blood; her cries pulled him apart as the coven fed on her. He could see their eyes, unblinking and hungry, like Eryn's now.

He felt himself being consumed by her mind, unsure anymore if these were her memories or his. *I can't.* Her words pierced his psyche. Quin pulled himself forward, his mind shattered between the reality of the apartment and the one in her mind. He felt the dirt between his fingers as he desperately reached for her, for him. Alexander's body was in front of him, his dead eyes unfocused. *I can't.* His vision blurred with her tears, the memory so clear. He felt the ice of Alexander's skin against his hand. He felt loss like a stone in his chest as they began chest compressions, too weak to make it matter. Quin knew Eryn's fear, then, and how to reach her.

Her fear wasn't the loss of her husband. Eryn's fear was rooted in the loss of herself that he symbolized, and the hunger that threatened to take away what was left. It chewed at the resolve that kept her from becoming the monsters that had destroyed them both. Taking his knife, Quin gambled on both their lives.

The steel bit deep into his collar bone, the warmth of the blood soaked his shirt as it burned down his chest. Arms wide, he was ready to take the full force of her weight should she lunge. Still her eyes begged him to run, to leave before it was too late. '*I can't become them.*' Her emotions flickered like candlelight. Control all but lost, he knew she couldn't resist much longer.

"Come on." Quin smirked, ready to grab her.

Any semblance of self was lost. Eryn lunged. Nothing but need, hunger, and pain as her teeth bit into him deeper than any blade. The sting of it was astonishingly sharp as she slammed into him. All he could do was embrace her as he fought every instinct to escape. Trapping her to himself, he never realized just how much smaller she was than him. The force of her had pushed him on his ass. His knees bent, she sat in his lap, her legs on either side of him. Quin wrapped his left arm almost all the way around her, leaning back on his right. This feeding felt different than before; this time it was just hers. There was no link, and no reprieve from the pain.

"Save your breath," Quin whispered to Marc. "I fucked up."

He tried not to cringe when he looked over to meet Marc's gaze; what he found as he looked at his friend was an odd mixture of sorrow and yearning. Marc didn't have anything to say to him, no lectures, and no snide remarks. He was lost within his own mind, here but not really present with them.

"She isn't Michael, I won't let what happened to him happen to her," Quin hissed, feeling Eryn bite down once more.

Quin wasn't sure how to reach Marc and pull him back to the present. He hoped that his words would be enough for now. Besides, he had to focus on not passing out from the pain or blood loss. The urgency in which Eryn fed was slowing, her hold on him easing as she relaxed into him. Her mind was less and less isolated from him until finally he could escape into the pleasure of it with her. Quin adjusted his hold on her slightly, allowing her to collapse into him. Before, he was afraid she'd try to break away from him or resist like the last time she'd refused to feed. Quin hadn't realized just how empty he felt when her mind withdrew from him, at least not until now. Slowly he threaded their connection, pulling her closer to him as he did.

Quin could feel the limits of his body, exhausted he delved deeper, losing himself in the chaos of her mind. For a second he wondered whose need was greater; they both found peace and serenity within the blood that nothing else could provide. Reluctantly, Quin knew it was time, unless he wanted Marc to pull Eryn off him. He found within her the remnants of what kept her human and pulled them to the surface where she could see them. This was her loss, her pain, and her will. It was the sorrow of him, the agony of their bites, and her resolve to never become them.

Quin felt her responding to him, felt her guilt and shame as she released him, her head heavy against his chest. Quin held her to himself. He didn't do so out of some selfish need for himself; he did it because he knew she needed someone to hold her together the way Alexander had so many times before him. He'd stay here for as long as she needed – he owed her that much after what he'd put her through.

"This makes us even." Quin spoke quietly against her messy brown hair. "Your maker told me I was only alive because of you."

It took him a second to realize that she wasn't going to answer, her eyes closed as she slept. Quin could just make out the faint glow of light from behind the curtains. She didn't stand a chance. Shifting, Quin sat up to inspect her wound. Nothing was left of the lacerations from earlier, not the one he had given her or the jagged ones she had self-inflicted.

"I need you to take her from me, I don't think I can stand." Quin watched as Marc moved slowly toward him, unsure at first how to grab her.

Quin was instantly cold and somehow weaker at the loss of her touch, almost as if their connection could be perpetuated by physical contact alone. He watched as Marc held her small blood-covered form. It reminded him of when she'd been carried up the stairs of the safe house. Then, just like now, it had been Marc who stepped in, saving them both from themselves. Quin lay back and closed his eyes; he deserved every bit of this exhaustion. The next thing he knew, Marc was pulling him to his feet, helping him to the couch in a nauseating lurch of movement. The world was spinning. Desperate for it to stop, Quin clung to the couch. He heard Marc laugh, clearly amused by his plight.

"You're an idiot."

"Yeah, maybe." Quin giggled. "Would you have done it differently?"

"No," Marc answered solemnly.

Quin struggled to keep his eyes open. "Her maker, when she touched me—" he paused, yawning. "—she burned me. Melted my skin. And her eyes – you didn't tell me her eyes were red." Quin struggled to turn over, forcing himself to sit up. "She bit me, Marc, like she just wanted to taste."

He was starting to feel high from the weird combination of sleep deprivation and blood loss. Marc moved closer, forcing him to lie back down.

"At the docks, she told me that you wouldn't suffer like I had. I thought she meant because she was going to kill you." Marc was beginning to sound as exhausted as Quin felt. "Who's to say she won't change her mind, though; in the end it's going to come down to you or her. We both know that."

"After what happened today, it'll be me. We don't stand a chance." Quin tried to get a feel for the damage done to his neck and collarbone, but Marc quickly stopped him.

"You can still get infections; leave it alone and let it heal. It probably feels worse than it looks," Marc scolded.

"Feels like hamburger."

"It looks like hamburger." Marc's serious tone shouldn't have been comical, but Quin was running on fumes.

An odd mixture of laughing and snorting revealed just how exhausted Quin was. Marc smiled down at him, and despite all his lecturing and name calling, even he was not immune to the hilarity of Quin's absurd laughter. Quin's amusement faded quickly, though; the physical act of laughing created a surprising amount of sobering pain as the bits of slowly healing skin reopened. Marc was forced to retrieve a dish towel to stanch the bleeding.

"If she had wanted to kill us, we'd already be dead, Marc." Quin tried to sit up, but again Marc forced him down, Quin's tiredness was quickly turning into delirium. "Remember what you said, about the hunters?"

"Yeah, I remember. It's not going to happen." Marc held him steadfast.

Quin didn't understand how he could be so sure. Marc hadn't been there, hadn't seen the look in her eyes when she bit him. The look of satisfaction and joy on that perfect, pale face of hers haunted him. They couldn't beat her. He'd never met a vampire that could embody fire and destroy so easily with a single touch. Few things scared Quin, but fire and the thought of blisters forming on his skin, and the agony that would ensue – that scared him. It was almost as unnerving as the thought of becoming one of them. There were worse things than death, of this Quin was sure. Nervous energy evolved into an almost drunken and unfaltering resolve; he'd never be one of them – at least not for long.

Marc sensed this shift in him. "It's not going to happen."

These words spoken earlier had been said defiantly, but now were dark and resonated with an unspoken promise. The two of them shared a knowing look. Regardless of how they felt, it was a shared truth of their pack: hunters don't become vampires.

The greatest enemies to hunters were not necessarily vampires, but one of their own. With the attack last night, Quin knew he and

Marc were not going to be alone much longer. While this brought some reassurance, it also brought the terrifying knowledge that Quin was going to have to justify his actions and stand before the guild. He knew they would not take kindly to his secrecy; Marc had warned him there would be consequences for his actions. What neither of them said was who paid the price.

"How long do we have until the others are here?" Quin had given up on fighting Marc, his body was too heavy to resist.

"A day at most." Marc peeked under the towel; he must have been satisfied with what he'd found because he withdrew from Quin.

"I'll bring her to the safe house tonight."

Marc took a deep measured breath in, slowly exhaling. He wasn't looking at Quin anymore; his gaze had drifted toward the bedroom where Eryn slept. Marc was transfixed, as if he was seeing something Quin couldn't.

"Marc, I'll bring her." His tone was unintentionally harsh.

This broke Marc's concentration, his dark brown eyes refocusing as he looked back to Quin. "It isn't up to me. Prepare her. If she resists, it won't be good for either of you."

There were no emotions; his monotone timbre was unsettling in Quin's ears. It stripped away the last of his fight. The hollow of Marc's tone had seeped into his features. Quin knew he wasn't going to like what happened next.

"Tell me what I need to do," Quin urged.

"There isn't anything left you can do." A look of frustration crossed his face. "You chose this route the second you didn't involve the guild, Quin. Depending on who shows, they'll want to make it hurt. Prepare yourself." Marc moved to leave, stopping short of the door. "Don't fight them; it will only make it worse for her."

The metallic click of the door latch popping into place as it slid across the strike plate was like a gunshot in Quin's ears. The others were coming, and they, alone, would judge his actions and the price of his arrogance. There were rules, rules Quin had bypassed when he'd tethered with Eryn. Not just anyone was vested by the guild; there were… prerequisites, one of which being that you weren't a part of the undead. The problem wasn't necessarily that he and Eryn were tethered; the problem was that he'd done so without the consent of the others, and with little concern of Eryn's wishes or her acceptance into the guild beforehand. Quin knew it was too late to change any of it, which meant that all there was left to do was wait and let exhaustion overtake him.

Unfortunately, sleep gave Quin no reprieve as he dreamed of teeth and the monsters attached to them. This was not a dream Quin had often anymore or would ever share. No matter how many times it played out before him, it always started and ended the same: with teeth, and the desperate, hungry grasp of his family's hands. Their fingers would break against his skin as their nails sliced into him and tormented his dreams.

CHAPTER ELEVEN

I woke to the feeling of hands greedily clawing their way up my legs to encircle my throat, suffocating me. This was a new nightmare and I could still see the dead faces looking up at me from the ground, broken and distorted in my mind's eye. It took me a while to fully pull myself from it, my other senses returning slowly as a pungent odor forced my awareness. Blood had hardened, coagulated in my hair and on my skin. I felt it cracking when I turned, peeling the sheets away from myself. Dark under my nails, it speckled my arms like copper. The metallic smell of the blood had mixed with the scent of lavender from my linens, intermingling with a distinct odor I quickly identified as Quin. My nose crinkled involuntarily. I couldn't stand the smell of myself or the feel of yesterday on my skin for another second.

Beelining for the shower, I didn't bother letting the water warm up before stepping in. It stung, creating goosebumps down my skin as it went. The running water enveloped and warmed me slowly. I closed my eyes, stepping completely under the stream as it stripped away the remnants of yesterday in a swirl of pink and red.

What it couldn't seem to take from me was the feel of Quin in my veins. I was intensely aware of him. His emotions filtered through me, the lines separating him and me blurred, yet defined; singular, yet separate; the connection between us stronger. Something had changed. It seemed that every time I fed I became more myself and less of who I was. The ease of it was startling, any earlier uneasiness gone as our consciousnesses brushed against one another.

Sufficiently warmed by the scalding water, I began the tedious process of scrubbing away what the water could not dissolve, my skin sore from the effort. Soon all I could smell was the warm vanilla of my body wash and the only pink tinge left was that of raw skin. Unfortunately, the stink of my apartment all but obliterated the clean smell of me as I dressed and examined the living room. A thought crossed my mind to just burn it. I could see traces of Quin's blood – and my own – across the carpet, on the couch, and finally in the kitchen. It was a murder scene of splatters and smears where he and I had been.

I left it. Not only did I not have the right chemicals to remove blood from fabric, but the old smell of it was making me sick. This was a battle I would face at a later time. Breath held, I cracked open the sliding glass door before evacuating. That was going to have to do until I returned. Donning my leather coat, I didn't bother locking the door as I set off in a new direction.

The streetlights looked like fireflies fighting to illuminate the seeping dark of the moonless night. They were just bright enough to create a faint trail of light along the cracked sidewalk, but no farther. It was nights like this that my imagination got the better of me. Shadows played at the corner of my vision as I walked, and childish instinct told me to just keep moving, that as long as I didn't stop, the shadows couldn't catch me. It quickly became a game as I plotted my path based on the closest lights, hopscotching my way through the city at an increasing pace. My earlier fear turned quickly into excitement as I darted through the playground of abandoned alleys and empty streets of the industrial district. It reminded me of my first night with Quin.

I didn't feel the ache in my muscles or lungs as I climbed. I was boundless, darting from obstacle to obstacle, pushing myself to go faster and faster until I found myself on the rooftop of an abandoned building overlooking the outskirts of the city. The lights were dim here, allowing the stars to break through the light pollution. I paused on the ledge, thrilled by the strength of my body and the beauty of the world around me. For a second I was able to just exist. Nothing else mattered and I just was. It was serene taking in the night air and stars.

I sat, not wanting to draw too much attention to myself. The cement edge of the roof felt cold even through my jeans. I kicked my feet defiantly at the ground below as I admired the river in the distance. It was nights like this that my imagination got the better of me, but this time I knew what I had seen as the shadows below converged on my location. A sinking feeling settled in my chest, kick-starting my adrenal glands and shattering my earlier calm.

The sound of footsteps on the rooftop behind me sent my body and mind into motion. Fight or flight, instinct at its best, I jumped. Everything inside of me screamed to move, to get off the roof and away. I hit the metal awning that covered the shipping doors of the first floor, ten feet below. The cacophony of my initial impact was almost comical as I scrambled to the awning's edge, dropping to the asphalt below in a flurry of movement. I was off. I hadn't felt the impact of my descent or the asphalt under my feet, and I didn't see the trap they had set for me – a trap with glowing eyes and sharp teeth.

Cyd waited anxiously; she'd never met another tethered and she was eager to introduce herself to the one named Eryn. She had followed her here, watching as she played in the empty streets and dangled from the rooftop. Oh, how she wanted to join in, to dance in the shadows, but now was not the time. Now was the time for a different kind of game, the kind that began with blood and ended with answers.

A boom of whining metal and squeaking shoes signaled the moment Cyd had been waiting for, the introduction. Stepping from the shadows, Cyd took her visible form and met the haunting emerald eyes of her fellow vampire with a sinister grin and every bad intention. This is how they'd learn not just what Eryn was capable of, but to which side she belonged. This was Cyd's favorite part because this was where she got to shine. Throwing herself forward, Cyd saw the change in the woman before her as she squared off, preparing to stand and fight. It was too bad that she'd never see Cyd coming; her footsteps faded into nothing and her form dispersed.

Moonless nights and hollow shadows: this was when Cyd was the strongest. On these nights she was infinite, vanishing in and out of the scattered street lights and the glow from the city beyond. Cyd chuckled softly, a chilling sound with no form to claim it. Eryn had braced, throwing her arms up in anticipation for a collision that would never come. Instead of hitting her head-on, Cyd had moved past her, waiting until the last possible moment to return; her weightless form suddenly had mass as she grabbed onto the back of Eryn's collar, using her full weight to slam her to the ground when she reappeared. Cyd was ecstatic when the sharp crack of Eryn's skull on the ground filled the air with the heavenly scent of blood.

"I'm sorry this is how we have to meet." Cyd spoke honestly as she put distance between herself and Eryn. "It's nothing personal."

Eryn rolled to her hands and knees, fighting to pull air back into her lungs. Cyd could see the blood on the ground where Eryn's head had struck, watched as it dripped down the back of Eryn's neck.

'Such a waste,' Cyd thought as she waited, watching as Eryn stood, finally able to catch her breath.

"If you want it so badly, then come and get it." Eryn held out her hand, blood coloring her fingertips.

Cyd smiled playfully in spite of the intrusion. She shifted again, fading in and out. Her shadows granted her an invisible and weightless form until the moment she wanted to strike.

"Quin didn't tell you, did he?" Cyd circled, feeding Eryn's confusion as she searched. It was clear she had no idea what Cyd was talking about. "This is your initiation."

Again and again, Cyd threw herself at Eryn only to watch with great pleasure when Eryn stood back up. It was easy to keep an opponent off balance when they didn't know where you were. All Cyd needed to do was keep her from running.

"What do you want?" Eryn all but cursed from the ground, hesitant to stand again. Her anger only served to fuel Cyd's enjoyment.

"Your answer." Cyd's lithe form towered above Eryn's. "You know the one," she teased. "The one that tells us which side you belong to. The question you should have been asked before you were saved."

Cyd watched as realization played across Eryn's features. She wasn't the first one to pose this question. What she couldn't understand was Eryn's hesitation; it was her uncertainty that frustrated Cyd. What was there to think about?

"It's not that simple." Eryn breathed, forcing herself to stand once more, the confusion in her tone only serving to fuel Cyd's growing resentment.

Like water, Cyd's form shifted as she readied her next strike on Eryn's now standing frame. Livid green eyes met Cyd's just before her next assault; all of her forward movement halted as gravity crashed down on her. It was unlike anything Cyd had experienced; the pressure took her breath away, forcing her to the ground in front of Eryn. It was an extraordinary sensation that penetrated her bones and crushed her skull with increasing severity. Eryn knelt beside Cyd's now flattened form. She winced, Eryn's voice resonating not in her ears, but sharply within her mind '– *Leave me alone,*' is what she said, but '*or else*' is what was meant.

The voice Cyd heard was angry and dark, much different than Eryn's spoken words. It made Cyd's hair stand on end, destroying her concentration and forcing her form to return as her illusion shattered, replacing all her earlier enjoyment with fear.

"Cyd!" Warren's voice cut through her panic just as light exploded overhead, saturating the world in white.

Cyd's mind snapped back to attention, no longer overwhelmed by the weight that Eryn had exerted on her. In the darkness Cyd was unrivaled, an unseen and haunting force, but it was in the light that she could be truly devastating – for it was in the light that her shadows were darkest. They'd have their answer.

———

Explosive light obliterated my vision, whitewashing the world around me before I was plunged into absolute darkness. Panic erupted within, engulfing me. I was being devoured as oblivion overtook me, instantaneously lost in the vastness of the darkness as it suffocated me. Claustrophobia robbed me of my reason as I fell to my knees.

My hands struck the asphalt below, stinging my palms; it was the sharpness of it that pulled me from my panic, my vision returning almost as fast as it had gone. The pounding of my heart felt like a kick drum against my ribcage, Cyd's sinister smile and glowing, honey brown eyes were all I saw in the renewed night.

"What do you want from me?" I yelled again, frustrated with this game of hers.

"Your answer," a male voice called, repeating Cyd's earlier words. He spoke slowly as he moved forward to stand beside Cyd.

The pair of them, they were the same as Quin and me. I didn't know if I should be relieved or afraid. I was being tested, which begged the question: what would happen if I failed?

"I'm not your enemy," I pleaded, genuinely confused and angry.

"And that's not an answer," Cyd quipped. "Not really."

"The thing is," the hunter began, voice flat, "we aren't so sure that's true. The way Marc explained it, you're still enchanted by that maker of yours, the one with red eyes."

Cyd made a point to close the space between us one long stride at a time. She looked insane – her eyes wide as she approached; they were the color of glowing amber as she circled my kneeling form. It took everything I had not to flinch when she reached for me, tracing her long, thin fingers through the blood in my hair. She stood before me, entranced by the glistening red painted on her fingertips. She took a step back, her eyes meeting mine as she licked it away.

"You haven't decided which side you owe loyalties to, have you?" Cyd's voice became increasingly menacing. "The side that saved you – that saved me – or theirs?"

"What would you know?" I spat, feeling my anger, guilt, and confusion stealing away my desire to engage further.

I didn't have an answer to give, and in this moment all I really wanted was to go back to my rooftop, to the stars and the distant river. For one night I didn't want to remember. I wanted to be left alone. Desperate, I moved to escape. The hunter's eyes instantly met mine, hazel flecked with a glow of amber. He had no intention of letting me escape as he drew on his connection with Cyd.

I caught myself responding to his threat, hating Cyd's demented smile as they prepared, ready to force my response. Taking a deep breath, I exhaled the last of my reluctance to fight them as I allowed my mind to extend farther outside of myself than I had before. Relief washed over me at the release. I'd been keeping myself confined, held tight like a fist for so long that I'd forgotten what it felt like to relax and stretch.

It got easier every time I fed; my mind didn't get lost in their thoughts or emotions. I was beginning to understand how to keep myself untangled from them. It would be easy to feed on them like this, psychically draining their energy, just as I did with my patients. Instinctually, I knew it would be unwise to outright attack them in that way. Stretching, I reached out and realized Cyd's emotions were more vivid to me than those of her counterpart, Warren. It took me a moment to understand why: she'd consumed me. I could feel my blood coursing through her, and knew she was no longer a threat to me.

...No one tells you how to be a vampire, because slowly, it becomes apparent to us all. Like the memories passed down through the blood, it is in the blood that we awaken and learn for ourselves who we are and what we are capable of.

I felt their intentions before they moved; I read their emotions as clear as a match lit in the pitch of night. I didn't have time to second guess myself as they charged, determined to force an answer from me. Cyd's form shifted like a mirage. What she didn't realize was that the more she did it, the clearer her image became. Her illusions had less and less effect on me until, finally, the shadows no longer hid her form. They were fast; the second I dodged one of Cyd's strikes, Warren was in her place. Their movements were rhythmic and practiced. This was what Quin and I could be.

It was their skill that would get the better of me. Their endurance and strength came from experience and training, mine was luck and I could feel it running out. It was getting harder to evade them the longer this dance of ours continued. It was tiring trying to physically and mentally stay a step ahead of them; each action they took was second nature and allowed little time for me to respond. Strategically, they'd been backing me into a corner, making it impossible for me to escape. In no way was I in control of their advance; the best I could manage was evasion.

Cyd's form shimmered as she lunged. Looking past her, I allowed her to believe I didn't see her coming as she reached for me. A smile played across her face just in time for me to dodge and smash the flat of my palm upwards into her nose, instantly erasing the upward curve of her lips. Without hesitation Warren advanced. His haunting, hybrid eyes caught me by surprise as he slammed full-force into me. I wheezed pitifully as his full weight pinned me against the brick wall of the nearest building.

"Enough running," Warren huffed, the hot air from his lungs an affront to my senses. "You owe us an answer."

Satisfaction burned within the hazel green and amber of his eyes as he held his forearm against my throat. I could feel his excitement as he pressed his body against mine, taste his pleasure at having caught me as he smiled down at me. Something in that instant brought me back to a dark place I didn't like to visit – the part of me that, time and time again, men decided they could take – and I snapped. With every ounce of my being I lashed out; I had to get the feel of him off me. Adrenaline pounded through my bloodstream as I sent Warren reeling with a concussive wave of energy. I watched as he tumbled, his entire prowess lost as he kicked up dirt and gravel. I was at his side before he had a chance to right himself, my foot quickly connecting with his ribs.

This time it was Warren that wheezed as his ribs cracked. I was lost in my rage for him, sickened by the warmth his body had left behind on mine. Distracted, I'd forgotten all about Cyd and her bleeding broken nose. She was quick to grab me, lifting me up and away from Warren. I struggled, but she held fast and her taller frame easily lifted my feet from the earth.

"Get up," Cyd spat, blood speckling the side of my face.

I met the fury of Warren's eyes with a smug, self-satisfied smile, honestly surprised at the ease with which he stood.

"Send her back, Cyd. Let her rot in the abyss," Warren grunted. "There's more than one way to get an answer."

I felt Cyd nod, watching as Warren pulled a flare from his jacket pocket. This time the world was drenched in red just before I was engulfed in black. I felt the familiar tug of panic setting in as my claustrophobia overrode me. My heart raced when Cyd tossed me away. Any sense of up or down was lost until I was reunited with the unyielding earth. The relief I felt as I struck the ground was short-lived, but it forced me to focus on the only other connection outside the abyss – Cyd and my blood within her.

It was a flickering light within the darkness; my earlier web receded, obliterating all outside connection as I fought against Cyd's darkness. I could feel her moving around me, acutely aware of her presence even before she struck out with her boot, reciprocating my earlier attack on Warren. Bile stung my throat as I coughed violently. Now that they had me, they weren't going to let up.

"Are you trying to protect her after everything she did to you? After what she did to Alex!" Cyd demanded.

"Shut up!" I screamed, fist pounding the asphalt below. "You don't know!" There was no way they could understand the hurt, rage, and betrayal I felt at their accusations and insistent questioning, demanding an answer I didn't have. What if the only side I was on was my own? What if I didn't want to be a part of either, would they let me go then?

Warren's hands found me once more, gripping my collar as he hauled me to my feet, lifting me up just to throw me back down. It was terrifying; no light could reach me here, and every time my feet left the ground I was more and more thankful to crash back down.

They did this until I tasted blood in my mouth, felt it on my hands and knees, warm and slick against my skin. This time it was Cyd's hands that pulled me up; my fears reignited as my connection with the earth was shattered once more. She held me up, her fingers firmly cemented in my leather jacket. I knew even without seeing her that she was smiling, thrilled by my turmoil.

"You don't know," I repeated, desperate to catch my breath.

"Give us an answer and this ends." Cyd's tone was sincere even if the brutality of her actions were not.

I laughed, my fear bubbling up in my chest as a nervous giggle took hold. I couldn't help it. My body, mind, and soul were drained by the never-ending rollercoaster my existence had created. Cyd slammed me back against a wall in an attempt to halt my laughter. It was too bad I wasn't going to see the look on her face when I took back what she had stolen. Focusing, I sought out every particle of myself within her before ripping it away. My world of black exploded with light and the red of misted blood as we both fell to the ground.

CHAPTER TWELVE

Q uin tried not to pace, he didn't want the others to see how uncomfortable he was. Occasionally Marc would shoot him a warning glance, telling him to sit down or stand still. With the help of binoculars Quin could just make out the trial below. He wasn't sure if he was going to be able to sit back and watch. Something about a two-against-one fight just wasn't sitting right with him.

"We have to be sure," Marc consoled. "If you were there, you'd only get in the way."

Quin shot him a glare. "Since when is torture a good indicator of truth?"

"Shut up and watch," Lucas, a hunter Quin had just met, spoke harshly. "This gives us a chance to see what she's capable of."

"Vampires, unlike humans, are born with their skills. Control is the only thing they learn," a female hunter named Clara chimed in.

This day had been filled with all kinds of new introductions, and so far the only one Quin still remotely liked was Marc. There was one other watching from the rooftop with them, a soft looking hunter with glasses named Rylan.

"You said her powers are psychic in nature?" Clara asked curiously, a mess of curly blond hair all but obstructing her vision.

Quin turned from Marc and Lucas reluctantly to answer her probing questions. "Yeah."

"Your connection, can she reach you from here, or you her?" Clara continued.

He didn't know how to answer. "Not really." Clara raised her eyebrows, waiting for him to elaborate. "Sometimes I feel things, but for the most part it's only when we're together."

Satisfied, Clara returned to her voyeurism alongside the other two hunters. Marc, ever patient, held out Quin's only source of connection to the trial below. He didn't want to watch as the other vampire toyed with Eryn in this fucked-up game of initiation, but in the end he didn't have much of a choice. Focusing the lenses, Quin moved his field of vision slowly until he found Eryn crumpled on the ground, Cyd standing over her.

He'd watched as the vampire blinked in and out of his field of vision, reappearing only to lash out. It was a dirty trick. The longer Quin watched, the angrier he became, until finally he was forced to look away again. Warren, the one Cyd was tethered to, still hadn't shown up; apparently Eryn had been able to give him the slip. That hadn't surprised Quin; she was surprisingly good at evading, but only when she could see it coming.

"Look," Rylan spoke up this time. "Cyd's down."

Quin moved too quickly, his vision swimming as he focused slowly on where Eryn was crouched over Cyd. The vampire was laid out beneath her, paralyzed. Quin smiled. Having been on the receiving end of this attack, he knew how much it hurt; and oh, how he hoped it hurt.

"What's she doing?" Clara asked excitedly.

"Crushing her," Marc answered after a while. "It feels like a thousand pounds compressing your bones."

"I think," Rylan said slowly, "that Eryn can see Cyd. Her eyes are always focused in the direction Cyd reappears."

Lucas, never looking away, pulled a radio from his jacket pocket. "Warren, Cyd is down. Hurry."

Quin glanced his way; Lucas's jaw was clenched. He was afraid Eryn might actually be stronger – afraid his stupid plan might end with the wrong person hurt. They were all tense except Clara, who watched with a crazed grin plastered to her freckled face. If Quin had to guess, she was probably a collector. That thought sent a chill through him. The idea of spending an eternity as some fucked up hunter's science experiment wasn't something he wanted to think about right now.

"She jumped off the roof, Luke," the radio squealed, the man's voice on the other end breaking. "Cyd can handle herself."

Silence resumed until a loud pop and flash of light lit up the buildings below, sending the shadows running.

"Now, the fight begins," Clara said quietly. "Let's see what your vampire can do, Quin."

Anger engulfed Quin and it felt like a black hole in his chest; he wanted to kick in their teeth. They were enjoying every second as they discussed each strike like commentators at a boxing match.

"They've caught her," Rylan said calmly.

Quin cursed, returning to his binoculars, but he wasn't sure what he was seeing. Eryn was on her hands and knees, clawing at the asphalt like she was afraid of falling up. That's when he saw her eyes. Two pools of black. It was the same darkness he now saw reflected in Cyd's once amber eyes.

"Get up." Quin's knuckles were white from gripping the binoculars too tightly; it was the only thing that kept his hands from shaking. The light from the flare faded slowly as the shadows returned to the road below, relinquishing their hold on Eryn.

"She's afraid of the dark," Clara laughed, addressing no one in particular.

Quin let out the breath he'd been holding, Eryn was back on her feet. He didn't like watching this game of theirs. She looked so small down there alone with Warren and Cyd. Radio static hissed around them; Lucas was flipping through channels, finally finding the right one before setting it at his feet.

A deep sense of betrayal gripped Quin's stomach as he listened to Warren's voice break through the static. Quin forced his attention on the scene below, refusing to acknowledge Marc or the other hunters' eyes on him. He watched as Cyd's spider-like limbs traced their way around Eryn as she circled, her sickly yellow eyes like those of a cat. Quin wouldn't give them the satisfaction of a reaction – or at least he hadn't intended to. He grew angrier with every question relayed through the static, realizing the extent to which Marc had sold Eryn out to the guild.

"Are you fucking kidding me? You tell them about her maker, but don't mention the shit that red-eyed bitch put her through?" Quin was livid as he squared up with Marc. He may still be smaller, but he was not weaker – not anymore.

Quin had Marc shoved back, off balance, and on his ass before the others could even reach him. Throwing his arms up, Quin dislodged Lucas's and Rylan's hold on him.

"I'm done." He moved to leave, tossing the viewfinders with enough force to shatter the lenses.

Rylan and Lucas made no move to stop him. Marc didn't even look at him; it was Clara that spoke from her perch, her attention never wavering.

"If you interfere or help her in any way, you'll be the next one interrogated." Clara's tone was cold, indifferent. "Marc's word won't be enough to protect you." Her pale green eyes met the blue of his then. "You're just one of them after all, a sliver away from awakened. I wonder what kind of vampire you'd make." A faint smile touched her lips before she resumed her observations.

Quin wasn't sure before, but now he knew what kind of hunter Clara was. She was a collector, or worse; by the way she examined the fight below he wouldn't be surprised if she was a creator. Marc was back on his feet, expressionless as always. He'd told Quin not to give them anything to use against himself or Eryn. Too late for that, he was gone; Quin would rather be on the street with Cyd's shadows than spend another second up here with them. He'd do what he was told, he'd wait and watch, but he wasn't going to pretend he was okay with it. Marc could play those mind games by himself.

Quin didn't waste any time skirting the side streets toward Eryn. The closer he got, the thicker the shadows became. Inky and thick, they clung to his clothes. Cyd was obscuring not only the trial but any that resided within; this would provide him and any other hunter anonymity and protection.

"Clara told me to meet you." A childlike voice whispered, catching him before he could wander any closer.

Silver eyes peered up at him from the face of a young boy, a vampire. His features soft and rounded, he couldn't be older than eight, but by the way he held himself Quin knew he was much older. He noticed Cyd's shadows didn't cling to the boy like they did him.

"I'll take you as close as I can," the child reassured Quin, his small hands tugging at his sleeve.

For a moment Quin was horrified and heartbroken as he was pulled forward by this child's cold fingers. Dark jeans, too long for his short frame, were cuffed over red tennis shoes. His small, zip-up hoodie flapped open. The striped shirt underneath only added to his childlike appearance. It was haunting to meet a demon cloaked in a child's skin.

"No farther, hunter; you can see from here, yes?" The boy asked sweetly.

Quin nodded; he could just see between the buildings. Cyd was holding Eryn from behind as Warren stood. He glanced down at the child beside him, his cold hand still encircling his wrist. Quin knew if he tried to interfere, he'd find out just how strong this monster that held him so innocently was.

Quin had made a mistake by coming down here. From here he could see the pain and blood on Eryn's face as they threw her to the ground. Cyd's boot hit hard enough to force the air from Eryn's lungs with a choked cough. Instinctually he tried to move forward; Cyd's last strike made Eryn writhe. As expected the child held Quin with a weight and grip that did not match the adjoined frame.

"Are you trying to protect her after everything she did to you? After what she did to Alex!" Cyd demanded.

"Shut up!" Eryn screamed, fist pounding the asphalt below. "You don't know!"

The pain and anger in her voice hurt Quin physically. He should have stayed on the roof with Marc. Now he had the pleasure of experiencing Eryn's pain first hand as Warren and Cyd toyed with her. They flung her around like a ragdoll, playing off her fear in an attempt to force a response.

The boy spoke softly from beside Quin, never relinquishing his hold. "She has the ability to feed by proximity, yet doesn't. Why?"

Quin looked down, meeting those silver eyes once more, realizing this child had not been a child in a very long time. The stink of blood clung heavily to him and his eyes held within them an inhuman fierceness.

"To protect herself," Quin answered.

It was the only reason he could think of. If she fed freely on the hunters Eryn would have condemned herself, giving Clara and the others all the proof they needed to mark her as an enemy.

"You don't know." Eryn's voice filtered through to Quin once more, breathless in her reply as Cyd held her up again.

"Give us an answer and this ends," Cyd answered, her voice absolute in Quin's ears.

Eryn's eyes were bottomless inkwells, a startling contrast to the emerald green they should be. Cyd's back was turned toward him as she dangled Eryn, she must have said something he hadn't overheard because Eryn was laughing. Quin winced involuntarily as Cyd slammed Eryn back against the brick wall. It took everything he had not to interfere.

No fight was a fair fight, but this was just cruel. From his interactions with Eryn, she barely knew how to defend herself. Eryn's laughter continued despite Cyd's attempt to quiet her; the sound of it was unsettling in the otherwise quiet night. That's when the smell of blood filled the air, sharp against the musk of the city air. Cyd's shadows disappeared – here then gone – as she collapsed to the ground.

Quin froze, confused by what he had just witnessed. A red mist hung in the air, frozen for a moment in the spot where Cyd had just been. That's when Quin saw it, the red reflected in place of black or green. It was the same red he had seen reflected in her maker's eyes. That's when the boy let go, just as the shadows fell.

The silence that followed was short lived. Warren sprang forth, reaching for something hidden, a curse just leaving his lips. Quin didn't remember stepping forward or the parts in between; he just moved, finding himself face to face with a man he'd never met and a pistol pointed at his face.

CHAPTER THIRTEEN

In one swift movement, Quin swept his left hand up and grabbed the gun, encircling the slide just before the trigger was pulled and effectively prevented the bullet from cycling. Without hesitating Quin pulled the gun away, the skin of his left palm bleeding from where the gun had pinched him. Warren stepped back, realizing what he had almost done.

"It's over," Quin warned, tossing away Warren's pistol.

Cyd's sputtering cough caught Warren's attention then. It looked like she'd been shot with birdshot; tiny puncture wounds speckled her body, coating her in blood. I could just hear Cyd cursing me, the sound of her voice distant in my ears as I teetered forward into Quin. I used him to slow my descent, catching the sleeve of his jacket as I lowered myself to a crouching position.

Quin didn't move, his back turned to me as he placed himself directly between me and the other hunter.

"You were here the whole time?" I asked, shakily clinging to his sleeve.

He glanced at me quickly before looking away again. I read the regret there, like a knife in his gut as before I reached out mentally. The connection felt comforting and familiar despite his turmoil. His mind was racing, chaotic against mine as bits and pieces of his memories played back to me. It was disorienting, seeing myself through his eyes. He'd been here, forced to watch as Cyd and Warren *tested* me.

"That was incredible!" A tiny woman with wild blond curls bounded forth, startling me.

As she neared, she began clapping, pausing only to catch her breath. A small boy followed in tow and I was instantly aware of what he was. His movements were unnaturally precise and his eyes were the color of moonlight reflected on water. Just the barest hint of blue mingled with silver, the contrast was striking against the mahogany color of his skin and the innocent smile on his face.

"The two of you should fight again once this one is better trained, Cyd; maybe next time we can pair you both off." The woman's voice was shrill in my ears, her excitement unsettling. "Maybe by then your hunters will have learned a thing or two about restraint?"

Neither Cyd nor I acknowledged her statement; it seemed that her presence was unwelcome by all. From the look on Warren's face, she was someone to be feared.

"So," she announced, her full attention now on me, "tell me what you just did."

Pale eyes stared down at me, the color lost to me in the dimness of the night, curiosity pouring from her and onto me like tar. Her emotions were vivid across my mind and I could sense her impatience. Any niceties she was affording us were just a front to her hidden nature. It was then that I understood the group's wariness of this woman.

Contemplating my response, I answered carefully. "I took back that which belonged to me."

I looked then to Cyd, meeting her weary yet intense gaze. Confusion played across her features before realization took hold. Humiliation evolved into respect; she'd been bested, and despite her earlier hostility, she seemed humbled and relieved now that it was all over.

"You control the blood, all blood?" the child asked, the weight of his presence sent a chill down my spine.

The energy I felt spilling forth from him was enormous. I was certain the vessel before me harbored a very real threat. He was a wolf in sheep's clothing. I watched as his smile shifted slightly, it was the barest of movements at the corner of his mouth; perhaps he was not used to being recognized for what he was.

"No. Only mine. I could feel it in her and have felt it in Quin." Fear made me forthcoming, and though his four-foot frame stood innocently, I knew I shouldn't give him any reason to question me further.

Slowly, others had begun to emerge, all of them hunters from what I could tell. The only vampires were the two before me now. It was unnerving being surrounded by them. Quin was the only one who stood opposed, his body still placed between them and me. The only other face I recognized was Marc's; the tension between him and Quin palpable.

"Marc tells me you can feed on the energy of those around you; show me." I felt a shift in her then as dark curiosity gave way to her true nature.

"You want me to feed from you?" I asked, surprised.

159

A smile touched her pale lips. "Show me."

Each word was precise, the twinkle in her eyes sinister. She didn't want me to show her, she needed it. Watching Cyd and me was just a way to whet her appetite; now she needed to experience firsthand what I could do. I think I understood Quin's contempt now. The woman before me never wavered – not as I forced my way into her thoughts, and not when I took from her every emotion she had to offer. One by one I erased her excitement, fed upon her intrigue, and stole away the energy she had to smile until she was breathless from the effort of fighting me.

I stole her name and the names of her companions from the depths of her psyche, and learned why she was so interested in me and my skills. Clara was a collector. I could see within her the lives of others like myself whom she'd studied, trapped, or killed. Not all of those I saw within her memories were vampires, though; some of them had been hunters. With every memory I stripped away, I found no remorse; this was why the others were so hesitant. This woman was an ally to none. So I consumed recklessly. The more Clara fought, the harder I tore it from her. It wouldn't satiate me, but I didn't care, not as long as it hurt.

Clara held her hand up then, a weak smile returning to her face as I abstained. She teetered, dark circles now present under her tired eyes. I'd given her exactly what she wanted.

"You can do that whenever you want?" Clara asked dryly, her excitement from earlier lost.

I nodded, returning to my feet; glad Clara and Alistair were no longer able to loom over me. Though Clara's tuft of wild curls gave the impression of added height, I was a good three inches taller. Stepping back, I cemented Quin's position between them and myself as I took in Alistair's unassuming stature. The completeness of his charade was unsettling and I wondered just how many he had killed disguised so innocently. The scent of blood emanated from him, and I quickly realized that the smell wasn't coming from him, it *was* him.

"Are we done here?" Quin asked quietly, his eyes never leaving Clara, who was still fixated on me.

Warren and Cyd had made a point to retreat when the others had shown up, making room for them to close in around us, Marc being the only exception. Lucas, a man with spikey blond hair and a chip on his shoulder joined Clara. He made a point to stabilize her while the other flanked Alistair. This second man was about my height with dark hair and eyes; his name was Rylan. I got the distinct impression that he was analyzing me, much as Clara had, but in a far less intrusive way.

I wasn't sure whether it was her exhaustion that finally won out or if it was the look the others gave her, but either way I was thankful when Clara finally replied: "For now."

'*Hello,*' Rylan's greeting filtered through to me.

Satisfied that I had heard him, he nodded a greeting. His mind felt different from the others, more precise. He had been analyzing me and wanted to test my ability for himself.

"You never gave an answer," Lucas pointed out as he pulled Clara away. "There's really only one choice."

"Fuck off," was Quin's only response and he spoke it like a goodbye.

Clara smiled at his response. "We'll have your answer once we find your maker."

Her voice trailed off as she was pulled away. Rylan lingered a moment longer, though. Out of curiosity, I reached out, touching his consciousness with mine, probing just enough to let him know I was listening.

'Which side will you choose?' Rylan's words felt heavy in my mind. 'Either way, I look forward to knowing you.'

Had I not just delved the depths of Clara's mind, I might have been surprised by his comment. Fortunately, his words were just that: words. He'd kept his memories to himself. Alistair was the last to leave, his innocent smile never wavering as he bounced away after Rylan and the others. Quin, Marc, and I were the only ones left. The tension from earlier faded quickly, erasing the headache-like pressure that had been building in my skull.

"I need a drink," Quin stated, starting in the opposite direction of the others.

Marc waited for me to fall in line beside him before setting off after Quin. My body ached like I'd run a marathon. I was healing slowly as we made our way back toward civilization. I did my best to clean up before reaching town; using my shirt, I wiped my face and hands. I was thankful my leather jacket hadn't been ruined as I zipped away the blood stains. There was no hiding the torn knees of my jeans; hopefully wherever Quin was leading us was dark. The fact that it was well after midnight meant that wherever we went, people would already be too drunk or high to notice us anyway.

"Why didn't you warn me? Why didn't either of you warn me?" I asked Marc bitterly, wiping the rest of the blood from my hands and onto my jeans.

Quin was too far ahead of us to hear; his one-track mind led us forward in a nearly blind manner. I could tell by the tension in his shoulders and the pace of his stride that he was trying not to explode. His anger weaved around him like a cloud, ebbing and flowing as he replayed the events of the night.

"We lost that option the second Quin hid you from the guild and you reached out to your maker." Marc never looked at me; his tone didn't match the sterility of his words.

He was angry, maybe even more so than Quin. Worse, though, were his feelings of guilt. I couldn't tell if it was for me or Quin, and I assumed maybe that it was a little bit of both.

"You could have tried; at least I would have known I wasn't alone." That was it, those were the words.

Marc glanced down at me, and there was the guilt I had felt as his mask of indifference shattered. Pain reflected within the depths of his brown eyes and the fine lines of his face. I don't know what my goal had been at eliciting these emotions from him, and I found myself regretting it as he struggled to find a way to respond. Thankfully, I didn't get the chance to hear his response as Quin ducked into an over packed bar, beckoning us to follow.

The smell of cigarettes washed over me, instantly causing me to cough. The music vibrated through my chest and teeth, not a single soul within sober, save for us. Marc and I stood in the doorway; the cool, clean, outside air was instantly replaced with the stale air that was created when too many bodies were packed in a small space. Breathing the stagnant air from strangers' lungs and inhaling the smell of their bodies was quickly becoming more than I could handle.

"Come on." Quin had doubled back, a drink in one hand as he pulled me forward and through the crowd.

His grip on my wrist felt protective – maybe even a bit possessive – as he led me through the crowd, his body again positioned between me and those who stood in our way. Marc followed in our wake and together we all settled on the balcony upstairs. From here I could look out across the bar, taking in the people below. Quin pulled us toward a corner booth next to a window. The sliver of night air that crept through in no way aired out the stench, but it did make being here bearable.

Quin quickly sat down, spreading his arms wide along the back of the booth, this only served to force me to sit with his arm around me, though thankfully not on me. Clean air was worth the minor discomfort. Marc, on the other hand, must have seen it as a show of possession – there wasn't enough room for both of them in the booth – and sat in a chair just opposite of us.

"What happens now?" Quin asked Marc, not waiting for a reply as he finished his drink, slamming the glass down hard enough to break it. "How long until we're all a part of Clara's collection?"

Marc didn't feed into Quin's anger; instead, he leaned forward, letting out a sigh of relief, his hands shaking. Quin took note of this, caught off guard by the sudden show of emotion. We all stopped, maybe for the first time since it was all over, and took a breath. Marc's lapse in composure exposed his thoughts to me. Again, I was disoriented seeing myself reflected in someone else's memories; the whole time the only emotion I read there was fear.

Marc was afraid for me and Quin, but not selflessly. *Michael*: the name brought with it a new understanding of the man in front of me and the image of a vampire I knew was dead. Marc's loss mirroring my own, I winced as I withdrew, regretting my intrusion. Maybe we all needed a drink.

"Why are there collectors?" I asked no one in particular, needing the feel of Marc's mind to leave mine.

"Sometimes, it's the best way to know your enemy," Marc answered absently, regaining his composure as a waitress deposited three shots to our table.

Quin divided them up, two to him and one to Marc. The clear liquid could have been anything. I watched as they both drank it like water, no hesitation. If it burned on the way down, neither one acknowledged it.

"Funny thing, she wasn't only collecting vampires; I think she was making them." Their responses told me this was not news to them. "So it's okay if you guys do it?"

I hadn't meant to defend one side over the other. My rash response was just that, a quick reaction; one that did not go unnoticed.

"I didn't mean –"

"It isn't." Quin cut off my apology. "It's never okay."

Quin was finishing his second shot just in time for the waiter to circle back and deposit three more glasses of clear liquid. He must have told them to keep them coming; his heightened metabolism wouldn't work in his favor here, especially not at this pace.

"You might want to take it easy with those." I suggested point-lessly as he downed another shot.

"Why, do you want one?" Quin teased.

"You can't coexist." Marc contemplated his second shot warmly. "They'll find her. There isn't a choice, not really."

His words mirrored Lucas's. I could feel the alcohol numbing the periphery of Marc's mind, softening the edges of his exposed and exhausted nerves.

"If they have their way, they'll make you kill her." Marc leveled his eyes with mine just before downing the glass of clear liquid.

That was an unsettling thought that instantly put me on edge. Surprisingly, Quin responded in much the same way: defensively.

"You really want to bring up sides now? You told them whatever they wanted to hear today with no concern for what happened to her." Quin's arm had made its way around my shoulder, pulling me closer to him.

I tensed involuntarily against the feel of him, the smell of liquor washing over me. Marc was again an open book, alcohol made him exceptionally vulnerable to me. His thoughts tangled as he tried to formulate a coherent reply.

"Knock it off. If he had tried to defend me, they would have turned on him in a heartbeat." I retorted before Marc could stumble through a response.

Sighing, I leaned forward and away from Quin to rub my temples. I was getting really tired of this fight of theirs. I had to force Marc's mind from mine, not liking the hopelessness I found within. There were too many people around me. The smell of them thick in the air, the taste of cigarette smoke at the back of my throat, and their spinning drunkenness made me want to gag. The weight of their inebriated minds against mine made it feel like they were touching me. I had to focus; it was becoming difficult to speak when others' thoughts were bouncing around my skull.

"How long? How long until they find Selene?" I strained to speak, realizing a little too late that I had said something I shouldn't have.

"How do you know her name?" Quin's unfocused eyes were suddenly sharp as he locked onto me.

I swallowed hard, mouth dry, as I looked at him through my fingers. I had stopped rubbing my temples, my hands frozen around my face.

"Did she tell you?" Quin asked, but what he meant was: *Did you meet with her again?*

I sat up, straightening slowly as I let my hands fall away from my face. "I heard it, the night you were attacked."

I've never been a good liar, not even when they were half-truths. Quin didn't believe me for a second. I saw it in his eyes and the way he smiled when he turned toward me. He closed the distance between us once more, his right arm resting on the table in front of me while his left circled around the booth behind me. I could smell the alcohol on his breath; he was purposely trying to make me uncomfortable.

"From whom?" He loved seeing me squirm; even before I was like this, he got a kick out of having the upper hand.

I shook my head, refusing to retreat from him despite my discomfort. "Not from her."

I knew this was why Marc didn't trust me. It was because I couldn't pick a side, because I was still unsure. I saw it on their faces. My uncertainty scared them, scared the other hunters, and it scared me. I didn't understand why I wanted to protect Derek – if that was

167

even something I could do. Maybe it was my sense of loyalty to one of my kin, or maybe I just didn't want to be alone. I saw the flecks of green in his eyes long before I felt him in my mind. It was a dirty trick, using me against myself. He was an extension of me. The feel of his senses mixing with mine was familiar and not unlike and embrace.

Quin looked around in amazement, as if he was truly seeing something for the first time. He could feel the bar's occupants all around him in the same way I did, and he loved it. Everything I was becoming so, too, was he. The only difference: he didn't have to think about it and he didn't doubt it. Quin really was the better monster, and the more I grew the stronger he became.

"Your sentiment for them will get you killed." I felt it then. Quin's resentment was a coal burning in my chest.

I was thankful that the resentment wasn't directed toward me. It was a general hatred that he somehow waived for me – a sort of blind spot. I realized that, perhaps, it was because he had accepted me in a way I had yet to accept myself. He knew what I was and didn't care.

"If Selene attacks openly again, it won't take long. It's when the makers hide that killing them gets tricky. They feed less and less frequently as they age." Marc's mind again wandered to the past. "I tracked one for fifteen years."

Again a face flashed in Marc's memories; this time I wasn't the only one who saw it. I watched as Quin flinched. It was a nearly imperceptible movement followed by a wave of recognition. Quin knew exactly who this face belonged to and it made his heart drop.

'*Michael.*' The name bounced between us in a hushed acknowledgement.

"Whatever it is you think you need from Selene, I suggest you figure it out quickly. I wouldn't count on Clara's patience." Marc spoke plainly, sensing my hesitation even if he didn't understand it.

Quin nodded his agreement as he leaned back to revel in the intoxication of the bar. From the outside someone might assume he was hallucinating; his connection with me allowed him to pick up on the internal conversations and sensations of those around us. Our abilities were continually evolving and thankfully he no longer needed to draw from me to maintain it. It was more of a give and take of our combined energies and senses, making it easier to process the information.

"I don't understand why you don't want her dead." Quin returned his focus to me, bringing with it Marc's own curiosity. "He's dead because of her; whatever hold she has on you can't override that."

An innate sense of déjà vu overcame me, like a memory I couldn't quite recall. What was it? Quin must have felt it too, circling just out of my reach as I tried to remember; it was lost.

"I can't make sense of what really happened." The feeling of déjà vu faded slowly until I wasn't even sure what I might have been recalling. "Why can't I remember her at the coven, the transference? Why are none of my memories from her?" I paused, hoping Marc would interject and give me some sort of insight, but he didn't, so I continued. "It would be a shame, to never even know the one who made me."

These words didn't make sense, not to me and not to Quin. My emotions were all I had to explain, so he took them, internalizing my feelings of loss, of hatred, of the neglect I felt when I thought of her – of my uncertainty. It was the gray area that held me. I was certain something was hidden, but didn't know what or why it was so important.

"I think there is a part of me left that I need from her." I didn't look at either of them; I didn't want to have to defend myself for the second time tonight.

I could feel Quin trying to digest the rush of conflicting information I had given him. It wasn't black and white anymore, and I didn't know when that had changed.

"Your sentiment could get both of you killed," Marc repeated, adding his own twist. "I've seen makers force their offspring to do things they wouldn't normally." The familiar lecturing tone had returned to his voice. "So, unless you willingly attacked those people on the docks, Selene has already shown that she has the ability to manipulate you."

I thought back to that night and the way she had led me, like my own feelings and thoughts were numb compared to hers. I'd done the same thing to Rey, forcing him to take medications and follow me, controlling him. The only thing that continually challenged my thinking and kept me honest with myself was Quin. I didn't like it: the thought of not being in control, of not knowing if I could trust myself.

A smile played across Quin's face, but this time it wasn't mischievous or mocking. He'd followed my train of thought and for once I was grateful for his intrusion. It was more than that, though. I needed to be able to trust him explicitly no matter what, no matter what I thought was right or wrong in the moment. The only other person I'd ever trusted like that was dead, and that trust had been built over years and years of growing together.

"If I can't trust myself, then I have no choice but to trust you." It came out as an insult. My doubt wasn't directed at him, though; it was directed at myself.

"I haven't let you down yet," Quin joked, but I could feel his confidence and excitement just under the surface.

He was right. He hadn't. Every step of the way he'd been pushing me and challenging me, changing my understanding of myself and my limits, forcing me to grow. The idea terrified me; it wasn't something I could tiptoe into. Trust. I either did or I didn't, and if I did and I got hurt... I knew the pain of it would be shattering. Letting down your armor to truly let someone in – it's like handing them your heart and hoping they don't crush it. To be honestly vulnerable with someone again scared me. That was the level at which I needed to trust Quin. I had to believe that no matter what he'd pull me back when I was lost.

"Okay." I breathed out slowly, trying to calm my nerves.

"I'm glad we're finally on the same page. Maybe now we can figure out what we're capable of." Quin's words were sincere and sounded odd without his habitually dismissive tone.

For the first time since I buried Alexander, I didn't feel so alone. This wasn't the partnership I had in mind, but somehow it was exactly what I needed. Besides, this wasn't the first time someone had forced me to be their friend – of course no one had ever went as far as to stab me for it before now.

"About time," Marc scoffed, standing to take his leave. "I was beginning to think you two were never going to get along."

"Me either," I admitted, smiling up at him.

Marc lingered a moment more, the alcohol had loosened him up, but he was still uneasy with today's events and his part in them. Regret: it was a sickening emotion with deep roots. Quin looked as if he'd just noticed his friend's inner turmoil.

"Go home, we're good." He smiled faintly at Marc, waving him off.

It was a simple gesture that dismissed any earlier disagreements. Or it would have been had Quin not flipped Marc off as he left. I felt his inner satisfaction; he was pleased with himself, mentally patting himself on the back. I'd be lying if I said I didn't find it amusing; they acted like siblings. Quin was obviously the younger and more unruly of the two.

Three more shots were delivered. I realized it was going to be a long night when Quin finished off the shot he'd been holding and prepared to tackle his liquid diet without taking a breath in between. By the timing of the drinks, I surmised this was a place Quin frequented often, which meant the wait staff knew he could drink his weight in alcohol – that or they just didn't care. Again, I'd be lying if I said I didn't find it amusing.

CHAPTER FOURTEEN

I t took eight shots before the alcohol hit Quin fully; that was counting the double he'd had when we'd first sat down. I felt when his buzz had shifted into full-blown intoxication. I knew what he was chasing. I also knew he wasn't going to find it in the alcohol. No one here was finding what they needed in the bottom of their glasses, yet they still drank. I guess we all need a way out once in a while, even if it is non-productive. The whole bar was fuzzy and numb and I was enjoying the feel of them now, taking in bits and pieces of them for myself.

"Come here." Quin's voice was low and unexpected.

I shook my head left and right slowly, unsure of what he was after. He was too close, but then again, he always was.

"You can either keep feeding on the people around us, or me. We both know which you'd prefer." He patted the space between us. "Trust me."

Cautiously, I probed his thoughts, surprised when I was met with no resistance. Nothing was concealed in the pages of his mind – no mischief or hidden agendas. He sat with his arms wide, nonthreatening as he invited me closer. He met my hesitation openly and without expectation, calming my uncertainty.

"Does anything make you uncomfortable? How is all of this just normal to you?" I was confused, astounded even, by his acceptance of me – and every damn situation that seemed to arise for that matter.

Quin shrugged. "It's what we are now; why would I waste my time fighting it or feeling *ashamed*?" Quin chewed on the word; apparently he'd never experienced that emotion before me. "Besides, it's not all bad."

He was right, it wasn't all bad. God, I hated admitting that to myself. I was getting too good at hating myself. It really was a waste of time, fighting what I was now, what we both were. If I gave into it, though, accepted it, would I be just like *them*?

"Come here." Quin's expression had changed, his features softening. "I think we both deserve an escape."

Addiction, that's what this was. His now teal eyes combined our need for instant gratification; I could feel it stirring within him and me. It really wasn't all bad. Reluctantly, I scooted closer, closing the distance between us. Trust is much easier in theory, I thought, trying to relax. Slowly and as respectfully as he could, Quin reached out, his arm crossed in front of my body to rest on my hip as he scooted me the rest of the way to him, his body leaning in and across mine. Instantly panic flared in my mind.

"Calm down." His tone was soft, reassuring me.

I realized that by turning toward me and pulling me closer he had placed himself in such a way that shielded me from onlookers. Effectively exposing his neck and shoulder to me, I had to remember that I wasn't the one in danger, he was. The smell of him surrounded me; honey, vanilla, tobacco, and alcohol as he metabolized the clear liquid from his system. I looped my right arm under his and up his back. Digging my fingers into the collar of his shirt, I revealed the crook of his neck and a handful of smooth, crescent shaped scars.

I hesitated, looking up at him, his face was turned away from me, but I could just see a smile tug at the corner of his mouth. His hand moved from my hip, tracing its way to the back of my neck. His palm warm against my skin as he pulled me in. It was all the permission I needed. But for the first time, I felt him flinch at the touch of me. The last time I had fed on him, I had done so with no regard for him, blindly digesting him. He was anticipating the pain, sharp against his skin. I regretted this, knowing that I was the cause. If I was going to sustain myself on him, the last thing I wanted was for it to hurt.

I breathed out slowly against his skin, feeling a shiver work its way up his spine as I pulled him into me. I felt him resisting, hesitant to give me control. I waited, not wanting to force or compel him to give into me. Slowly, Quin relaxed in increments as I replaced his anticipation of pain with memories from before. He never felt the quick pop of his skin as I dug my teeth into him, both of us lost. I reveled in the taste, savoring him and the pleasure of it. We were drunk off one another.

It was an excruciating exchange; there was never going to be enough – not for him and not for me. I had to fight the urge to bite harder, desperate to drink more of him in. This time it was Quin's mind that met mine and together we shared in it, neither of us overtaking the other. Somehow he was supplementing my need for blood, mentally fortifying our connection and the blood alike.

I was pulled in by him, devouring the very essence of his being. One by one I took his emotions, his fear and excitement, the pain and pleasure, down to the very joy he obtained from the drug of me until his need was no more. Our hunger satiated, I withdrew, slowly following him down before finally pulling myself away. For the first time since my awakening I didn't feel the ache and need of the blood clawing inside my veins. This was what it meant to feed. Before, no quantity was ever enough.

I felt alive, never realizing just how much pain I was in until it was finally gone. I watched as the green in Quin's eyes faded, stealing the intensity of our connection. I shared in his sense of relief. Watching as he leaned back against the worn cushions of the booth with a heavy sigh.

"It figures that's what it'd be." Quin laughed. "What are you talking about?" I asked, finding my own place against the cushions and away from him.

The alcohol was just hitting my system, this was better than second hand experience any day. I was floating away on a sea of foam cushions and tequila. It dulled my senses and the thoughts of those around me. Lost in it, I struggled with the effort it took to listen as Quin spoke. He'd sat up to smile at me, eyes gleaming in the dim light.

"You weren't much of a drinker before, were you?" He was visibly enjoying the sight of me drunk.

"Shush," I said too loudly, blindly striking out. I was pleased when I managed to smack his arm. "Can you just let me have this?"

Thankfully, he relented, returning to his cushion and remaining shots. It couldn't have been more than fifteen minutes before the onslaught of people and noise returned to me, no longer obstructed or hindered by the alcohol. I let out a long and overly exaggerated sigh before returning to Quin and whatever he had tried to mumble at me.

"Okay," I said begrudgingly. "What was it you were trying to say?"

"It looks like we've found your *vice*." I didn't like the way he said that word, like a secret – one he fully intended to hold above my head.

"You know I could just take it from you, right?" I threatened.

"You could try." Arrogance poured from him; it changed the feel of his mind, surrounding him in an aura of red.

It was just a hint of color, fading away quickly once I blinked. God, he was competitive. Was everything a game to him? He made a point to finish another shot before turning toward me, squaring off. His childishness was baffling for someone in their mid-thirties.

I met Quin's eagerness with confusion. "Okay, I give. What's a vice, you drunk?"

"Think of it like a signature. Every vampire has one – a compulsion, something they need in order to truly feed." Quin leaned forward, grabbing his next drink from the table. "It felt like you were erasing me until all that was left was the relief of it, of not feeling."

My stomach sank; the horror of his words caught me off guard. "Just like a signature," I agreed stoically, recalling the feel of the coven as they fed on me. "Each one was different."

"Hey." Quin had set his drink down to physically restrain me. "Don't."

He held my hands, blood under my nails; I'd dug them into my arms involuntarily when the memories of them resurfaced. The eight red crescents faded just as quickly as they'd been placed.

"I'm sorry. I lost myself for a second." I swore I could still feel them, just under my skin.

Quin let go slowly, watching me skeptically as I wiped my fingers on my already soiled pants. I hadn't meant to harm myself. Working in the psychiatric field, I understood why he was hesitant to release me. We both had an innate instinct to protect others.

"I didn't understand what it was; when they fed off of me, each one brought with them a different pain." I paused, trying to remove myself from the fear of them.

I could feel him searching for me, our connection distant. I was in a place he couldn't follow, a place I wasn't able to share, not even with myself. There was nothing for him to find but fear and suppression.

"You aren't them." He pressed, trying to pull me back. "If you were, we would have killed you back in that basement."

"Isn't that what you did?" I joked, regretting the guilt that flickered across his mind. "I didn't mean that. I wouldn't be here if it wasn't for you and Marc. Thank you."

I meant the words, maybe for the first time in a long time; it was getting easier to still be here. I didn't know if I was ever going to completely heal, but at least it didn't always hurt anymore – that was a start. It was enough to just be alright again. It took me longer than I would have liked to pull myself from my thoughts, but slowly I was able to return to him. I really didn't want to be alone right now.

Quin didn't hesitate; perhaps it was his lack of inhibition mixed with intoxication that stole away his remaining reservations. I felt Quin as an extension of myself, and while his thoughts, emotions, and sensations were clearly his, I internalized them as my own. The cool shot glass in our hand, the taste of tequila, the heat of it burning our stomach, and the way the world spun, all of it his yet mine. It made me dizzy.

"Lightweight," Quin laughed. His eyes were glassy and unfocused.

"I think we've both had enough. Come on." I stood, swaying a bit as I struggled to differentiate his body from mine. "I'll take you home."

CHAPTER FIFTEEN

Cyd watched as Warren paced the safe house. His shoes squeaked across the hardwood every so often. They'd been bested, and while it was surprising, it was not unheard of – especially when they let their tempers get the best of them. As far as she was concerned, this was how they got stronger, and besides that, they had been told to hold back. He was just going to have to get over his bruised ego. Closing her eyes, she could hear his feet transition from the hardwood of the kitchen back to the carpeted living room. He'd pause now and again to peer outside before getting right back to it. It was rhythmic, relaxing even if he would stop dragging his feet across the hardwood.

"I don't get why you're still so mad," Cyd called out, annoyed.

Peering through half closed eyes, she could just make out the disgruntled look on his face. Cyd couldn't help but smile. He was pouting; the absurdity of it almost made her laugh, but she knew that would only embarrass him further. She could tell by the look on Warren's face that he was trying to figure out what to say, to find some way to disprove her statement. Frustrated, Warren collapsed into the chair across from her. His slumped form only added to the hilarity of it all. Of course, his brooding and defeated form was only funny to her.

"I almost shot her Cyd," Warren said finally.

"That's what you're upset about?" Cyd sat up in disbelief, swinging her legs to the floor; she wanted to make sure she'd heard him right.

Warren nodded, refusing to look at her. He was bouncing his legs nervously from where he sat. He hadn't been mad; he'd been scared and afraid of what he had almost done. Cyd's laughter bubbled out slowly. She'd tried to fight it, but in the end it just made it that much funnier.

"Knock it off." Warren stood to leave, his face flushed with embarrassment.

"No. Come on, just wait." Cyd barely got her words out between laughs.

She'd just been able to snag the back of his shirt before he could leave, her long arm anchoring him to the couch. Cyd held him, forcing him to stop, waiting for him to calm down again. After a few minutes he relaxed, letting out a long, jagged exhale. Satisfied he wouldn't bolt, Cyd released him.

"I thought she really hurt you – all that blood, like you'd been shot." Warren stood, leaning in the doorway that separated the living room from the rest of the house, his shoulders still slumped.

"It felt more like being stabbed, honestly. Her blood felt like needles, but instead of going into my skin, she pulled them out." Cyd's tone was completely opposite of Warren's; she was excited, intrigued even, by the experience now that it was over.

In the ten years since they'd been bonded, not once had they come away from a fight with the same experience. Warren was always protecting her; more often than not, it was from herself. Maybe it was because he was still human. Death was always a certainty for him; it

181

defined his actions and the risks he was willing to take. Cyd, on the other hand, didn't have that fear anymore. When and if she died was no concern of hers and as a result she was always pushing her limits. Maybe that's why it was so funny to watch him worry over another vampire's life.

"I've never seen anything like that before," Warren admitted, joining Cyd on the couch, his own curiosity taking hold.

"She's strong; it means killing her maker is going to be even harder." Cyd reveled in this, excited by the prospect of another fight. "Maybe we'll even need Alistair's help."

Cyd was elbowing Warren, digging her bony limb into his side. Playfully he shoved her away; the last thing he wanted was Alistair's help, and she knew it. Neither one of them played well with other vampires – especially the ones Clara kept. This was their purpose: to eradicate every last vampire until all that was left were the tethered, and then not even them. It was the reason they had nowhere to call home. For ten years they had hunted together, bound by blood magic and a purpose. In their ten short years together, they'd only met one other set of tethered: Quin and Eryn. There was no way to tell if the bond would form between a hunter and an unawakened vampire; more often than not it ended in the loss of the hunter and the newly-awakened vampire alike.

"This will make fifteen," Warren said, following Cyd's train of thought.

It had been a hard-fought number. Many hunters never got into the double digits before being killed. Old age wasn't an option for their kind. With every vampire killed, often three or more hunters were lost. Their only saving grace was that vampires reproduced successfully only once or twice for every ten attempts. Of the failed attempts, seven would likely become ghouls, and if the human was lucky, there was a one in ten chance of just dying. With their numbers dwindling, many vampires had begun to form covens in an attempt to bolster their numbers. Within the last year Cyd and Warren had seen the number of deaths from vampires and ghouls double; desperation fueled their attempt to procreate.

"That's a good number." Cyd yawned, sprawling back out across the couch, ignoring Warren's protest as she wedged her feet underneath him for warmth.

"I think it will have to be us, Cyd; the fact that Eryn has any reservations –"

"I know." Cyd cut him off; she didn't like discussing this topic with him.

Warren met her amber eyes knowingly. Hunters thought it was so simple to end a creator's life. It wasn't. Even when you hated them. Of the fourteen they had killed, only one had been a maker: Cyd's maker. It'd taken them three years to track down the bastard who had devoured her family. For three years she had thought she was ready, engraving his crimes in her skin until she no longer knew pain; until, in turn, she could do the same to him, cutting every letter into his flesh; until there was nothing left of herself in the names she'd left upon his skin – the names of her family. Cyd died again that night. She'd never tell Warren that though. Her first life lost – taken by the creator; the second ended with the loss of him. She'd carved the memories of her creator and family in her flesh until all that was left was a shell.

The person she was now didn't care what happened anymore, live or die; all she wanted was to destroy every last one of them, even at the cost of herself. Where Cyd was chaos, Warren was order. He was always there to pull her back from the darkness, not just that which they found in the world, but also within herself. The night they'd found her maker, Cyd had lost herself in his destruction.

She wasn't going to be satisfied until he felt the full force of her anguish. If she concentrated hard enough, she could still recall the feel of his body underfoot. Remembering the way his blood coagulated in sticky pools around him and the crunch of his bones. The amount of mutilation required to deplete a vampire's healing and make the body forget how to put itself back together took time and commitment. Warren was ultimately the one to erase him; he had to. It was never going to be enough. No amount of pain Cyd could inflict upon her creator was ever going to make up for his evils.

"In the end, it isn't up to her," Cyd concluded, hiding her remorse behind a façade of resentment.

"You're right," Warren agreed, shoving her legs away from him. "The sun will be up soon. You should probably head downstairs, we'll figure out where to start tomorrow."

"Afraid I'll catch fire?" Cyd joked, exaggerating the effort it took to stand.

"If only. It would be much easier to get rid of you then," Warren teased, laughing at Cyd's feigned hurt.

"Imagine how easy it would be if all we had to do was drag them outside." Cyd chuckled, pushing her way past Warren.

It was a short walk down the hallway that led to the secured basement. Most of the safe houses had one; this one just happened to be finished. No boarded up windows and tin foil this time; it was a rare commodity, especially since the basements were mainly used for torture. That thought shouldn't have excited her, but the idea of blood flowing freely from wounds she created was her one true joy. Probably only one other thing in the world could rival it.

"Are you coming?" Cyd called from the base of the stairs.

"Again?" Warren responded above, feigning irritation.

Cyd laughed. "You've never complained before," she called back, amber eyes ablaze.

Warren stood at the top of the stairs, the light silhouetting his frame; she didn't need to see his expression to know he shared her hunger. His hazel eyes were backlit with the amber of hers; he was never able resist her, not that he ever tried.

"I'll be nice." Cyd's smile widened, revealing nothing but sharp teeth within.

Warren scoffed at this. "Don't make promises you can't keep," he replied, meeting Cyd on the last step.

Her wicked smile told him she was going to be anything but. As he removed his shirt, every inch of him foretold just how nice she could be. White scars adorned every inch of his skin; the newest ones were still pink, healing from the last time she'd fed.

"Do your worst," Warren said, leaning in to meet her chaotic energy head-on.

The first cut was always the worst – anticipating the sting of it; sometimes it blinded him. Other times the pain focused him; her need of it always drove the intensity. Every time was different; sometimes it was just the act that she fed on, others it was the feel as she internalized him. This time was slow, her blade poised between the two of them as she pulled him further into the darkness.

Just the pressure of it against his skin created a thin line of blood. Cyd's breath caught at the smell of it; every time was like her first, the hunger overwhelming. It was the best part, her absolute need of it – of him. Warren matched her sharp smile, the blade sliding deeper; it wouldn't be long now. Once his blood spilled she couldn't last long, no matter how she tried. All he'd have to do was pull her in, but the anticipation was almost as good as the end. He'd let Cyd think she was still in control and wait, building his own excitement.

The sting of her mouth was warm and insistent against his flesh. Her blade poised just above his hip, she was always careful to never inflict more trauma than he could prepare for. The blade trembled against his skin; she was trying to resist the urge to bury it in him.

"Do your worst," Warren repeated, feeling her smile against his skin.

The pain was outstanding as the cold steel plunged deep into his abdomen. The ease at which she slid it through skin and muscle was amazing. Blood seared its way past the icy steel. It was exactly what she'd needed: the unexpected eruption of his pain. Unintentionally Warren braced himself against her, locking her body against his, preventing either of them from moving. Pain was the catalyst that sustained them both as she fed. It was a good thing he was a masochist.

Steel against concrete, her blade fell away. Cyd lingered against his skin, returning to herself before pulling herself free. A thin line of blood was the only tell of her presence left against his skin. Her ability to heal him was nearly instant; it had to be with the way she fed. She would delight in the savory taste of him until day robbed her of consciousness. It was the best way to fall asleep: with a full belly.

Warren left Cyd to the cool sanctuary of the basement, locking the door behind him. She wore him out; feeding her two or three times a day was starting to take its toll. He had to be careful. No matter how strong her healing was, he was just one man. Her need of him always seemed to grow between kills, and while it had been a while, there had to be another way to keep Cyd satiated.

Smiling, he leaned against the cool wood of the basement door to trace his new scar; there were worse ways to go. He sighed, the weight of the last ten years settling on his shoulders. He didn't know the meaning of peace anymore. Maybe a shower would clear his head. It wasn't just keeping up with Cyd that was wearing him out; it was ten years of slaughter. He didn't know how many years he had left in him or how many more times Cyd could heal his body of scars before it would give out.

Undressing, Warren tossed his clothes into a sink of peroxide before rinsing the last traces of Cyd's trespass from the fabric in cold water. That was all the energy he cared to expend on laundry. He was much more interested in cleaning himself and getting to sleep. Luckily, blood was easier to remove from skin than fabric. His room and adjoined bathroom were just opposite the laundry room, convenient considering how often his clothes were soiled.

Steam filled the bathroom, fogging the mirrors and humidifying the air. The warm water served to erase the stress of the day and steal the smell of her from his skin. There weren't many places left that Cyd's blade hadn't claimed; more of his scars were from her than their fights. He'd never forget the first time she'd cut him.

It happened just after they killed her maker – after *he* killed her maker. This scar was the faintest. Soon it wouldn't even be visible. This cut had been deep. The white line left behind was jagged where the blade had not only cut, but torn him open. She'd channeled every bit of her rage into him. Running his hand over it, he recalled the pain. It started at his left hip, ending just below his navel. Cyd had struck out at him when he had interrupted her to put a bullet in the skull of what was left of her creator.

'*What did you do!? I wasn't done!*' He could still remember the venom in her voice and the look in her eyes. Her anger blinded her to him, nothing left but anguish and self-hatred. That was the first time Warren had been afraid of her, the first time she had attacked him, and the first time she had truly fed on him. The second scar she'd given him ran straight across his chest where he had pinned her and the knife against himself. He'd effectively trapped Cyd and the blade against himself as she fought to tear him apart.

In doing so he'd left her no choice, ensnaring her. He knew better than most that a vampire would always resort to biting – especially when there were no other options. Her teeth had sunken deep; that was when he'd felt every bit of her hunger and the agony within. Something about the way she fed on him that time was different. Cyd's emotions set his blood on fire. Every sensation was amplified as she tore through him, both excruciating and exhilarating.

She was inescapable. His only choice was to be destroyed by it, by her – or consent to it. Funny thing about pain: once you acknowledge it and accept it as a part of yourself, it loses its control on you. That's when Cyd stopped fighting him and stopped running. Every cut since then had been something they shared, making them both stronger.

Warren turned the water off, taking one last glance at his scars before stepping out to dry. Over the years, they had met countless vampires, each one with a difference vice. Maybe vice wasn't the right word, he thought; it was more of an addiction or compulsion – one that they couldn't control. Collapsing into bed, Warren flung the disheveled bedding over himself. The cool sheets felt amazing after the day he'd had. Warren felt the weight of his exhaustion settle over him. It wasn't the worst vice.

CHAPTER SIXTEEN

Controlled chaos was the only way to describe the grueling descent from the second floor of the bar as I pushed my way through the crowd herding a drunken man. It was miserable trying to figure out Quin's address in the mess of his memories. He insisted on singing a song the whole way; the melody bounced around his head and reverberated in mine like a bad joke of "Row, Row, Row Your Boat."

I was forced to hang onto him the whole way; his inability to walk in a straight line greatly slowed our progress. I wasn't completely sure if he knew I was still there as I propped him against the front door to fumble with his keys. It was a bit comical watching him. Eventually, though, I had to intervene.

"Okay, which key is it?" I leaned in, holding the keys like a fan.

It took him a moment to focus his eyes, but eventually his drunken mind connected the memories of home to the cut metal and I was able to decipher which one would let us in.

"That one." Quin burped; he could have blown us up by the smell of it – thankfully there weren't any open flames.

Plugging my nose, I quickly unlocked and flung open the front door. "Home sweet home, stinky."

Quin laughed, stood straight for all of two seconds, and then began tilting on his axis. Reaching out, I caught him just before he could go ass over teakettle. Stepping inside, I again found myself under his arm, steadying him as he attempted to kick off his shoes. It might have been easier if he wasn't so much taller than me. Even with my grasp on him he managed to pull us both off balance and into a nearby wall. The weight of him forced the air out of my lungs.

"Y're cute when yo mad," Quin laughed, his words slurring.

"Walk," I grunted, forcing him off me, his feet all but tangled in mine.

He just managed to kick off a shoe as he went. "Oops," he said absently as it crashed through the darkness of his living room.

The unevenness of his now one-shoed gait was infuriating as his still-booted foot drug along the carpet. This had quickly become tedious, all earlier amusement gone. To top it off, he was singing again. Though it was slow, we did eventually make it to his bedroom. His drunken mind was making me sway again. Repositioning myself, I grabbed his hips, forcing him to sit on the edge of the bed.

"I could'a mad-it home, ya'no," Quin exclaimed, falling back against the bed, unable to keep himself upright.

I smiled, just making out his sentence. "Uh-huh," I agreed sarcastically as I pulled off his remaining boot. "Give me your arm."

Slowly, he sat up like a corpse rising from a grave and faced me, eyes unfocused. The room was spinning slowly within his mind. Doing as instructed, he held his left arm out to me. I'd like to say he was the first drunk man I'd helped undress, but that'd be a lie. More often than not, it was drunks whom we both helped at work; at least this drunken man didn't curse at me. Getting his left arm free, I finished peeling off his jacket.

"It'll be mornin' soon," he said, collapsing onto his pillow.

I nodded my acknowledgement before lifting his feet into bed; he didn't need to tell me. I felt the day weighing on me just as heavy as he'd been a few minutes ago. The thought of going home to the bloody mess I'd left behind wasn't ideal. I'd probably sleep in the bathtub; at least it wouldn't smell in there.

"Stay 'ere," Quin slurred, his eyes already closed.

"You'd like that wouldn't you?" I mumbled under my breath, turning to leave.

Quin's arm caught mine. "Don' be stupid."

"Let go." I didn't want to admit it, but he was right.

I had stayed out too long and wasn't going to be able to make it home, or anywhere else, before the sun came up. The overpowering and sedating effect of morning sapped my energy better than any sleeping pills. I could just see the light changing, brightening the living room; the sight of it gave me a headache. Quin's arm slipped away then to dangle over the edge of the bed. He'd fallen asleep, his breathing deep and slow, he was almost handsome now that his mouth wasn't running.

The feel of his mind slipped from me, freeing me from his insistent, intoxicated singing. I covered him up before stealing his extra pillow and blanket. Exhausted, I closed the bedroom door, sealing myself off with Quin. The ache behind my eyes vanished instantly once I blocked out the early morning light.

The room stunk of Quin, alcohol, and now me. My clothes reeked of blood and dirty rainwater, the grit of it heavy against my skin. Quietly, I stepped into the bathroom; I could live with the smell of Quin as long as it didn't mingle with the foul smell of old blood. Maybe it was instinct that drove my need to escape it; I assumed it must be my equivalent of rotten food or spoiled milk.

I paused, unsure of my intrusion. I'd just have to ask for forgiveness tomorrow, I thought, riffling through Quin's closet in search of clean clothes. I settled on an older looking t-shirt, I couldn't afford to be picky. At this point I'd wear anything as long as it wasn't what I had on now; blood had soaked the fibers, and the taste of it in the air was sour against my palate. I stripped, any earlier reservations gone as I sealed the dirty clothes in the bathroom. At least I'd be comfortable now.

Draping myself in the stolen blanket, I slid down the wall, tucking my knees in as I padded my back with the pillow. I leaned back; the world around me fading to black as unconsciousness claimed me.

I dreamt of Selene, her red eyes like fire in my soul and across my skin. I looked down, trying to free myself from her blistering grasp, but it wasn't me she held on to; it was Quin. Then, just as I looked up, it was me I saw, my eyes mirroring the red of hers as blood exploded around me. I jerked awake, my head hitting the wall behind me. Quin jolted awake at the sound, striking out as he awoke from his dream.

"Dammit, Quin, keep your dreams to yourself," I hissed, rubbing the back of my skull.

I could feel his confusion as he pieced together how he'd gotten home, why I was on the floor, and what I was saying.

"Is that my shirt?" He asked, voice thick with sleep.

"Go back to sleep, Quin. I can't be up yet." My head throbbed, and not from denting his drywall.

Leaning back, I stretched my legs out in front of me, the abyss of sleep pulling me back under to numb the internal – and external – pain of my head. I could just make out the sound of Quin stirring; his footsteps were a million miles away as I sunk deeper into sleep.

"Cover your eyes," Quin instructed.

It was the only warning I got before he lifted me from the floor, jolting me awake once more. Before I could protest, we were out in the full light of the living room, pain exploding behind my eyes. I turned my face into him, clutching desperately at his shirt to shield myself against the piercing brightness. I heard the distinct click of one door opening and closing, and then another. Slowly, the pain behind my eyes subsided.

I don't know how long it had took me to notice that we'd stopped moving, my eyes and face still shielded against Quin. Wherever we were now was much cooler than the living room. It was the warmth of his arm under my bare legs that reminded me that all I had on was an old t-shirt and underwear; he could have at least grabbed the blanket, too.

I loosened my grip on him, hesitating to open my eyes. When I did I realized that we were sealed off in a different, smaller room. My confusion quickly replaced with a surge of nausea; being awake at this hour made me physically ill.

"Marc told me to make a space for you," he said proudly as he sat me down.

He'd converted one of his spare bedrooms into a sanctuary – for me? The furniture within was simple. The bed I sat on was small and nestled against the far wall, a matching desk and chair just opposite of us. I wasn't sure how he kept the light from peeking through the window or under the door, but I was grateful.

"Thank you." I didn't know what else to say.

Something told me he hadn't done this just because Marc had told him to do so. The amount of effort put into this room was evident – hell my apartment only had blankets covering the windows. He'd installed internal shutters with thick drapes; no light was going to get through unless I opened them.

"Yeah." He brushed off my thanks as he turned to leave, my eyes closed before he even made it out the door.

One click, then two. Two doors led in here, preventing all outside light from getting in. It was smart and reminded me of the sally ports we used at work to prevent people from eloping. It was quieter without Quin's snoring and it smelled better too. Honestly, at this point I could have slept anywhere, but here felt nice. It didn't take me long to settle into sleep once more.

My dreams shifted around me, familiar at times and abstract at others. Faces came and went until I found hers; it wasn't the same face I'd seen in Quin's dream. This was the face she'd shown me. It was the face with pale blue eyes and a gentle smile. Her presence pressed in around me, the smell of the woods and ocean encompassing me.

Her face was the same, yet different. I couldn't place the tears in her eyes or the words she said when her lips moved.

'*I said I'm sorry.*' Her voice shattered the image before me.

When I found her again, it was at the docks, the river black behind her. There were no lights here, just her, the swaying dock, and the black river that surrounded us. There was nothing before me but her, and nothing beyond her but darkness.

'*You were never meant to be alone.*' Her image rippled before me as her eyes glistened.

It was familiar, the look on her face, but I couldn't remember why as her tears fell like warm rain. I felt them warm on my face, and everything shifted again. Cool earth cradled me, her eyes the color of blood as her tears fell around me.

'*I'm sorry,*' her words came to me over and over until I remembered why, until I recalled where I'd seen her like this before.

The taste of blood filled my mouth, her blood, as she leaned over me. My body broken underneath her, the coven lay dead all around us as I fed. She tasted like tawny port, rich and thick on my tongue. The pain of it was excruciating as her blood tore its way through my body until nothing human was left. My vision blurred as darkness closed in around me. The last thing I remembered was her desperate attempt to feed a corpse, the eyes of my husband unseeing as her blood streaked his slack face.

'*They're coming for you,*' I said into the darkness. I could still feel her tears on my skin and taste her on my tongue.

When I opened my eyes I was alone, the image of Selene and her presence slipped away from me. Her words haunted me as tears stung my eyes. I was never meant to be alone. My mind still foggy from sleep, I was sure I hadn't imagined her.

It shouldn't have made me feel better, but it did. It didn't change the fact that I was alone or that he had died, but a part of me was still thankful knowing she had tried to save him. I sat with this thought for a long time as I hid under the covers. I wanted to disappear and pretend for a moment that I wasn't facing another day without Alex.

I let the loss and despair wash over me as I had done so many times before, allowing myself to digest and acknowledge the pain as it ripped open my chest and twisted my guts. I had to force air into my lungs; the physical act of taking a breath was no longer autonomic. *Just breathe*, I thought, the pain in my chest sharp like a knife as its serrated edge stole my breath. For just right now I didn't have to be okay, I needed to breathe and let the moment pass. Because that's all it was, just a moment: a moment filled with all our what-ifs and a lifetime of memories lost. Eventually, though, it did get easier; my tears and energy spent, I was numb again.

I lay curled up in my cocoon until eventually the stale and humid air within forced me to emerge. Listening carefully I could hear Quin stirring, the smell of laundry and burnt toast wafting underneath the doors. I took a moment to stretch and make the bed, taking notice of the quality of the blankets and furniture within. I wondered how long this room had been set up, just waiting for me to use it. I decided not to dwell on the idea for too long; the thought of it made me uneasy.

Warily, I stepped through the sally port and into the empty living room, the thick carpet perfectly concealing my progress. Quin was in the kitchen cursing and tossing what looked like two chunks of charcoal into the trash.

"That is my shirt," Quin announced, doing a double take before returning to his breakfast. "I washed your clothes; they're in the bathroom down the hall."

I thanked him under my breath, doing my best to pull the shirt down around me as I went. Quin, as always, was instantly aware of my discomfort. I didn't need to be psychic to see the enjoyment he got out of watching me leave, my underwear and ass partially exposed. I should have stolen some sweat pants when I had the chance. I all but ran into the bathroom, my face reflected bright red in the mirror within. At least Quin hadn't lied; my clothes were washed and waiting for me. I might have appreciated his act of kindness more had he not just embarrassed me. I already felt awkward enough having just stayed the night. Showering quickly and getting dressed even faster, I was glad to finally be rid of the smells from yesterday.

Making my way back to the living room, I found Quin stretched across a shabby recliner. He spread out across its entirety, one leg draped over the armrest as he drank a cup of coffee.

"You know I never liked this stuff before you?" He smiled into his cup before taking a sip, obviously still amused by our earlier encounter.

"I'm sure you never had a darkroom before me, either," I quipped, leaning against the kitchen counter. "Why'd you really build it? And don't tell me because Marc told you to."

"He did tell me to," he conceded, "but that's not why I did."

I watched as Quin straightened, setting his coffee down so he could lean forward to rest his elbows on his knees. His apprehension made my stomach lurch. His whole demeanor changed from playful to contemplative.

"Why, then?" I asked, trying to stomach his apprehension.

"After everything that's happened, do you still want to be a nurse?" All mockery was gone from his tone. "Do you really want to take care of people like that *forever*?"

I thought about what he was saying and what he wasn't. I'd never thought about what I would do if I wasn't a nurse. I'd been working in hospitals in one capacity or another since I was sixteen. Perhaps more concerning was the way he said "forever"; it made me realize he'd been considering what he would do if he didn't have to be a nurse anymore.

"It's all I've ever wanted to be, and in a lot of ways it's the only thing I've ever been good at," I answered honestly, unsure of what he was getting at. "Maybe not forever, but I don't know what forever means yet."

"What do you think will happen in ten or twenty years when you never change? Or when you refuse to feed because you're too stubborn and you attack a patient? What about when you can't get home on time?" he paused to let his words sink in. "What happens when more people die because *we* didn't do what we're supposed to?"

"What we're supposed to?" I scoffed. "According to whom, your guild of psychos?"

"No," Quin answered. "You and I, we can prevent someone else's family from getting ripped apart. Could you honestly live with yourself knowing you could've done something and didn't?" He leaned back, hands tangled in his hair. "I couldn't. What kind of nurse would I be if I just let them die?"

I knew my answer before he finished talking. When I looked up I expected to see disapproval in his eyes. What I found instead was sympathy. The second I had been tethered to Quin, I knew my life wasn't my own anymore. I exhaled slowly, realizing I'd been holding my breath; it shuttered out of me, threatening to catch in my throat.

"We don't get to have normal lives anymore," Quin said softly; he looked like he was a thousand miles away. "I'm not saying you aren't a good nurse, but there are a hundred people that can replace us at Oceanside. None of them can do what we're doing now."

My heart was in my throat. I knew he was right, but nursing was my last connection to who I was before. I knew it couldn't last forever, this life of in-between I was trying to live.

"So, what happens now?" I asked, struggling against the lump in my throat.

"Nothing has to change right now." He tried to assure me, but he was just as hesitant as I was.

I turned from him, focusing on the dirty dishes in his sink and the residue on the kitchen counters in a desperate attempt to hide the tears in my eyes. I wasn't sure if I could stop them once they started, so I distracted myself, clearing my throat as I looked around his minimalist house furnishing. Other than his hand-me-down chair, there wasn't much in the way of anything here that screamed: Quin.

"I'm going to clean your apartment," Quin announced, returning his dishes to the kitchen. "By the way you responded to your clothes, I bet you haven't been able to stomach the place. After that, we hunt. Warren and Cyd are waiting."

"How do you know I haven't cleaned it yet?" I asked, thankful for the change of subject.

"Experience," he said simply. "That, and you couldn't even keep your own clothes on."

"What's that supposed to mean?" I ask defensively.

"Have you cleaned the place or not?" Quin asked, his eyes daring me to lie as he fought the urge to laugh.

"No," I answered, irritated.

"It's because you can't." He said knowingly. "None of you can. The smell of old blood repulses you."

I was genuinely surprised, realizing my own guess hadn't been far off.

"We use it as a form of deterrent sometimes," Quin admitted absently. "Come on, we can stop by there before we head out."

"I can clean it – "

"Not a chance," Quin interjected, grabbing his shoes and coat to leave. "It's partially my fault your place got wrecked, and I don't know if you've thrown up yet, but that's a hundred times worse than what's going on in your apartment right now. Even I can't clean up the mess that would make."

I hadn't thrown up, but I knew what he was referring to: purging, a vampire's way to rid its body of unwanted contaminants, and it wasn't pretty. It's what would happen if I ate food my body no longer had the capacity to digest. The response would be dramatic, messy, and violent to say the least.

"Fair enough," I conceded, tossing on my coat. "Lead the way."

CHAPTER SEVENTEEN

"They're here," Cyd announced, shimmering back into existence.

"How can you tell?" Warren wondered. They'd been waiting here for the last hour, and as far as he could tell they were still alone now.

"She's in my head." Cyd smiled sharply, tapping the side of her temple. "Kind of hard to forget the feeling."

It was a subtle and eerie pressure, almost akin to paranoia. The exception was that Cyd knew Eryn was there eavesdropping from somewhere nearby.

"Try not to get carried away or you'll scare them off," Warren warned, to which his only reply was a weak shrug. The last thing they needed was for Cyd to lose control and get stabby in front of new hunters. As long as there wasn't an audience, Warren couldn't care less how she dispatched their prey. Cyd could reduce them to pulp and bathe in her handiwork, whatever made her happy, just not tonight. Crunching gravel announced their arrival long before Warren spotted their approach. Cyd hadn't had the pleasure of truly meeting Eryn's hunter last time. He was taller than Warren. His blue eyes and black hair contrasted the light brown of Warren's. He also looked older and rougher around the edges somehow. Quin was his name, and he shared the same mischievous smile on his face as she had on hers.

'*Perfect,*' Cyd thought. "Let's get started. I promise to be gentle with you."

The look of disgust that crossed Eryn's face was priceless. Good. At least Cyd could get under her skin – which was fair play if Eryn was going to be bouncing around inside her head.

"They don't usually line up to get killed do they?" Eryn's tone was flat, unlike her earlier expression.

"All we have to do is follow the blood; you can smell it can't you?" Cyd smiled ardently, her eyes bright with excitement; tonight they'd show the new hunters what it meant to hunt.

"Just don't get in our way or get yourselves killed. We can't afford to be the only tethered," Warren chimed in, almost kindly, before he and Cyd set off. They'd waited an hour for the two of them to show; he wasn't about to waste any more time.

Cyd didn't even bother to look back as she went. They'd keep up or they wouldn't; it wasn't her job to coddle them. Besides that, the air was sweet with the scent of blood and rain – it was too delicious not to enjoy. Cyd shouldn't have been surprised when Eryn didn't smell it right away. She'd learn; it was only a matter of time before it became second nature. Her outline flickered then dispersed, and just like that she was gone.

Warren didn't bother trying to keep up with Cyd; she'd make her presence known again once they got closer. Quin kept up easily enough, even slowed his stride to match Warren's while Eryn trailed behind. Her face was upturned, eyes reflecting the gray skies above. Warren looked away just as she turned her attention toward him. He made a point to refocus his effort on navigating the broken sidewalks and side streets. Alas, he couldn't help but feel guilty for their last interaction. His palms were beginning to sweat as he ruminated; he knew he needed to say something, but what?

"Look," Warren sighed, needing to clear his conscience. "I didn't mean to take things so far the last time we met. I'm sorry I made it personal."

"You aren't sorry for that." Quin's teal eyes blazed. "You're sorry Clara saw you protect Cyd." Quin blurted, laughing manically as he left Warren where he stood.

Dumbfounded, he watched as Quin bolted ahead, only to pause once out of striking distance to tap the side of his head. Quin had been in his head the whole time before darting off.

"Motherfucker." Warren exhaled the word, completely caught off guard.

"Yeah," Eryn agreed. "I'm sorry too."

With that, she ran ahead, matching Quin's pace. What was she sorry for? Warren felt a little stupid – first for caring, and now for letting Quin get the upper hand. He had no doubt that had Cyd been here, she too would've laughed at him. Maybe he had been worried for nothing, but he couldn't risk conflict with these two, especially if they were going to be hunting together.

Shaking off his embarrassment, Warren quickened his pace. They had a job to do and he couldn't afford to be distracted. It was their responsibility to teach the newly tethered and keep them from making the same mistakes they had. Drawing on his connection with Cyd, Warren readied himself to head off Quin and Eryn. He took the scenic route, knowing their head start wasn't going to be enough. They'd never be able to match his speed. This city had one thing going for it: old buildings with countless fire escapes. It was easy to take the high ground, and somehow freeing to leave the cluttered city streets below to sprint across the flat rooftops.

He ran full force across the tops of the buildings. He'd never be as quick or as graceful as Cyd. It didn't matter, though; he was fast enough and every bit as reckless. In one long, leaping stride Warren cleared the twelve-foot gap between two buildings. Rolling on impact, Warren was back on his feet in seconds, none of his earlier speed diminished. It felt good to stretch his legs; his heart pounded, breathing even and rhythmic as he prepared for his descent.

The fall was the best part; he loved the way his stomach dropped as the ground rose to meet him. Warren felt Cyd's strength surge through him, lessening his mass and strengthening his bones as his feet connected with the earth once more. Normally he'd roll to reduce the force of the impact, but for showmanship he merely bent his knees, absorbing the shock with no risk of trauma. He returned to his full height, smirk in place as he confronted Quin; this time it was his eyes that reflected an inhuman glow from within.

Warren was pleased with the look of shock and admiration that Quin gave him, lost for a moment in what he'd just witnessed. Eryn met his gaze, a half smile in place as she shook her head. It was hard to tell, but he thought perhaps she had enjoyed his theatrics. Quin at least had been impressed – of that much he was sure. The point wasn't merely to show off; it was meant to inspire and encourage them to imagine what they, themselves, were capable of.

"Come on, we're getting close." Warren took the lead again; he could feel Cyd's hunger within him. She'd found the blood.

It wasn't until they neared a fenced-off construction area that Cyd graced them with her presence. The entire first floor was nothing but columns and rubble; it looked like the whole place was resting on cement stilts. A look of satisfaction was plastered to Cyd's face, her smile wide and sharp, eyes glowing with crazed excitement. They were getting to her favorite part of the hunt: the kill.

"Can you smell it now?" Cyd leaned against the fence, fingers laced through the chain link as she breathed deeply. "We've found the feeding grounds."

With minimal effort, Cyd forced the lock that held the gate before her closed; her form shimmered in and out of view as she ran ahead to dance among its skeletal pillars. The air was stagnant. Thick plastic hung lifeless, creating makeshift walls that trapped the humidity within. It was the perfect place to feed undisturbed. The smell of blood engulfed Cyd and instigated her hunger.

"Ready?" Warren held the gate open. "Let's go."

He was glad to see Quin's excitement; Marc had told him Quin was experienced despite being new to the guild. The one Warren was really concerned about was Eryn; this was her first hunt. It wasn't self-defense. They were actively seeking the end of one of her kin. He'd have to keep a close eye on her – not only to ensure their safety, but to make sure she wasn't overwhelmed. No one wakes up ready to kill, no matter the reason for it. Entering slowly, they found Cyd perched on a pile of jagged concrete and rebar, and above her was an opening to the second floor. With a little effort they'd be able to climb up.

"I don't think they're still alive." Eryn's voice was muffled.

Looking back, Cyd was confused by the sound until she realized Eryn had buried her face in her jacket to shield herself from the smell. Standing slowly, Cyd dusted herself off, her eyes never leaving Eryn.

"If you fed more, the smell wouldn't bother you as much." Cyd recognized the look on Eryn's face all too well. The problem wasn't the smell; the problem was the temptation that it brought with it. If left unchecked it would envelop your senses and pull you forward blindly. It was insatiable, the smell, and Cyd knew by the look on Eryn's face that the hunger was waging a war for control.

"I'm fine," Eryn responded through gritted teeth.

Cyd pressed on. There was no point in arguing with her, so she climbed. If Eryn couldn't continue, then she'd be Quin's problem; it wasn't her job to keep her fed after all. The unmistakable smells of dust, blood, and unwashed bodies hit Cyd as she ascended. This place was probably being used as a makeshift homeless shelter before the monsters with sharp teeth and glowing eyes ripped their way through.

Cyd was able to actually see the blood now; it began as a few drops here and there, leading her forward until it was nothing but red. Cyd reveled in the mouthwatering aroma, thick and tangible in the air around her. Curiosity getting the better of her, Cyd looked back. Eryn's eyes burned with hunger, the pain of it quickening her breath as she slowly advanced to stand beside Cyd. To them, this was Christmas. The air stunk with the smell of iron, pooling in gray and black puddles where the dirt had settled within it. Cyd's enjoyment stopped there as the faint smell of rot broke through the initial, overwhelming sweetness. The blood had acted like camouflage, hiding away the undeniable scent of death and decaying flesh.

It was too late, though; they'd wandered in too far to back out now, especially when they'd brought dessert. Ghouls, unlike vampires, were not satiated by blood alone. They needed the flesh and bones, the shit-filled intestines, and all of the bits in between. They needed to devour. Cyd threw her arms wide, stopping Eryn in her tracks. She'd stopped at bloody footsteps on shifting rubble and the wet sound of their breathing as it rattled out of them; every sound set off an alarm in her head. Everyone knew then, as the smell and sound of them broke through the pungent iron and silence. They were not alone here.

"Ghouls," Warren cursed, nodding at Cyd as he armed himself with two wicked blades. The black steel was all but invisible in the dim light, save for their serrated silver edges.

Quin responded in kind, gripping the leather handle of his hunting knife tightly in his left hand; it wasn't as impressive as Warren's double blades, but it would get the job done if one of the fuckers charged him. The plus to fighting mindless ghouls was that they didn't strategize. They only had one driving force – to feed. Survival, beyond that, like self-preservation, was null; their bodies rotted at a rate faster than they could repair.

Relaxing, Quin reached out to Eryn, her thoughts frantic against his calm. His mouth went dry as a wave of terror washed over him and threatened to blind his senses. She was back at the train tracks. He could hear the laughter echoing in the recesses of her mind as flashes of the vampire played out before her. She saw him now, dancing away his life, clutching the leathery form of his lover as she tore him apart. If she couldn't pull herself from it, she'd risk not only her safety, but his.

The putrid smell of rot and infection assaulted my nose, pulling me back to a place I didn't want to be. I froze, paralyzed by the memories of the railroad and the dance of death that had ensued there. Protectively, Cyd slammed her arm across my chest, halting me unnecessarily; I couldn't have taken another step if I'd wanted to. All I saw was blood and the haunting dead eyes within. Their bodies shifted forward, broken and lopsided in their advance. They weren't the same as the woman I'd met at the train tracks; their bodies wore the recent and telling trauma that had led to their demise.

"Move!" Cyd's voice commanded, but it wasn't enough to break the spell.

I watched her step forward, slamming the first ghoul to the ground with a wet thud; a weak wheeze escaped its dirt-and-blood-caked mouth, speckling her with stinking innards. The next one came right for me, its breath hot on my face as it slammed into me. Jagged and broken teeth tore into my shoulder, shredding my leather jacket like paper as we both fell to the floor.

The pain of it took my breath away as it twisted and jerked, desperate to rend flesh from bone. Its sinewy arms wrapped around me, constricting my chest and trapping my left arm at my side. My right was sandwiched between our two bodies. Pressing back, I fought against its vice-like grip, wincing when its fingers clawed into my back. The sound of it chewing and ingesting me collided with the terrifying realization that I was being eaten alive.

A cacophony of curses bounced around my head then as Quin darted forward, his boot catching the ghoul right in the side of the face; a resonating *CRUNCH* told me he had caved-in a portion of its skull as it flew backwards and away from me. I yelped when he hauled me to my feet, blood pouring from my sleeve to slick my palm. The amount of it was alarming as it mixed in the dirt below.

"Whoever they were before, they wouldn't want to be this. If you can't help, then get out of the way." Quin stepped past me as he drove his knife deep into the throat of the ghoul with the broken face.

Its eyes went still, fixed and unseeing as blood spilled forth from the wound, seeping slowly from its mouth and nose. The skin around the silvered blade blistered. I watched, motionless as Quin followed the body down, sinking the knife to the hilt before twisting the handle. The crunch of separating cartilage foreshadowed the violent yet beautiful severing of the ghoul's head from its body. An arc of black blood trailed from his blade like a ribbon until all that was left was sizzling tar on its edge.

This was who he was; it was what he was created to do, and there was no hesitation as he cleaved open the next rotten body. I could see the anger on his face and feel his resolve, cold in my veins. This is what it meant to be a hunter. Their combined disgust slowly erased my fear; Warren's hatred was an ember of resolve while Cyd's burned like napalm. They all hated the creatures before them in different ways; for Quin, it was sorrowful. I had let myself get lost in the horror. Quin was right, they wouldn't want to be like this and there was nothing I could do to turn them back. The blood was warm in my palm, but this time it wasn't going to be just mine.

I imagined a blade, just as sharp and deadly as the silvered steel in Quin's and Warren's hands. I focused on it, preparing myself for the force it would take to break the sternum and pierce the heart hidden within the cage of bone. I poured myself into it, crystalizing the blood around my fingertips until I was sure I could end it in one blow. No pain, no dread, no knowing. Just death. I lunged; the blood was warm in my palm, but this time, it wasn't mine.

CHAPTER EIGHTEEN

I'd buried my arm elbow deep in the ghoul's chest cavity, splintering the sternum and rendering the ribs useless as I ripped the sinewy heart to shreds. Just like carving pumpkins, I convinced myself, before pulling free. The innards within spilled from the orifice I had created. Steam rising around them, it reminded me of when I'd hunted with my father; on those cool mornings the guts of the deer would react in the same way. Task completed, I relinquished my makeshift blade. The blood that had hardened around my left arm dripped away, leaving me weak from the effort as my shoulder screamed in pain.

Spent, I fell back, my legs unable to hold me a second longer. I landed hard on my ass, Cyd and Quin surrounding me before I could right myself. Warren, on the other hand, was busy wiping his blades on the tattered shirt of his last kill.

"Did you know you could do that?" Cyd's amazement was lost to me in the concern that marred her face. She'd knelt beside me to probe the bite in my shoulder.

"Don't you think I would have used it on you if I had?" I hissed, grimacing as her fingers dug into my skin and peeled my jacket away.

"Fair enough," Cyd chuckled. "You need to eat; we can wait." She stood, looking between Quin and me expectantly.

"I'll be fine." I lied, feeling Quin's eyes on me as I tried to hide the damage from him.

"Don't be stupid," Warren chimed in. Using a dagger as a sharp finger, he pointed to the corpses. "These bodies are riddled with bites. Whoever did this was trying to turn them. We aren't done here and you aren't healing."

"How often?" Cyd questioned, her voice humorless as she directed her full attention from me to Quin. "How often is she feeding?"

"Twice a week, maybe." No hesitation; they could have been discussing the weather.

"You're starving yourself." Warren's tone cut through Cyd and Quin's banter. "What good are you if you can't heal?"

Cyd waved an arm at Warren dismissively. "What about your vice?"

"It's none of your business," I breathed. The world was beginning to spin around me; it was stupid move, drawing from myself to create a weapon.

"Just once," Quin answered, matter-of-fact; his voice sounded distant in my ears.

I was acutely aware of the blood trickling from my shoulder and down my biceps as it worked its way across my forearm to drip from my sleeve. The color was brilliant, so much brighter than the blood around me. I watched it fall from me, the pitter-patter of it muffled by the dust below. My trance was immediately broken when Quin's cold hand encircled my wrist, hiding the flow of it from me.

"You'll have to build up your tolerance." Warren spoke slowly, his eyes on Quin. "It gets easier."

"Every other day is fine until you figure out how to balance feeding her and yourself," Cyd added – and though she was speaking to him, she was looking at me.

"Hey." Quin forced my attention, lifting my face to look at him instead of the intricate ways the dust was dancing in the blood below. "Easy way or the hard way?"

He was joking, no real menace in his tone. His concern was a welcome interruption to Warren's frustration and Cyd's curiosity – neither of which was helpful.

"Easy way." I smiled half-heartedly; even with him forcing my attention I was having a hard time hearing his words. Everything else seemed so much more interesting and I wondered if it was his pulse or mine I was listening to.

"Hold on." He warned before picking me up.

I didn't want to want it as much as I did. The hunger had a way of erasing everything else and I was afraid I was going to hurt him again, unable to hold back.

"We'll catch up," he spoke over his shoulder, distancing us from them.

I've never been as thankful as I was in that moment. I knew Quin had no qualms with me feeding, which meant he had distanced us purely as a courtesy to me. He waited for Cyd and Warren to vacate before settling in beside me on a bench-sized chunk of rubble. Distracted, I was vaguely aware of him shedding his jacket before eventually helping me out of mine.

"This way I'll know when you're healed," he reassured me, defensively justifying his reasoning as he exposed my torn shoulder, the fat and muscle clearly visible.

"I'm sorry," I apologized, leaning into him. "I hesitated."

He shrugged a reply of indifference before lifting his arm over and across the front of my chest. His skin was cool against the fever of mine. I didn't want to fight it. The smell of him surrounded me as I pulled him closer, firmly tucking myself under his arm before biting down. The connection between us was instantly fortified as I ingested. The act was somehow made easier when I just gave in; almost as if resisting only served to destroy my control. The pain in my shoulder lessened immediately, replaced instead by faint itching as my skin stitched and pulled itself back together.

Quin's mind was distant and unfocused as he took in the blood-bath around us. Heavy, the pressure of his thoughts weighed on my psyche until I could no longer ignore it. Within the smoldering bodies of the ghouls, he saw a face. Familiar yet unfamiliar, I recognized it from the dream a few nights ago. This face was the same one that clawed its way up my legs with dead and broken fingers. They reached, cruel and malformed to encircle our throats, but just as quickly as the memory came it went, faded and gone before I could make any sense of it. The earlier weight lifted, Quin's mind returned to me.

It was then that he drew on me, desperate for an escape, his need overtaking my own. His addiction was absolute as he pulled me physically and psychically closer. From the outside I could feel him shifting and turning so that he no longer sat beside me. My back, once nestled against his side, now met his core as he wrapped his free arm around my other shoulder. His head rested against the back of mine, face buried in my hair. I couldn't have stopped if I wanted to. His emotions flooded me as he, in turn, devoured mine, desperate for anything that wasn't him.

I accepted, greedily erasing him within myself until there was nothing left but the feel of our combined relief and his high. Mind lolling against mine, he was content. It was then that I slowed and his grip loosened. I withdrew, letting Quin's arms fall away from me, the only evidence I'd fed was the faint line of red against his skin.

"Don't ever let them know what your vice is." Quin spoke languidly, taking his time to stand. "It's one of the ways we hunt vampires. Don't give them anything they can use against you."

Meeting his eyes, I saw all the seriousness his tone had lacked. It made more sense now; Quin hadn't shielded me from Cyd and Warren as a courtesy; he'd done so to protect us – to protect me. Hesitantly, I followed him back through the caved-in section of the floor where Cyd and Warren waited for us.

"That was fast," Cyd teased, animalistically sniffing the air for Quin's scent, visibly pleased when she found it.

Her eyes met mine, playfully questioning me. Her curiosity and intrusiveness was exhausting; it reminded me of how younger siblings sometimes acted. Thankfully, her interest faded quickly once she realized neither of us was going to respond to her inquiry.

"What now? We can check a few more places around here." Quin's tone was casual – relaxed even. It was like we hadn't just massacred the feral corpses above.

The tension I was used to seeing, like he was waiting for a fight, was gone. I couldn't tell if it was just because of our exchange or because he'd been able to dispatch the rotting corpses above us. Regardless, I'd never seen him so calm. He was in his element and it showed.

"No." Warren quickly warded off Quin's suggestion. "It'll take too long. We had an idea, but it all depends on you." Warren had shifted his attention; the soft hazel glow of his eyes moved from Quin to me.

"How close does someone have to be for you to listen in?" Cyd smiled eerily.

Quin sidestepped, purposely destroying my strategic wallflower positioning to include me in the now-oblong huddle. All eyes on me, I was caught off guard. I didn't have a sense of distance; the few times I'd been able to stretch and let my mind wander, there either wasn't much to listen to or it all became noise, individual thoughts amalgamating into one chaotic and indiscernible hum.

"I don't know." I admitted sheepishly, "Some people are louder than others."

"Whoever did that," Warren replied, voice shaking, his anger barely hidden as he gestured behind me, "is going to be loud."

Something about his tone and the feel of his anger popping against my senses like oil on water had set me on edge. It filled the air around me, humid and sticky; it clung to my skin. Shoving back, I removed him from me. The gravity of my irritation forced him back. Unfortunately, Warren was not the only one caught within. Quin, having felt Warren's onslaught, laughed when Cyd and the other hunter withdrew, physically uncomfortable. It took me a moment to reign in my emotions and withdraw from them. I hadn't meant to act defensively.

"I'm not making excuses." I spoke apologetically, understanding Warren's misplaced anger. "I'm also not going to hear much if you can't control the noise in your own head."

Thankfully, neither of them had anything to add, both of them still visibly shaken by my intrusion. I didn't know where or how to begin. I had to do more than just block them out; I had to find a way to block myself out too.

"Just give me some space…" It was harder than I thought to find a spot within the skeletal remains of the first floor to hide. Maybe hiding wasn't exactly what I was trying to do. I needed to be somewhere Cyd's prying eyes couldn't see. Their yellow glow like a cat's, I was amazed some of us passed as human.

I settled along an outer wall. The fresh air cleansed the smell of death from me. I let my mind wander, relaxing as I reached out, straining to listen… That's all I was doing. At least that's what I'd told myself as I sifted through each subconscious mind, one by one. I passed over them, soft as a paint brush, with my consciousness. Some were but a whisper. These were sleeping minds, I decided. They were soft and self-limiting as I passed over them. Others were harsh, the noise of them reminiscent of a migraine as they grated against me. Soon I was flipping past them, like the pages of an old magazine. I didn't know what I was looking for, but I assumed, much as Warren had, that it would be loud.

The longer I listened the harder it was to hear or to see, my other senses numb from the overload of internal stimuli. I slid down the column at my back, covering my ears and closing my eyes as I went. Focusing, I desperately tried to process as little information as possible in my search. Their emotions flooded me regardless, bursting like fireworks in a closed fist. I felt every ounce of their aggression, contempt, remorse, disapproval, awe, optimism, submission, and love. I was riding a rollercoaster with no end, but still I searched, certain that if I delved a little deeper I would find what I was looking for and be free.

The wheel of their emotions spun, threatening to rip me from my axis. Distraction, when muddled by surprise, creates amazement. Pensiveness smeared in sadness creates grief. Boredom degrades to disgust, then loathing. Annoyance and anger blend to create rage. Interest and anticipation evolve into vigilance. Serenity and joy ascend into ecstasy. Acceptance and trust combine to form admiration. Finally, apprehension to fear until all that's left is terror.

Terror. It rippled through me like a shockwave, and just like that I was swallowed whole by it. My mind snapped free from everything else except it and the tearing pain that ripped through my body as my psyche fractured.

———

Quin winced, rubbing his left temple; an immense amount of pressure had started to build there. His vision blurred, forcing him to blink.

"What did you say?" Quin shook his head, distracted.

"What's it like, always having someone in your head?" Warren asked again, concerned.

"Right now, it's really fucking loud." Quin turned; he could have sworn someone just whispered in his ear.

He vision wasn't clearing no matter how many times he blinked. Next was his hearing. It felt like he was underwater. Balance compromised, Quin reached out, feeling himself tip backwards. Cyd and Warren each took an arm, helping him down.

"I'm okay." Quin spoke slowly, unable to hear himself. "She's blocking out my senses; just give me a second."

That wasn't completely true. His senses weren't blocked, per se, as much as they were obsolete in the face of so much other information. He was hearing and seeing plenty; the problem was that none of it was his. He was watching a movie on fast-forward and none of it made any sense as scene after scene ripped past him before he could comprehend. Eryn was flooding his perception, her mind rapid-firing in every direction, trying to find the one thing that was unlike all the others.

Nausea hit him in waves. The images and emotions were moving too fast – there and gone. His head ached. He was trapped in a spin cycle. Around and around he went. More disturbing, though, was the immediate and terrifying halt as his vision and hearing snapped back – but what he saw didn't belong to him.

Terror ripped through him, blood spilling warm and wet across his lap as intestines tangled in his hands – hands that were too small to hold back the torrent of insides that tumbled out. Fear. That was all he felt; not the pain of it as the man before him pulled away what Quin was so desperately trying to keep inside.

"And who are you?" The voice was wet, mouth full of stinking blood, eyes like inkwells.

The blood, his blood, didn't feel warm in his hands and across his legs anymore. So tired; he wasn't strong enough to hold back the dam of viscera. His world faded to black. This was death. It wasn't so bad. Except for the fear, it felt good to sleep and let the nothingness claim him. It encompassed him, erasing everything he thought was important. It was pleasant here in the quiet dark of nothingness, he thought, until it was ripped away and placed back inside him.

Awareness brought with it the horror of what he'd just experienced. A searing pain tore across his abdomen; its intensity forced him to pull his shirt up, certain he'd find the gash from before. Warren and Cyd had descended on him. The concern in their eyes pulled him back to reality.

"Eryn!" Quin cried out as he struggled to his feet. The pain, even without true injury, slowed his progress.

———

I heard Quin call out to me, but my voice was gone. I let my head fall back; the cool cement column helped ground me in reality. I could still feel intestines, sickly slick, sliding between my fingers, her blood warm against my skin; the phantom sensations faded slowly. Quin's panic was better than the terror resonating within my mind. I let it wash away the fragments of her death as he pulled me to my feet, checking me for injuries.

"I found him," mind exhausted, I spoke the words without feeling as Quin inspected me for damage.

"What the hell just happened?" Cyd asked.

Concern mixed with confusion, the emotions tasted bittersweet as I ingested them, taking just enough to feel something. She thought we were the crazy ones. That was funny coming from her.

"You told me to find him, and I did; that's all that matters right now." I was spent. This must be what introverts felt like every day. "You saw it?"

Quin didn't have to answer; I knew by the way he guarded his abdomen, inspecting me in much the same way. He'd been right there beside me.

"I'm sorry." I apologized for the second time that night. "He isn't far."

"Wait." Warren's voice was filled with doubt. "This isn't going to be like the ghouls. Just show us where to go."

"No." Quin and I spoke in unison, his anger caustic.

"Let's go, then." Cyd smiled, a flash of red shifted around her. The color was reminiscent of the auras that often surrounded Quin; they were kindred spirits of rage and unspent energy.

Mind made up, Quin shoved past Warren as he went. His brisk pace forced me to jog. Thick, icy fog filled the streets outside; the weight of it stung my lungs. Quin pulled away from us, pushing past the broken fence and reaching the street before we could clear the building. He searched blindly for direction.

"Show me," Quin demanded as the memory of the woman's organs spilling from him replayed in his mind.

I didn't have a choice as he ripped it from me, prying the lost connection from me easily. He followed the vector, sensing the entity just as I had before breaking into a full sprint. No hesitation in sight, his feet pounded the pavement faster than I could keep up, his form lost to me in the fog.

"Damn it. Cyd, keep up with him," Warren cursed, slowing to match my pace as Cyd, too, disappeared. "What the fuck did you two see?"

"He's tearing them apart while they're still alive," I spat between breaths, bile burning the back of my throat as I ran. "I felt it. Quin felt it."

Warren matched me step for step as I retraced the maze in my mind. At this rate Quin would be there long before we could catch up. We were close, though; the unmistakable smell of viscera filled the air. The bastard wasn't even trying to hide. This realization hit me hard: he was expecting us. I'd interrupted him, disrupting his feeding, and intruding on his vice. He'd sensed us there. Frantically, I reached out to Quin, but it was no use; his anger blinded him to me. Dread, like molten lead, settled in my stomach.

CHAPTER NINETEEN

Silas was careful, oh so careful; he knew exactly how much pressure it would take to crush her windpipe. But there'd be no fun in that. The wheezing squeaks she made under his boot were music to his ears as she fought for consciousness. He still had two more guests stopping by. The other one he'd ensnared was making noise, too, but not the kind he liked.

"Shut up or I'll make you." Silas's musical tone did nothing to hide his malice as he struck the hunter with teal eyes.

He was going to have fun with that one. Although Silas wasn't completely sure how, he thought it had been this hunter who'd rudely intruded earlier. Hurried footsteps on broken tile and scattered carpet signaled the arrival of Silas's last two guests. Good. It meant the fun could begin.

"Cyd!" Warren barked, equal parts scared and angry.

Instantly annoyed, the last thing Silas needed was another talker; all this chatter was going to ruin the orchestra of music he was trying to create with their suffering.

"Enough! Or you'll join her." Silas spoke pointedly, a perfect smile painted across his face. "I doubt you can withstand quite as much pressure, hunter."

As he expected, the one who shared in Cyd's amber eyes lashed out. Silas watched as the hunter pulled a gun from the small of his back and pointed it directly at the vampire pinned underfoot. He'd been in control of the second hunter the second he trespassed; his puppet strings were securely connected to the vampire blood which flowed through Warren's veins. Cyd squirmed, eyes wide, as her hunter aimed right for her, finger quivering over the trigger as he fought for control.

Silas took in the exquisite hue of their amber eyes; if his hunch was correct, that meant the one on the ground grunting and cursing belonged to the one who stood just out of his reach.

"Join us or I'll kill them all." He didn't bother hiding his temper; he was hungry and the night was getting bright.

The woman who filtered in behind the gun-wielding hunter was smaller than the others, her green eyes like emeralds. He was sure she belonged to the teal-eyed hunter. Silas watched, both intrigued and infuriated that she had read his ability. Now she teased him, evading him as she skirted his grasp.

"You've figured it out, then?" Silas hissed, grinding his boot into the throat of the one named Cyd.

"Not me, her." Eryn gestured toward Cyd.

Silas watched her curiously as she circled in a futile attempt to reach her hunter. Territorial, he stepped toward her, forcing her retreat. That was his prey; he had caught him and he belonged to Silas. Cyd, free of Silas's weight, sucked in air desperately. The sound sent chills

225

up his spine. He'd have plenty of time to create a symphony if he could just catch the last instrument.

"That's how you found me then; you're a listener." Step by step, he pushed her back. "If you prefer, I can just as easily kill them in front of you."

With a gesture, purely for performance, he forced the hunter with teal eyes to his feet. Oh, how he loved it when they fought; the hatred that poured from those insane teal eyes was delicious.

"Fuck you," Quin cursed.

Silas felt the force of the words, wet in the air as the hunter tried to spit on him. That was a mistake – one he was sure to regret.

"I told you to shut up," Silas reminded the man coldly.

It really was a shame they could still talk. Silas had a remedy for that; he had warned him after all. With one quick movement Silas punched Quin in the throat. The cartilage underneath shattered with a satisfying CRUNCH, and just like that, the night air was filled with wet and choked wheezes. Silas reveled in the sound and the look of hatred that reflected in the green eyes of the vampire before him.

"That's better, don't you think?" Silas asked, proud of the music he'd created.

"Don't touch him –"

"Or what?" Silas snapped. "You'll make me stop?" A show of force was the only thing hunters understood anymore; so to make his point he pulled the other two to him, their movements stiff and lacking of grace as they fought to break his hold.

With a flick of his wrist Silas had the three of them arranged just so. He poised the men, guns ready, safeties off, and fingers resting against the triggers. Silas staggered them: Warren standing, Cyd sitting, and Quin prone – a beautiful row of toys set out before him. He took a moment to look over his arrangement. Something was missing.

"I'll make you a deal. You come closer, play my game, and I promise to let them go." Silas inspected his display, finding the missing piece to his showcase.

Stepping forward enthusiastically, Silas relieved Warren of his silvered blades. He held one out to Cyd. Her hand shook as she reached out. The terror on her face as she accepted his gift – eyes never leaving the silver edge – was exquisite. Slowly, she positioned the serrated blade tight against her own chest like a stake. Her shirt was the only thing that kept her skin from blistering.

"Here's the deal." Silas called out. "For every minute you survive, I'll let one of them go."

He hated the silence that hung between them; it bored him, and he grew tired of the stalling. Needing something, anything, to fill the dull sound of their breathing, Silas trailed the edge of his new blade against Cyd's exposed forearm. Her skin erupted in blisters, the flesh below eventually bubbling and falling away where he touched. He loved the tenor of her scream as fear contorted her features, sweetly filling the air with music.

"Deal," Eryn agreed hastily.

"Let's begin, then." Silas smiled, loving every second of her resolve.

"Don't" Quin croaked; his voice broke, hoarse as it passed through his barely-healed windpipe.

Oh, how Silas loved a show. Glancing between the two, he knew Eryn's mind was made up. There wasn't any anger or fear to be found, just calm knowing. He couldn't wait to see that look turn to regret.

"I don't have to win," Eryn replied under her breath.

Silas couldn't have agreed more as he watched her willingly step into his web. Her courage was almost as impressive as her strength. Where the others had resisted physically, she fought mentally. What she didn't realize was that he controlled the very essence of their being. As long as he was stronger than them, their blood was his to control.

"Let's see how long it takes to you break." Silas's mask fell away, revealing with it all his cruelty and ill intent.

———

This was more than compulsion; it was ownership. No matter how I fought it, I couldn't break free of him, and was terrifyingly aware of everything he was doing. He let this realization sink in, building my anticipation of the first strike. Even if I could've avoided it, I couldn't escape the unsettling darkness of his black, pupil-less eyes. My vision swam as the force of his punch drove the air from my lungs. This wasn't just about feeding. This was for fun. *I don't have to win*, I reminded myself. Three minutes. I just had to last three minutes.

"Focus." His blood-stinking breath was hot against my face, fingers tangled in my hair as he pulled me up from the concrete. "It's no fun if you check out. I want you to feel it."

I felt it. What he really wanted was to hear me scream. He needed it. He wanted me to cry out the way Cyd had – the way the woman before me had as he ripped out her intestines. My voice, it was the only shred of control I had left and I'd be damned if I was going to give it up easily. Vision focusing, I sucked in air greedily, my body heavy as he forced me to my feet. My neck craned painfully as he forced me to look at him, his hand still tangled in my hair.

Two minutes. I just had to last two more minutes. But two minutes might as well have been eternity as he slid Warren's silvered dagger into my abdomen. I didn't feel it at first, the blade too sharp; it slipped right past my ruined leather jacket. It was the twist that made the pain real, the jagged blade simultaneously tearing and incinerating me. I screamed then, doubling over. I'd given him exactly what he wanted. He followed me down, much like Quin had with the ghoul. His grip never left the handle. He wanted me to feel every inch of serrated steel and silver as he dragged it free. The relief and pain of it confused me. My body fought to repair the damage as he pulled the silver free, innards boiling, desperate to seal themselves once more. I would have given anything to pull away – free of him and this pain – but he held me frozen. For the second time this night, blood pooled in my lap; at least this time it was mine.

One minute. Just one more minute… I could endure anything for one minute. The first time I'd had someone's fingers inside my chest, the white hot pain had almost made me pass out. This time was nothing like that. This time my vision sharpened as the agony of it erased everything else. Nothing existed but the pain. I couldn't breathe, I couldn't fight, and I couldn't scream. It stole from me my thoughts, my strength, and my will.

"There you are. I knew you couldn't hide forever." He spoke intimately now, the satisfaction in his voice palpable as his fingers strummed my innards like guitar strings. No words exist to explain the despair of it or the enjoyment I found in his eyes. I knew, though, when my time was up.

Silas froze, and though he couldn't see them from here, he could feel them, his control wavering. Quin and Warren lowered their weapons. Cyd discarded the blade at her chest with great disdain. The sound of steel hitting concrete was music to my ears as I pulled myself free from the vampire named Silas and lashed out with the last of my strength. Striking him across the face, I was sure I'd just struck a cement block, shattering the bones in my right hand. It didn't matter so long as it got me away from him. My attack had thankfully caught him off guard. Silas's balance faltered, giving me enough space and time to push away before the first shot rang out.

Blood exploded from Silas's shoulder as Clara's unmistakably cheery voice rang out: "I guess Rylan was right; you are just like a ham radio."

Clara's crazed eyes affixed Silas. Just behind her Lucas brandished a revolver, the stock of it looming over her head like a cannon.

I never saw Silas move, but I heard when he stopped; it sounded like a sonic boom. He crumpled before the new group of hunters. The shock of what we were witnessing was plain on our faces, including his. Silver eyes reminiscent of liquid mercury peeked out from behind Clara. They were unwavering and held Silas where he fell.

"He's a feisty controller, but then again, most are." Stepping forward, Clara sat beside Silas; the pale green of her eyes scared me every bit as much as the silver ones. "You've been busy, haven't you? I can't have that, especially when you're going to involve my hunters." Her voice was sweet, reassuring even.

"I'll leave," Silas pleaded, any earlier malice lost in his now weak and defeated tone.

Clara smiled wide. "No, you won't."

I'd never seen anything like it, and I hoped I never would again. Exsanguination. The medical term came to mind as I watched every ounce of blood ripped free of Silas's now-husk of a body. This was why Alistair smelled of blood. The form before me wasn't a child's anymore. It was a spattering of pulsing red blood, a literal vortex of death swirling around silver eyes and the faint silhouette of a child. He hadn't smiled at me the first time we met because I had interested him; I had merely amused him with a funny party trick – one he knew much better than I did. Horrified, I watched with morbid fascination, unable to turn away as every drop of Silas was absorbed. Alistair, no longer engulfed in the sea of blood, stood beside Clara in his sweatshirt, cuffed pants, and red tennis shoes. There was not a single drop of blood on him.

"What the fuck was that?" Quin cursed, almost screaming in my face.

"You're lucky we were close," Clara said, nonchalantly stretching a leg out to prod Silas's bony and leathery remains. "It's been a while since I've encountered one like him."

"He was a controller," Cyd responded to Quin, knowing full-well his question had nothing to do with Silas. "That's not going to heal if there's any silver left in you."

Quin reached out and I flinched, slapping his hand away. "Stop it. You're acting like this is the first time I've been stabbed."

Annoyed, I freed myself of Quin and Cyd's concern, making my way to Clara and the others. Each of them regarded me with differing levels of interest. Clara smiled up at me from beside Alistair, no longer intrigued by Silas's now crumbling corpse.

"You're lucky he didn't want to play Russian roulette," Lucas joked dryly, his revolver hanging loosely at his side.

"Yeah." I agreed weakly. "Thanks."

"There is weakness in invariability," Alistair responded, watching intently as what was left of Silas turned to dust. "A controller holds power over any vampire weaker than themselves."

"How's the hunt for Selene?" Clara interrupted, gaze unblinking.

Gasping, I turned from her, thankful for a reason not to answer. Cramping, twisting pain all but doubled me over as my guts pulled themselves back together. I felt them twisting under my skin as connective tissue pulled everything back into place.

"We haven't seen her," Quin snarled, again finding a way to place himself between them and me.

"You mean you haven't been looking," Lucas retorted, a warning tone in his voice.

"Lay off." This time it was Warren who spoke up, blatantly annoyed by Lucas's remark. "This is the first chance we've had."

"Don't wait too long." Clara's voice rang out loud and clear; her irritation silenced any further crosstalk. "Or," she added, voice cheerful again, "We'll be the ones hunting."

"Yeah, we know." Quin met Clara's crazy eyes. "You need a new threat."

If looks could kill, Lucas would have added Quin to the body count. Hell, I wasn't completely sure he wouldn't shoot him now. Thankfully, Clara laughed, somehow amused by Quin's opposition.

"It'll be light out soon." Clara remarked, blond curls every bit as wild as her eyes. "Don't make us save you twice."

"Thanks," Warren said sincerely before turning to leave.

Curiously, I waited, watching as Alistair lingered just long enough to drag a small tennis shoe through Silas's dust and scatter him to the wind. The gray powder seemed to evaporate – all except for a child-sized foot print.

The tension left Cyd's mind the second Clara and her gang departed. Looking back, I saw her inspecting Warren's other dagger, my blood caked around the hilt. There was something dark about the way she turned the blade over and over, entranced.

"He's a Progenitor," Cyd said after a few more twirls, the blade dancing in her hand, eyes distant.

Warren glanced at her before reaching out to reclaim it; she offered it up without hesitation.

"I don't know what that means," I sighed, the painful churning of my insides finally subsiding.

"The safe house isn't far." She stood, her lithe frame shimmering before us. She didn't leave right away, though.

I watched as her form shifted in and out of my perception like smoke. Her mind beckoned me to follow, though I wasn't completely sure why. Thankfully, neither was Warren; his confusion mirrored mine even if he didn't show it. Quin, completely unperturbed by the offer, hesitated only long enough to spit where Silas's remains had once been.

"Alright, let's go," Quin said, satisfied with himself. He strode off in the direction Cyd had headed.

Apparently he was no more disillusioned than I by Cyd's tricks. Warren waited for me to fall in line beside him, the same apologetic look on his face from before. This time, though, Quin wasn't around to make fun of him.

"Are you alright?" Warren asked carefully.

"I'll heal," I replied. He was much more perceptive than Quin.

"That's not what I meant." He countered gently, eyes meeting mine. "Something happened when you were searching, didn't it?"

"I could show you, but I don't think you want to know," I answered sadly, feeling the woman's death shroud me. I didn't even know her name, but her pain would stay with me. I was surprised, though, when he didn't immediately refuse me.

"I'm sure I don't. Is that how you found him, you saw him killing?"

"No." I shook my head, pausing as we went. "I never found him, I found her."

Warren and I had run through the building so fast that I hadn't noticed the smell. This was the floor where she died. I stood in the open doorway, the spots of red and chunks of gore led my eyes to her. There wasn't much left in the way of a body – Silas had made sure of that. Warren didn't press any further as we continued our way outside; there was nothing either of us could do to help her now. Vampires seemed to enjoy their abandoned buildings. It would probably be months before anyone found the remains, especially with the cold weather. It would take a while for the body to start stinking.

"Thank you," Warren said, finally building up the nerve; he didn't know I was listening to him trying to thank me this whole time.

"Cyd saved us. I just bought us time." I countered. I wasn't trying to disregard his sentiments; I just didn't feel like the self-sacrificing hero he was making me out to be in his head.

The nurse in me couldn't let go of the life lost. I'd felt her death and the peace of it wash over me, stealing her pain and terror away. The part that hurt most was the loss of her dreams. Just before it all faded to black and I was returned to the skeletal columns of cement. I was aware of her consciousness and the sadness within as she took her last breath. I had within myself the regrets of a woman who died too soon.

"Warren." I stopped just short of the safe house. "I'm not alright."

The words shuddered out of me. I couldn't carry the burden of the day anymore. My adrenaline was spent, muscles weak – it crashed down around me. Mind, body, and soul, I had nothing left. I stood distant from them all. Sensing my hesitancy, Warren stopped halfway up the steps that led inside to Quin and Cyd. He turned to face me, his hazel eyes every bit as tired as I felt.

"All you can see right now is the death; it's harder to see the ones you saved, the ones who will never know what we did today." He spoke these words, not just for me, but for himself. "Come on." Warren held his hand out to me. "It doesn't get easier, but at least we don't have to face it alone."

It was the worst silver lining I'd ever heard; at least we could suffer together? It shouldn't have been funny, but his sincerity was overwhelming; he had really meant it, and somehow it had made me feel better.

"Nothing is easy anymore," I added sarcastically. "But you're right; at least we can be miserable together."

Warren grinned, caught off guard, my innate pessimism twisting his meaning. "Pretty much, yeah, but it isn't all bad."

These last words resonated within me, reflecting my own thoughts. "It isn't all bad," I agreed, but my mind was reeling.

The weight of the day pulled at the last of my reserves as I took in the hunter before me, his mind searching for some way to comfort me. I realized, maybe a little too late, that he'd been afraid today would end this way for me: with my resolve broken and mind confused.

"Come on." Warren turned, finishing his climb to the front door.

But I was gone, his voice barely audible to me as I ran, leaving him, Quin, and Cyd behind.

CHAPTER TWENTY

I closed my mind, delving deep within myself, hiding in places I didn't want to be – but I needed to be somewhere Quin couldn't follow me, a place so dark even I couldn't see: to the beginning, back to her. It wasn't memory or compulsion that drove me forward. I ran, led by blind instinct. It was the same instinct that drove animals to migrate, determined to find their beginning.

Quin clawed at my mind. The feel of him was sharp against my consciousness as he struggled to find me. I covered my ears, quickening my pace; I was lost in the fractures of my own mind. His fear and confusion were unable to break through the surface and reach me. Where I went, he couldn't follow. I don't know how long I wandered like this, pulled forward by an invisible, yet powerful, string. But I knew when I had found it – when I had found her.

She smelled deeply of the ocean and woods that ran along the coastline; her red eyes burned like a fire through my soul. The heat of her was agonizingly warm. It radiated through me, erasing the chill of the night and the pressure of Quin in my mind. For the second time since my awakening, there was silence. My hands fell away from my ears, the hum of the city and waterway all around me. Euphoria. I closed my eyes, taking in the silence she provided. The relief of it was astounding, her presence the only thing I could feel.

"Why?" I asked, opening my eyes slowly. "Why us?"

Selene stood, frozen in contemplation before a serene and pitying look overtook her features. She took me in, weighing her words. I was tattered and disheveled, frantic in my search for her and for answers.

"I didn't choose you." She spoke softly, the warmth of her all around me. "You called out to me."

Pressure built behind my eyes and in my skull; this time, though, it wasn't Quin; it was something forgotten and hidden just under the surface. Slowly, she advanced, sensing my distress.

"What?" I grimaced, taking a step back, the pain intensifying the closer she was. "Why would I call to you?"

Concern filled her ruby eyes as she reached for me, the touch of her fingertips scalding, and for a second she forgot herself. Her eyes and the feel of her cooled – blue pools replaced the red as she grasped my hand, keeping me with her.

"There's still so much you don't remember." Selene spoke cautiously, her hold on me barely a caress, ensuring I could pull away.

"Why would I call to you?" My voice broke. "Why would I ask for this?" I didn't understand, couldn't.

Selene's features changed again, her own distress apparent to me. A deep sadness settled within the porcelain of her face. This was the face she had shown me all those nights ago. It was a face I knew well, a face I had worn myself. This was the face of sorrow and regret, at not being able to save someone and feeling their life slip from your grasp. I understood this sorrow, having felt it time and time again in my profession as body after body crumbled under chest compressions – sometimes no matter what you did or how hard you fight, they just died.

"It'd be easier to let you hate me." A sad smile touched her lips, the same smile from my dream. "I won't shield you from it anymore."

Selene's lace-like grip slipped away, her grasp but a whisper as she distanced herself from me. Azure blue melted into lavender until her eyes were again fully saturated with red. There were no more expressions to be found in the elegant curves of her face as she pulled up her sleeve. The pale skin of her forearm and wrist clearly exposed, she reached out, offering herself to me. Warmth again flowed from her, this time it was soft – inviting even – as it washed over me in waves. It mixed with the cool night air, creating an updraft that tousled her silk hair and tugged at her long coat.

She was hauntingly beautiful, reaching out to me. Here lay my choice: to drink of her once more, to choose her. It was my choice, but I knew I couldn't turn back. The only way was forward, and she was in my path. I entered the maelstrom, her energy pushing and pulling at me, encircling us both. Purposefully, Selene pierced the palm of her left hand with the thumbnail of her right. Their perfect sharpness was something that I had previously overlooked.

Rich blood pooled perfectly within her palm; it was intoxicating, the smell of it surrounding me. She'd waited until I was sure, knowing I wouldn't be able to resist the taste of her. I drank deeply, her blood heavy and saccharine across my palate. Selene's mind was absolute; there was no beginning and no end. Centuries of her passed before me, the knowledge of her soul so much deeper than anything I could possibly comprehend. Selene's blood was fortifying me as her strength poured into me, changing me once more.

"I'm sorry," Selene said, shattering our connection as she pulled free of me.

For the second time, her blood ripped me apart. Doubling over, the high of her was completely erased from my mind. It felt just like when she'd created me, but this time I wasn't sure what would be left. Selene burned through every inch of me, simultaneously destroying and rebuilding.

The fog of her lifted from me, her invisible chains breaking as the memories within her blood – of Alexander – returned to me all at once. Realization paralyzed me; in those moments before unconsciousness consumed me, I knew he was always going to die. It had nothing to do with her or the coven. Cancer had been devouring him long before she'd ever found us. I was always going to be alone, and it wasn't anyone's fault.

I gave in, letting the pain of her tear through me; at least within it there was feeling. My psyche truly exhausted, I could not endure the loss of him another time. There was no anger, no sadness, and no one left to bargain with as my vision went black and I fell to the cool earth.

———

He was getting close. Derek spat, remembering the taste of Quin's blood in his mouth. It was time to go; they couldn't afford to wait around for the other hunters to catch up. Eryn had made her choice; Selene wasn't going to let her go a second time. Quin's boots pounded against the pavement; he was too close. Derek wasn't about to let him interfere – not after how long Selene had waited.

He contemplated killing Quin. It would be easier with one less hunter, but he knew having Quin's death on his hands would make things messy. It was going to be inconvenient no matter what he did, so he might as well introduce himself. Derek didn't bother trying to hide his presence as he stepped into the open and directly into Quin's path.

He stood, hands buried deep in the pockets of his coat, his stance relaxed but strategic. Quin's pace slowed, stuttering to a stop as he neared, his breathing made ragged by his efforts. Derek smiled wide; Quin knew exactly what he was. Without hesitation the hunter drew his gun, its aim low but direct.

Within the space of a few seconds, Quin fired, the stink of gunpowder stung Derek's nose as he advanced. He was slow without his connection to Eryn. This was going to be child's play. Derek stopped inches from Quin; to a human it would look like he'd just appeared out of thin air. Their exchange was over before it had even begun. Derek's blade kissed the underside of Quin's chin. Blood trailed down the black steel to meet his fingertips.

"You go no farther." Blue eyes met black, Quin's focus just catching up with Derek's movement.

The two men were in a standoff, their weapons pressed tight against each other, but only one of them in control. The smell of Quin's blood disgusted him: human yet inhuman. It was an insult. Derek could drive his blade straight back, burying it within the cartilage of Quin's trachea and watch as he choked to death on it. Unfortunately, he'd have to settle for his ghosts. Sidestepping, Derek was careful to keep his blade pressed just deep enough into Quin's skin to prevent him from healing. He wanted to see what fed this man's nightmares.

Before them stood the supple figures of a woman and small child, their significance initially lost on Derek. He waited, watching as Quin's finger trembled against the trigger of his Ruger. Quin didn't see Derek anymore. It was the dead that stayed his hand, their faces as real to him as the ground beneath his feet.

"I'm sorry." Quin let the gun fall from his hand, desperate to touch them – to feel her skin alive against his. He needed to hold her and their child once more.

Derek took in the sight of them. The woman's skin and hair were bright in comparison to the child's olive skin. He saw no discernable resemblance between the two as they stood before Quin, their images shifting as Derek delved deeper. This wasn't going to be a happy family reunion. He needed to know why they haunted Quin. He wanted to feed on his memories of them. If he couldn't kill the hunter, then at least he could make Quin wish he was – even if his blood was disgusting.

A sharp pain stung Quin's right shoulder, but he didn't care; he needed to touch them, to remember the feel and smell of them. She hadn't changed; her eyes were just as bright and beautiful as he remembered. Every line etched in her face was a reminder of his life before. Their hands reached out to meet his, the fullness of them disintegrating until only withered hands held him. The pressure at his shoulder grew more persistent as the pain intensified. Quin could just make out the familiar, yet sickening, sound of feeding as his girlfriend's eyes hollowed. Any life he'd seen in their faces was now gone. Their nails fought for purchase in his flesh, tearing into him just as sharp and insistent as the pain in his shoulder.

Quin screamed. The illusion of his girlfriend and daughter shattering suddenly as searing heat ripped through his body to release him from his nightmare. Derek couldn't move away fast enough, his vice interrupted as Quin tore free from him, collapsing to the ground. The taste and smell of him had changed. Circling cautiously, Derek knelt beside the now writhing hunter.

"What did you do to me?" Quin bellowed, doubled over in pain.

Derek took a closer look. Grasping Quin's chin, he forced the man to look up at him. Red reflected back at him and he realized that what he had tasted was the beginning of Quin's awakening.

"You're changing," Derek answered venomously before releasing Quin.

"Bastard!" Quin moved to strike out, his attempt easily swatted away by the monster before him.

"I'd rather kill you." Malice tainted his voice. "This is your doing. This is her blood running through you." Derek spat the words in Quin's face.

It served him right. Now the hunter would become what he hated. Standing, he left Quin to his pain. The other hunters would soon find him. It felt appropriate, leaving him there like that to be killed by his own kind. Quin could die in the street, just as the vampires that had come before him. Derek didn't look back; he'd let the agony of the change rip Quin apart before the people he trusted most put a bullet in his skull.

Derek would love to see the destruction of the hunter, but he'd have to settle for second best: the sound of Quin's screams and the horrors of his ghosts. The taste of Quin's loss still sweet on his tongue, he wished he could have seen his vice to fruition. There was nothing was worse than a story left untold. He'd just have to find another way to satiate his curiosity. Returning, Derek found Selene crouched beside Eryn, her long blond hair shielding her face from him. He could smell her blood, see it as he approached, dried and cracked against the pale skin of her wrist and palm.

"You stink of him." Selene spoke quietly, turning to face him. "Bring her; we need to go to ground."

Derek wiped his mouth absently, Quin's blood lost within the fibers of his coat as he crouched down to retrieve the small body of his blood sister. Her eyes opened, but only briefly, revealing to him the same red that had been reflected to him in Quin's. He didn't understand how a false bond could unite a vampire and human; it sickened him. The idea of hunters feeding from them like parasites, sapping their strength and abilities, was a disgrace.

Lifting Eryn, he realized the weight of her was too light for one of their kind. One so young shouldn't be starved, and this was why the hunters shouldn't meddle where they didn't belong. They had no idea what it took to satiate a new vampire or the time it took to teach restraint. They were the reason death plagued the city, because when the elders are killed, the young never learned.

CHAPTER TWENTY-ONE

Consciousness disrupted the peace of oblivion as my mind and body fought to forget the memories Selene's blood returned to me. It was the smell of ozone, chemicals, and decay as cancer ate Alex alive from the inside and radiation killed him from the outside. The worst part wasn't the burns as his skin sloughed, or the loss of his independence as I cleaned him, or the pain as it eroded him. We could anticipate all of that as we spent night after night on the bathroom floor together. It was the loss of his mind as the tumor grew and destroyed his memories.

It was the fear in his eyes when he forgot who he was, when he could no longer play the guitar, when he started to forget me – all the while knowing something wasn't quite right. The pain of these memories was worse than the havoc of the blood as it shredded my insides; at least when that pain became too much, I could return to the darkness.

I'd stay there forever in the nothingness of unconsciousness. Was this really what death was, just beautiful emptiness? A place where nothing and no one could reach you, no more pain… no more anything. It was the feeling of cold dirt falling around me like rain that pulled me back, forcing the memories to return as we went to ground. Selene's warmth around me fed the agony of her blood within as Derek covered us like a gravedigger of old and blacked out my perception.

I remembered the first night we spent in the hospital. The radiation had destroyed Alex's taste buds; no matter what I tried, he couldn't eat.

"It just tastes like metal..." his voice replayed weakly as the nurse chided him for not eating again.

These were the last of his sick days before I took him home, before we stopped treatment, before he asked me to stop fighting. We'd skipped right past stage I and II, and by the time we caught it in stage III, the treatment only served to weaken him further – before stage IV and palliative care began. For a moment we forgot about death as his strength and appetite returned in the weeks that followed, but it was just a honeymoon period of wellness before the inevitable.

Shovelful by shovelful, there was something comforting in the weight of the earth as it surrounded me, erasing a sense of vulnerability I hadn't realized was always present when I slept alone. Derek and Selene both so near, for the first time since the loss of Alexander I wasn't sleeping alone. Their arms held me, warm in the cold of the grave as I waited for the nothingness to consume me once more.

We'd lain like this our last night together; Alex and I, buried under the blankets – nothing but the weight of the comforter and his arms around me. For just a moment there was no cancer, no end to him and me, and no loss of my best friend. For a moment we talked like there was no expiration date. His warm brown eyes focused for the first time in months as clarity returned to him. We talked about growing old, how we'd love each other even more with the wrinkles we'd earn together after a life well lived.

Like a web, Selene's control had veiled from me the loss of my partner and of her mistake. Drop by drop her blood had allowed me to pull apart the strands that had obstructed the truth of our loss. This was the last time I'd dream of the coven as they ingested and destroyed what was left of my husband.

CHAPTER TWENTY-TWO

Bile seared the back of Quin's throat; the sting of it inconsequential compared with what felt like the rupturing of his organs. He puked; acid and chunks spattered the asphalt. He couldn't move, and he believed he was dying, or at least he hoped he was, and soon. The acrid smell of his own vomit didn't make matters any easier, especially when he couldn't get away from it. Was this really what it felt like to become one of them, to change?

Quin reached desperately for his gun, the cool metal teasing his fingertips, but all he managed to do was push it farther away. He'd rather eat a silver bullet than change, but that wasn't up to him anymore. Infuriatingly curly blond hair bounced into view. Even if Quin could have grabbed his Ruger, Clara would never let him use it. He never believed in God, but in that moment, he prayed for death as his insides churned once more and his vision went black. Clara's voice was lost to him as he fell forward in his own mess, unconsciousness claiming him.

"I told you to roll over…" Clara whined; she hated cleaning vomit.

Quin lay before her in a heap, torn shoulder still bleeding and vomit soaked. Tonight was getting better and better. At least she'd have something new to play with. This was where she excelled. Lucas didn't have the stomach for it, and Alistair only cared if he got something out of it. Carefully, she retrieved Quin's firearm before rolling him onto his back to secure his knife; if he had anything else on him, she'd find it later. She took solace in the early morning light that filtered between the tall apartment buildings; even if Quin did change now, he'd be incapacitated.

It took Rylan longer than she would have liked to help her retrieve Quin. At least if anyone noticed them, they'd probably just chalk it up to strangers helping their drunken friend home. *No abduction here, no sir.* Clara smiled to herself as they tossed Quin's limp body into the back seat of their rental car. It had been Rylan's idea to keep an eye on the newly-tethered; they had no idea it'd pay off so soon, though.

"What's the plan?" Rylan drove slowly, dividing his focus between the road and the back seat where Clara and Quin resided.

"We wait," Clara didn't bother to hide her excitement, "and see how he turns out."

Rylan considered the idea for a moment before saying, "And if he doesn't turn?"

"Then he's bait." She shrugged. "Until Eryn surfaces we can't very well let our only leverage go." Clara's imagination was starting to get the best of her.

She wondered if the two of them would still be connected. Clara had never had the chance to study the effects of vampirism on a tethered hunter. Would Quin still be bound by Eryn's blood or manifest his own abilities? Essentially, a tethered hunter was just piggybacking on the fledgling's awakening. It was a weakened union, but one that nonetheless left many hunters dead. The real question was: why now?

If Quin was going to change, shouldn't it have happened when he'd first tethered Eryn?

"The one that bit Quin, that's all it was, right?" Clara wanted to be sure she hadn't missed anything.

"Yeah, it doesn't make any sense to me, either. Why now?" Rylan hadn't seen anything to suggest Quin's encounter with the male vampire would activate the infection already present in his blood.

They were both silent now, forming their own theories and ideas on the matter, each a scientist in their own messed-up way. The remainder of their car ride together was quiet, Rylan and Clara both lost in thought. They weren't returning to their safe house tonight; tonight they'd go where no one could hear the screams of their experiments.

It was a secret place – a place Quin and all the others only suspected existed, but never knew for certain. Those who came here rarely left. Moving as one, Clara and Rylan transferred and secured Quin. They made a point to remove any excess clothing and stow his weapons where they couldn't be easily accessed. Years of practice had made them efficient and precise; they were collectors after all.

Four cells lined the circular walls of their underground mortuary. All of the cells' entryways faced the medical theater the two of them had worked tirelessly to create. Surgical steel glittered against the sterile white tile that lined the walls and floors; in the center was a modified autopsy table. It was perfectly centered above a drain for easy cleanup. It was also their most used toy. This was where they restrained Quin.

Their more inventive toys were secured down the only other hallway. The equipment stored within that room was reserved for their more time-consuming experiments. Clara and Rylan stood on opposite sides of Quin, triple checking the restraints. The key to imprisoning and keeping a vampire was to make death their only means of escape. They had a lot of ways to ensure their captives complied; one of those ways was woven within the very restraints that now held Quin.

Satisfied he was secure, Clara took to her tools, fingers dancing across their surgical steel surfaces. Each one was laid out just the way she liked. Rylan waited, watching for any sign that the blood within Quin had taken hold. Neither one dared make a move – not until they were sure. To hurt another hunter would mean their end. But a vampire? It didn't matter what they did then.

Rylan, allowing his curiosity to get the better of him, pulled on a pair of black gloves. In two long and deliberate strides he placed himself at the head of the autopsy table and methodically began his examination. Technically he wasn't breaking the rules; this part of his job was benign – innocent even – as he inspected Quin for the telltale signs of awakening. Clara, usually uninterested in this part of his job, leaned in. She was just as eager as Rylan to see what his inspection would reveal.

Clara's skills resided solely in her tools. Her surgical precision and speed were a thing of beauty, but this was Rylan's skill – the assessment and dissemination of vampires. He had single-handedly cataloged six different strains of vampirism and their distinct features, tracing the lineage back hundreds of years through the archives of the hunters. Each strain brought with it different strengths, weaknesses, and costs. Quick and careful, Rylan knew what he was looking for.

The tricky part was that tethered hunters often took on characteristics of the vampires – sharpened teeth, enhanced sight and smell, inhuman healing and metabolism, or fortified bones just to name a few. Each new vampire was a chance to see how the strain acted on the human physiology. Rylan had been born into a family of collectors; he lived to discover and test every genealogical anomaly he could get his hands on.

Clara took note of every movement; she'd become intricately aware of Rylan's tells – for example: the way his hands paused when he inspected Quin's eyes told her there was something of interest there. It was the same way she knew when he was disappointed. The speed at which he moved through his assessment usually dictated the amount of information he was able to gather and its importance.

She watched him stop on three separate occasions of his head-to-toe assessment: eyes, wound, and abdomen. Clara didn't pretend to know what his pauses meant, but she knew it must be important. In the eight years they'd been working together, very little made him pause anymore.

"What do you see?" she asked finally, unable to stand his quiet contemplation any longer.

Rylan began as he always did, by showing her. He started by returning to the head of the table, revealing Quin's eyes. From what they'd seen of his and Eryn's connection, the hunter's eyes reflected teal when they were linked. What Clara saw as Rylan lifted one heavy lid was red. It was the same red they'd seen reflected in Eryn's eyes when she attacked Cyd. Clara assumed it was probably the same red that Marc and Quin had encountered when meeting Eryn's maker.

Next, Rylan drug one gloved finger over the viscous blood caked against Quin's shoulder. He held it out to Clara, as if he was preparing to show her a magic trick. Leaning closer she watched as he brought his extracted sample back toward the wound. If Clara had blinked, she would have missed it. The blood pulled itself free; like a magnet, it returned to where it had originally been collected. Rylan then gestured at Quin's physique, the near bareness of it exposed before them. She knew better than to ask any questions before Rylan was ready to answer, so she waited for him to summarize his discovery.

"His change is much more advanced than that of Marc or Warren – which is interesting considering that both of them have been tethered longer than he has," Rylan stated before returning to his side of the table, hands carefully pressing into Quin's abdomen. "I can't be certain, but there may be some atrophy present. It's hard to say if this is merely from being tethered or if it is the beginning of his awakening."

They were both well versed on the internal workings of a fully awakened vampire; their anatomy was drastically different than their human counterparts. The most distinct changes occurred in the small and large intestines, mainly the shortening of both. This led to the thinned and often hollowed-out core seen in vampires. Quin by no means fit that description, quite the opposite actually as his enhanced metabolism and healing served to create the well-muscled physique before them. What Rylan was referring to was an internal shift felt upon palpation.

"So we still know nothing." Clara tapped her tray of instruments impatiently. "This could very well be nothing more than a shift in the blood bond."

Rylan nodded, remembering the changes they had studied in Warren after his discovery of Cyd's vice. The shifts in his abilities were notable, but nothing as violent as what they had witnessed in Quin tonight. It was for this reason that they weren't sure if Quin was turning. Truth was, there weren't many tethered for them to study; their research resided more in the discovery and destruction of vampires.

Clara grew bored of staring at their incapacitated hunter. Quin's breathing had slowed, even and heavy from sleep. Her own exhaustion was beginning to weigh on her; they'd been busy, and not just from earlier rescue and reconnaissance. They'd been working on a different project since arriving in the great northwest.

"What do you say we check on Hannah?" Clara suggested, a wide and sinister grin playing across her lips.

Rylan stifled a laugh. "Determined to kill her or just testing the limits of your new invention?"

"Come on; give me more credit than that." Clara feigned innocence. "You know it's a little bit of both."

Energy renewed, she bounded down the long hallway, beckoning Rylan to follow. This was the side of her only he saw. Their spirits shared an insatiable need to push the limits of discovery – no matter the cost. Collectors didn't play by the rules of society; they did things no one else could or would. It was fine by him. Rylan never needed anyone but himself and his experiments. They'd remember his name when he eradicated the vampires that ate their families. They'd thank him then for all the things he did that they never could.

Their footsteps reverberated off the tile and down the narrow hallway. If Hannah wasn't awake before, she would be now. Even in the early morning, she was able to fight sleep. Perhaps it was terror that kept her eyes from closing. Just as Rylan had suspected, Hannah sat wide eyed and alert within the confines of her personalized cell.

"Shall we begin?" Rylan asked clinically. He carried within him none of Clara's malice.

Lucas had called them Jekyll and Hyde once, and though Rylan was sure he meant it as an insult, he and Clara found the comparison amusing. The truth was, they were both Hyde; he was just better at hiding it. You couldn't be a collector if you didn't enjoy the process.

"Experiment thirty-six: silver emersion." Rylan turned the valve that bathed Hannah in silver mist.

Her screams filled the room as Clara all but threw herself against the cylindrical glass that entombed the vampire. Again and again they'd done this, bathing her in silver until her skin melted away. Each time, they extended the exposure time. At five seconds, her skin was all gone. At ten her adipose tissue sloughed off, exposing the muscle. It was at this time that Hannah lost the ability to scream, the silver eroding her vocal cords.

Each and every time, Clara met the fiery pain in those auburn eyes. *Burn*, she thought, watching muscle give way to ligaments and bone. Fifteen seconds, Hannah was no longer able to support herself as the silver emulsion picked her bones clean, spilling what was left of her innards to the grate below. Rylan spun the valve, nothing but bone left. Twenty seconds, that's what it took to render all but the strongest of tissue. Clara examined it, certain there was no more meat or viscera left.

"Well?" Rylan joined Clara against the glass cylinder, examining what was left.

"Nothing," Clara spat. "It can't penetrate."

"No, not yet," he agreed, watching as Hannah began to heal.

Muscle sprouted, stitching what was left of Hannah back together. Her regeneration always started at her core, working up her spine and through her chest cavity. She was a truly rare specimen; they weren't even sure if melting her brain would finally kill her. They couldn't be sure until they perfected the emulsion, though. They had thirty-two chances remaining to get it right; after that, she was Alistair's. They had one attempt for every life she'd taken.

Rylan stayed, watching over Hannah long after Clara stormed off, aggravated by their failures.

Veins and arteries laced their way to organs not yet formed, creating an intricate network reminiscent of spider webs as the capillaries burst forth. She healed this way every time – from the inside out – until her skin spilled forth to seal away her vital insides. Curiously, she always grew her hair back; he'd never seen a vampire have so much control over their molecular structure. He was sure this was something he'd never seen another vampire repair. The rich color of it perfectly matched her eyes.

"You're slowing," Rylan pointed out matter-of-fact. "Perhaps even you have limits. Has the thirst begun to take hold?"

She didn't answer him. She didn't have to, though; her eyes spoke volumes – the reddish brown glow of them screamed for release; the hungrier she became, the less human they were. He circled her glass prison, taking in her naked form: not even one scratch was left on her perfect skin. There was so much he still didn't know about her abilities.

"I have a theory," Rylan said quietly as he popped open a small pocket knife. "I think this isn't your true form."

His eyes never left her face as he pricked the tip of his finger. That got her attention. Hannah's eyes fixed on the drop of red that welled against pale skin. Rylan held it out to her, watching as Hannah's jaw clenched and unclenched, fighting the urge to throw herself against the jar-like prison in which they kept her.

"Show me." Rylan spoke evenly.

If she was able to shift, his offering was the only that wouldn't hurt. Clara didn't believe in patience; if you didn't tell her what she wanted she'd just rip it from you. Hannah's auburn eyes were backlit with hunger and resolve. Rylan moved to leave, calling her bluff, satisfied when she stirred, hands slamming against the cylinder.

Her auburn hair corkscrewed, the color fading slowly to expose familiar blond curls. She stood, her skin losing the bronze glow to reveal perfectly pale skin. Rylan watched, amazed at her transformation. Before him stood a near-perfect replica of Clara – all except those haunting eyes. It all made sense now, why it had taken them so long to find her.

Sixty-eight had died before Alistair captured her. Sixty-eight children were lost to this monster that wore the face of their mothers. Rylan smiled – one of the few times Hyde could slip out; he put his finger in his mouth and opened the valve. He'd carry the sounds of her screams into his sleep with him.

CHAPTER TWENTY-THREE

The smells of infection, old blood, and bleach pulled Quin from the oblivion of sleep. The odor was an odd mixture of clean and dirty that he wasn't accustomed to, but then again, he wasn't accustomed to waking up half naked and strapped to a table, either. The lights above him resembled the ones used in emergency rooms, the blinding white of their circular beams painful even against closed eyelids. Quin had just enough slack to prop himself up on his elbows and look around. He was in an oversized operating room – the only difference being that most operating rooms didn't have cells.

The last thing he remembered was the sensation of his organs ripping and tearing themselves apart, then puking. The taste of it still lingered in his mouth – and then… blond hair. Fear hit his stomach like a brick; the realization of where he was cemented his terror. Quin panicked, testing the strength of the restraints. That battle was short-lived, though, as blades, razor-thin, revealed themselves within the leather and steel. The more he struggled and pulled against it, the farther the blades pushed into his wrists and ankles.

"Shit," he cursed, slamming his head against the cold metal beneath him.

The wounds itched around his wrists where the concealed edges broke his skin. These restraints, he realized, were created for vampires; and while Quin couldn't be certain at this point, he believed the itching was a good sign. He knew what silver did to vampires. The fact that his flesh wasn't violently reacting to it made him feel marginally better. Frustrated, Quin thumped his head a few more times. The soft sound of his skull banging against the metal was somehow reassuring in the face of silence.

He'd just have to wait and hope beyond all odds that he could find some way out of this hellhole. He really didn't want to know what the instruments on the tray beside him were for. Their precise and organized placement made him uneasy; whoever used them took great pride in their work. Quin forced himself to focus instead on his anxiety, desperate to regain control of himself and his thoughts.

Concentrating, he searched for the connection he'd grown so accustomed to. Quin didn't know if he could reach Eryn, but he had to try – even if it was just a way to distract himself. The thing was, he had always been able to feel her within him, but to what extent was always up to her. Sometimes he could draw on her and pull her closer, tracing the bond. Last night was the second time he'd been completely unable to find her.

Quin felt Eryn's absence like the death of a loved one, her strength, the feel of her ever present in his mind, just gone. He'd grown comfortable with it – complete even. Something had happened to them last night and it scared him. The vampire that had bit him had fucked with his mind; said Quin was changing. He couldn't explain it, but he knew something had changed, smelled it in the stink of his now dried blood. It was more pungent than when Eryn fed.

Even without her, Quin felt a peculiar extension of self. It was more forceful and concrete within his mind, less explorative and all his own. Quin was about to give up searching, but just as he was about to withdraw, he felt her. Eryn's mind stirred, meeting him with the fog of sleep as their connection combined their senses.

The ease of it was astounding, both intimately aware of the other. Dark vs light, damp dirt vs sterile steel, and both lost in their new locations – but that's all he got before she was again lost to him.

"Dammit!" Quin slammed his head again, hard enough to see stars this time.

The mixture of anger and frustration as Quin lashed out sent the tray of instruments beside him flying. A sharp and painful cacophony loud enough to wake the dead ensued, effectively causing Quin's adrenaline levels to spike again. It was in the following silence that Quin realized he was not alone.

The presence he felt shared with him the same panicked realization: they were trapped. Looking back, Quin was immediately aware of a hallway he had originally missed in his earlier investigations. Down that long, narrow hallway, he was sure something or someone was held every bit as captive as he was. A tapping sound, soft and persistent, just reached his ears before screams rang out, silencing any further noise from the back room.

"How did you do that?" A voice called out from above, it was familiar yet distorted through the static of a speaker.

"Fuck you," Quin cursed; it was his default. "Come down here and I'll show you!" He yelled, instantly regretting the response that followed.

"Okay." This voice he knew; it was Clara's, and he could hear the smile in her response.

Cold sweat stuck him to the table below. Even if he could force his hands free of the bladed manacles, he'd never be able to get his feet out without incurring major damage, damage he wasn't sure would heal in time to matter. As if sensing his desperation, the restraints were suddenly and painfully pulled tight. The undeniable click of gears below him forced his legs and arms around the edge of the table. The tension on his shoulders and knees was excruciating; it effectively took away any range of motion he previously possessed.

"Comfy?" Clara called, her voice no longer distorted by technology.

From what he could tell, she was keeping her distance, probably standing close to the stairs that lead up and out of this fucked up operating room. The pain in his joints only served to fuel the anger he felt for the bitch with blond hair. What he wouldn't give to wrap his hands around her throat right now.

"I believe you had something to show me?" Her smug and self-satisfying tone filtered over to him; she was patrolling the room, working her way slowly closer.

"Fuck you," Quin replied once more through clenched teeth; he could just see her in his periphery.

"You already said that," Clara retorted, unperturbed by his expletives.

She was busy scanning her scattered tools; she was looking for one in particular – a corer to be exact; it was used to carve and remove circular chunks from overgrown potatoes. Its sharp, tong-like design was ideal for removing someone's vision. It even had a rounded, spoon-like curve on each finger to ensure the eye didn't go rolling away once excavated. Finding the tool she desired, Clara gasped excitedly.

"Now," she declared, fully stepping into Quin's view, "I believe you had something to show me, and I, for one, would love to see those red eyes of yours again."

Quin tried in vain to push away from Clara. Her form leaned over his, a sharp, spoon-like tong in hand. Panic replaced any of his earlier anger as he pulled against his restraints; the warmth of his blood was shocking against his cold skin. It wasn't until she lunged that he lashed out defensively with a force he had only ever been on the receiving end of. He'd effectively sent Clara and her sharp spoon whirling.

It felt like he had physically shoved her, just the same as he would have done had his arms been free. The clang of her body against the tile and scattered steel was satisfying, but his joy was short lived. Clara's laughter floated up to him from where she'd landed.

"Loosen him." Clara's tone was light again, filled with a humor Quin did not understand.

Joint-relieving slack returned to the restraints, but still they held him. He was thankful when feeling returned to his arms and legs.

"You've gotten stronger." It was Rylan's cold and calculated tone that filtered through the static – the same as before, Quin realized.

Of course they were both collectors; he felt stupid for thinking Clara was the only one, especially after the way Rylan had regarded Eryn's abilities.

"Tell me." Clara's face and tangled blond curls popped back into view. "Are you still human or has the blood corrupted you?"

Again, Quin was desperate to escape her closeness. It was an odd sensation, the violation of his personal space. Maybe it was his lack of clothing and freedom, but he doubted it. It probably had more to do with the way Clara was looking at him.

"I'm human." He met those pale green eyes and saw nothing staring back at him. No emotions and no sign of a soul within. It was for this reason that he feared her. These eyes – he'd met them before – but when he stared into eyes like this, the people that they belonged to were committed.

"We had to be sure. The way we found you, writhing in the street, you looked like one of them." Clara stepped back; her tone no longer held any laughter within. "That and you lost her. Or perhaps she left you?"

Quin didn't consider himself an emotional person, but for the second time in a five-minute span he contemplated de-gloving his hands and feet over the knives of Clara's words if it meant escape. He felt stupid. How was she able to cut him deeper than the blades around his wrists? The pain of it hollowed him and he shut down. It wasn't something Quin did consciously; it was maladaptive and only effective for one thing: hiding.

"You don't know what you're talking about." Quin's voice was sobering; its cold indifference was something Clara wasn't expecting.

She knew in that moment that she'd get no further with him. It wasn't that Clara didn't know how to break him – oh she'd love to take a hammer to the walls he was surrounding himself in – but to do so now would be suicide. Clara hated losing the upper hand, but she'd just have to find another way to settle the anger growing inside her chest.

"I want to show you something." She smiled too sweetly.

Quin sneered; he didn't have the patience for her games. His disdain for her was making his blood boil. If he had a free arm he'd find a way to break her teeth, but he didn't, nor did he have a choice but to participate in her sick games. Quin watched as she circled around to the foot of the table. A loud click sounded and they were off. She was rolling him down the narrow hallway where the screams had sounded only moments before her arrival.

The smell from earlier grew stronger as they advanced, but it wasn't until they crashed full force through the double doors that the stench of infectious rot and blood hit him fully. It assaulted him, forcing him to look for the source of his discomfort. In the center of the room lay a bubbling mass of bone and flesh contained within a cylindrical, tube-like tank.

"This is the best part," Clara breathed, close to his ear; he jerked away, attempting to turn his head, but she held his jaw tight. "Watch."

He did as he was told, unable to look away once he realized the festering mass of rot was still alive, the bones beneath desperate to escape the liquid silver that had dissolved the flesh. The jaw hung open, silent screams of agony apparent even without the sinew required to make sound. Eventually it was all that was left: bones and silver. The horror of it left him in awe. Clara's fingers dug into his skin painfully, her excitement sticky in his mind. It was nauseous, the feel of her emotions mingling with his, but he couldn't move, and soon he realized why Clara was so persistent.

Quin stared in amazement, breath held as the bones shifted. Free of the glittering rain overhead, he watched as they violently snapped back into place. Ligaments bloomed from nothing to tie it all back together. Organs burst forth as the visceral peritoneum stitched itself together, the veil of membrane and vessels hiding it all away. Next came the muscle and fat; the globules of it revealed to Quin the shape of the woman underneath until she was whole again and sheathed in skin. Her eyes were wild, meeting Quin's. He could taste the death of her on his tongue.

"That was number thirty-eight." Clara freed him from her grasp, leaving Quin so she could tap the glass. "Very soon she won't be able to come back anymore. We're so close."

Clara's excitement hit him again. Quin wasn't used to the feeling of it, the only emotions he'd ever felt from another person were Eryn's. That's when a stronger emotion pulled at him, demanding his attention. Quin was lost in the pain and fear of the woman trapped in the cylinder. Her hunger ripped through him. Clara was right, she was dying. The fear he felt was the vampire's knowledge of her end, and the agony she would still have to endure until then. Quin almost felt sorry. He'd been fed on enough times to understand the hunger that was consuming her mind.

"She eats children, doesn't she?" The realization erased any of his previous empathy.

Clara's brow crinkled, confusion pulling her away from her prize. "Did she tell you that?"

"Get me out of here or turn that thing back on." Quin met the panic in those auburn eyes, and suddenly the smell of her rotting and melting away wasn't so bad.

'Thirty-nine,' Quin thought, catching the twinkle in Clara's eyes as the female vampire – Hannah – screamed until her vocal cords melted away. Again, he couldn't look away, but this time he didn't want to. Quin needed to purge the feel of her hunger, desperate to replace it with anything else – even Clara's psychotic thoughts.

"Her bones – they're starting to pit," Clara announced. Her unabashed sense of accomplishment was exactly what Quin needed to cleanse the remnants of Hannah's hunger – and her vice – from him.

Curiously, Quin was aware of another presence. He couldn't explain how he knew, he just did. Was this how Eryn felt, like a radio antenna picking up on every frequency that crossed her path? It was distracting. Much like Clara had, Rylan circled, regarding Quin curiously. It was the same look he'd given Eryn at her trial, and soon he realized why.

'*Are you just like her?*' Quin heard the question, almost as clearly as spoken words and completely ignored it.

He returned his attention instead to Clara and her morbid curiosity. He wasn't going to be a willing test subject, not for anyone.

"Did you show me this to scare me?" Quin spoke low, indifferent to the suffering of the monster before him.

"Maybe, maybe not." Clara half turned, her athletic frame leaning casually against the glass container. "How do you think Eryn would fair in there?"

It was all Clara needed to get her point across, a simple but clear threat. Quin's resentment was palpable; he'd kill her if given the chance. Rylan and Clara's beady, rat-like stares were really starting to piss him off. They were looking for an excuse to add him or Eryn to their collection. It was clear Clara was just trying to antagonize him, desperate to test his limits while Rylan took note of every reaction or lack thereof. The thing was, Quin knew a thing or two about psychoanalyzing people and he wasn't fooled – not by their threats or by the instruments they displayed. He hadn't turned, not yet, and until then he was off limits.

"Let's see if we can't make you a bit more comfortable, shall we?" Quin didn't like the tone in her voice or the look in her eyes as she approached. She spun him away from Hannah and back down the long tiled hallway.

CHAPTER TWENTY-FOUR

Q uin was careening forward at an alarming speed, the rubber wheels clacked and whined across the tile like machinegun fire. He'd driven with drunks that scared him less than Clara did running down this hallway. Thankfully the ride didn't last long as the wheels caught, slamming back into their locks in the center of her and Rylan's morgue-esque operating theater. The suddenness of it sent Quin sliding forward, the skin on his back burned against the unforgiving metal table.

"Now," Clara exclaimed breathlessly. "Easy way or the hard way?" Her green eyes sparkled; a sinister yet playful look resided there as she repeated Quin's words back to him.

Confusion, realization, and finally anger, it threatened to consume him; she knew just how to push his buttons. "Hard way ."

"Did you know," Rylan interrupted, "that tethered hunters, while technically not vampires, share some of their same weaknesses?"

The hissing of pressurized air pulled Quin away from his staring contest with Clara as he searched for the sudden and alarming source of the sound. Rylan cradled a small tank in his left arm, tubing tangled in the grasp of his right.

"Don't worry, this won't kill you, but it is going to hurt." Quin met Rylan's empty eyes, feeling in this man nothing but cold calculation.

He was a fool, overly confident that he could get out of this situation unscathed. These people were no different than the monsters he hunted every night. Something about the emptiness he met in Rylan told him that this man wasn't above hurting him, especially if it meant getting what he was after.

"This will go a lot faster if you don't fight." Rylan suggested, knowing full well Quin wouldn't listen. That was fine, he was curious to see how long Quin could stave off unconsciousness.

Their hands held him tight, an aerosol mask pressed hard against his face. Quin smelled the plastic of the mask long before the acid within stung his throat and filled his lungs. He choked on it, thrashing against them, but it was too late. Pain turned into panic as his vision swam and the burning in his chest traveled through his muscles, every cell screaming for oxygen. He fought for every stinging breath, wheezing. Those dark eyes watched, unblinking as Quin succumbed to hypoxia, his airway sealing against itself.

Rylan was always careful, he'd learned through trial and error when enough became too much. Paying close attention, he looked for the exact moment Quin's eyes lost focus, his chest rise paused, and his flailing limbs fell slack. They had to be quick, the effect didn't last long. Thankfully Clara was three steps ahead: Restraints loosed, bed unlocked, and cell door open. It was with little grace or concern that they then deposited Quin's body to the concrete floor.

"We should really hire someone to do the heavy lifting," Clara complained, slamming the cell door closed.

Rylan nodded his agreement more out of habit than actual acknowledgement. He was preoccupied – body crouched, eyes focused intently on Quin. He watched for chest rise, waiting for the sputtering and choking coughs to begin. He'd used a higher percentage than normal to induce the pseudo-anaphylaxis; while he couldn't be sure, he had a hunch that Quin was more vampire than human these days. He had to be sure Quin didn't wake up before they got him in the cell.

One minute turned into two, the time excruciatingly slow until, finally, Quin stirred. His blue eyes focused once more and, for a second, Rylan was sure they'd flashed purple before he started breathing again. Wheezed coughs forced their way past a narrowed airway. The sound of Quin's choked gasps were music to their ears. Rylan's mask broke; peering in at Quin, he couldn't help but smile.

It was faint, nothing compared with Clara's, but attached to it was all the same malevolence and morbid curiosity. He'd never seen a hunter so completely bond with their counterpart and still manage to keep their humanity. Rylan wondered how much further Quin could change before completely succumbing. Confusion played across Quin's features, eyes wide as he took in his new surroundings, the fog of unconsciousness lifting slowly.

"Comfy?" Clara leaned in, resting her forehead on the steel bars of Quin's new prison.

Not surprisingly, Quin lunged, faster than Rylan thought possible; his arm hooked through the bars, grasping Clara by the back of the head. His hand tangled in her hair, forcing her attention and pinning her in place. Light lavender transcended to the deep red they'd seen reflected the night before.

"Going to kill me, hunter?" Clara met his eyes, daring him.

Rylan observed, unmoving. She had hoped it would come to this; Clara was nothing if not persistently antagonizing. It was her way of getting at the person you really were, the one you tried to hide away. She was good at finding the true nature of every monster they trapped within these walls.

Quin didn't respond, his grip on her unforgiving as he pulled her to her feet, his face close to hers. He could crush her against these bars, of that he was certain. Something within told him the feat was not beyond his current abilities.

– *'Vampires are born with their skills; control is the only thing they learn.'* Quin dropped Clara, doubt consuming him; was he really willing to hurt another person?

One step at a time Quin distanced himself, stopping only when his back met the far wall. It was there against the seamless cement wall that he saw himself, his reflection mirrored in the steel backsplash of the prison-sanctioned bathroom. These eyes, his eyes, they were the ones that haunted his dreams – just like Selene's. With calm clarity that he realized why he was here; it wasn't just to satiate their intrigue.

"Marc." Quin turned away from his reflection, meeting his captor's unblinking eyes. "He's my executioner."

Rylan nodded again, acknowledging his statement. He had no intention of following through with Quin's request. Quin would meet his end should he turn, but not until he and Clara had first been allowed their just dues. Quin didn't need to know that, or at least not right now.

"Just let me die before I lose myself completely." Quin's eyes locked on Rylan's. "If I turn, give me that much."

Rylan's smile bloomed fully across his face; he should have known Quin was just like her. "This, I swear." There were some requests even collectors couldn't ignore.

"Rest up; we'll find your vampire," Clara said with certainty. "If you can't control her, we will. A few months with us should help change her perspective."

Rylan stood, taking in the now despondent man before him. "If you know where she is or can reach her, she needs to present herself. If she resists, I can't promise we won't hurt her."

Quin said nothing; he wasn't in control right now, and until he was, he had no room to argue. He despised the smiles they both wore. They'd won, each one so smug. Thankfully, neither one felt like gloating as they cleaned up the mess he'd made of their tools; Clara even made an effort to toss his clothes through the bars for him.

"We may be collectors, but we aren't completely uncivilized." From crazed to nice in the same breath, Quin was convinced this woman was bipolar. "These will have to do for now."

He wasn't about to thank her, a shrugged acknowledgement was the best he could offer as he pulled his pants over his boxers and re-laced his belt, forgoing the blood-caked shirt; the smell of it made his stomach churn. His repulsion of it did not go unnoticed. Clara held her hand out for it, for which he was grateful, and a part of him felt intensely uneasy of this newfound aversion.

"Interesting." Rylan said to no one in particular; his intrigue often made him forget his manners. "Are you hungry?"

"Not for what you're insinuating." Quin backed away from the bars again, pacing the five-by-eight cell.

"Is there a chance that your repulsion has more to do with your connection to Eryn?" Rylan gestured to Quin's eyes, knowing that tethered hunters drew more from their counterparts when their eyes changed colors.

Again Quin shrugged; it was hard to tell how much of this was Eryn when she wasn't here. It could be her hunger that drove him now, or maybe it was a deeper need within his own blood. He really hoped it wasn't the latter.

"Do you know what happens when a vampire tries to eat food?" Rylan asked.

"I'm guessing it's why you have a toilet in here; that and a drain," Quin remarked, annoyed by Rylan's tone.

"Good. That will be your first test, then." Rylan turned to leave, Clara's sharp gaze upon him; she'd just finished putting her tools back in their designated places.

"If he purges, you're the one responsible; no offence." She glanced back at Quin. "Once was enough for me."

Quin ignored them, distracted by the waking pull of Eryn's mind against his; he was aware of the cool earth around her and the smell of it as it fell from her skin. Relocating slowly, his perspective was fractured by Eryn's. He stretched out on the cot within. His limbs felt distant and numb compared to the sensation of Eryn's as she pulled herself free. He had to concentrate – first to make sure his movements were controlled and natural, and second to ensure that what he said was actually said and not just thought as Eryn's psyche overlapped his own.

"I prefer savory foods of the medium-rare variety." Quin did his best to mock them. "And apple juice. If I'm going to puke, it should taste good at least."

Neither seemed interested in arguing with him; perhaps – despite the countless times they'd undoubtedly dealt with bodily fluids – their stomachs were still weak to the idea of cleaning up after others. Either way, he was grateful when they finally left. It was disorienting, trying to fight the pull of her perspective. He'd felt this way before, their senses intermingling but still separate. Now it felt like they were becoming one person, both aware and equally in control.

Quin draped his arm over his eyes, unaccustomed to the mixing of images. "Why'd you run?" There was no hiding the hurt he felt, not from her. She smiled, strained and sad, as she dusted the earth from her clothes.

'*Would you have let me go?*' Eryn's guilt stirred within him, '*What I needed to do, I couldn't have done with you.*'

Eryn's encounter with Selene replayed in his mind, granting Quin a greater understanding of her grief, the changes they'd both endured, and the cost she'd paid for the knowledge.

'*I choose freedom, both apart and a part of,*' her resolve caught him by surprise.

"There's no such thing as freedom," he said coldly. "Not from them."

This time, he pulled her to him, letting her see the bars that held him and the perfectly displayed tools left out for his viewing pleasure.

'*If they catch us, this will be our eternity,*' He didn't dare say the words out loud, he wasn't even sure he should be thinking them. "Sometimes, we just have to pick a side."

'*Then pick mine...*' her voice pleaded before her mind faded from his.

Quin struck out at the concrete wall, feeling his fingers give as the manmade stone cracked underneath. She was going to get them both killed.

CHAPTER TWENTY-FIVE

Selene waited, looking after her children until they rose. Derek first, his blood was stronger, followed by Eryn after a considerable amount of time. Selene had felt her stir earlier, her hunter interrupting the peace of sleep. Even now, as Eryn rose, Quin reached out to her. Selene sensed their connection, feeling the pressure build before fading away. Pain played across Eryn's features, her hurt reflected in the red of her eyes. Perfect, the less distracted she was, the more Selene could teach her.

"You don't need him; you aren't alone anymore." Selene spoke softly, lifting her child's face to look at her. "It's time you learned what you are from your own kind."

Dirt and beautiful, ruby eyes, Selene knew Eryn was still processing her blood and the knowledge that whispered to her there. To be truly awakened, Selene had so much to teach her – but first to the bath. They needed to wash away the earth, and with it, her human life. A baptism, of sorts, to the night; it was purely ceremonial, but still powerful. This old building with open rafters and exposed brick was the beginning of their coven. It had been a church once, and while not all churches had a baptism pool, this one did. Selene often enjoyed cleaning herself there after going to ground and swore it cleansed her better than any shower.

"He's a part of me," Eryn said, finally able to break free from the whispers.

"Of course he is," Selene agreed, liberating her youngest from the earth that weighed heavy against her still buried legs.

There was a process to being born, a process that Quin had interrupted. Selene was going to make it right, though, and give her youngest the knowledge and strength required to be a creator. It was the least she could do after failing to save her family; she would give Eryn the power to create her own one day.

Step by step the dirt fell free as the blood awakened in Eryn's veins. Centuries of knowledge lived within – knowledge she couldn't begin to understand – but that was alright; Selene would teach her.

"Why does it still hold her?" Derek asked, helping Selene guide Eryn upstairs.

"It whispers something different to us all upon waking. It has been so long since you were born, you just don't remember," Selene said softly, not wishing to break the spell the blood still held. "Now leave us."

Derek stepped aside, lingering at the threshold only a moment to watch as Selene led Eryn into the baptistery. She removed Eryn's dirty clothes with a delicateness he thought beyond her capabilities. The light caramel skin was clean beneath the tattered clothes save for where Selene's blood held the dirt to her. Derek observed as Selene treaded the water, her dark dress flowing around her in the clear blue of the pool, arms outstretched. She reminded him of an iris, her gown flowing around her like petals, the fabric entwining them both as Eryn stepped into the water to meet Selene.

He left then, abandoning Selene to her ceremony; he'd never seen her behave this way. Not with him anyway. He didn't understand why she'd waited so long to claim what was hers, but it was beginning to make sense. Those red eyes, they were the same as hers. Derek wondered if Selene would be just as keen of Quin if she knew how her blood had changed him.

If there was anything left of their previous coven, Selene might not be so careless with an unaligned fledgling. Her recklessness, Derek feared, was going to get them killed – if not by the hunters, then by the Progenitors; they were the unseen watchers, the ones trusted to safeguard and control the covens and vampires within. Derek was worried, certain his maker was lost, lost to him and to herself.

———

Their words started off soft, distant yet near, surrounding me until there was nothing left but their harsh and demanding voices. I almost understood them as they whispered to me, but the more I focused on one voice, the more the others distorted and cried out to be heard. Some of them were reassuring, while others chided. I'd heard them on the first night I awakened alone. It was the blood that guided me, telling me what I was and what I would become. This time, though, these voices were not of the ones who had made me. These voices belonged to the ones who came before.

This was transference; everything we were and would become was carried in the blood, in our blood. It was creation and destruction, life and decay, beautiful yet ugly, just as likely to save as it was to kill – if you knew how. I couldn't tell how many lives existed within our strain; I lost count of the voices in my head as she washed me, cleansing me of who I was before.

The pressure of them fighting in me was enough to make me forget myself, each life within desperate to share, teach, and protect. This was how we survived, how we ensured our bloodlines survived when the hunters came, because they always came. My mind ached with the weight of it all.

"Stop, please," I begged; it was too much, I couldn't process the noise of them. "Please."

I felt her then, warm hands cupping my face. The sensation of her pulled me from myself. Selene's face came into focus. The blue of her eyes and gold of her hair was mesmerizing. She gave me a way out of my head, an escape from the cacophony of it. Was this what schizophrenia felt like? The turmoil I'd found in those afflicted had been horrendous, but the possibility of actually experiencing it for the briefest of moments was engrossing and terrifying.

"Please," I pleaded again, but this time to Selene. "Make it stop."

"It will not stop." She spoke kindly. "Not until the blood has taught you all you need to know, and even then, it can still call to you."

This truth was hollowing. It meant there was nothing I could do but wait. To this I nodded, accepting the cost of knowledge and of the truth I'd sought. I could hear it now, the whispers calling to me, urging me to take heed, to hear them, to listen. It was all I could do as Selene pulled me from the water, clothing me before leading me farther into the sanctuary of the old church. This is where she left me, but not alone. Derek sat among the scattered pews, waiting until he was sure Selene was gone.

"Has your hunter turned?" Derek's mind burned; he was just as curious of me now as when we first met.

"No." I paused, waiting for a lull, the hushed tones like static on a TV I couldn't turn off. "That's not how we are made."

Pain exploded behind my eyes, instant and unforgiving. The ferocity at which the voices converged on me was extraordinary; had I not already been sitting, the force of it would have dropped me. It took everything I had not to scream as I clenched my jaw, forehead pressed tightly to the dusty floorboards. If I didn't know any better, I could have sworn I felt dozens of hands pressing me there, holding me captive in the error I had made: this knowledge was not to be shared, of this I was certain.

I wasn't sure if it was obligation that drove Derek to me, but I was thankful. He hesitated, reaching for me slowly before gently resting his hand on the back of my neck. His palm was rough and cool against my skin; the distraction of it soothed me. This was not the first time he'd helped someone like me. He was concerned, the feel of it thick in my chest.

"You need to feed," Derek consoled, just the same as he had in the alleyway where we'd first met.

"I'm not hungry," I replied, the voices within barely restrained by my psyche. The distraction his present provided me was just enough to relieve the pain from my earlier mistake.

"I didn't ask if you were hungry." The irritation in his voice made me regret his closeness and his grasp on my neck. "This is why the hunters should leave well enough alone. They do more harm than good." I heard Derek sigh, his mind frustrated and angry before settling once more. "Feeding will ease the pain."

Derek's earlier irritation made sense to me; between his mind and the whispers I understood his meaning. The truth was that I was always hungry. My vice may satiate, but the urge to feed and the desire for more never vanished. I didn't need it, but I always wanted it. What I realized was that by not feeding more, I was creating a deficit. My avoidance prevented me from learning control.

"I can't." I felt the thirst stirring within me, the ache of it always present. "Not like you."

"There is more than one way to feed." I expected to be met with irritation or disgust at my response, but instead found sincerity and understanding. "Not everyone we feed on is unwilling."

I nodded, finally able to pull myself back to a seated position. His hand fell away from me, obsidian eyes unreadable as he sat beside me, waiting without expectation.

"Do you kill them?" My eyes never left his, recalling the smell of him when we'd first met, his clothes saturated with blood.

"Do you believe there are no humans deserving of death?" Derek smirked, sharp teeth visible through his half smile.

I found no doubt within the vault of his mind. Neither was there guilt, remorse, or hesitation… To be so certain, it was exciting and horrifying.

"No," I conceded, there were plenty of people who deserved to die.

"There are worse predators in this world than you and me," Derek stated plainly. "Live long enough and you'll come to understand the insignificance of a life."

The black pools of his eyes held no emotion, no empathy; I wondered how long he had lived to care so little. His stoic features and demeanor reminded me of Marc. There was a darkness too, again reminding me of Marc. Derek seemed distant, but not uncaring. I let my mind wander as his did, taking in my surroundings. Pews lined the outskirts of the church's sanctuary; they'd been scattered haphazardly to allow for the open space Derek and I now occupied.

Bare wooden rafters and intricate archways decorated the ceiling overhead, merging perfectly with wooden columns in the exposed brick and broken plaster. A circular alter sat at the deepest part of the sanctuary, pristine except for the overturned pulpit. Stained glass lined the back wall, its half-moon shape complimenting the curve of the stage. I could just imagine the light of early morning illuminating this room in shades of blue, red, and gold as the sun hit it. They'd been renovating, clearing the church of its unnecessary parts in order to create a home – to rebuild the coven.

My stomach sank, the voices whispering once more of bloodlines, survival, and the death that was required in creation. My nature betrayed me, threatening to overtake my reason as my head began to swim again. The demons in my blood were gnawing at me, the pain of it sharp in my veins. They spoke to me, promising sweet relief in the nectar of another's life. The urge to consume was stronger than before.

Amongst the commotion and noise stirring within my mind was a soft, yet clear, voice – one that spoke of the bonding of the coven through the sharing of blood, and fortification of the young by the old. The first time Selene had fed me it had torn through me and healed the damage done. The second time destroyed and rebuilt what already was. This was forced evolution. Selene had fed the curse, strengthening

282

and changing my being at a much faster rate. The forced growth of the young ensured our survival, but there was danger in providing the young ones with strength not earned and powers beyond their control.

I groaned, feeling her blood and hunger burn through me. Any semblance of control I'd learned with Quin was lost in the face of this new and extraordinary desire to devour. How was it that something could feel so good and bad at the same time? I felt my panic then, like ice in my limbs and across my skin. I didn't know what I was capable of anymore; could I stop? Was I strong enough to resist and fight the urges overtaking me? No. This was bigger than me. Stronger. Darker. This was something instinctual, and it was devouring my self-control. This was the price of strength and knowledge not earned.

Sensing my impending frenzy, Derek wrapped an arm around my waist, lifting me from the floor. He held me to him, twisting my left arm and pinning it behind me while his right arm looped under my right to cross my chest before firmly grasping my throat. With his added height and strength Derek easily lifted me from the ground, his hold on my throat just tight enough to make my eyes water. Reaching up with my free right hand, I was just able to pull against his hold, affording me enough relief to breathe. Everything in me screamed to fight and break free of him. It was hard not to react, but I sensed no danger from him, or at least none so long as I cooperated.

"If you fight it, it will blind you. Control isn't learned with avoidance." His breath was warm against the side of my face, the tone of it heavy in my ear.

That's when I understood. Selene had returned. I smelled it on her, saw it red on her lips. The same beautiful color reflected in her eyes. There were three too many people within the confines of this church. I could hear their heartbeats as they neared.

"I thought you'd be hungry." She said knowingly, beckoning the first beating heart forward.

He would be the first one I killed; fear erupted through me as Selene led him to me. I struggled then, the smell of him too near, but Derek held me tight. The closer he got, the more I wanted it. My grasp on Derek loosening as I reached for the man behind Selene.

"Don't worry," Derek whispered. "I won't let you kill them, unless you want to, that is."

I shook my head, my eyes never leaving the man in front of me. I had no doubt that if left to my own devices there would be nothing left of this stranger. There would also be nothing left of me.

"Suit yourself; it will be harder this way." The implications of his words were lost on me as he relinquished his hold.

I was vaguely aware of the scars that laced the man's throat where I bit. Selene's look of approval was all but lost to me as I fed. I was engrossed; there was nothing but me, the man named Evrett, and his blood as it spilled from him to me. His memories flooded my mind as I drank him in, greedily swallowing his hopes and dreams as I erased his very identity. There was nothing but the taste of his blood and the feeling of pain – his or mine I was unsure – as they ripped us apart.

I hit the ground hard enough to bounce, dust exploding from the floorboards. I inhaled it, choking as I fought to catch my breath. The loss of Evrett was maddening. Derek had said it would be hard, but this, this was worse than hunger. This was addiction, but not just mine. Evrett called out, his pain and mine alike, both of us desperate for a second more. I moved to oblige him, everything in me willing to take back what I'd said to Derek as his size-twelve boot pinned me back to the floor.

If there had been any air left in my lungs I would have cursed him. Hungry and desperate, I struck out, his weight doubled, threatening to crack my ribs. It took everything I had to lace my fingers around his boot and grant the slightest bit of reprieve in which to breathe. His obsidian eyes stared down at me, daring me to try fighting him. The pain of it was sobering.

"It will pass," Derek assured me.

It didn't feel like there was anything but this need. It was a cancer that eroded my bones, breaking me apart a little bit more every time I gave in.

"Savor it." I heard Selene's voice call out to me, my next victim tangled in her arms.

If I could have, I would have screamed. Derek was right, the need of it was fading. I didn't want more, didn't want to feel the loss of myself again so soon. His boot had become my safety net, holding me back. He saw my hesitation, reading the fear in my eyes.

"This is how you learn." No sympathy, no malice, just the loss of his restraint as he released me.

Selene brought another to me, the smell of this woman just as enticing as Evrett had been. I reeled back, desperately trying not to lose myself, and what was left of my restraint, at this woman's throat. I didn't get far; my back met the cool brick wall just as Selene forced the woman to her knees before me.

"Slowly," Selene demanded of me, dragging one clawed finger across the woman's collarbone.

I flattened myself against the wall, my feet finding no purchase as she leaned into me. Warm blood dripped across my bare leg and, again, I was lost in the taste of it. Lacey nestled in my lap as I fed. Slowly I took her in, entwining my being with hers as I digested her drop by drop. I plucked away her fear, savoring the taste before moving on to the next emotion. I had to fight not to take it all away at once like I'd done to Evrett.

Lacey's body responded to me as she processed the high, finding her escape within me, just like Quin. She gave me freely the things that hurt her: the memories of her lovers' faces, the feel of them, and the pain when they left. With every piece of her I consumed, she too fed – internalizing the relief that came with forgetting and the bliss of being truly needed, even if it was by another monster.

We spiraled, her need of me fueling mine until, again, I was ripped away from the ecstasy of feeding. Once more Derek held me; my head spun with the loss of her. He used my disorientation to lift me to my feet. His hand pressed just under my neck as he pinned me to the back wall. I couldn't focus, my body drunk on them, confused. I didn't understand why he had pulled me away, and it made me angry. I tried to break away from his grasp, needing to return to the sweet abyss of Lacey's demons. It was easier there. I didn't have to think, didn't have to care, and didn't have to be.

"This time," Derek leveled his eyes with mine, voice serious, "you're alone."

"No." I shook my head, drunk. I couldn't pull myself from the taste of them on my lips or the feel of them in my veins. The escape I found within the beating of their hearts as I ingested their emotions was captivating. The taste better than the air I breathed.

The next one called to me in a way the others hadn't. His turmoil and the way his mind called out for an escape was louder than the rest. I knew this song well; it was the same one I heard every night in Oceanside. This was a song sung by the ones who suffered beyond repair. Derek's grip fell from me. I was mesmerized by the black aura that rippled around the damaged man before me. I'd never seen so much violence and hopelessness reflected within one person. It was enchanting. His energy captivated me as he drew near.

His dead eyes met mine. "She said you might need encouragement." His deep voice held no inflection as he drug a knife down his forearm.

I met his outstretched arm, breathing in the jam-like sweetness of his blood before taking hold. Crimson-slick, it trailed from him to me before I could bring it to my mouth. I felt him relax, hearing him sigh as I enveloped him. Slowly, just like before, I needed to know why his suffering called to me, why it drew me to him.

There was something about the way he felt – his subconscious was heavier, guarded. He wasn't giving me what I wanted. Selfishly, I began picking apart his psyche, taking what I needed in order to truly feed. To feed and be fed upon was a give and take, or at least it was for me.

Brick by brick I tore down Neil's walls until there was nowhere left to hide. He tried to pull away, the lull of his high interrupted, but I held tight, sinking my teeth in deep. His blood poured into me, securing my grasp on him mentally and physically as I pulled him back under.

He was thirteen, the stench of gunpowder, singed hair, and burnt skin made him want to puke. Pulling the trigger hadn't been the hard part, it was aiming. He'd pulled the trigger until the revolver in his hand click-click-clicked, his hands numb from the recoil. They'd told him it had to be him; they'd never expect a kid, so he did it. He wasn't sure why it had mattered, but he liked the way it felt, and now they all seemed to like him. He'd call that a win.

His emotions burst forth, hot in my chest; he was proud of his accomplishment, indifferent to the cost. Better the other guy than him.

He was eighteen and today he was happy. Today they had a different job for him, which was nice. He hated running from the cops; being caught wasn't so bad, but he was too old for juvie now. Now when he hurt people he didn't have to worry about getting hurt back. It was pretty easy; they said it would be. Neil just had to be sure they talked before he finished the job.

Again, Neil's pride flowed through me; he'd earned this promotion and the respect that came along with it.

He was certain he got everything he'd needed from this man. His face was swollen and split; he was sure he'd broken all of his ribs, too. All he had to do now was make sure no one could identify the body. His muscles already ached from his earlier efforts, so he wanted to make this quick – that and he had a date to get cleaned up for.

It was easier than he thought it would be, placing this man's open mouth over the edge of the cinder block. Then again, it was hard to resist when you were unconscious. Neil wasn't even sure if the guy would feel it. No matter, he didn't have to worry about causing pain now; this was about finishing up.

The first stomp snapped the man's jaw loose, the heel of his boot crunching through the back of the already cracked skull. By the third and fourth, he wasn't moving anymore – and on the plus side: he'd knocked out a bunch of teeth. That was going to save him a lot of time. He'd call that a win.

Neil's emotions burned through me as I swallowed more of him down. Every one of them came to life within me. The power he felt as he drove his boot down – over and over until it was finished – radiated through me; next came the odd satisfaction he got as another tooth broke loose, despite the tediousness of it; then his relief at having finished another job; and, finally, the satisfaction he felt at having destroyed another man.

The deeper I went, the closer I got to the energy that drew me to Neil, and the louder his subconscious called. Something in him resonated with me in a way that I couldn't ignore. I let instinct drive me forward as I held tightly to him; I was vaguely aware of the pain I was causing him. Neil was no longer a willing victim, and he knew it as I forced my way deeper into his mind.

He remembered the blue of her dress, the way the fabric felt on his skin, the way she smelled – soft like silk and flowers on a warm summer day. He remembered the way she could make him forget about work, the way she made him smile...

A familiar pain ricocheted through me – loss. Neil struck out, knife in hand. Even if he could have stabbed me with it, the steel wouldn't have left much of a mark. As long as my mind held him, he'd never be able to hurt me. My right hand caught the wrist of his left, crushing the bones just as he'd done to so many others. I twisted his right forearm at the same time, feeling the joint give at the elbow as it tore free of his flesh. The pain of it dropped him to his knees. I held his arms in mine, turned at impossible angles as I bit into his throat.

Blood: it was all he smelled anymore. It was in his pores, stuck under his nails, staining his soul. It coated his hands, sticky and cold. He told her to stop, she couldn't leave, couldn't just take their kid. So he hit her and kept hitting her until she didn't move anymore. He'd hit her until he couldn't remember what her face looked like; until he couldn't remember why he was mad.

I tore his memories from him, absorbing his anger in order to catalyze my own. The harder he struggled the more I consumed, until he was breathless.

'Look at what you made me do!' Neil screamed, knuckles swollen. She'd taken everything he loved, without her he was nothing and now, now she'd be nothing. Her and their child…

It hurt worse than the crushed, throbbing bones in his wrist; worse than the twisted, burning joint of his elbow; worse than the migraine that was exploding behind his eyes; and I understood. I understood the tearing and suffocating finality of loss that squeezed his chest. Slowly, I pulled away, watching as his blood trickled down his chest.

"Look at what you made me do." I whispered, burying the steel of his knife between the third and fourth rib, puncturing his heart; at least it wouldn't hurt him anymore. That was what he wanted after all, why his mind called out to me. It was too bad he hadn't realized what he'd been asking for this whole time was death.

Fireworks exploded in his ribcage, his heart pumping harder and harder against the steel edge, shredding the muscle to pieces as it fought to supply oxygen to his brain and muscles. Desperate to escape, he pushed away. The edge of the blade scraped against his sternum as he fell back. The tearing pain built until the pressure of it forced blood from the wound. I could feel him dying.

Neil looked down at the wound, confused by the warmth as it leaked from him, near black against the blue of his shirt. He understood now, his mind heavy as hypoxia blurred his vision; a choked laugh left his lips.

'*This is what it feels like to die*,' he thought; the realization brought with it a spark of fear, followed by acceptance; the loss of him was dark and absolute in my mind as the weight of what I'd done slammed into me. The blade fell from my hand. The harsh clang of steel against wood severed my connection in the oblivion of Neil's lifeless mind; I couldn't get away fast enough – not from him and not from myself.

The church was filled with the smell his too-sweet blood, suffocating me until I escaped the confines of its walls. The night air wasn't any kinder; cool and sharp, it burned its way down my throat. Every inhale was painful as I tried to slow my breathing, my mind racing.

"Don't," I snapped, feeling Derek's approach. Head swimming, hands shaking, I tried not to hyperventilate. He thought I was weak; his face may have been blank, but his mind wasn't – not to me.

Anger bubbled just under the surface; Derek's thoughts kept tugging at my concentration, testing my self-control. He couldn't understand why I was upset. They'd known from the beginning what Neil was. Made sure to save the monster for last, that way if I broke the promise to myself at least I'd be able to say the world was better without him; because then at least I wouldn't have to feel bad; because then I'd realize…

"Stop," I cursed him, my fists clenched, desperately trying to keep myself contained.

"Why do you mourn him?" he asked.

"You. Promised." My voice shook, each word forced.

"You're mad at me?" Amusement flickered in his eyes.

I unclenched my fists, exhaling slowly the last of my restraint. "You. Promised." Gravity shifted around us, crushing the scattered leaves and branches in the courtyard, and suddenly Derek didn't look so amused.

I sensed his intentions long before he moved to meet me, blade drawn. I had no doubt that had he reached me, I wouldn't have lasted five seconds. His strength would win every time – but strength was not where my power lay as I drove him to his hands and knees.

———

Derek lunged, meeting the gravity of her mind recklessly. The force of it was extraordinary as his knees buckled; the gravel of the court-yard bit deeply into his palms as he struggled to hold himself up. Eryn's anger pierced his temples like a knife, burning through him as it blinded his other senses.

"You promised." She spoke the words again. Her anger shifted. The piercing white hot of it twisted into a sticky and dark self-loathing. The promise broken was not his, but her own.

Her hold on him weakened slowly, her thoughts turning inward. When Derek could fully stand again, he was met by the effervescent green of her eyes. Pain was reflected there. He understood then, just before her mind completely slipped away from his. She hated the ease at which she had killed him, angry at how good it felt to take his life. She knew, time and time again, that no matter how much self-control she learned, she'd kill Neil every time.

The promise had been hers; Eryn was upset because she knew it was one she'd never be able to keep again, not after this. She'd fed on his death and it completed her vice – as it did each and every vampire's. Sweet and dark in her mind, the consumption of a person's very last moment was better than the blood.

CHAPTER TWENTY-SIX

Selene watched from the church as Derek chased after her youngest. It was amusing, if not a little tiring, looking after them. She had to ensure neither one truly hurt the other. They'd just have to learn each other's boundaries. It amazed her just how strong they were, both in character and abilities.

She never expected her blood to express itself so differently between them – but then again, she was nothing like her own maker. She should be pleased by their differences; the strength of a coven depended on the diversity of its members after all. The commotion of their presence destroyed the quiet serenity of the courtyard. She'd almost intervened when Derek threw himself forward, his intent as severe as the blade in his hand.

That's when she felt the concussive force of Eryn's mind, it was enough to drive Derek to his knees. Eryn's mind pried at her unsuccessfully as Selene walled herself off, forcing the pressure of it back. As most young did, Eryn relied heavily on her emotions to actuate her innate abilities. This meant the effects were not only limited, but weak.

As expected, Eryn's control faded quickly from Derek. There was much they needed to teach her. Selene wasn't sure what had transpired between the two, but she was pleased to see them regard each other a bit more kindly, if not a bit more hesitantly. This fighting was to be expected, especially between siblings.

"You were never going to be able to keep that promise." Derek spoke first, softer and quieter than Selene was used to – except when speaking to the women he killed.

Selene was curious now, watching the two of them. The glowing red of Eryn's eyes softened, turning a delicate shade of brown and hazel until the green fully returned. She wasn't looking at him – or anything, Selene realized, the focus lost in the gleaming emerald pools. The clean linen dress she'd put Eryn in clung to her frame, blood adhering the fabric to skin and painting red down her arms and legs.

"I know." Eryn exhaled the words, speaking them both as an acknowledgement and as a defeat before stepping past Derek, pausing as she met Selene in the doorway.

Selene had no words for her and no way of understanding; this is what she had seen exchanged between the two of them: understanding. All she was capable of was indifference. She knew not how to relate to the struggles of the blood that her youngest faced. This is where Derek thrived. Selene could keep Eryn alive, feed her, but despite all of the primal mothering she provided, Selene knew she was incapable of truly nurturing anyone. There was only survival.

"Clean yourself before you start to stink; tomorrow we begin anew, until you learn." Selene's tone held no softness, only expectation.

There was no time for coddling. The Progenitors would call on her soon. Selene had to be sure they could survive. Eyes low, Eryn left them. Derek hadn't moved. His stillness was uncanny; he might as well have been a statue, dark hair and eyes against olive skin. He'd always passed more as human than the others, except for that predatory stillness. The sickly, sweet concentrate of Derek's blood filled the courtyard; it dripped from his palms to the autumn leaves below. He needed to feed, but Selene had given up trying to keep him fed long ago. She was beginning to think starvation was part of his ritual.

"How long will you torture this one?" Selene smiled; the stink of his blood all around her.

"Is that what you think I'm doing?" Derek asked, no hint of a question in his tone.

"I'm sure I do not wish to know what it is you take from those women." Selene could see the hunger in his eyes, his blade still poised at his side.

"Perhaps not," Derek answered simply. "When's the last time you fed on anything other than their terror?" His dark eyes locked on hers. "I don't know how you stomach the taste of it."

"My," Selene spoke languidly, "how brave you are when you're hungry."

She'd stepped from the doorway as she addressed him. Jaw clenched, he craned his neck as she neared. Silence was all he gave her, his tall frame towering over hers. Derek didn't dare move; he'd learned a long time ago to never turn from her. As much as Selene hated insubordination, she loathed cowardice more. Violence and blood, it's all she was anymore. Until Eryn.

"Go," she said finally, seeing no fight in him. "Bury the body. I have more pressing matters to deal with tonight." Out of respect, she stepped aside for him, a sense of pride washing over her at his determination to face her despite the fear seeping from his pores.

Four long strides and he was gone. Selene could hear his footsteps resonating in the church, stopping once he met the corpse named Neil. Silently, she crept back in, looking to Derek's crouched form in the pool of what was left of the blood. He'd never put away his knife. Selene had a sneaking suspicion why just as he dragged it across Neil's skin.

She didn't need to see Derek's face to see the enjoyment he got out of doing this. Even the dead couldn't keep their secrets from him; he was the only one she knew who could convene in this way. He was feeding, but not in a way Selene recognized. It was perverse. Say what he would about her, but at least she was honest; she didn't sustain herself on the secrets of the dead and dying. In the end, she didn't really care what he did with the body. He could carve it up and feed it to the children of the city so long as it was gone when she returned. Selene left the same way she'd arrived: silently.

The old stone fence of the courtyard was bathed in the silver light of the moon, the air cool and fresh. It was always about to rain in this city; she smelled it in the air, felt the moisture around her. Sometimes, she even caught the scent of the ocean, the salty air close and familiar to her heart. Selene never considered herself the nostalgic type, but now, as she left the church in her wake she couldn't help but think she might be leaving something behind. She realized, as her mind wandered to times long past, that it felt like home. Their coven wasn't perfect, but it was finally complete; she wouldn't apologize for that.

Selene had no destination in mind when she departed, just an insatiable urge to return. Every night since siring Eryn she had set out like this, awaiting the night she'd have to answer for the lives taken and the coven she'd destroyed. There were laws, though not set in stone, and she had explicitly defied them.

The memory left a bad taste in her mouth as she recalled the betrayal of her kin. Their corrupted attempt to create had nearly cost her both of her children. One lost to their hunger and the other almost stolen by the hunters. Anger burned inside of her like an ember. What they had done was devour, none of them strong enough to sire.

Fists clenched, Selene's pace quickened as her body heat rose. She wasn't out here to hide, she wasn't going to plead, and she didn't need to be forgiven, not after what they had done. The coven hadn't acted in its best interest. No, they'd taken from her, sealing their fate before Selene had ever burned them.

The corners of her mouth lifted; a cruel and crazed smile shattered the porcelain of her face. Selene took great pleasure in melting away their flesh, the heat of her cracking their bones, engulfing them until all that was left was dust. The pain she'd caused them was nothing compared to the pain they had inflicted. They'd bitten and force fed, recklessly consuming and poisoning the bodies of her children. Even if she had been able to revive Alexander, his body was too damaged. Parts of him had been torn to the bone; even her blood couldn't heal what was left of him.

They'd started with him, she was sure of it – breaking him as they fed, testing their theories on him until either his body gave out or the poison of them destroyed him. The violence of it was an abomination of the laws, the sharing of the blood, and the life that was to be given instead of taken.

They had wanted so badly to create that they risked the manifestation of ghouls, creatures without minds and of rotting bodies. For years she had denied to share her knowledge, denying their requests to strengthen their numbers – for even more unlawful than the killing of your own was the creation of another without permission. They'd known Selene had been waiting for the right time to claim her chosen children. What she didn't understand was why they couldn't wait, why they'd stolen them from her, why they thought they needed to force her hand.

No, she didn't regret killing them – not as they screamed, their blood boiling and bursting from them just as black as the charcoaled bones underneath. She'd gladly do it again just to feel the slickness of their organs in her hands. She'd destroy them the same way they'd destroyed her children, tearing them apart piece by piece until nothing was left. There was never going to be enough violence or blood to satiate the hatred she felt for them.

Every night she set out with no destination in mind, only to return to the skeletal remains of brick and mortar, bones of charred steel peeking through the devastation she had wrought on the coven. Soon there would be nothing left to remind her of them and this place; the humans would reclaim the land and erase from it their presence. Maybe then she could stop returning, stop reliving that night, stop the sorrow and anger that played in her mind.

CHAPTER TWENTY-SEVEN

Rylan watched her chest rise and fall, he was so close. He knew if they had a little more time he could find a way to kill Hannah.

"That was sixty-eight, one for every family you destroyed." He clapped; it was a slow, soft noise, signaling his defeat and the acknowledgement of her abilities. "It's too bad; it really would have been easier for you to die here."

Hannah's form had begun to show signs of damage; the bruised color under her eyes and the thinness of her skin was truly beautiful. It was only a matter of time before she'd completely lose herself; there was a price for her powers and if she didn't feed soon, it wouldn't be Alistair that killed her. The curse would consume her, cannibalizing her mind and body in a desperate attempt to sustain itself. She'd become a ghoul. He doubted that even she could reverse that damage.

The hair on the back of Rylan's neck stood on end; he always knew when Alistair was present even when he never made a sound. It was beyond his comprehension how silent they could be. Alistair's small frame stood just through the double doors, no sway evident in the hinges.

"As promised, she is yours. If we had more time, I'm sure we could find a way to break her." Rylan turned to meet those silver eyes, startled by their brightness – even under fluorescent lights.

"She's paid your price; release her," Alistair demanded.

Rylan hesitated, watching as Hannah's starved and crazed eyes took them both in. Alistair's focus shifted from Hannah to him, silver eyes slow to acknowledge him. Rylan had no doubt Alistair could just as easily kill Hannah inside the cylinder as out, but he wasn't going to argue. Despite the childlike tenor of his voice, there was no innocence held within.

"Fine." Rylan agreed unhappily. Maybe he'd get one more chance to kill her himself, though he doubted a silver bullet would do much.

Doing as asked, Rylan disengaged the locks at the base of the cylinder. This would allow the mechanism overhead to lift away the enclosure. It was a slow process, one that gave him plenty of time to move away. Strategically, he placed himself behind Alistair, fully expecting Hannah to charge; in the face of his own death, Rylan liked to imagine that's what he'd do. It was better to die fighting than cowering, but that's exactly what Hannah did as the safety of her glass prison lifted away: cower. Muscles emaciated, she crawled backwards. Not even her own freedom or hunger was enough to make her fight.

It was pathetic and bewildering. Had she preyed upon children because she lacked the ability to kill anything stronger than herself?

"Oh," Clara exclaimed with false surprise as she stumbled in. "Playing with her, then?"

Rylan watched as Hannah forced herself to her hands and knees, desperate to escape. Alistair waited until she settled against the back wall before advancing. In the sixty-eight times Rylan had tried to kill her, she'd never spoke to him; never pleaded, just screamed; but now, the words spilled from her freely as Alistair approached.

For months he'd waited patiently for her confession, needing her secrets and pitiful negotiations. It was insulting to see her so scared now, after all the things he'd done to her. Hannah's words fell from her, frantic and fevered; her arms outstretched to ward off Alistair's progress; his slow stride never changing. Rylan was curious to hear what it was she was so desperate to share.

"No." Her voice cracked like glass. "I've paid the price, please. I'm sorry." Hannah was huddled in the corner, knees pulled in tight; her long auburn hair was all that clothed her from them.

Alistair either wasn't listening or didn't care as he met her. Rylan circled, gaining a better view of them both. Auburn fire pleaded with liquid silver. Clara stayed in place; she'd afford no more of her energy to lost prey.

"They're dead; they're all dead." Her eyes searched Alistair's for understanding.

"We already know about the children," Clara barked, annoyed. Unlike Rylan, she didn't enjoy the pleas of the dying.

"No." Hannah shook her head. "It wasn't me. The others, they stole them, and then her eyes." She was trembling now. "Like that hunter's."

Rylan felt Clara's eyes on him. "Which hunter?" she asked.

"I paid the price," Hannah pleaded, groveling at Alistair's feet. "She killed them for stealing them. Selene, the one with red eyes, destroyed the coven when they tried to create."

Alistair didn't move, not to distance himself from her failing body and not to address the hunters waiting behind him.

"Please," she groaned into the floor, too weak to hold herself up.

"Did you know she could lead us to the creator?" Clara asked, her features harsh.

"My actions are not dependent upon your understanding, hunter." Alistair spoke slowly, never turning from Hannah.

"Maybe not *Progenitor*, but even you must answer to laws," Clara retorted with a seriousness that gave Rylan pause.

He'd had never heard Clara speak to anyone the way she spoke to Alistair now. The air between them was statically charged; it made the hair on the back of his neck stand on end once more.

"Ask, then." Alistair turned, a smile marring his features, the demon underneath barely hidden.

"Are you still bound to our service, Progenitor, or is your task done?" Clara never wavered, her eyes just as intense and unforgiving as those that peered back at her.

Rylan didn't assume to know anything of what they spoke. In every district they served, there was always one like Alistair, always bound to Clara. Never once had he questioned the alliances formed; neither had he ever seen Clara question the alliance. Perhaps more concerning was the way she stood, her body clearly placed between Alistair and the only exit. There was only one way they could stop Alistair, and it didn't involve either of them escaping with their lives.

The intensity of his smile never faded and for a second Rylan thought they'd call each other's bluffs – but Clara didn't bluff; there was a failsafe, one Rylan was sure not even Hannah could survive.

"I am bound yet to you, Clara, but my task is not done." He bowed mockingly. "Should our paths diverge, you will know." Alistair returned to his full height. "Now," he said decisively, "I need you to feed her."

"You can't be serious? She'll bleed us dry." Rylan laughed, forgetting himself.

"If she wasn't willing to earlier, she won't now." Alistair replied confidently.

Rylan all but gawked in disbelief. He couldn't be serious. But when he looked back, expecting the same reaction in Clara, he froze. Her green eyes set; she'd made up her mind.

"Fine," Clara growled.

Rylan watched, unsure of his role as Clara peeled off her extra shirts. Three layers lay at her feet before she revealed the last layer: a thin silk tank top with lace straps. He hadn't realized how thin she was or just how many scars she bore. How had he never noticed? Her body was malformed in the places she'd been cut or bitten to many times to heal properly. Her pale eyes didn't meet his as she moved past to confront Hannah's withered frame.

Clara forced the collapsed monster to sit up. She did this with no pretense of kindness or patience as she crouched behind Hannah. She wrapped an arm forward and around the vampire's neck, simultaneously supporting and pressing herself to the monster.

"You stop when I say or Rylan will put a silvered hollow-point in your skull. I'd love to see you heal around that." Clara looked at him, unflinching, as Hannah bit down hard.

Without hesitation Rylan met Clara on the floor, the barrel of Quin's Ruger pressed tight against Hannah's skull. He may not understand what was going on, but this he could do.

"Thanks," Clara whispered apologetically as Hannah consumed her.

For the first time, Clara looked truly exhausted, her eyes closing after a few minutes. He didn't know what to say to her, so he counted... sixteen... twelve... eight, her respirations slowing. When she opened her eyes again, they were unfocused and heavy.

"That's enough." Clara pulled away, meeting no resistance from Hannah as she shoved the vampire away harshly.

Hannah grunted from the abruptness of it. Clara's blood spilled from her mouth to streak the white tile red beneath her. By the look in her eyes, Rylan thought she might try to reclaim the lost sustenance; alas Hannah composed herself before doing so.

"What now?" Clara hissed, bracing her arm tight against her chest.

"Now, we find the creator," Alistair answered nonchalantly. "This one will show us where to find Selene, and then her life is her own."

Clara smiled weakly at this, but agreed. "Fine, but tell me this. Knowing what you do now, will you still kill Selene?"

Alistair paused, contemplative. "I don't have an answer yet. It seems she may have done us both a favor by destroying a coven full of heretics."

Before Hannah could register the threat in Alistair's tone, Clara stole all intended serious as she vomited, violently splattering the red tinged tile with yellow bile and stringy saliva.

Alistair didn't hide the look of disgust on his face or in tone. "Clean up. Tonight I hunt."

"Not without me," Clara spat, clearing the last of the bile sinuses.

"I can't wait for you," Alistair answered, matter-of-fact.

Rylan thought for sure Clara was going to pass out. The human body could withstand massive blood loss, but not at the rate Clara had been drained. It was no surprise she was symptomatic. Her skin was damp with sweat, lips and gums gray. If she didn't compensate soon, he'd be forced to intervene. That idea terrified him; he wasn't medically trained, at least not enough to treat humans.

"Then the guards," Clara answered, swallowing hard; it was all she could do to keep from puking again.

"Name them," Alistair called, his back already turned to them.

"Lucas and Marc," Clara groaned, slumping into Rylan, too weak to hold herself up.

Though it pained her, Clara watched them leave. Alistair's sneakers squeaked across the floor as Hannah padded silently beside him. Small bloody footprints were the only thing left in their absence.

"Can you stand?" Rylan knew the answer before he asked, but out of respect, he gave Clara the benefit of the doubt. He could feel her stir against him, her breathing quickening as her body fought to oxygenate.

"Only if you want me to puke again," Clara joked, barely able to catch her breath, her saliva thick in her mouth. "I forgot how fast they can drain us. I messed up."

Shifting slightly, he braced Clara's frame against his, preparing to pick her up. She gave him no indication to stop, her skin cool against his. She was going into shock. Rylan wasn't a fighter; he didn't train with Clara and Lucas. He knew how to shoot a gun and how to dissect what they brought to him. Despite this, and to his surprise, he was still able to lift Clara with relative ease. It helped that he was taller and probably outweighed her by eighty pounds.

It felt like he was carrying a child, but even children got heavy after a while. His grip was slipping, and he'd have to set her down; it would be easier if she wasn't just dead weight. Quickly and with a surge of energy, Rylan managed to clear the last few feet of the hallway, depositing Clara's body on the examining table with a loud, huffed exclamation of effort.

"What are you doing?" Quin's voice cut through the silence, concern pulling him from his prison-style meal.

Rylan didn't know how to answer at first; he'd completely forgotten about Quin, fear clouding his judgment. "She fed her, Hannah. Clara fed her, but…"

"Let me out." Quin dropped his sorry excuse for a peanut butter and jelly sandwich, true concern spilling from him at the sight of Clara's unmoving form.

"You'd help her?" Rylan asked uncertainly.

"I'm a nurse, Rylan, let me out." Quin insisted.

Maybe it was the look in Quin's eyes or just the urgency in his voice, Rylan wasn't sure. All he knew was that he didn't know how to save a life and Quin did. Rylan opened the cell; Quin darted past him and to Clara's side. Without hesitating, Quin tore his belt free to tourniquet her bleeding arm.

"Put oxygen on her," Quin demanded, darting back toward the wall of open supplies.

Rylan hadn't realized he might be familiarizing himself with their supplies, but it made sense. What else was he going to do? In a flurry of movement, Quin was priming tubing with saline. Rylan used the bags to infuse silver intravenously.

"Where are your IVs?" Quin barked, tearing through the supplies again. He managed to find what he was looking for long before Rylan was able to give any sort of direction. "Oxygen. Now."

With fumbling fingers Rylan did as he was told; they didn't have normal oxygen tubing, so he just ripped the nebulizer off the end of what he had. A nodded acknowledgement told him he had done something right as Quin established venous access. Rylan was impressed by his speed and skill.

Quin moved with the same practiced precision he'd witnessed in Clara, muscle memory guiding him as he worked. Saline held high, Quin squeezed the bag, draining half of it instantly. His focus quieted Rylan's questions as they both waited, watching as Clara's breathing eased and her color returned.

"She's okay," Quin said shakily, loosening his grip on the saline bag. "I think her response had more to do with the speed at which she was fed on than the volume lost."

As if to prove a point, Quin raked his knuckles up the center of Clara's chest. He'd be lying if he said he didn't enjoy seeing her pain response, her crazed eyes slowly coming into focus.

"How long was I out?" Clara groaned, trying to sit up.

Quin pressed her back just like Marc had done to him when Eryn had ripped apart his shoulder. "I could have put air in your line. I want you to remember that. Now stop moving."

Quin fully expected her to argue, but to his surprise she lay back as he took the oxygen from Rylan, trading it for the saline bag. He made a point to twist the valve tight as he turned it off. Quin doubted they'd be able to easily use it against him now. He returned to their wall of supplies to grab rags and an ace bandage. He could make a pressure dressing at least.

"Hungry?" Clara teased, wincing as Quin pressed the course rags against her tattered skin.

He wasn't going to give her the pleasure of a response; instead, he squeezed her arm as he tugged the belt free, the pain of returning blood flow and the pressure of his fingers where the only answer she deserved. The way she squirmed, trying not to fight him was adorable. He almost felt bad as he wrapped her arm.

"Why'd you let her go?" Quin asked dryly.

"We didn't have a choice. Progenitors don't play by the rules," Clara blurted. "I guess, in a way, neither do we."

"I don't understand." Quin moved slowly back to his cell, snagging his sandwich and juice, careful to keep an eye on Rylan in case he got any bright ideas. "Drink this."

With as much gentleness as he could muster, Quin helped Clara sit up. Again, she did as told without much of a fuss. He waited patiently for her to finish; this probably wasn't the first time she'd woken up like this. If the scars across her body were any indication, she'd been fed on more times than Quin could count. Sections of her skin were hollow, shiny scars stretching over where tissue no longer grew.

"There is no 'us and them,' Quin." Clara spoke low, like she was telling a secret. "Alistair isn't tethered, not to us and not to his own kind. The laws are as much for them as they are for us."

"What the fuck are you talking about?" Quin scoffed, taking a bite of his sandwich.

"It's a balance," Rylan interrupted before Clara said too much. "We help them, and in turn they help us. That's all you need to know."

"So," Quin sneered, "this is them helping us? Looks like you're food to me."

Clara laughed weakly. "How many scars would you have if you couldn't heal? Don't pretend like it isn't something you enjoy." She sat up slowly. "At least when I feed them I'm not getting off on it."

Quin didn't have a witty comeback; her pale eyes saw right through him. "Why did Alistair take Hannah?" he asked, changing the subject as he removed Clara's IV.

"She knows where to find your vampire," Clara teased.

'There she is,' Quin thought, seeing the glint in her eyes as she held the information he wanted just out of his reach. Carefully, she dropped from the stainless steel table to stand beside Rylan.

"No one is stopping you from leaving." Clara smiled; she could just see the color changing in his eyes. "We aren't in control anymore, Quin. Alistair made that abundantly clear."

As a show of good faith, Clara waved her arm wide, directing Quin forward. She still felt like shit, but at least she could stand – well almost. Rylan kept her steady as they made their way toward the stairs.

Quin followed, never taking his eyes off her. To be fair, she hadn't given him a reason to trust her, and probably wasn't going to start now.

Clara felt the sweat on the back of her neck, trailing down her back like ice; she had to stop and catch her breath. Fluids were great, but they didn't replace red blood cells. She'd give anything not to puke again. Three flights of stairs stood between her and the surface.

"This is going to take all night," Quin complained, backtracking. "Come on."

Clara looked at him, puzzled by his offer. He'd turned his back to her, squatting down just low enough to provide her an easy climb up.

"You're going to carry her?" Rylan remarked, just as confused.

"Unless you think you can," Quin quipped, remembering how Rylan had struggled earlier. "Hurry up."

Surprised, Clara realized he'd been looking back because he was worried about her and not because he thought they might mace him again. Though she was sure his mistrust still played a part, perhaps it wasn't as prevalent as she originally thought. Hefting her weight without so much as a grunt, Quin set off at a brisk pace. It wasn't the most comfortable way to travel, but it was certainly faster.

"Thank you," Clara spoke sincerely.

"What's a Progenitor?" Quin glanced at her from the corner of his eye, taking the stairs two at a time; he was determined to leave Rylan behind.

"This is more than a war, Quin; it's survival. What they don't tell us when we sign up is whose." Clara sighed; she might as well be explaining the intricacies of Mozart to a baby. "Progenitors are the keepers of the laws, the ones who get to say who lives and who dies.

They are the monsters that wiped out our numbers thirty years ago. All they care about is balance."

"That sounds like forced compliance, not balance." Quin slowed, his pace reflecting his uncertainty as he advanced.

"Not exactly." Clara shook her head, blond curls all but swallowing his field of vision. "It's like how you and Eryn are tethered: it's symbiotic. The cost of living versus surviving was too great, so hunters learned how to coexist. That's what we're doing, sacrificing the few to save the many."

"In nursing they call that downstream thinking," Quin grunted, shifting Clara's weight. "It's fine as long as you aren't the one slipping through the cracks."

Quin sensed Clara's inner turmoil, the closeness of her made it easier to internalize the emotions. He knew they were at an impasse, but not because they didn't agree; it was because she had no choice. Cooperating and living by their laws had saved lives, saved hers. It wasn't right, but it was better than death.

"For now, it's all we have." She sighed, her mind and body exhausted.

"Just because I don't agree doesn't mean I don't understand. I just didn't know," Quin admitted, trying not to let the new information distract him.

"Why would you? Hate to break this to you, but you're expendable – or at least you were," Clara chuckled. "You newcomers get excited at the idea of guns and monster hunting, never stopping to ask the real questions – never make it far enough I guess."

Quin shrugged; she wasn't wrong, though that wasn't his only reason for joining. He hadn't waited for the promise of guns or killing.

No, he became a hunter the night he came home to his daughter's half-eaten body. He'd found his girlfriend elbow deep in her chest cavity while another ghoul ate her legs to the bone. At some point the ghoul had infected his girlfriend, who in turn infected his daughter like a fucked up buffet line. The memories, once buried deep, emerged easily now.

That vampire he'd met two nights ago had fucked with his head, dredging up things he'd tried hard to keep hidden. Thinking back, Quin realized that if Marc hadn't found him, he'd never have lived long enough to make it here in the first place. To him, it was never about surviving, no matter what Clara said; he couldn't just let people die. No greater-good mentality would ever convince him otherwise either, not after what he'd been through.

"What now?" Quin asked, setting Clara down at the top of the narrow landing.

"Now." Clara drew out the word, stretching as she bought Rylan time to catch up. "We meet up with Lucas. Marc shouldn't be far behind him. I need to make sure Alistair plays by the rules."

CHAPTER TWENTY-EIGHT

Lucas never liked hearing a knock on the door; no one good ever tapped on a door after midnight, and tonight wasn't any different. Silver eyes peered at him through the half-opened door; his revolver's aim hadn't even been close. The best he could have hoped for were wood splinters in Alistair's creepy, unblinking eyes. Anyone else would have opened the door to greet a child this late at night, but this was no child, and no matter how he hid behind the childlike visage, Lucas despised the form.

He hated the adorable red shoes and way Alistair's pants were cuffed; he even hated the way his oversized hoodie made his frame seem smaller and somehow more vulnerable, its sleeves just a little too long. Lucas wondered how many children this monster had stalked in order to perfect his disguise. How many children shared the story of the silver-eyed demon that learned how to play and act just like them?

"Where's Clara?" Lucas asked, peering past Alistair; he didn't like looking at him for this long. She should have forced her way inside already, Rylan in tow. He was starting to get tired of being the only 'normal' hunter.

"Clara has appointed you and Marc in her place tonight. She wasn't feeling well." Alistair chewed on the words, picking them carefully; the less he had to explain, the sooner he could find Selene.

"Perfect." Lucas lied, feeling a piece of himself die a little inside. "Tell me, what's so important that Clara needs us both looking after you?"

Lucas regretted asking as a smile played across Alistair's features; it was too perfect, the way he mimicked the innocence of a child. The last thing he wanted to do was run errands with this abomination.

"I know where to find her, the creator."

Lucas shivered, even the tone of his voice held the tenor and joy of a child. He wasn't going to enjoy this night. At least he didn't have to do it alone. Stepping aside, he left Alistair in the open doorway. He needed to grab some supplies if they were facing a vampire strong enough to be a creator. Good thing he always had a bug-out bag packed for just such an occasion.

"Lead the way," Lucas huffed, slinging the leather duffel bag over his right shoulder.

"No." Alistair shook his head. "You and Marc are merely there to watch. If she spots you, she will not come."

Lucas stopped, fixing Alistair with a steady and unwavering glare. "I do not take orders from you. Clara declared Marc and me act in her place, correct?"

Alistair's smile faded to an unreadable and expressionless mask, the stillness of him unsettling as he regarded Lucas. He'd made his point. He may not be Clara, but that didn't mean he was naive to the laws required of him *and* the Progenitors. Lucas would ensure they both acted accordingly.

"You won't see us," Lucas reassured him. "Not unless the situation calls for it." He paused, crouching to meet Alistair eye to eye. "And as long as you stay in radio contact."

Lucas presented him with a small black transmitter and wired microphone from the duffle bag. The hair on the back of his neck stood on end. His instincts told him to run, telling him that what he faced was something much more dangerous than himself. Lucas held fast; it had been a long time since he'd let fear dictate his actions and he wasn't about to let that change now.

"I see why she named you." Alistair smirked, accepting the wiretap. "Retrieve the other; then, and only then, can we begin."

Lucas was immediately relieved when Alistair finally left, his shape melding into the shadows as he went. It reminded him of the way Cyd and Warren could vanish, but when they left they didn't carry with them the distinct smell of blood.

"How soon can you be here?" Lucas asked, finally releasing the transmitter button tucked inside his sleeve.

"Fifteen minutes." Marc's voice broke through the static.

"Perfect." Lucas spoke the word with the same lack of enthusiasm as before. "Fifteen minutes," he repeated, switching to Alistair's channel.

The reply he received was a haunting whisper of a child's voice. The hollowness of it sent a chill up his spine as he wrote down the address, all too eager to end the exchange. Whatever Clara was doing, she'd better finish up quick; something about this didn't feel right.

Alistair had been too eager to give orders, orders that limited their ability to interfere or participate in the exchange.

Out of habit, Lucas popped the cylinder on his revolver, spinning it a few times before slamming it back into place. Something about the sound of gun metal locking and the click as the cylinder spun helped calm his nerves. Now was not the time for worry; now was the time for quiet focus.

———

Alistair hated the smell of the charred bricks, melted wires, and smoke-ridden remains of the building before him. This was near where he'd first met Hannah. The smell of death had brought him to her. He'd expected to find a ghoul, but instead stumbled upon her, desperately clinging to the tattered body of a child. Nothing left but a cherub face with dead eyes and bones picked clean.

Hannah was not the first vampire he'd met with the need to completely consume and she would not be the last to do so recklessly. It, unfortunately, had been something he could not ignore. The laws kept them safe; what he hadn't anticipated was her connection to Selene. In delivering Hannah to the hunters, Alistair had thought her crime merely that of gluttony. He knew better now, but not enough.

The hiss of static forced his attention; he winced at the sharpness of it, clenching his jaw. He wanted to crush the device and rid himself of the hunters' prying eyes, but even he must follow the rules placed before him.

"Incoming," Lucas warned Alistair, needing an excuse to elicit a response.

Alistair turned, scanning the rooftops, both thankful and disturbed that he was unable to spot Lucas or Marc. Hannah approached him; her form changed but not her scent. Corkscrew curls framed a face too perfect for humans, her warm, ebony skin flawless. She must have fed again.

Side by side, they could be easily misconstrued as mother and child. She had mimicked the shape of his nose and eyes; it made him wonder if she remembered her own shape anymore. Had he met Hannah a few centuries ago, he had no doubt they would have made the perfect killing team.

"Tell me." Alistair gestured through the fence that barred entry to the ruins. "Why do I smell so much death?" The earth was drenched with blood, but not that of desecrated humans; this was the blood of vampires.

There it was. Fear. As clear to him now as when they'd first met. He didn't mind the taste of her fear, sharp in the air around him. Anything was better than the remnants of the dead hidden among the bricks. Her silence excited him; she knew something he didn't and it was driving him crazy.

Alistair didn't mind waiting for Hannah to make her way past the barricades, leading him to the truth he sought. Every step across the building's skeletal remains shifted the rubble below, the smell of decay barely veiled by the thin layer of dirt that concealed the bodies underneath. Interestingly, the farther Hannah led him, the less she was able to hold her form. Whatever had happened here was bad enough to make her forget parts of her form.

What she showed him next was worth the wait as she excavated each brick. Though she was a vampire, strength was not one of her natural abilities. She struggled to expose the bones below; they lay scattered, partially incinerated and cracked. Only fragments were left of Hannah's coven. It was perhaps the only reason she had survived. A lesser vampire could not have survived the inferno that was Selene's rage.

"Why?" Alistair had to keep his hands buried deep in his pockets to stop himself from ripping the truth right from her lips.

"Why indeed?" Clara's voice broke through their morbid preoccupation, her teeth bared.

Within the span of a breath, Alistair became acutely aware of three things: the absolute certainty of Cyd's abilities, Clara's mimicking of a gun as she pointed at Hannah, and red eyes.

One simple movement was all it took to obliterate the entirety of Hannah's spine as a .50 caliber bullet entered and exited her body with no more resistance than the motion of Clara's hand through the air. The stink of fresh blood and viscera filled the air, speckling the perfect cleanliness of Alistair's clothes with carnage.

Hannah gasped as she was thrown back to join the dirt and bones of her kin. She couldn't regenerate fast enough; panic slowed her abilities as she tried desperately to escape the taste of their death on her tongue. She clawed hysterically for purchase in the scattered bricks. That's when Hannah saw the red of Quin's eyes, just like Selene's. Quin enjoyed every second of her terror, especially when he was able to pull it to the surface, ensuring it was all she could find.

Alistair shared Clara's same snarled expression, anger replacing his earlier excitement as he absorbed the bits of gore that threatened to ruin his clothes. He could feel every beat of her heart, and for a second he wanted nothing more than to spill her blood.

"Clara." He spat her name, unable to express himself further without resorting to violence.

"Alistair." She met him with the same venom. "Why don't you tell me what it is you're trying so hard to discover?"

Alistair met her unyielding stare, her unwavering conviction reflected within. It was clear Clara would leave with answers or blood, and nothing was worth the aftermath of a broken pact, not even the life of a creator. If the hunters didn't kill him, his own kind surely would. So Alistair yielded, making a point to step aside, despite the pain it caused him. Clara stepped forward then to peer at what Hannah had struggled to reveal.

"Bones? Or what's left of them. Why are we here, Alistair?" Clara asked, her irritation evident in her tone.

"I have to be sure." Alistair dared not meet her eyes. "Hannah was here. The laws favor hunters; I need to be certain."

He hated speaking openly; Clara was the only one who understood the balance. This was more complicated than some rogue vampire creating at will; it was too calculated. Alistair still feared. He feared that all Clara would see was the life taken. Laws forbade the creation of another without consent. He hoped doubt was enough to stay an execution… those left that could sustain the vampire race were rare. This was his truth, one that he'd never share.

Clara took in his words, hearing what he was saying and what he wasn't. He was desperate to prove Selene's innocence; she just didn't know why. There were no gray areas, no loopholes, and no wiggle room, at least not regarding Selene. No matter Alistair's reasoning, she would not let a vampire live that had condemned another.

"Humans don't live long enough for a vampire's certainty," Clara answered carefully. "But that doesn't mean I'm unwilling to see what else *we* can learn."

Clara had been met with enough patience from Progenitors centuries older than herself to afford Alistair the same kindness now. Compromise was the foundation of the alliance between the guild and Progenitors – even if their motives weren't always clear. Maintaining balance and mutual survival was the keeper's sole purpose of existing.

Quin sensed a shift in Alistair and Clara, their earlier animosity dissolving into an odd feeling of admiration. Hating the way Cyd's ability clung to his clothes, Quin distanced himself from her. The way the shadows reached for her made him uneasy. He much preferred the feel of the earth under his feet, even if it meant being loud. He was sure he'd float away if he lingered in Cyd's shadows too long. Hannah's eyes met the cooling teal of Quin's. He kept her in his sights, enjoying the fear he read in her. He was sure this was what it felt like to be the boogeyman.

"I've underestimated you, Keeper." Alistair spoke honestly, before returning Lucas's device.

He was glad to be free of it. Clara had surprised him, not only with the abilities of her hunters, but with her openness. It was rare to find a hunter who didn't differentiate between human and non-human. She'd been just as willing to persecute her own people as his; it was a rare quality.

Hannah groaned, the last of her skin stitching itself together, all eyes now on her. The ones of amber were the only ones that took her in with genuine awe. She had been the one who snuck up on them; her ability to hide was absolute. Hannah would trade all of her regeneration for that gift right now; she was growing tired of dying and the pain of returning. Each time her mind faded, her abilities ripped her back. It was beginning to take a toll.

"Please," Hannah begged, her plea falling on deaf ears. How many times could she die before her mind didn't come back, before all that was left was the darkness; she couldn't take much more.

"Knock it off," Quin demanded, her pity party was wearing on his nerves. He couldn't wait to hear her side of the story. Quin hadn't been able to identify just why this place had felt so familiar to him, but it was all making sense. This was where Eryn had been created, and the vampire in front of him had something to do with it. In his book that made her just as despicable as Selene.

"Cyd, return for now; it appears Quin has some personal business with this one." Clara waved her away; the fewer involved, the less she'd have to explain. Things were getting complicated as is.

"Speak and you'll be free," Alistair stated dispassionately regarding Hannah's cowering frame.

Her mind raced; Quin was just able to decipher the bits that flashed before him as she spoke.

"Months she stalked them. Selene, she was infatuated. Every night I'd watch her go to them. Always observing but never taking." Hannah spoke quickly, the sound of it weak and trembling made him sick. "So they took them for her."

Hannah tried not to remember, focusing instead on the dirt and bones beneath her, but his red eyes had reminded her too much of Selene's and soon the taste of the man played across her tongue, richer than the first time.

"She was going to turn them, spoke of it to her kin in the early light. The others, they couldn't wait..." Again, the memories played out before her. Their screams, the way it felt holding them down. "Selene didn't like that."

Quin saw every lie as it played out in her mind, she was completely blind to the vile acts of her kind. Quin saw Hannah rip Alexander and Eryn from their home, already beaten and bloody. He felt her excitement when they converged on them.

"The coven defied her, took what was hers." Hannah shivered, recalling the way the flames had liquefied her. "She turned them after she destroyed us."

Quin didn't have to fight for these memories. Hannah was no more able to block him out than she was able to sense his intrusion in the first place. He tasted Eryn's blood then, sweeter than anything he'd consumed before. It coated his mouth like melted chocolate. Quin spat, fists clenched, and the only thing he felt next were flames. He watched it play out across Hannah's mind as Selene cremated them one by one, until the only one left was Hannah.

"Tell me." Quin forced her attention. "Who tasted better, Eryn or her husband?" He stepped to her, livid. "Better yet, why don't you tell me why all of you took turns feeding them?"

Alistair saw the confusion play across Hannah's face, followed by the horror of understanding. Quin had seen it all. Rage erupted from Alistair as explosive and violent as a bomb. He made no apology as the force of his anger hit them like a shockwave, driving them back. From their perspective, it would look like he was being swallowed by the darkness, from his he was expanding, shedding the limitations of his form. This one was infinite, ebbing and flowing freely like a wave of pure energy. He didn't know if he could destroy Hannah, but he was going to try. They hadn't merely stolen from Selene; they'd forced themselves on humans.

Clara smiled wide and wild, her hands clenched tight to the cemented rebar in front of her. Quin didn't stand a chance as the full force of Alistair's anger converged on him and Hannah. Debris exploded outward – shrapnel of steel and rock. This was the strength of a Progenitor. Clara would give anything to dissect one so far removed from human. What happened next, Clara could only describe as violent.

Alistair's small frame was suspended in a flowing black mass. It appeared liquid at times, shifting and pulsing, and smoke at others. The only light inside was the silver of his eyes. He was ripping Hannah apart. The ink of him was simultaneously dissolving and digesting as he dissected and disemboweled her. Hannah's cries for mercy grew weaker and weaker each time she reformed. This was the fate of those who broke the law, the ones who took and gave without permission.

This was justice, Clara thought, completely absorbed in Hannah's destruction. Less and less of her came back as her regeneration failed. Her body, now malformed as her mind broke, forgot how to put itself back together – Alistair was destroying the part of Hannah that remembered how. A sick look of satisfaction etched itself into Quin's features; Clara had a sneaking suspicion the he was enjoying every ounce of Hannah's suffering.

It didn't take long, the massacring of Hannah. In the span of three minutes Alistair had destroyed her more times than Rylan or her could have managed in a lifetime. All that was left when Alistair returned to himself was a huddled mass of ill-formed bones and skin, stretched too tight. This was her last life, Clara was sure of it. Hannah had lost the ability to form her limbs and all her insides were out.

It was startling, the serenity on Alistair's face as his small fingers dug through Hannah's misshapen chest cavity. The sound as he forced his arm past her ribs, cracking and wet, made Quin turn in disgust. Clara was fascinated; never had she seen a Progenitor kill one of their own so intimately. That's when Clara saw it, the pleading in her auburn eyes as Alistair took her heart in his hand. She didn't scream, no, the sound that left Hannah was not one of pain as he took from her one last time.

Despite all of Alistair's anger and disgust, he did not enjoy killing his own – but she had left him no choice. He just hoped he wouldn't have to kill another for the same mistake. The desire to create was not uncommon, but the ability and strength to do so was.

Quin felt when her psyche shattered, knew when there was nothing left, and experienced Hannah's end. He didn't enjoy the suffering of others, but he had enjoyed this. Since being tethered, he had lived the nightmare Hannah and the coven had initiated; he had experienced every ounce of pain, terror, and loss as his own. What had surprised him more than the violence was the kindness as Alistair released Hannah. His childlike features had softened, making him appear even younger than he already did. Quin could sense his sorrow at ending Hannah and the acceptance they both shared in the end.

"It was her. She was the one who took them," Quin reiterated. "She wore the face of a friend." If Alistair heard him, it didn't show.

"Why would they feed off them like that if Selene was planning on doing it herself?" Quin spoke a bit louder, seeking clarification.

"She wasn't going to, you idiot," Clara snapped. "Or at least not like that." He really didn't know how to read between the lines. This was exactly what she hadn't wanted. What happened next was going to blur the lines between hunter and vampire. This is why Alistair had sought secrecy. Now, they'd have to confront the sire, not to kill her, but to bring her to trial. There was a reason Progenitors were kept secret; it was the same reason keepers and collectors were not well known: hunters only saw in black and white – us versus them, right and wrong, life and death; things got messy when the ideals of either side were tested. Clara sighed. She hated playing the middleman.

"Now we wait. We have to find Selene and determine *whether* any laws were broken." She made a point to emphasize the last part for Alistair and Quin in an attempt to reassure them both. "That being said, Selene isn't the only one we need to find."

Alistair nodded, knowing that whatever happened next was out of his control. Whether Selene lived or died was up to what they learned from her and Eryn. All of this would have been easier if the hunter had left well enough alone, but Alistair knew it wasn't that simple. The truth of the matter was that a new vampire, whether forged by a hunter of the sire, was always better off if they weren't alone.

"She won't approach willingly with all of you here." Alistair knew how it sounded, but one as strong as Selene didn't get that way by being reckless.

Clara considered his statement; this wasn't her realm of expertise. She didn't *talk* to vampires, at least not in the way that was required of her now.

"How many?" Clara asked.

"Laws required you; blood requires him." Alistair gestured toward Quin. "No more."

"You've got to be shitting me." Quin laughed. "What happens when she realizes we're there to kill her? You think she'll wait for us to get back up?"

The change in Alistair was subtle yet significant, his outline blurring, anger renewed as he faced Quin. "You will do nothing. You're in over your head, hunter. The only reason you're still here is because you are bound by the blood."

Clara felt Alistair's threat; the tension of it was thick in her lungs and against her skin. Quin's wide-eyed expression told her he could feel it too. Alistair had made a point to verbally and physically affront him. His message was clear – he would tolerate nothing but absolute compliance.

"Observers," Clara agreed. They didn't have a choice. It had been a long time since Clara had been afraid; this was not an ideal situation, but it was par for the course. She didn't have the luxury of picking sides.

"Observers," Quin repeated, fighting the urge to escape Alistair's piercing gaze, any earlier kindness gone.

"If you find Eryn, so too will you find Selene." Alistair spoke casually as he kicked debris over Hannah's scattered remains. "Until then, we wait for her to return here."

"What makes you so sure Selene will come back here?" Quin asked, skirting the shallow grave to stand beside Clara.

"She'll smell Hannah. You don't destroy your home and forget the person that drove you to it. She'll come." Clara offered clarification when Alistair didn't respond; she just hoped that when Selene showed up, it wasn't to burn them alive.

CHAPTER TWENTY-NINE

Derek let the weight of the knife decide the cut he left on Neil's corpse. The tissue beneath wept as the steel separated its layers: skin from skin, fat from fat, and muscle from muscle until he hit bone. The sudden stop vibrated the steel, solidifying his connection. It was all he needed to pull apart and ingest the man before him, taking from him the sins etched in his bones – sins that not even death could purge. His obsidian eyes wandered the faces of Neil's dead; their hollow forms only served to incite his hunger. Derek felt their touch as they pulled themselves free from the incision he had created. Like whispers, they danced across his skin, leaving traces of themselves behind. Unfortunately, without a live host he couldn't truly feed on the memories. The pleasure and pain of his hunger was excruciating as his veins cried out for sustenance and his mind struggled for control. His hunger was maddening and magnificently clarifying. Even now, eager to feed, it served to sharpen his senses and drive his focus.

It was the excitement of balancing between frenzy and control; every smell was enough to throw him over the edge, and the taste of them… he had to fight every drop he consumed, careful to not kill his prey instantly or, worse, lose himself. Tonight he would enjoy the meal he'd been meticulously preparing for the last three weeks. It was time to quench the thirst that burned his body and threatened to erase his mind. It was a game, one he'd learned to play a long time ago as a way to savor the kill. Taking all he could from the corpse before him, Derek withdrew; the audience he'd dug from the skin faded from him like a mirage. The dead made for poor sustenance, even for him.

With a long, shuddering breath, Derek stood, removing himself from temptation. He'd do as Selene ordered and bury Neil. The act of digging would clear his mind and rid him of the deep, visceral odor of death. It was with learned practice that he put spade to earth, making short work of the overgrown courtyard, the shovel easily rending the ferns, wild flowers, and creeping vines free of their roots and the dirt they clung to. He'd long accepted his role as undertaker, digging mindlessly until it was done and four perfect walls of dirt were erected around him, wrapping him in a cool embrace.

Derek apathetically set out to finish his task. The only sound, as Neil's corpse puffed into the loose soil, was a wheeze of escaping air from long dead lungs. Bits of the rich soil clung to his shirt, attracted to the smear of blood that Neil's weeping body had left behind. He breathed it in, enjoying the smell of it as it mingled with the forest, sweet and thick in his nose and on his palate. He could finish filling the grave and cleaning the spilled blood later. Now he needed to feed. Derek afforded his appetizer no more thought as he set out, instinct driving him.

The night was alive all around him, like a heartbeat; the cars, lights, and people were the blood that fed it. Derek knew his path well and wasted no time as he advanced through the winding streets of downtown. It was nights like this, polluted by the living, that the stars were lost and the shadows ran. Despite his hunger, it was not an unpleasant adventure to walk among the people they fed upon every night.

Derek didn't linger with them long. Something about their world and lives brought about a darkness within his soul he dared not explore. It was an unsettling disconnect that made him question his place in a world ever changing. It was this separateness that haunted him at the oddest times, but always more so when he was alone. Derek slowed, surprised by his revelation. He was never truly alone, especially not now that he'd found his way back to her.

This was their secret place, Derek's home away from home: the place he kept his captured prey. Even now, as he rested his head against the heavy metal door, he could hear her stirring within, smell her, sweet and warm against the harshness of the city all around him. Derek held fast to the metal of the barn door that led to Hailey; it was all he could do not to lose control. His vision dark around the edges, tonight he'd add her to his sins.

It was rare that he found someone as fearless as her. No, that wasn't it. She feared him plenty; her hands shook as he stepped over the threshold; metal cried out against the unforgiving concrete below, shattering the peace of the loft. He'd been gone too long. He could see it in the wounds that adorned her dark skin. She'd been fighting it, trying to prolong the effect he had on her.

Hailey's dark eyes searched Derek's as she paced the back wall, fiercely defiant of him and her need he created in her. She dug at the cuts, craving the release they'd provided her – the relief he'd provided her. He was infuriating, just waiting for her to succumb. She'd told herself she wouldn't, not this time. She repeated the same lies in her head: that she could leave; that she didn't want him; and that she was stronger than her need. Even now, with all her anger, she knew it was a lie. He was like a drug, one she needed. Her whole body ached for it – for him.

It began the same way every time, with him circling slowly toward her, his movements slow and unnaturally precise. His posture was relaxed as he casually advanced. Each time he returned, it was the same. Loft door wide, Hailey could taste the night air and her freedom. Thing was, she knew she'd never escape, not when Derek was her salvation and her end.

Step by step, they circled each other until their positions were swapped, her back to the open air and his resting against the bricks. He was expressionless, drinking her in.

'*Just one more step*,' Hailey thought, '*and I could be free of him.*'

Would he really let her go? She'd never know. Metal against concrete, the barn door protested as, yet again, it was forced to move, this time closed. Hailey's forehead pressed against its icy frame. Exhaling slowly, she never heard his approach. Her refusal to leave was all the permission he needed. His closeness made her tense as he overtook her.

Derek's hunger betrayed him as he advanced; he'd given her the choice to leave, to live, but now she was his. He breathed her in, smiling into the tangles of her curly hair. Derek held Hailey tightly against himself, preventing her escape as he drew a blade. They always wanted it until they remembered how the steel serrated their flesh. Hailey was no different, her body tensed and twisted against his.

Little did she know, the more she fought the hungrier he became; it was no fun if they didn't resist. Derek lifted her, taking pleasure in the way she cried out as he pulled her away from the doorway, spinning them both to face the empty loft.

Her breath caught, steel against flesh, Derek pressed the blade against her collar bone. Her body, once rigid, relaxed as she sighed with relief. Blood stained the mirrored blade red and spilled across his fingers, sticky and hot. He brought it to his mouth, consumed by the pull of Hailey's mind and the taste of her across his tongue.

Drop by drop, Hailey bled them out, tears stinging her eyes; she wiped them away furiously, angry every time their faces were obscured by tears, her emotions betraying her. It wasn't enough. To see them there was a cost, one she gladly paid.

"Who are they?" Derek breathed, leaning in, his hold on her shifting. His right arm rested across her shoulders, blade poised against her flesh.

Hailey flinched, both at the sound of his voice and from the sting as he inflicted yet another cut. "My family," she whispered, their forms becoming clearer and clearer with every drop she bled.

Derek watched them fill the space before them, tracing his knife across Hailey's skin slowly until there was nothing left to draw out of her. The stink of her blood surrounded him just as her loved ones did her. He took it in, watching as the familiar faces danced around them.

It was a reunion unlike any Derek had seen. Grandparents embraced her, their touch as real to Hailey as the one his blade left. The memories of their voices were long lost, but still they called to her wordlessly as children weaved their way past to tug at her blood-laced hands. He'd been building her to this moment, cut by cut; he freed her mind and fed himself upon her life.

"Why do they not speak to you?" Derek asked, curious of the mumbled and unclear hum of voices that filled her memory.

"I can't remember the sound of their voices," she admitted sadly before stepping into the maelstrom of bodies, desperate to feel them again.

Derek watched as they ebbed and flowed; she was their gravity, pushing and pulling them as she frantically tried to recall them all. He could feel her need resonating with his own. What she wanted would cost more than she'd given – it would take more than the bite of a blade. Derek followed where she led; each droplet she left behind hypnotized him. His heart raced as he advanced, razors tearing at his veins with every lost drop. He'd waited long enough.

Hailey fought his grip, desperate in her search; she had to find them. They had to be here somewhere – otherwise she was truly alone, forgotten by them not once but twice. Pain bloomed in her left shoulder unlike anything she had felt before, simultaneously sharp and crushing, as Derek pulled her back to him once more. This was more than a cut; his left arm trapped her while the right forced her head back and to the side. He was *biting* her, she realized.

Fear and confusion took hold of her just as sure and unyielding as the monster who now consumed her. Hailey screamed, tears once again stealing their faces from her.

"Please!" she sobbed, hands scrambling against his crushing grasp. To her relief, Derek's hold softened and the pain in her shoulder eased.

"Find them," he whispered against her skin, his voice wet and thick before he started to feed again.

It was with great restraint that Derek slowed, coaxing Hailey's body and mind with his. Her blood unleashed the full extent of his abilities as he ripped from her the memories she'd been so fevered to find. They lay buried deep within her subconscious, too far gone for recall without assistance.

Hailey's blood filled him, restoring to Derek a semblance of control. To feed and be fed upon was more than the taking of another's life. It was an exchange – one that, until now, had been one-sided. Derek was not Selene; his connection to the blood and those he fed on had always called for more tedious requirements.

He closed his eyes, searching Hailey's memories; with each heartbeat he helped bring her closer, pulling from her the fragments of her life until she was able to evoke and bring to life what it was she so desperately sought.

One by one they faded from her, each face painfully beautiful and sorrowful as they went. Hailey knew she'd never see them again; this was her end... it had to be worth it. The vast loft, once filled with the laughter and smiling faces of her family, was now vacant. Save for the two before her now.

Hailey didn't feel the pain of her shoulder or hear as Derek drank her in; all that was left was her and them. These were the faces of her parents – parents she hadn't seen since she was five. Their arms enveloped her, and finally she wasn't so alone. She was a child again in their arms; suddenly everything made sense again, because for the first time in her adult life, she was whole.

She breathed them in, a wave of nostalgia taking hold. Her father always smelled faintly of tobacco and cologne she'd never been able to find. It was a pleasant mix of leather and coffee, rich and deep against her senses. Her mother was just the opposite, soft lilac and sugar sweet. Their faces and the feeling of them mended all of her broken edges. She was the perfect mix of the two, strong and soft. Hailey stared into the eyes of her father, just the same as hers. The fullness of her mother's features mirrored her own.

Here, with Derek, she wasn't the last of her bloodline. Here she had them all back, each face a reminder of where she'd come from and how hard she'd fought for her life, earning every foothold. She didn't have to be strong anymore, not now that they held her – now that they could see who she'd become. It had all been worth it to get to this point. The weight of her sorrow faded away as Derek consumed.

He drank in her death. Consuming not her despair, but the beauty of a life well lived no matter how short and harrowing. Hailey didn't regret any of it as she fell asleep in his arms, the last remnants of her family guiding her into the afterlife. All that was left for Derek was the smiling face of his prey, Hailey's body small against his as her spirit joined the faces of the others that had come before her. Not everyone shatters, some of them accepted Derek's offer. Hailey had been the later, welcoming the chance to be whole once more.

She had been his best meal since, well, he couldn't remember. Maybe the best he'd had in years. As easy as it was to feed on the shattered dreams and despair of the dying, their joy tasted so much sweeter across his tongue. Derek wasn't done, though, not when there was still so much left to consume of her.

CHAPTER THIRTY

Bits and pieces of the night's events played out behind my eyelids, keeping me from true slumber. Some of it was mine while some of it was Quin's. His mind was pulling at mine, fighting against the chaos of Selene's blood and the memories of those I had consumed.

'*Find me*,' he called, mind half asleep, the urgency of his words twisting my dreams. It was like reaching out in pitch black night, lost until I found him. There were no images within our restless sleep, just the emotions of the day warping between us.

The familiarity of Quin's mind was like an embrace, calming the whispers and tangled flashes of the night lost. There was a certainty within his mind that I did not possess. It was his unwavering confidence that settled my soul, even if just temporarily. His dreams were just as scattered as mine, but one thing was for sure: yesterday had been good. We'd won. I didn't know how or why, but it felt good finding peace within him even if it was just for right now.

Still, despite the solace we found in one another, his urgency persisted, disrupting the peace and forcing my mind fully awake. His apprehension ripped away any remnant of sleep I had left. My head ached, not just from the pressure of him in my mind, but with the earliness at which I'd risen.

"He's a persistent one," Selene's voice called out, her body dusted with the rich soil where she'd slept.

I didn't know how to answer her, my body stiff from sleeping upright. Despite her insistence I hadn't been able to join Derek and her in the earth beneath the church. The act of burying myself willingly was too macabre.

"Both of you need to learn how to be quiet," she stated as she stood. "Announcing one's thoughts when the other is already listening is pointless. Come. There is a lesson to be learned in waking early."

It felt like I was walking into a solar flare, the gray light filtering through the stained glass of the sanctuary's windows sharp against my retinas. For once, as I peered up the stairs at Selene, I met the blue of her eyes. There was no hint of discomfort to be found as she waited patiently for me. My stomach churned, dizzy and disoriented even in the dying light of the day.

"You need to suppress it; mask your nature and your abilities in order to dull your senses. The light is not what hurts, it is the way we perceive it." Her voice was soft, limiting the reverb in the empty rooms; she waited with expectation.

I swallowed hard, focusing intently – not on my surroundings, but on myself. In the beginning I fought every day to bind myself, withdrawing from those who surrounded me, lest I be overrun by them. It was easier than I thought, shutting myself off from the outside. What I hadn't expected was the vulnerability of it, at the loss of my added senses.

I wasn't perfect, and more than once I had to pause to concentrate, but eventually the light and feel of the day was no more than a dull ache. I'd never been much of a morning person, but after months of hiding it was a treat to experience it.

"There are some of us that aren't even affected by it." Selene continued quietly through the church. "No matter how we achieve walking during the day, one thing is certain: it makes us weaker."

I nodded my understanding, taken aback by the beauty of the old church's architecture in the fading light of day, the thick rafters above like exposed bone. Tarnished steel brackets were the joints that held the beams in place while aged brick and plaster rose to meet the high ceiling and hanging lights. The wood beneath my feet was worn and scraped; each piece of its being told a story of use, repair, and eventual neglect.

I was captivated, pondering the history of a place so old. How many families had it watched grow, how many times had it been restored only to break apart again, and how many times had its floors been scrubbed of blood? There was no way to tell; no amount of coaxing could bring forth the memories etched within these bones. Dismayed by the thought, I returned my attention to Selene, her dirty footprints betraying her advance.

I followed them past the open sanctuary. The only remnant of my earlier trespass was the clean spot on dark wood. I made a point to circle past as I entered the wide hallway beyond, disturbed by the memory. Before me lay a rec room, scattered with old toys and broken chairs; it was eerie, covered in a thick layer of dust. Farther down was another abandoned area, the kitchen. It was sparse, most of the appliances probably taken for scrap long ago by squatters. Lastly was a bedroom, and the third exit from the church. I found Selene within the last room.

"You're not the first I've met who prefers to sleep above ground, and though it makes you more vulnerable, you may use this space as your own." She gestured with one sweeping arm, her lack of interest apparent as she stepped aside, allowing me to examine the space.

It wasn't much. There was a large bay window that took up most of the outer wall. A mix of tattered curtains and overgrown shrubs from the courtyard all but completely obscured the view. This room must have been used to house the priests, for stored inside was a wardrobe, what used to be a table and chairs, an old metal bed frame without a bed, and a private bathroom. The entire space was laden with the same thick layer of dust as the kitchen and rec room, probably untouched for years. Despite this, I found myself enjoying the privacy it would afford to me.

Much like the inner sanctum of the church, the wood floors and walls told a story. They were battle worn and scarred from being well lived in. I could see where the chairs had eaten away at the plaster where they had resided too close to the wall. The gouges in the floors almost read like cursive where the furniture had been rearranged time and time again. I wandered the ten-by-ten space slowly, rummaging through the closet and wardrobe as I went. Stored within were an assortment of curtains, tablecloths, and runners for the altar and pews. Anything of value had been pilfered long ago. The bathroom wasn't any better stocked than the room itself. Thankfully, everything seemed to be in working order.

Nothing left to investigate, I turned to leave, all but meeting Derek's chest with my face as he hovered just outside the bathroom door. Instinctually, I turned to flee, startled by his presence as I cursed under my breath. I had forgotten myself, angry at my mistake and Derek's intrusion. The look of amusement that replaced his normally indifferent expression did nothing to alleviate the matter.

"What is it?" I asked, settling my initial panic and anger over being scared, forgetting myself and the person to whom I spoke. I had no doubt that had he been Selene and had I responded in kind to her, I would not have liked the outcome.

"I didn't realize you could be snuck up on," he joked, finding amusement in my embarrassment. He was right; I shouldn't have been caught off guard. My senses returned to me in my panic, my earlier focus forgotten. I could smell the earth ever-present against his skin and hear Selene's approach.

"Yeah, me neither," I answered halfheartedly at Selene's return, the earlier grime cleared from her hair and skin. The look on her face was sinister.

"Time to go." Selene smiled wide and wild, and for a second I saw Clara reflected in her excitement. It was this comparison that solidified my reservations as she bounded forward and from the church.

Derek urged me forward with a quick nod. "It will get easier.""I know," I answered grimly. "That's what I'm afraid of."

One foot in front of the other, I stepped into the heavy night air. It was cool and humid against my exposed forearms. Selene ahead of me and Derek behind, I fell in line, stepping into the narrow alleyway that ran along the building. If I was being honest with myself, it wasn't the feeding that truly scared me. I was afraid of the nearly constant pull of Quin's mind. If he found me now, he'd see right through me and know exactly what I'd done. Would he understand? Could he? When next we met would he recognize me? I hoped so.

Selene pulled ahead, her gait long and strong, the energy pouring from her reeked of excitement and power. It was infectious, stealing away my hesitation; she was alive in the freedom of the night. Eagerly, I let her emotions wash over me; it was empowering. Her confidence, much like Quin's, was a breath of fresh air. I wasn't the only one drawn in by Selene's influence, though it was hard to tell if Derek wasn't just more relaxed after feeding the night before. He'd returned early this morning – his clothes and skin saturated in blood and gore – drunk and full. That was when I realized ghouls weren't the only ones that consumed flesh.

The thought gave me goosebumps as I recalled the decaying woman at the train tracks, her belly swollen and tight from the one she'd ingested. The thought of Derek consuming in that way both terrified and intrigued me. I had no idea what he or Selene were capable of – or what I was capable of anymore – and it terrified me. Had they always been the ruthless, unapologetic, and dangerous creatures I saw now?

How many lives had they taken, how many did it take before it became second nature, before it was easy? Looking between the two, these thoughts sobered me, breaking Selene's spell. No longer in thrall of her, I became aware of a faint aroma. Selene hadn't been wandering blindly in search of our next victims; she was following a trail of blood, richer and deeper than that of a human's. This was the blood of an elder, someone like Selene, leading us haphazardly through the overgrown city.

Their senses were sharper than mine, and every time I lost it, they were able to pick it back up, ushering me forward. It quickly became a game, my need to discover the blood's origin overriding my judgment. A drop here, a drop there, I was infatuated. I followed blindly, chasing after Derek and Selene. I rounded the final corner, out of breath once I'd caught up; we'd arrived at our destination.

The owner of the blood was just inside the unassuming bar before us. Selene didn't hesitate in her advance. She pushed her way inside, features awash with the neon glow from the broken open sign. Derek had slowed, waiting outside with me, his eyes intense and unwavering as he closed the space between us, forcing me to look up at him.

"You won't regret this; we don't always have to hide." His voice was intimate and kind, reassuring me as he stepped back to hold open the door open.

Derek was either telling the truth or he was a good liar. I guessed I would figure it out once I entered. The moment we stepped in we were swallowed by the bodies residing within; it didn't take me long to realize what kind of place this was. Their eyes shined like stars within the abyss of the crowd; each one carried their own orbit of people. Greedy hands pulled at me, quickly overwhelming me with the sheer number of them as they converged.

Men and women alike reached out, their fingers grasping wherever they could find purchase. Their closeness ignited my hunger as their minds begged for release. For a second I lost myself, drawing on their desires to feed my own. I was an alcoholic let loose in an open bar. Before I knew it my hands reached out, just as eager. It was the familiar steel grasp of Derek's arm around my waist that pulled me from the crowd and to my senses.

"You need to pace yourself," he warned, leading me forward, and away from the first onslaught of people.

It took me a moment to register his words. Fighting my urges, I took a deep breath. My focus no longer held captive by the immediate entertainment of the night. We were not alone here. Their eyes found me, their curiosity just as bright as the shine of their eyes. This was a den, thick with hungry monsters. My once eager and careless mood now stoic and guarded, I felt Derek's hold tighten as he ushered me forward.

"Humans aren't the only ones who want to meet you." He leaned in, waiting for the music to ebb. "It has been a long time since any of them have seen a new vampire."

It was hard to tell if his words made me anxious or excited as the music drowned out my ability to think. It pounded through my chest and resonated in my bones, inciting the crowd and changing the energy of the bar. Their emotions became mine as I took in the hungry eyes of vampire and human alike. I drank it in, relaxing once more as I met the embers of Selene's eyes.

Tonight was for us, there was no space here for anything but the pleasure of the moment. Tonight I'd forget who I was. Insistently, Derek led me to an alcove just off the main floor. He pushed past the thick curtains to reveal the circular room within; it was here that I learned the origin of the blood that had led us here.

The green of his eyes was lighter than my own; they reminded me of the coast where the forest meets the sea, the blue hint reminiscent of sea foam. They shone brightly against the paleness of his skin and the fire of his red hair. Instinct told me I needed to tread lightly; his whole being stunk of blood and death. It was not unlike the scent I found upon first meeting Alistair. Unlike Alistair, though, he did not meet me with hostility at being so easily spotted.

"She's intuitive. Good." He smiled wide, exposing the fang-like quality of his teeth, any likeness to the humans around us completely lost in that moment. "Sit."

I felt the security of Derek's hold slip away from me as he joined the others in the comfort of the booth within the hidden lounge. Scattered about the crescent hideaway were oversized pillows and a low table in the middle. It currently served as a footrest for the man with red hair, his arms stretched wide across the back of the booth. He was the epitome of comfort, his body language easily read as open and welcoming.

I did as I was told and sat on the floor just opposite Derek to face the man with ocean eyes. I leaned back, letting the base of the booth support my back as I tucked my legs to one side. The opaque glass table was the only thing between him and me. The smell of him came over me once more as he leaned forward, elbows to knees, resting his chin on his clasped hands as he took me in.

The more I looked back, the less human I thought he actually was. The angles of his face were stronger and harsher than I'd seen before, and despite his relaxed posture and fit of his clothes, I was sure there wasn't an ounce of fat to be found on him. However old he was, he had not gotten this way without fighting for it. He was leaner and shorter than Derek, but not by much.

"I was wondering when Selene would bring you to me." His smile widened. "The name's Oran. Welcome to my Den." There was something odd in the way he introduced himself, a certain hesitancy I couldn't quite place.

"Thank you," I answered honestly, taking in the surroundings once more.

The music had changed tempo, and the people just visible beyond the thick curtains slowed as they swayed methodically to the new beat. It was mesmerizing, each of them eager to be fed on. I reached out, caressing their subconsciouses; all but a few were aware of my intrusion. I couldn't help but draw on and ingest their energy.

"You're a channeler," Oran stated smugly, forcing my attention. I met the green of his eyes once more. "That's not all, though, is it?"

All eyes were on me. Derek and Selene's interest piqued, and suddenly the lounge seemed too small. I sat up a bit straighter, narrowing my vision at our host. Had I not been brought here I might have felt threatened by Oran's intrusion, but something told me he meant no harm in his questioning. In fact, I got a very distinct sense that he did not want easy answers, but instead to learn… to appraise.

"Are you a channeler?" I deflected, turning his words back on him.

"No." Oran laughed deep and melodic. "My abilities do not lie within the mind."

Maybe it was his openness or, perhaps, it was the ease with which his emotions came through to me that put me at ease. He was genuine in his interest and intent to know me for no other reason than to be acquainted. It was refreshing to speak with someone who wasn't looking for weakness or a reason not to trust.

"Don't worry; you'll know me soon enough," Oran stated plainly. "But tonight is for you, a welcoming party. And now that you've arrived–" He clapped his hands together, his speed startling me. "–we should get started."

The lights dimmed and, for a single breath, the whole place was silent. As one, I felt their anticipation and excitement build within me just as the music began to swell. It was a low rumble that began in the floor boards, building until slivers of silver light broke through the darkness. That was all it took to break the trance. The glow of the lights reflected in the luminescent eyes of the monsters within as both sides lost control.

I waited, frozen by the unison of bodies before me, expecting nothing but blood as my breath caught, sure of the worst and surprised by the outcome.

Oran's words broke through the boom of the music resonating in my bones. "Still so human." He smirked, eyes piercing in the dim light. "We are more than just our impulses. If you feed, you do so in private. We are not all monsters, young one. Now go."

A part of me felt ashamed of my assumptions and the other part hurt by his dismissal, but I stood, ushered off by Derek as Selene stayed. She and Oran did not intend to join the party; their intent was made clear as, one by one, the bodies filtered in to meet their hungry mouths. The smell of it was mind numbing as it mingled with the pull of the people around me. I bit the inside of my cheek; the sharp tang of my own blood and the pain it caused kept me from losing myself.

"It will pass." Derek spoke the words again, like somehow they'd make it easier.

"That's what you keep telling me," I said through gritted teeth, searching for the nearest exit.

His grip on my upper arm was painfully tight, erasing any chance of escape. "If you let it pass instead of fighting it, the urges will subside. Breathe it in, enjoy it, and move on," he chided. "And if you're too weak, that's why I'm here."

Derek spoke the last words like an insult, pleased with himself for getting under my skin just before he shoved me into the open arms of the dance floor. There was no hiding as the mass of people swarmed and swallowed me whole. If there was an end to their minds and my own, I couldn't find it. It was dizzying, the way they moved around me. Little by little I took from each person that rose to meet me. Their perverse need to dance with death was tantalizing, and it seemed that no matter how much I stole from them there was always more – so I indulged, drunk on their excitement.

With every encounter I lost more and more of my self-control. It was easy to breathe them in, to enjoy it, but it wasn't enough, and soon my body ached as my veins burned. I didn't have the calm of Quin's mind to pull me back. I was backpedaling, trying to remove myself from the temptation. Every second spent tangled in their greedy arms was harder than the last, and I could feel myself drowning in them. There was no calm to be found here, no way to escape the feel of their skin on mine or the way their minds begged for an escape. They were like a drug and I was the junkie, desperate and unable to escape my need of them.

The truth was that we were just as much their drug as they were ours, and they knew it. It was for this reason I couldn't escape them. No matter how far removed I was from them, they followed. I retreated until my back was against a wall and his arms caged me in. I could just see the red of my eyes reflected in the brown of his. He smelled like one too many whiskey sours; the warm and sweet smell of alcohol, molasses, and lemon was not completely unpleasant – neither was the fuzziness of his mind or the unfocused look in his eyes.

"Looked like you were having a hard time deciding; thought I could help." He smiled down at me, the full weight of his drunkenness hitting me.

He was a drink of ice water after running a marathon, his mind lazy and numbing against mine. I leaned my head back and let the feel of him wash over me as I erased everything else except him. His eyes widened, feeling the weight of my full attention press in on him.

Of the minds I had encountered thus far, they all seemed to want one thing: oblivion. Each time, I'd obliged. This was especially true of Quin, but this one was different. Jordon wasn't trying to escape anything, so instead of taking, I gave. Sharing in his nervous curiosity, I let him guide the experience, heightening his euphoria as I erased the fear.

"Thank you." I sighed, feeling my senses return as I withdrew, thankful for the barrier he'd provided me.

For a moment he was confused, a flash of disappointment mingled with the sharp realization of rejection; each emotion crossed his mind quickly before he resigned, not completely ungrateful for the interaction. The warmth of him slipped away as he went, and again I could breathe. He'd been just the calm I'd needed.

Now that I'd had a chance to filter out the extra noise and energy of the bar, it was easier to keep myself separate. The initial plunge had caught me off guard, my instinct to feed stronger than my reason when there were so many welcoming throats. I did as Derek had instructed and just enjoyed it, letting the urges pass from the safety of my wall.

"You think I don't see you hiding? Why are you still holding yourself back?" What I couldn't hear of Derek's words I picked from his mind. The music was a living, breathing thing, pulling at each and every one of us as it vibrated through our bones.

"What would you have me do, Derek, feed on each and every one of them that crosses my path in hopes that I'll grow tired of the taste?" I didn't mean to snap at him. "You and I both know that won't ever happen."

His relaxed stance changed quickly; where he had been standing beside me he now faced me. I felt the impulsiveness of his mind, and for a second feared he'd throw me back into the grasp of the crowd.

"You will learn, either by your own means or *hers*. Trust me, you won't enjoy the latter. How much longer do you think she'll let you play this game?" Derek's voice, though harsh, was sincere and earnest; a warning of things to come should I not obey. "Feed, because if you don't, she'll make you, or she'll make me do it."

I met the unblinking abyss of Derek's black eyes, and for a second I saw it; the truth of his words cut deep within his mind as he relived Selene's methods. It was quick, more emotion than image, gone before I could process what it meant. I saw, maybe for the first time, the two sides of the person before me. The side I saw now and the side he showed when around our maker. How long had he spent hiding from her, alone, until now?

I stepped away from him, grabbing the first volunteer; I needed to erase the taste of Derek's fear. More importantly, I needed to ensure I never came to know it. He'd told me my choices, feed or be fed, and I knew which one I preferred.

She smelled of cigarettes and beer; her scars and the eagerness with which she followed me into the lounge told me that she didn't care much for wooing. Red and white crescents laced both of her arms. It was haunting, the varied healing of these scars, but the smell of her blood pulled me away from my inquiry as she created the next scar herself.

Just like that, she was in my veins. Her intoxication was exquisite. I let her infect me; sharing in her drunkenness was sublime. I drank her down just as quickly as she could give. It was too easy to just take and take… Derek's grasp on the back of my neck was just painful enough to bring me back to myself. I slowed, acutely aware of the drunken woman's labored breathing, despite her insistent hold on me. I hadn't even bothered to learn her name, mindless in my need. I might have regretted it had I not been drunk. I released. Derek did not.

"Again, but this time, enjoy it. You can feed psychically; use that to catch your breath." He instructed.

It wasn't long before the next person filtered past the heavy drapes, almost like an open sign hung just outside. Again I was met with those brown eyes and the smell of whiskey as Jordon stepped through. Who was I to say no twice?

CHAPTER THIRTY-ONE

Quin stopped for the second time in the span of thirty minutes; it was just like the night Marc had found Eryn down at the docks. She was feeding, and by the feel of it her drug of choice was still alcohol; it was distracting and slowed his progress. One after another each person lasted a bit little longer than the one before. It was an odd sensation, his mind fracturing between the solidness of the world around himself and the phantom sensations of hers.

With each drink, Quin got closer. It was cute just how drunk she was after so little. He was thankful because it was working in his favor. The more inebriated she became, the easier it was to sneak past the barriers she'd put in place to keep him away. What he could do without was the persistent sound of music. Drunk he could do any day, but the music was infuriating. It bounced around his mind like a bad joke of "Row, Row, Row Your Boat."

Clara and Alistair could wait for Selene at the grave. He needed to move. It was stupid, and Quin was sure that was exactly what Marc would say if he got himself killed tonight. It didn't matter; he had to find her. He needed to understand, and the only way he was going to get answers was if Eryn couldn't hide from him.

His plan relied heavily on Eryn's inability to pass up another alcoholic, so Quin nudged, pausing for the third time that night to indulge in the feel of her hunger. Just because they weren't directly connected didn't mean he couldn't shift and manipulate their connection. He'd done it in the past, using her against herself. He let her emotions cascade over him, enjoying them long enough to give them back.

It was a subtle dance, one that made him grit his teeth as he fought not to spit, the taste of blood filling his mouth. There was a drawback to not being the one fed on; the illusion and seduction of the act was completely lost. Quin clung to the parts that didn't make him want to puke: the dying ache ever-present in her veins, and the relief it created as she forgot herself.

Whatever was left of Eryn's barrier that kept him separate came crashing down, and suddenly the blood didn't taste like blood anymore and he could breathe again, the fractured connection of their minds made whole.

"I found you." They both sighed, he into the night and her against the flesh of her latest victim.

———

Derek was surprised when Eryn pulled away long before he would have intervened, a smile playing across her face; it was uncharacteristic. Perhaps her insistent ingestion of the intoxicated had finally satiated her weird desire to be disoriented. It wasn't something he'd ever enjoyed, himself.

"He's coming," she giggled, red eyes unfocused.

Derek considered her words a little too long – confused first, in disbelief second, and furious third as he forced Eryn to her feet. "Who?" he demanded.

"Quin." She grinned, depending solely on Derek's grasp to stand. "He found me."

Derek could have screamed a thousand obscenities at her, but there wasn't time now; and if there was later, he was sure it would be Selene's fury that reached her first.

"Move." Derek dragged Eryn forward, the force of his voice and disregard for her comfort making her wince; but she did as told.

"He doesn't like you," Eryn said, eerily sober despite her dependence on him to remain upright.

Her eyes focused again, locking with his, and for a moment Derek got the distinct feeling it wasn't Eryn looking back. They were her eyes, but the intensity behind them was not; this was the same look Quin had given him the night they'd met, blade to hunter's throat. Derek shoved her away, delivering her unceremoniously at Selene's feet.

"The hunter, she's called him to us," Derek proclaimed, disgust twisting his tone.

Selene met her youngest where she fell, her clawed hands framing her oval face like a vice, nails pricking the surface of Eryn's skin. Now, Selene had her full attention, glowing pools of blood no longer unfocused. The embrace could have easily been confused as tenderness; the way Selene leaned over Eryn's small frame nestled on the floor, lifting her to meet her livid gaze.

"If you bring him here," Selene whispered softly, "I will kill him in front of you."

Fear. It was the only tool Selene required; not kindness; not admiration; and not respect. Fear held people stronger than any bond she'd ever seen forged – even love, for in love is fear: the fear of loss. It all came back to the only emotion that drove humanity, and with it, Eryn complied – her green eyes wide. Selene smiled, feeling the quiet of Eryn's mind as she erased herself from the hunter and bound herself within.

"Good girl." Selene kept her voice low, releasing her hold. "If you'd like your hunter dead, there are easier ways than bringing him here. Now go."

Eryn's drunken scramble might have been comical had she not just threatened the safety of The Den.

"Another time, then?" Oran grinned, amused by the troubles of the young and the frustration of the parent.

"Until next time, Oran," Selene agreed, glancing back to meet the humor in his eyes before departing.

"I had hoped to meet the man who stole from you and lived," Oran called in her wake, enjoying the way his words fueled her anger; poor fucker didn't stand a chance.

It didn't take Selene long to catch up to Derek and her youngest; the smell of alcohol alone could have led her to them. She had to fight not to turn her nose up at the scent of it. It would take Eryn all night to process it.

"Call to him," Selene instructed once they'd stepped from the road more traveled. "Let's see what your hunter wants, shall we?"

"No," Eryn pleaded, settling to the ground between Derek and her.

"Why?" Derek asked, leaving Eryn to her own devices.

"Because," Selene snapped, her body heat rising. "I am tired of him and I will not lead him to our home. Call to him or I will make you."

It wasn't Selene's tone that scared him, or the feel of her anger as it burned away the cold night air, it was the look in her eyes as she fought to keep her temper in check.

"No." The word was not spoken bravely, and there was no assertion or strength behind the two letters. It was a weak refusal cast from trembling lips and downturned eyes.

"I won't ask again," Selene threatened, her eyes and voice devoid of emotion.

It wasn't Selene's threshold for violence that paralyzed Derek; it was her lack of remorse. She was destruction: pure, and without caring for anything caught in her path. So he did the only thing he could and buried his knife into Eryn's exposed thigh. What he hadn't expected was the explosion of pain that followed.

Vampires were experts at hiding; suppression was only one of the ways that they had adapted – but no matter how far removed they became, one thing could always bring them back: instinct. It was the instinct to defend herself and to survive that Derek exploited. What he didn't understand was why there were hundreds of red needles buried across his skin or why he couldn't move. All he knew was the pain of it as they melted into his flesh and the look in the red of her eyes as she held him captive.

———

Quin cursed, almost toppling from the sudden loss of his connection to Eryn, her senses and strength completely gone from him. He'd been so close, and now all he had left was the insistent sound of music… Music that wasn't just in his head anymore.

"They're close, Clara," Quin huffed, adjusting his earpiece for the third time; the thing was hard to run with. "Clara!?" he yelled.

"We heard you," she announced, clearly annoyed by his impatience.

"I lost her. She was here." Quin had to force the air in and out of his lungs; he was not a runner.

"Spectator, Quin. Nothing more," Clara reminded him. She was beginning to sound like a broken record.

"Yeah, yeah." He waved her off as if she could see his physical disregard for her. He didn't have time to argue, he'd promised not to interfere with Alistair but he'd made no promises regarding Eryn.

Fatigue and the accumulation of lactic acid forced Quin to slow; he was out of breath a block ago. He'd forgotten how hard it used to be before he was tethered. Sure he was stronger, but muscles ate up a lot of energy and oxygen, two things that seemed endless when fueled by the metabolism of a vampire. At least he'd finally found the source of the music, even if the discovery brought with it a new obstacle of the red-headed variety.

"Listen, I don't want any trouble." Quin wheezed between breaths, hands on his knees. He didn't dare get any closer, not to the man or the bar.

"Best turn around, then; you'll find nothing but trouble here." Oran spoke calmly, body poised lazily in the doorway; the red curls atop his head just long enough to fall loosely to one side when he cocked his head sideways to take in the winded hunter curiously.

"Thing is," Quin said, straightening, "I think a friend of mine is in there."

Oran smiled wide and sharp. "Would you like to come in?" he offered sincerely. "I warn you, though, you'll find no friends here, especially not alone."

Quin was surprised when the man stepped aside, granting him a clear view in. "You don't cross me as the lying type," Quin stated plainly. "And I never said I was alone."

Oran looked around, making a point to exaggerate his effort. "You look alone to me." His voice was predatory yet playful, stepping forward slowly.

Quin squared off, expressionless, as he assessed the very real threat before him; he was a sitting duck. "Tell me, do all of the old ones reek of blood?"

"Perhaps," Oran chuckled, nothing but the narrow street between them now. "Do all tethered smell of the vampire they've captured?"

"Yes." Alistair's voice was small yet severe, carrying with it the hauntingly soft and adenoidal tone of a child not yet grown.

The speed at which Oran's features changed was startling, his curious, yet aloof, nature now dark and intense. The grin on Alistair's face was a polar opposite: light and full of amusement, but nonetheless unnerving. They were electricity and water.

Their interaction was almost as unnerving as the pain in his right thigh and the warm, wet sensation that followed; for a second, he thought he might have pissed himself. Mind fractured, his perspective collided with Eryn's once more. All her pain was his as the ice of her fear shattered against him. Looking through Eryn, Quin saw the spray of blood like broken glass, the knife buried deep in her thigh, and Selene's joyous face. He wondered if she would smile at him that way when he showed up with a Progenitor.

"The two of you can settle this pissing match some other time," Quin stated, matter-of-fact. "She's waiting for us." Blue eyes shifted to lavender, until red was the only color that bled through.

CHAPTER THIRTY-TWO

W e were in a stalemate. I couldn't feel my body or the knife sticking out of my leg, but I could feel *him*. Derek was just as trapped as I, but unlike my paralysis, his was not without pain as I crawled through his veins like ice and tore at his mind. He didn't resist as I carved my way through him, shredding the calloused and dead parts of him until there was nowhere left for him to hide. I found the center of his chaos bound within three little words: *I had to.*

The truth of the words broke against me, revealing shards of Derek's existence. *I had to.* I could feel Selene tearing him apart piece by piece, his terror still so vivid. *I had to.* His memories screamed as she broke him down over and over. *I had to.* He reasoned as she starved him, stripping from him his ability to resist her. *I had to.* He pleaded as she burned him. *I had to.* The words and their meaning consumed him as he justified his actions, all of them to protect me from her. *I had to*… I let him go. I had to.

With the release of him, there was nothing but waiting dread. It was worse than Cyd's all-consuming abyss. I would be forced to watch as Quin faced Selene alone, helpless. I sensed as he drew near, his excitement startling, but in the end it wasn't his eyes that I met when the footfalls ceased. These eyes were the color of liquid mercury, bright and vibrant against dark skin, the molten pools trapped behind the guise of a child.

A new fear crept into me, not the fear of loss or of pain; this was fear born of certainty – the kind of fear you can't reason with, can't hide from, and can't escape. Before me stood death, and he hid behind a shroud of innocence. The pain started slowly, stinging and irritating until the full weight of the damage returned to me. It radiated through my thigh, severing the muscle below and splintering the bone within.

Had I not already been on the ground, I would have collapsed from Derek's attack. I'd broken bones before, knew the pain well, but never without the mind-numbing rush of adrenaline. The worst part: I knew it wouldn't heal until the steel was removed. Derek released his hold. His stance shifted as he turned, placing himself in front of me and just behind Selene. She faced Alistair, shielding us as she stepped forward. I realized then, why Derek had freed me; this was not the time to fight amongst ourselves. They knew as well as I did that Alistair had not simply stumbled upon us, especially not with two hunters in tow.

Selene was an inferno. The instant and intense heat of her immediately halted their advance. The air hissed, any moisture held within now vaporized. It was excruciating and utterly ineffective as Alistair met every bit of her fire with the tarry black of a form no longer human.

Viscous ink to liquid smoke, sharp then shapeless, Alistair was an endless, sticky, wet mist in the face of Selene's abilities. Both were terrifyingly resolute in their desire to destroy the other. Every slithering tendril and shadow Alistair brought forth she incinerated. It wasn't enough, though. The more Selene pushed back, the faster he advanced; little by little Alistair was smothering her. The air was thick with every piece she burned from him, caustic in our lungs.

I was staring into a solar eclipse; Alistair was the black center before us, and Selene the flame igniting the edges of him that dared get too close. The sight of it was frightening, yet beautiful, neither yielding.

"Will you burn us all away, Selene, just like your coven? Just like Hannah?" Alistair's voice was ethereal.

Satisfaction, pure and unapologetic: Quin's mind sparked at the memory of Hannah. It was her face that haunted my dreams. Teeth to bone, she devoured my husband, mouth slick with him. It made me sick.

"Yes," Selene hissed, meeting Alistair's shadows. "There isn't anyone I wouldn't destroy to protect them."

"Even yourself?" Alistair's words hung in the air, a sticky pause before he converged.

Derek didn't hesitate, his resolve every bit as cold as the steel in my leg. He moved for Quin and Clara, ignoring the collapsing black hole that had consumed our maker. Alistair was doing all he could to contain Selene. The intense energy within peaked through. She lit the darkness from within like a furnace.

Quin's psyche overrode mine; our senses combined and together we pulled the knife from bone. The relief of it stole my breath away. I held the handle tight, blood crystalizing across steel. The familiarity of the weapon and how to use it was all his. Smoke and embers erupted, the half-moon of Alistair's shadows now tattered and eaten by flames. Held within was Selene's shadow-bound form and the charred body of a child.

He'd started to ingest her just as he'd done to Silas. Steel to concrete, crystals shattering, Derek and I couldn't get to her fast enough. He met us, just as feral and sharp as the smell of blood and burnt flesh in the air. Lidless silver eyes met us; we didn't stand a chance.

"No," I exhaled the word as the tattered fabric of Alistair's form bound me.

He'd met Derek more violently, sharper than any knife as he riddled him with spikes, like black widow spider legs, his form suspended in air. Every drop of lost blood found its way to him, feeding his strength. Had she the ability, I believe Selene would have screamed, her anger white hot. Alistair held tight, forcing her to her knees, hands bound to ankles. The mist of him laced her throat, silencing her objections.

Alistair was done playing games, his anger like acid across my skin. "You'd defend her?" he demanded an answer of me, his flesh stitching itself together in front of my eyes.

The weight of his question held me tighter than the vice of his grip. His anger and inquiry, though clear to me, mingled with everything else: fear, hatred, indifference, realization, and uncertainty. It all mixed together, but perhaps the most notable was Selene's resignation and realization of who she faced.

'*Progenitor.*' The red of Selene's eyes faded blue. This was the second time I'd heard the word, and while its importance was lost to me, she surrendered to it.

The icy blue of her eyes was no less intense than the red; she was just as prideful and angry. Her arms and legs bound, voice stolen, this was the only show of compliance available to her. The anger burning through Alistair settled, his silver eyes regarding her carefully.

"Will you stand trial, Selene, even if it means your end?" His voice had returned, emanating just as soft and innocent as before.

"I will." Her voice broke as he released the hold around her throat.

Clara and Quin stood back, wide-eyed; Quin had been so ready to fight until he saw the full extent of Alistair's reach and the violence he'd resort to. Derek fell with a wet thud to the ground, a grunt of pain his only sign of life. Alistair had all but bled him dry. His shadows receded, settling around him like mist, save the parts of him that yet bound Selene and me.

"You destroyed your coven. Tell me, how many died that night?" Alistair's silver eyes bore into her.

"Seven," she spat, no remorse to be found. Their faces came to me in flashes of bubbling and blistered skin.

"Laws forbid the killing of our own," Alistair warned. "Who named you executioner?"

"They did." Selene spoke her words like curses, her pain and anger reflected within. Alexander's dead, unseeing eyes looked through her.

"What gives you the right?" Alistair met every ounce of her rage and sorrow. I saw his hesitancy then. How many of his kind had he been forced to end?

They were both haunted. Their emotions erased me. Alistair's crept over me, rising slowly like water while Selene's pulled me under like a cinderblock tied to my feet.

"They did." Selene spoke the words again, meeting his conviction with her own. "I found them poisoning the bodies of my children. I burned away their bloodlines for the change they tried to force."

Alistair turned, no longer dividing the hunters from us or us from them. "And what of you?" he asked. "Did you not give without permission?"

Those were the words that halted Selene's anger, sparking instead deep feelings of remorse.

"When I found them." The smell of our blood filled her nose. "What had been done." His body devoured to bone. "I had to."

Her mind pulled me back, and again I could feel them against my skin, trapping me just as Alistair trapped me now. I fought it – the memories of their teeth and blood-stinking breath, the way they tore at us, and the sound of his death when his voice could no longer drown out the sound of their feeding. The silence and chaos that ensued after she'd ripped them from us, the pain of her in my veins, was nothing compared to waking again; the nightmare of it all made real. Alexander was always going to die... Selene had tried to give us a chance.

"Let her go." Quin's voice felt distant in my ears, his fingers pried Alistair from me, hands shaking.

Maybe it was pity that made Alistair relinquish his hold. I couldn't tell anymore as I withdrew from all of them – all except Quin. There was no point in hiding from him, not now. I escaped into him, not wanting to be alone with myself.

"Will you defend her?" Alistair asked, his voice flat as he prepared himself.

"Yes." I held the word, nurturing it inside myself before releasing it. I didn't need to be psychic to feel the relief my answer provided.

Alistair physically removed himself from Selene, her body now just as drained as Derek's. Any signs of her earlier onslaught were completely erased from him as he returned to Clara. Selene was slumped over, fully prepared to die for her actions; shocked that she was still in one piece.

"What of you, then?" Clara called out, pointing rudely. "To us or them?"

"Neither." I laughed, meeting the blue of Quin's eyes. I spoke the word softly and with a finality that even he could not ignore.

Fear, uncertainty, doubt; I knew what I was asking of him. To pick me over his guild and accept whatever that meant. To be apart from and a part of the two worlds that made us who we were.

"There are easier paths," Alistair remarked, "than that of a Progenitor."

ACKNOWLEDGEMENTS

To my very first peer reviewers: Cassie, Janyce, Chi, and Andy; without your feedback I would have been lost. Each of you helped me step back, see the bigger picture, and mend the frayed ends of my story's edges. Thank you.

To my editors – through the muddled nonsense and errors you found me, gave my story a clear and concise voice, and helped me paint a clear picture within. Thank you.

To my Launch Team: what a crazy and hilarious ride. Your feedback and extraordinary commentary made every mistake worth it in the end. Thank you.

To my husband who stood by me when I was lost in the words and consumed by my work, you'll never know just how much your patience meant to me when I had none. Thank you.

Lastly, to Trina, thank you for all those recesses you spent herding us together just so I could read my stories aloud to all of you. Your sound effects and ecstatic reinterpretations will always bring a smile to my face. Thank you.